The Chagall Cello

Art Theft Mystery
Book 2

Bea Green

D1617292

ROUGH
EDGES
PRESS

The Chagall Cello
Paperback Edition
Copyright © 2022 (As Revised) Bea Green

Rough Edges Press
An Imprint of Wolfpack Publishing
9850 S. Maryland Parkway, Suite A-5 #323
Las Vegas, Nevada 89183

roughedgespress.com

Paperback ISBN 978-1-68549-170-3
eBook ISBN 978-1-68549-169-7

For my two brothers, both too far away,
one in Broxbourne and the other in Brazil.

The Chagall Cello

"An eye for an eye leaves the whole world blind."

—Mahatma Gandhi

Prologue
Rio de Janeiro

The first-class departure lounge at Galeão International Airport was busy, and to occupy the time Paolo Fernandes was studying the other passengers who were waiting for their flights to be called.

Turning his head, he caught sight of a little girl in a red dress, dancing in front of her parents at the other end of the lounge.

He grimaced, feeling his lips pulling over the hard plastic of his dentures as he did so.

The girl's dress was made of gossamer thin fabric, and multiple layers of the Venetian-red material fluttered against her legs as she moved from side to side, giggling.

Transfixed by her red dress, Paolo felt a familiar sense of panic hit him. For some strange reason, these days every shade of red, from ruby to magenta, cherry to maroon, took him straight back to his teenage years and the Night of Broken Glass.

The other passengers seated near the little girl were smiling at her in amusement and their admiration seemed to be encouraging her antics, much to Paolo's disgust. One onlooker, a middle-aged lady dressed in a white linen suit, was leaning forward and clapping enthusiastically at her performance.

The red dress bobbed up, down, up, down.

Gripping the padded arms of his wheelchair tightly, Paolo fought against the memories starting to resurface in his mind, trying as usual to extinguish them but knowing he'd never be able to block them out. Time and time again, like sadistic ghosts, horrific images from the past kept coming back to haunt him and pushed him to the edge of insanity. Even worse, it was happening more and more because in old age he was weaker and had less control over his mind.

It wasn't just the color red that invited in unwanted scenes from the Night of Broken Glass, there were many other triggers, too.

Dusk, for example, was a reminder of the time of day when Paolo's initiation into brutality had started. Any clicking noise would make him think of the sound of a safety catch easing off a machine gun. And a loud call, echoing up and down the street outside his home in Lagoa, brought back to him the sound of voices during that one memorable night in Germany.

He remembered with amazing clarity the chorus of heart-rending screams merging with the soldiers" aggressive shouts during the Night of Broken Glass. The screaming became the background music to the pillaging of generations of accumulated wealth and rounding up men of all ages from the Jewish quarter.

Bizarrely, even the white beaches of Brazil kept him trapped in the past.

Glistening in the sun, they reminded him of

nothing more than the diamond-twinkle of broken glass, strewn across German pavements and roads, crunching loudly under his booted feet.

Fear brought back memories, too. Paolo could smell and sense fear like a dog. It was a skill he had developed to perfection during the few years he had hunted down his fellow men as though they were vermin. In his old age, any acquaintance who suffered from anxiety brought out in him a sense of superiority and he would again be reminded of his past.

At the far side of the room, the little girl in the red dress began to spin in wobbly circles, squealing in excitement as she became dizzier. Paolo started to lose sight of everything around him as in his mind's eye the girl's dress spun outwards, then started changing shape.

The hallucinations had begun.

This isn't really happening, he said to himself.

It's not real. It's *not* real.

Layer by layer, the dress expanded, sprouting red streamers that curled their way into every corner of the lounge. Soon, pieces of red chiffon were swirling around in front of Paolo's face, floating on invisible currents from the air-conditioning.

Paolo felt as though a cloud had descended on his brain.

The caramel-colored wood in the lounge vanished, as did the smooth leather surfaces of the sofas and chairs.

The whispering television screen in front of him seemed to flicker once, twice, and then switched off completely.

Terrified, Paolo turned to look at the airport runway but there was no respite to be found there either.

The tinted windows, on his left-hand side, began to narrow and bend, pulling away from him.

Squeezed by a hidden force, the entire wall of connected windows diminished in size, until they became a thin, shimmering ribbon stretched out on the airport tarmac. Shining brightly in the sun, the strip of windows reminded him of a coral snake he'd seen sunbathing on the paving stones in his Brazilian garden, gaudy with its red, black and white stripes and highly venomous.

He stared, fascinated, as the long line of windows shuddered and then started to make its way towards him like a freight train, picking up speed.

Paolo groaned out loud and lifted a trembling hand to his eyes to try and stop the madness.

It was too late.

By the time his hand reached his face, the airport windows had disappeared, along with everything else.

Before long the only thing he could see in front of him was a mound of pale- skinned bodies. All of them men. Lying like discarded, broken dolls, they were stained with wet, crimson blood which was slowly dyeing the dry earth of the ground underneath a dark chocolate-brown.

Paolo's tortured mind, retreating into its shell, turned further inwards, and as it did so the soothing background notes of Elgar's *Salut d'Amour* in the airport lounge fell silent, along with the clink of cutlery and the chatter at the buffet bar.

And then there was nothing but the eerie, empty silence which had so often stalked his waking hours during the last eighty-two years.

"Are you alright, *Vovô*?" asked a concerned and

familiar voice, bringing him back to the present-day again.

Paolo turned and looked into the worried face of his grandson.

"*Si, claro*," he replied, smiling gingerly.

Alonso, relieved, smiled back at him and returned to studying his mobile phone. In his left hand, Alonso was holding onto the handle of his grandfather's old cello case.

The black leather case, positioned right in front of Alonso, was proving useful in sheltering him from view. Alonso was a quiet introvert and preferred not to attract too much attention to himself, but invariably he drew people's eyes to him because he was a handsome young man, whose classical features reflected a movie-star quality he was far from feeling.

A first-class seat on the plane had been reserved for Paolo's cherished cello, and as Paolo was rich enough to indulge his whims, no one had questioned his bringing along with him a bulky instrument that he was unable to use.

He's a good boy, thought Paolo, as he focused his mind on his grandson.

Well, not a boy as such, he reminded himself, more like a man, for he'd turned twenty-two in March.

Paolo shook his head as he remonstrated with himself.

He certainly did not want to recall what it was like to be twenty-two because it would again bring up the visions he was trying hard to forget. However, watching his grandson flicking his mobile phone screen with his thumb he couldn't help marveling at how different life was for Alonso compared to the turbulent years he had lived through at his age.

Out of concern for his grandfather, Alonso was accompanying Paolo to London for a week before returning to Brazil on his own. Paolo was the one who had insisted on Alonso's early return and Alonso, who was meek and hated confrontations, had reluctantly agreed to do so.

Paolo smiled at his grandson's bent, curly-haired head.

He appreciated having Alonso with him on this trip and hoped that having him around would give him the moral strength to follow through on his plan to atone for one of the many crimes he had committed during his reckless teenage years. Alonso, poor boy, knew nothing about his grandfather's past or his desire to return to a Jewish family something he had stolen from them many years ago during the Night of Broken Glass.

Paolo had also brought along his nurse, Luca Barboza, for the journey, not expecting nor wanting Alonso to take care of his physical needs. He was too proud to accept Alonso's help in getting to the toilet or to have him chop up his food into more manageable pieces. Luca was there to sustain him on the tiring journey to London, and after seeing Alonso off on his return journey back to Brazil, the two of them would then travel onwards to Switzerland for private medical treatment.

Of course, his family in Brazil had not realized that when Paolo had talked enthusiastically about "an inno-vative, specialized treatment for early dementia" what he had actually meant was "an end-of-life clinic". That was his little surprise for them and he was more than ready for it too.

His stubbornness and ruthlessness being legendary, none of his family members had done more than faintly protest against a voyage that seemed the height of lunacy at the age of ninety-nine. In their view no one so old should be travelling anywhere but all the doctors they had taken him to had declared him of sound mind, albeit also advising him in the strongest possible terms against undertaking such an arduous trip.

True to form, Paolo had ignored their well-meaning advice.

He was searching for some kind of last-minute redemption although he wasn't exactly sure why this would be the case, given he had been lucky enough to escape accountability and retribution for most of his long life.

Maybe this trip was a final, arguably desperate, bid to banish the memories that had plagued him so much over the years and to find some form of peace before he died. "*Senhor Fernandes*, we're ready to take you to the flight now," said a polished lady

in a British Airways uniform, as she walked up to them.

Alonso and Luca, who were seated on either side of Paolo, stood up and waited while the lady unlocked the wheelchair brakes and pushed it forwards.

Luca, dressed in a T-shirt and jeans, looked completely unprepared for a mid- October arrival in London. Paolo made a mental note to send Alonso out to buy him a suitable coat as soon as they reached their hotel.

There were uses to having a wheelchair, thought

Paolo, when he saw the other passengers looking enviously at them as they made their way to the doors of the departure lounge. They might be the first ones to board the airplane but in all likelihood they would be the last ones to disembark, so the final laugh would be on the others travelling with them.

As his wheelchair turned around at the double doors of the lounge, he caught a final glimpse of the girl in the red dress.

She was now seated placidly next to her father, sucking her thumb and looking down at a picture book on her lap.

1

Richard

DCI Richard Langley opened the car door and stretched his legs with a sigh of relief. Without a single pit-stop, they had been travelling in the car for four hours and his long legs were starting to feel cramped.

London now seemed like a different world, a million miles away from the Tudor- style, quaint buildings they had just driven past in Chester.

Richard felt a small tug on his heartstrings every time he left the hustle and bustle of the capital city. No matter how many times he travelled out of London and into the countryside, the change was always a shock to his system. For some reason, leaving behind the bubble of his life in London and learning to adjust to a slower, gentler pace outside of it didn't come naturally to him.

He had long decided that he belonged in the heart of London and to this day he hadn't been tempted to exchange his tiny flat in South Kensington for a more spacious house in the suburbs or on the commuter belt.

Some people living in the middle of the city worked miracles with a minuscule patch of green grass or a small patio, trying to recreate the feel of country living. He'd seen north-facing basement flats skillfully growing wisteria and clematis on the walls and stairs, filling several pots with bright floral displays from early spring.

However, he was content with strolling around Hyde Park when he felt the need for a greener landscape or ambling slowly through Kensington Gardens if he wanted to enjoy some pretty flower beds.

Richard got up from the passenger seat and slammed shut his car door. Turning sideways, he leant against the Land Rover Discovery and waited for DI Eilidh Simmons to get out.

They were on the outskirts of Chester and as he looked around he could see in the distance the River Dee and parts of the old Roman wall.

In the 1st and 2nd centuries, the city of Chester had been as important to the Romans as London, or Londinium as they called it. Richard found that very hard to compute because nowadays London was a gigantic sprawl of a city, with almost nine million inhabitants, whereas Chester had around 80,000 inhabitants. The comparison was mind-boggling.

Richard had visited Chester a couple of times before and he liked the black-and- white oak timber buildings in its city center, even though only a very few of them were genuinely from the Tudor era. Most of the striking black-and-white buildings were Victorian, mock-Tudor impersonations. Like many of the ancient cities in England, Chester was a diverse place with a confusing mix of medieval, Roman, Tudor, Georgian, and Victorian architecture in it.

And like other parts of England, some ancient Roman roads were in use, too. They were going to be travelling part of the way along the route of a Roman road that day, too.

After stopping at Chester for lunch, Eilidh was planning on driving them to Wales on the A55 for a three o'clock appointment at Penrhyn Castle with Peter Griffiths, who was the Lead Curator for the National Trust in Wales.

As was always the case when they set off together out of London, they were going to take a look at the location of a high-profile art burglary. Their meeting with Peter had been pre-arranged so he could discuss with them the theft of a multi-million- pound master-piece by the Italian artist Sandro Botticelli and show them around the crime scene at Penrhyn Castle.

Feeling out of his depth with the case, a detective from Bangor Police Station had wanted from the outset to request the support and involvement of the Art and Antiquities Crime Unit at Scotland Yard, but for some reason Peter Griffiths and the team at Penrhyn Castle had disagreed with this, asking that they be given more time to assess what had happened during the burglary.

Four days after the theft had occurred and at the point when it was evident the painting was not going to be recovered any time soon, Peter Griffiths finally decided to reach out to Richard's department.

Peter's phone call to Scotland Yard did not go to plan and must have made him doubt the profession-alism of the officers working in the Art and Antiquities Crime Unit.

Richard couldn't help cringing whenever he remembered the day Peter called them and he was sure that Eilidh felt the same, not that he ever reminded her of it.

Looking back to that inauspicious day, he reckoned it was sheer desperation over losing a priceless Botticelli painting that had stopped Peter from hanging up the phone and giving up on getting any help from them.

To start with, Peter was put on hold several times before the receptionist at Scotland Yard managed to transfer the call to Eilidh's phone extension.

This, sadly, was a frequent occurrence for their little-recognised department. The Art and Antiquities Unit did not feature prominently beside the other larger, more high-profile departments at Scotland Yard.

When Peter Griffiths' call did reach Eilidh's extension, a further setback occurred for the poor man because Eilidh immediately thought Peter was one of the lads from Homicide, trying to pull her leg again.

To be fair to Eilidh, she had been irritated beyond measure that day by several mischievous phone calls from her old colleagues on the sixth floor. Unlike Eilidh, who was snowed under with work, some of the lads from Homicide were having a quiet day at the office and were bored.

One of Eilidh's former colleagues, like a naughty schoolboy, had called her extension earlier on that morning and had asked her to verify an 18th-century gold thimble for him.

She fell for that one, gave out the contact details of a reputable antiques dealer in London, and then afterwards wondered if Scotland Yard had an inexperienced operator manning the phones at reception.

Next, someone else from Homicide had requested, in a truly appalling Scottish accent, that she come up to Dundee and value a priceless collection of Beano comics.

After a short interval, she received another phone call reporting that a Banksy mural had been bulldozed down in Hackney.

Lastly, someone trying to impersonate an old lady informed her that a portrait of the Queen had been stolen from the National Portrait Gallery and was now hanging up on the side of a Sentry Box at Buckingham Palace...

At which point, Eilidh had slammed the phone down.

Throughout the morning, the two sergeants seated near Eilidh had listened with amusement as she became increasingly irate with the prank calls from her former colleagues. Eilidh was always an easy target to wind up because she took her job a little too seriously and tended to be more gullible than the other officers on Richard's team.

Homicide would have known, too, of course, that as long as it didn't get out of hand, Richard would turn a blind eye to their behavior. Having a sense of humor himself, Richard had taken it with good grace on the few occasions when they had made him the butt of their jokes.

Peter Griffiths, therefore, was set up to be the unlucky recipient of Eilidh's pent-up wrath when his call came through to her.

"Eilidh Simmons," Eilidh had said, putting her phone on speaker while she typed away at her computer.

"Is this the art department?" Peter had asked, cautiously.

"For fuck's sake!" yelled Eilidh, giving Richard, who was working quietly at his desk, a fright.

He turned and stared at her in surprise.

Richard rarely heard Eilidh swear and it was one of the traits he liked about her.

Given the air was pretty blue at Scotland Yard, he suspected her restraint wasn't because she was particularly sensitive about swearing but instead due to her being a bit of a control freak and not liking to fly off the handle.

This time, though, her homicide chums had obviously gone too far and pushed her over the edge.

"I beg your pardon, I was just trying to speak with the art department," said Peter in a horrified voice.

Alan and Mario, the two sergeants seated near Eilidh, chuckled to themselves.

Richard watched, perturbed, as Eilidh, summoning up what seemed to be one of her mindfulness techniques, shut her eyes and took a deep breath.

Then she opened her eyes again and glared down at the telephone.

"Look, get lost the lot of you or I'll come upstairs and speak to Lionel," she said, angrily. "He'll have all of you suspended for harassment towards a female officer. Enough is bloody enough, OK?"

"I'm afraid there's been some misunderstanding. I've been told to speak to Richard Langley, at the art department in Scotland Yard," mumbled Peter, sounding as though he was regretting his decision to call.

Something about Peter's voice made Eilidh blanch.

"I'm sorry, where are you calling from?" she asked in a much quieter voice.

"I'm Peter Griffiths, the Head Curator for the

National Trust in Wales. I'm calling about a robbery at Penrhyn Castle."

Eilidh cleared her throat.

"I'm so sorry, Peter. I've been plagued with quite a few nuisance calls recently and I thought your call was yet another one." She scowled at Alan and Mario, who were sniggering next to her. "I do apologize. By the way, for future reference, we work in the Art and Antiquities Crime Unit, not the art department," she explained, kindly. "Though I'm sure they understood what you meant at reception. I'll put you through to him now."

She put her phone on mute and turned an anguished face towards Richard.

"Man, this is so mortifying! It's Peter Griffiths, Head Curator in Wales for the National Trust," she said to Richard, looking shell-shocked.

Richard shrugged his shoulders and then waited for her to transfer the call, trying hard not to laugh at her.

Eilidh stuck her tongue out at him and transferred the call.

"Hello, Richard speaking," said Richard on answering his phone.

"Ah, finally," said Peter, sounding relieved. "I've been on the line for an eternity trying to get hold of you."

"I do apologize. I'm afraid that can often happen if you call the central number for Scotland Yard. Remind me to give you our department's direct number. Is there anything I can help you with, now that you've managed to reach us?"

"Yes, there is." Richard heard Peter sighing with exasperation on the other end of the line. "A Botticelli painting has been stolen from Penrhyn Castle and we're needing your assistance, if at all possible. Inspector Thompson at Bangor Police Station recommended I speak to you."

"Good grief! A Botticelli, you said?"

Eilidh and the two sergeants swiveled their heads and looked at Richard. None of them were making any pretense at getting any work done.

So much for having an open-plan office, thought Richard. It was far too much of a distraction in his opinion.

He motioned for the others to get back to work again.

"Yes," replied Peter, his unhappiness echoing down the phone line. "The Botticelli painting was placed in the castle office, prior to hanging it up, and was stolen from there."

"Hold on a minute," insisted Richard, dragging a piece of paper towards him and grabbing hold of a pen. "If you could just start from the beginning for me, please." Peter sighed, as though he had repeated the story one too many times. "When did the theft happen?" asked Richard.

"It happened during the night, on the 8th of October. In the early hours of the morning. I think from what the security guards said the exterior alarm in the Housekeeper's Room went off at around 3.30 a.m. I should explain that "Housekeeper's Room" is a bit of a misnomer. The room isn't just used by the castle's housekeeper, it's used by other members of staff who are responsible for the cleaning and maintenance of the artifacts in the castle."

"But I thought you said the painting was in the castle office."

"Yes, it was, of course, but you can't enter or exit the castle from the office. When the guards heard the alarm, they walked past the office on their way to the Housekeeper's Room and noticed that the office door had been wrenched open, breaking all three of the mortice locks and badly damaging the door frame. When they looked inside the office, they found the open crate with its packaging tossed on the floor and an empty picture frame."

"What's the painting valued at?" asked Richard, a question he had to ask, even though he knew any genuine Botticelli oil painting would be worth millions and therefore justify his department's involvement. Only recently, Botticelli's *Young Man Holding a Roundel* had been sold via Sotheby's for nearly 65 million pounds.

"It hasn't got a valuation as yet, I'm afraid. It has only been certified recently by an academic from Oxford University."

"I'm afraid I'll need to, at some point, come up with an approximate estimate of its value for the sake of our departmental procedures. It's a real pain, I know, but we're a small unit and we're always stretched. I have to defend the use of our limited resources."

Richard coughed with embarrassment. It was shameful, in his view, how little funding and support their department had.

"Was the Botticelli artwork painted on wood paneling or canvas?" he asked, moving on swiftly. "As you probably know, if it was painted on canvas then the painting must have been destined for a nobleman's house when it was made. In which case, it would almost certainly have been painted by Sandro Botticelli himself, not one of his studio minions. That's an important distinction as far as the value of it goes."

"It was a canvas painting. It was cut out of its wooden frame."

"Well, that was very foolish of the robber," commented Richard, starting to doodle on his sheet of paper under the word "*canvas*." "A painting without its original frame is worth a considerable amount less."

"I think when you hear the rest of my report, you'll see why the thief removed the frame," said Peter sharply, offended by Richard's casual tone.

"Fire away, Peter, I'm all ears."

"When they reached the corridor leading to the Housekeeper's Room they saw a man at the other end, holding onto the folded canvas. He was dressed in black and wearing a balaclava. Both security guards, by the way, are adamant it was a man. The build of him, I think is what they said. They rushed to the Housekeeper's Room only to see the thief climb through the open window, drop down onto the carriage forecourt, and run off at full speed towards the castle grounds with the canvas flapping at his side."

"*Carriage Forecourt,*" "*Housekeeper's Room.*"

Richard thought Peter's tale had all the romance in it of a Mills & Boon book. The robbery was beginning to sound totally unreal to him.

It had to be the first time he'd heard of a Botticelli painting in Wales, too.

Then he suddenly remembered Botticelli's *Virgin and Child with a Pomegranate* at the Cardiff Museum. For decades, it had been hidden in storage until experts from the BBC television program *Britain's Lost Master-*

pieces had declared it as a genuine Botticelli painting or, at the very least, produced in Botticelli's studio.

Was this painting another remarkable Botticelli find?

For a moment, he felt as though he was falling down a rabbit hole alongside Alice in *Alice in Wonderland.*

"So, Peter, I take it the guards chased after the thief? I mean, they did know he had hold of a Botticelli painting?" he asked, trying to focus once more.

"The two of them had been told there was an item of great value in the office but they didn't know it was a Botticelli. Don't think it would have meant anything to them, if we'd told them."

Fair enough, thought Richard. Why would two security guards be interested in art? Art wasn't everybody's cup of tea.

"They did run after the thief," added Peter, in defense of the security guards. "Or at least, from what I understood, one of the guards followed the thief through the window and ran after him but beyond the carriage forecourt, in the total darkness outside, he soon lost sight of him. He did have a torch on him but unfortunately Baqir's not very fit. In fact, he's got a substantial paunch so I'm surprised he managed to even run after the thief. But in any case, he lost sight of the thief in the undergrowth near the Heather Slope, which is where the other guard, Dylan, joined him."

"Sorry, what did Dylan do while the overweight guard chased the thief out of the window?"

He heard Eilidh gasp next to him.

He turned and shrugged at her again. There was no

way of sugar-coating "substantial paunch". It was what it was.

"Dylan went out of the main entrance of the castle. Which is fair enough, in my view. It's quite a drop down to the carriage forecourt from the window..."

There was a long pause at the other end of the line and Richard guessed Peter was thinking things through.

"Neither guard saw a car anywhere, other than a Ford Focus and a Nissan in the car park, both of which belonged to them. You get a very good view of the surrounding area from the castle grounds and the lack of transportation has us all puzzled. You see, there are many acres of land around the castle, which means that it would take the thief at least 40 minutes to walk to the nearest village. Not an easy thing to do in the dark, even with a torch."

"What about a bicycle?" asked Richard, as he sketched the shape of a car under "*no getaway car*" on his piece of paper.

"None of the guards saw a bicycle or any bike lights, but in any case it was a horrible night. It had been raining heavily and the sky was overcast so it was very dark. In my view, those are not ideal conditions to be cycling in but I'm no cyclist, so I'm not really qualified to judge that."

"I imagine if he's done it many times before, it wouldn't be too hard for the thief to cycle in the dark."

"I disagree. Both guards said it was pitch-black that night. I don't think there's any way a bicycle could have managed along that bumpy road in the dark. The guards wondered if there could be a car waiting for the thief further down the road, perhaps, but they walked around the castle and along the road and didn't spot any headlights or hear a car engine. Although with the noise from the alarm going off it's not surprising, really, that they couldn't hear anything."

Richard grunted.

"So, at what point did the Bangor police get involved?" he asked. Peter cleared his throat.

"Well, the police took ages to turn up. I don't think they fully comprehended the magnitude of the theft."

Probably not, thought Richard. After all, even the security guards at the castle hadn't had a clue what they were dealing with.

He resisted pointing this out to Peter.

"The guards called Bangor Police Station to report the theft and then Baqir decided to call up three of Penrhyn's long-time members of staff. They all live locally in the village of Llandygai. By this time, it was around four o'clock in the morning, I think. Anyway, the other members of staff all drove up to the estate and with torches joined the guards in searching for the thief in the grounds."

"And I take it they weren't successful in finding anything," said Richard.

"No, they weren't. The police turned up two hours later. Shockingly late, in my view. They had a good look around but by eight o'clock in the morning everyone decided it would be best to refer the matter to myself and Stephanie Meadows, the onsite curator at Penrhyn Castle. Stephanie Meadows called me as soon as she heard about the robbery. She was utterly distraught, of course."

"I hope Bangor police called forensics in?"

"Yes, they did. Once they realized the value of the stolen painting, that is. No new leads came up with forensics. What confused us all is that the window in the Housekeeper's Room was unlocked from the inside, not the outside."

"It sounds to me as though the thief was a professional or else that an insider was responsible."

"I know, that's what the staff have been saying. They're all saying that the few people who knew about the painting were involved in its theft. I've been pretty stern with the staff at Penrhyn and told them to stop making slanderous accusations, based on no foundation whatsoever. It doesn't make for a very pleasant working environment when there's a witch-hunt going on amongst the staff to find the culprit."

"No, of course not," agreed Richard.

However, he was inclined to agree with the staff at Penrhyn because many art experts reckoned that up to 80 percent of art theft cases involved insider participation of some kind. Very few of these corrupted insiders were ever caught.

He could tell this wasn't something Peter wanted to hear, though, and there was plenty of time for all that later. Art crimes were seldom resolved in a short time-frame; it could take months, if not years, for some artworks to be traced and restored to their rightful homes.

Richard didn't like to think about the many valuable artworks that were still missing, with little hope of finding them. It kept him awake at night.

"Could you tell me a little more about the Botticelli painting, Peter?" he asked, instead.

"Yes. It's been renamed *Two Angels above the River Arno*. It used to hang up in a dark corner of the chapel corridor because no one had really established who the artist was. It was a quasi-religious painting, badly in need of some restoration, but we had several other, more important paintings lined up for the conservator-restorer. Or so we thought at the time. Everyone assumed the Botticelli painting was insignificant and therefore worthless. There was no mention of the painting in the family's records either, which in itself was unusual."

"I see," said Richard dryly, thinking to himself that surely between two experienced art curators they could have spotted the work of a genius Italian Renaissance artist.

"The Botticelli painting was dark with grime, and had discolored, yellow varnish on it," added Peter, as though excusing his error in judgement. "And we look after so many renowned artworks. Penrhyn Castle has a stunning collection of paintings, which includes works by Canaletto, Hans Holbein the Younger, van Dyck, and Gainsborough. All owned by the Penrhyn Family Trust, of course."

"OK," said Richard, scribbling down Penrhyn Family Trust on his paper. He wondered how they were feeling about the theft. "When did the painting get authenticated?"

"Only a month and a half ago. An art history professor from Oxford University, Professor Marco Balboa, took the painting away and studied it extensively, with kind permission from the Douglas-Pennant family. He declared that in his professional opinion, the painting was a masterpiece by Sandro Botticelli."

"Did the other experts on Botticelli agree with his diagnosis?" asked Richard, knowing full well the jealous and competitive environment these so-called "art experts" operated in. He wouldn't have been surprised if a number of them were reluctant to concede to a member of their clan any fame for discovering a hitherto unknown masterpiece.

"Well, in actual fact, the leading Botticelli academics he consulted with did agree with him. The proof was irrefutable, that's probably why. He investigated the painting fully, using infrared analysis and hiring an expert conservator-restorer to remove the dirt and old varnish."

Peter gave a long sigh on the other end of the phone.

He was wearying but Richard felt he hadn't lost him yet.

Peter knew how pertinent Professor Balboa's research would turn out to be if they ever found the painting again. If the masterpiece was recovered, the research done on it would help identify the painting as the stolen, Botticelli original.

"Professor Balboa established that the artwork had all the features, technique and style of Botticelli's work," continued Peter, as though repeating a mantra. "He's studied the draftsmanship under the paintwork in great detail with scans. He's looked closely at the brushstrokes used in the flesh tones. There was the use of the pigments in the painting, with the enamel-like effect of the paint layers which was so distinctive in Botticelli's work. The green color in the angels' garments and their garlands has turned brown because of the artist's use of copper resinate in his pigments... It's all there on file."

"OK. Professor Balboa had the painting. I presume he then returned it to the castle after his investigations?"

"Yes. He did, of course. When we found out the painting was a Botticelli we wanted to put it up in a more secure and illustrious position within the castle." Peter sighed. A sigh that denoted disappointment more than anything else. "The plan was for the Botticelli painting to be put in the same place where Rembrandt's *Catrina Hooghsaet* painting used to hang. In the Breakfast Room at the castle."

"The Catrina Hooghsaet painting?"

Richard knew he had heard of the painting before but was struggling to recollect when and where.

"Yes, you might have heard about it," said Peter, uncannily reading Richard's thoughts. "The Catrina *Hooghsaet* painting was sold by the family trust a few years ago for 35 million pounds and, after much controversy over a UK export license, it was placed on long-term loan at the National Cardiff Museum in Wales."

Now Richard remembered it.

He did indeed recall the outcry caused when Rembrandt's *Catrina Hooghsaet* was sold by Sotheby's in the summer of 2015. Quite apart from anything else, there had been significant press coverage about the painting.

The Art Fund had been wanting to spearhead a campaign to buy the Rembrandt painting and preserve it for the British public but, at the last-minute, the request for an export license for the painting was withdrawn and it was declared the picture would be kept temporarily in the UK.

In 2025 the anonymous owner would be entitled to reapply for an export license for the painting and who knew what would happen then? Would the Art Fund be able to raise the money required to buy it, when in all likelihood the painting would have gained in value?

"Anyway," Peter said, carrying on regardless of Richard's musings on the *Catrina Hooghsaet* painting. "The Botticelli was only in the office for one day before it was stolen. It was placed in the office awaiting its re-hanging because space needed to be allocated to it in the Breakfast Room. The office, of course, is closed to the general public."

It was stolen after one day?

Richard was stunned. Someone on the inside must have been involved, he thought to himself.

After that surprising statement, Peter didn't have much more to tell Richard.

Richard, still digesting the extraordinary fact that Botticelli's *Two Angels above the River Arno* had been stolen after sitting in the locked castle office for only one day, managed to say they would be in touch very shortly to arrange a visit to the castle.

He also asked Peter for Professor Balboa's phone number and rang the academic straightaway to request as much information as possible on the painting.

Later that day, he received a file in his email inbox with every detail of the professor's research and some enticing photographs of the painting. Richard scrolled through the attached close-ups on his computer, admiring the painter's technique and use of color.

The Botticelli painting had two angels in it that were flying above a river, and according to Professor Balboa the architecture of the buildings in the distance suggested the river was most likely to be the Arno in Tuscany.

The angels in the painting were carrying thick,

colorful garlands consisting of roses, irises, cornflowers, jasmine, carnations, and lilies.

Some of these flowers were used as Christian symbols, others had mythological associations. Irises were used as an emblem of Florence during the Renaissance, which further corroborated the painting as a masterpiece from Botticelli's home city and era.

All the botanical features in the painting were executed in a similar way to Botticelli's famous *Primavera* painting, although the Penrhyn masterpiece had a simpler composition and was much smaller, hanging at 1.37 meters wide and 1.04 meters high.

So, two days later, armed with plenty of information about the painting, Richard and Eilidh were on their way to Penrhyn Castle.

The theft had occurred six days ago now, which left Richard wondering why it had taken Peter Griffiths and his team so long to report the crime to the Art and Antiquities Unit, but that was a question for later that afternoon.

Right then, though, Richard had other, more important, matters on his mind. He was hungry and wanted some food. Due to Eilidh's phobia of being late, they had driven continuously for four hours and hadn't even stopped at a service station for a packet of crisps. Having only had a black coffee for his breakfast, Richard was feeling one step away from starvation.

Eilidh knew a long-time friend in Chester and had organized for them to go to her house for lunch, so he was going to have to wait for his food. Lunch with a friend made perfect sense to Eilidh because their meeting with Peter wasn't until three o'clock that afternoon and she hadn't seen her college friend for several

years. In effect, their trip to Wales would be killing two
birds with one stone for her.

Richard, however, would have preferred to have
used the spare time to look around Penrhyn Castle
before their meeting. He understood Eilidh's natural
desire to catch up with a friend from her college days
but he felt the more time they had to look around the
crime scene, the better. He was kicking himself that he
hadn't been firmer and voiced his objections.

Quite aside from everything else, his hunger would
have been sated by now if they had just stopped and
grabbed some sandwiches on the way...

2

Richard

Resigned to his fate and gearing himself up to be sociable, he followed Eilidh along the pavement and up the steps to her friend's home in Chester, an old, red-brick house listed as number 23 Queens Park Road.

While Eilidh pushed on the doorbell and waited for the front door to open, he turned around and studied the street they were on.

The first thing that struck him was that it wasn't a peaceful location for a residential home because there was a school directly opposite the house. A minute ago, the school bell had blasted out and now the tarmacked playground was packed full of school children running about, shrieking, yelling, and generally expending all the energy they had built up inside the classroom.

The noise coming from the playground was joyful but Richard wasn't kidding himself that school was the place to produce happy memories. To this day, he couldn't recall anyone he knew saying school had been the best experience of their life, which suggested to him that there was something wrong with the education system in the UK. Maybe too many square pegs—children who were perceived as different—were being forced to squeeze into bog-standard, round holes.

In contrast to the chaos taking place in the playground opposite, the garden at number 23 looked as though it had been groomed to within an inch of its life, each blade of grass standing to attention alongside perfectly manicured rhododendron and camellia bushes.

Two regal stone lions sat on either side of the front door, and next to them were two matching olive-green pots, each containing a pruned basil tree.

Impatient as ever, Eilidh pushed the doorbell for a second time. They heard the doorbell chime again and then, at last, the dove-grey door opened wide. From the doorstep Natalia Symanski, Eilidh's erstwhile friend, smiled cheerfully at them.

"Come in! Come in!" she screeched happily, standing back and waving them in. Natalia reached forward and hugged Eilidh as she walked into the hallway, wrapping her arms around her shoulders and kissing her on both cheeks.

Amused to see this effusive continental greeting, Richard wondered how Eilidh felt about it.

He knew Eilidh wasn't a touchy-feely kind of person so he was surprised to see Eilidh taking Natalia's hug in her stride, returning it with gusto. Clearly, a close friendship existed between the two of them.

Turning around, Natalia reached out and shook hands with Richard, her head tilted to one side as she looked him up and down.

"Welcome to my home, Richard. I've heard an awful lot about you from Eilidh," she said, her pale-blue eyes appraising him. Not in the least bit disconcerted by her scrutiny, Richard smiled back at her.

He decided he liked Natalia's vibe. She seemed very eccentric, which he hadn't expected because her front garden, conservative and tidy, looked like something out of a landscape gardener's manual.

Dressed in a lemon-yellow floral dress and cardigan, Natalia was wearing several brightly colored plastic rings on her fingers and a pair of black, diamanté glasses that wouldn't have shamed Dame Edna.

Her curly, blonde hair was pulled back in a ponytail and tied up with a dark-red scarf, exposing a square-shaped face with an aquiline nose and thin lips.

She wasn't a beauty, by any means, but Richard thought she came across as a mesmerizing and attractive character. In his opinion, charisma was a trait that you couldn't hide and it seemed to him that it flowed out of Natalia in bucket loads.

The delicious aroma of what Richard guessed was a lamb casserole filled the hallway. He thought he could detect the scent of tomato, basil and rosemary, as well as lamb, but it was possible his hungry mind was just imagining it. To his acute discomfort, his stomach growled loudly as Eilidh and Natalia exchanged pleasantries.

The ravenous complaint from Richard's stomach was enough to prompt Eilidh and Natalia to start making their way down the hallway to the back of the house, both of them politely pretending not to have heard his stomach rumble.

Richard was about to follow them when he caught sight of a cluster of black-and- white photographs hanging on the hallway wall.

Unable to suppress his curiosity, he stayed behind for a moment to study them.

Each photograph on the wall appeared to be a snapshot of a farm, with the camera lens focusing on details such as a barn door, a frosted window and a pot of soup boiling on an Aga oven.

Some of the photos were more natural than others, capturing a hen pecking at some grain, for example, or a hay bale sitting in an empty field.

All of them had rustic charm but Richard noticed that a few had been taken at an awkward angle or were slightly out of focus, revealing the photographer was something of an amateur.

Rubbing his chin thoughtfully, he wondered if Natalia had taken the photos and whether she had sentimental links to the farmhouse.

With that intriguing question at the back of his mind, he hurried after Eilidh and Natalia, who by now had reached the entrance to the kitchen.

Natalia's kitchen was a room whose style was completely different to the homely farmhouse photographed in the hallway.

The room was large and modern, with several glass doors facing out onto a big garden with pleached trees around the perimeter, giving it some privacy from the houses nearby.

Richard, who was inclined to favor the traditional over the modern, found himself admiring the contemporary décor in Natalia's kitchen because the room's design seemed to embrace the old house and make use of its features.

Part of the building's original, red brickwork was exposed above the cooker and worktops, contrasting with the dark-grey cabinets and white marble surfaces.

Navy, velvet stools surrounded a kitchen island. The island itself was bright orange on all sides with a white marble top, enabling it to mesh with the orange-red of the brick wall opposite it.

The floor, meanwhile, consisted of patterned white and grey tiles.

Not a color combination or style Richard would have dared to use in his own small kitchen but somehow in Natalia's house the brave color choices, the different tones and textures, seemed to blend together and work.

After Natalia had encouraged her guests to take a seat, she went and fetched a bottle of red Bordeaux from the wine rack, placing it on the table in front of them.

"No, thank you, Nat. We're both taking turns driving, I'm afraid," said Eilidh, smiling apologetically.

Natalia pouted in disappointment, her hands on her hips in a very Gallic posture.

"No? Are you sure you won't even have one glass?" Both Richard and Eilidh shook their heads.

"OK, fine. Would you like some mineral water or soft drinks?" Natalia asked, accepting defeat.

"Mineral water would be great, thank you," said Richard.

Eilidh nodded in agreement, so Natalia, making a face, went to search in her double-doored fridge for the water.

She reappeared shortly afterwards with a bottle of mineral water in her hand and poured it into their wine glasses, leaving the rest on the table for them.

Undeterred from having some wine herself, Natalia

reached for the bottle opener, pulled the cork out of the Bordeaux, and poured herself a large glass of wine.

Sitting down, she took a sip of wine and smiled at them over the rim of her glass. "Well, it's lovely to have you both here. It's been a long time, hasn't it, Eilidh?" Eilidh nodded.

"Yes, nearly four years I think."

Natalia groaned and drank some more wine.

"Now you're making me feel old," she said at last, looking sad. "It's true what they say about time going by faster the older you get. My biological clock's ticking and it's starting to freak me out. I know I'm going to end up at the local sperm bank."

Richard and Eilidh glanced at each other as Natalia finished her glass of wine and topped it up again.

"What's your line of work, Natalia?" asked Richard, keen to change the subject and break the awkward silence.

"Hasn't Eilidh told you? I work as interior designer. I'm lucky, I've got a group of loyal clients who want me to do up their homes every couple of years or so, so it means I don't have to go out touting for work."

"She's very well-known and successful," Eilidh explained to Richard. "She does up the homes of some Man City and Man United football players."

Natalia chuckled.

"Yes, but don't tell them that, for heaven's sake. Both teams are mortal enemies."

Much to Richard's relief, Natalia opened a bag of pepper Kettle Chips, poured them out into a wooden bowl and offered it to them.

Both Eilidh and Richard tucked in heartily.

Richard, having grabbed a big handful of crisps in a

manner that would have drawn a stern rebuke from his mother, proceeded to munch them up as fast as he could.

Natalia, on the other hand, seemed to be content to drink her wine and watch them.

"Where were the photographs in the hallway taken?" asked Richard, having taken the edge off his hunger sufficiently to be able to concentrate on other things.

"Those photos are of my parents" farmhouse in Poland. It's where my heart will always be," replied Natalia, smiling at him. "I go there as often as I can. I took the photos myself, as you can probably tell."

"They're very attractive. A different way of life, I'm guessing," commented Richard.

"Yes, it's a way of life that's vanishing fast in my homeland. Speaking of being far from home, what are you guys after up here? I'm very curious. Has a Leonardo da Vinci or a Rembrandt gone missing from a stately home?" asked Natalia, as she finished her second glass of wine.

"Something like that," replied Richard, with a grin. "To be honest with you, some of the artworks hiding out in the Welsh countryside are absolutely incredible. It's astonishing, actually."

"It's not that amazing," remarked Natalia, looking down the stem of her wine glass. "A country estate has always been the must-have of most upwardly mobile people. I should know. I spend half my bloody time crisscrossing Wales and England as I try to find my client's latest holiday home and I often get lost down winding country lanes in the process. I can't imagine it was any different back in the day."

A bell pinged from the oven, startling them.

"Just as well I put the timer on," said Natalia wryly, as she got up and opened the oven door, letting out a potent waft of lamb stew.

Lifting the lid of the casserole dish with a padded glove, she poked about expertly with a knife.

"Nice and tender. Perfect."

She replaced the lid and lifted the heavy casserole dish onto a placemat at the table.

Richard bit back a smile when he caught sight of the expression on Eilidh's face. She was staring at the casserole dish in front of her, oblivious to everyone else. He could tell that, like him, she was ready to wolf down some food at the earliest opportunity.

Prolonging their agony, Natalia went to the sideboard to pick up a basket of what seemed to be homemade bread, with each slice showing a fluffy white underbelly beneath its thick crust.

She placed the bread basket on the table and then, before serving up the stew, went to check the oven was switched off.

When Natalia finally seated herself at the table and took the lid off the casserole dish, Richard found himself shutting his eyes in bliss as he breathed in the delicious smell.

The mouth-watering aroma only became more potent as Natalia started to fill up the bowls in front of her with a soup ladle.

Living on his own in London, Richard seldom had the opportunity to eat a decent home-cooked meal and so Natalia's cooking was a real treat for him. He had, of course, forgotten that he had ever wanted to stop and grab a sandwich at a service station.

He heard the sound of muffled laughter and opened up his eyes to find Natalia and Eilidh watching him in amusement.

"Honestly, Richard, I can't take you anywhere," remonstrated Eilidh.

"It just smells so heavenly," explained Richard apologetically. "I might not be a decent cook, in fact my cooking to be honest with you is appalling, but I do know how to appreciate good quality food."

Natalia beamed across at him.

"Well, I think that's the nicest compliment anyone's ever given me on my cooking.

Tuck in," she said, handing him a bowl filled to the brim.

Richard soon lost track of the conversation after he started eating. Eilidh and Natalia had gone down memory lane and had begun to discuss people and places he didn't know but he was quite happy to be left out. Savoring each mouthful of his meal, he was focused on the food in front of him and content to do nothing else for the time being.

Before he had finished his second helping, though, Natalia turned and looked at him.

"Where are you driving to? I might know the place."

"Penrhyn Castle," answered Eilidh. Natalia's eyebrows shot up.

"Really? That's very interesting. My goodness, what a surprise! I hadn't expected you to be heading there."

She smiled at them.

"You should know that Penrhyn Castle's a very

weird place," Natalia informed them. "There's a strange atmosphere in that building."

She fiddled with her napkin for a moment, as though unsure about what she wanted to say next.

"And many people have said that the castle's haunted by ghosts," she added, avoiding their eyes.

Richard and Eilidh gazed at her with mingled disbelief and interest.

"I'm serious," insisted Natalia, looking ashamed to have brought up the controversial subject of ghosts but determined to tackle it all the same. "There's been loads of recorded sightings and a lot of odd, unexplained things happening in the castle. You can read about it on their blog."

She swallowed some more wine and glowered across at them with defiant eyes.

"I think there's always going to be ghostly sightings in any historical building," said Richard, trying to introduce a more prosaic and level-headed tone to the conversation. "The past kind of gets people's imagination going, doesn't it?"

Richard wasn't someone who liked to ridicule other people's beliefs but he did not subscribe to thinking the supernatural existed or influenced events in the real day- to-day world. He thought those views were the remit of people with too much time on their hands, but he could see Natalia was offended by his dismissive understanding of the matter and that she wanted him to take her comments seriously.

The corners of Natalia's mouth had edged downwards as she pursed her lips, the smooth, unlined skin around her mouth revealing that this was not an expression commonly used by her.

"I don't think over a hundred sightings can be summed up as *"people's imagination,"* Richard," she said, sounding cross as she swirled the little wine remaining in her glass round and round in front of her. "And there's proof, you know. Some visitors to the castle have taken photos of Penrhyn's ghosts."

"Sounds a little bit too much like the Loch Ness Monster to me, Nat. People said they had photos of it, too," commented Eilidh skeptically.

"Come on, that's daft. There's no comparison between the Loch Ness Monster and what's going on at Penrhyn Castle. Nothing like the variety and number of reported incidents from visitors, volunteers, staff and even professionals like the engineer who works in the Railway Museum at the castle."

Eilidh shrugged.

"Well, I guess it's one of those things that's impossible to prove or disprove," she said in a neutral tone of voice.

Natalia sniffed, not looking convinced by this.

Richard smiled to himself. Eilidh would be the last person on the planet to subscribe to superstition but she was always diplomatic when she needed to be, making her an invaluable officer.

"Well, as you can probably both tell, I do believe ghosts are haunting the castle," stated Natalia, reaching for the wine bottle and pouring out her fourth glass of wine. "Everyone knows ghosts tend to haunt the places where appalling things have happened in the past. Take the Tower of London, for example, or the Royal Mile in Edinburgh. Anyone who knows Penrhyn Castle is aware of its shameful history. There's a whole load of ugly deeds associated with that building and its previous owners."

Sighing heavily, she ran a finger around the rim of her glass.

"Some of the stuff they did in the past might have been accepted and legal back then but nowadays, of course, it's seen as the height of monstrosity."

Natalia drank some more of her Bordeaux, then leaned forward, holding on tightly to her glass.

"Everyone hereabouts knows that Penrhyn Castle, all its land and its famous art collection, were bought with money made from slave labor," Natalia said, lowering her voice dramatically. "Richard Pennant, one of the head honchos at Penrhyn Castle, owned nearly a thousand slaves and it was the money from Jamaican slave labor that paid for roads, railways, houses and schools near here. And if that wasn't bad enough, conditions at the Penrhyn slate quarries were so bad it led to the longest strike in British industrial history."

Natalia tossed down the remainder of her wine.

"And," she said, raising her forefinger. "It's important not to forget that Richard Pennant spoke as an MP in Parliament *against* the abolition of the slave trade. Thankfully, a majority in Parliament didn't agree with him but still, where would we be today if his views had prevailed?"

Richard watched as Natalia stood up and poured the dregs of the wine bottle into her glass. Natalia was proving she had a high tolerance for alcohol.

He turned and looked out into her garden. Grey clouds had gathered during their lunch and the sky was now dreary and dark.

Sitting in the coziness of Natalia's kitchen, Richard

felt the darkness outside was heightening the impact of Natalia's storytelling. *It was amazing how the imagination worked*, he thought, when in reality what one could see outside of Natalia's French windows was just what one expected at this time of the year: yet another dull, autumnal day.

"Don't you guys wonder if there's any karma in life? Do you think people ever get what they deserve?" asked Natalia, a whimsical note creeping into her voice as she sat back down again.

"Nope. I don't think so, Nat. Life isn't fair and it never was," said Eilidh with certainty.

"I suppose I should expect an answer like that to come from a policewoman," remarked Natalia, a disparaging smirk on her face.

"I have to say, I kind of sit on the fence with that one," interjected Richard, his interest awakened.

Eilidh turned to look at him in surprise but didn't say anything.

"I do tend to agree with Eilidh that life in general is unfair and random," mused Richard. "But sometimes, I do think what goes around comes around. Cause and effect, you know. From what I've seen, grudges and hurts from the past have a habit of coming back to see justice done."

Richard tore off a piece of bread from the basket and dipped it into the sauce left in his bowl.

"I mean, it seems to happen all the time when countries or communities have been at war with each other. Even if the conflict occurred hundreds of years ago," he added, holding onto his piece of bread. "The historical undercurrents are always there in the present-day and it can become an endless cycle of tit for tat."

"That's exactly my point," agreed Natalia, leaning back on her chair and watching Richard as he ate his bread. "Injustice from the past will always come back and haunt the present. People don't forget. Therefore, in my humble opinion, all those ghosts up at Penrhyn Castle will never be able to rest in peace. It's my belief that the cruelty done by Penrhyn's past owners to the slaves and the quarry workers is the reason why their ghosts are still with us in the land of the living."

Richard and Eilidh were silent, not wanting to enter into a dispute with their host about the validity of her views.

In the background, a magpie suddenly chattered to itself as it bounced along the garden wall outside.

"I didn't think you were one to advocate the "an eye for an eye" way of thinking, Richard," said Eilidh, with mild disapproval.

"I'm not advocating it, Eilidh, but it doesn't mean it doesn't happen and that people don't want vengeance for past injustice. Sometimes they get it, sometimes they don't. That's what I was saying in a nutshell."

"This conversation's really a bit depressing," reflected Eilidh, as she picked up their bowls and carried them over to the sink. "I guess we should be thankful we live in a different age and time now. I think there are many issues to resolve, of course, but it seems to me that the majority of people want to try and move on in the right direction and heal wounds from the past. At the end of the day, most people want to live a peaceful, happy, and free life. It's as simple as that. It's the politicians in charge who tend to screw things up."

"No politics, please!" begged Natalia, raising both palms in mock horror. "I know I'm responsible for bringing it up but I can assure you, what we don't want is to have a political debate. It'll curdle the food in our bellies. Let's have some coffee and chocolate instead."

Eilidh looked amused but didn't say anything more.

After inquiring which of the grey cabinet doors had the dishwasher hidden behind it, she started stacking the bowls and cutlery neatly into it.

Richard looked at his watch and, with a shock, realized they would need to leave soon if they were going to make it up to Penrhyn Castle on time.

He got up hurriedly and helped to clear the table, wiping up the scattered crumbs and dribbles of casserole with a cloth from the sink.

"Honestly, guys, please just leave it. I've plenty of time later to get around to clearing up, and if not, my lovely cleaner, Amelia, will tidy this up in the morning," said Natalia, who was laying out three stoneware mugs on the work surface.

"Coffee, anyone?" she asked, as she reached across and began to fill up a cafetiere with boiling water from a separate tap.

"Yes, please," said Richard, feeling very grateful for the opportunity to have some caffeine. The massive lunch he'd consumed was now starting to make him feel very drowsy.

He stretched backwards and yawned, feeling the tears start in his eyes as he did so.

Needless to say, given Richard's sleepiness, it was Eilidh who drove them up to Penrhyn Castle half an hour later. Richard suspected she didn't much trust his driving skills anyway and even less so when he was tired. In any case, it suited him just fine to sit in a comatose stupor, gazing out of the car window at the passing Welsh countryside.

"Natalia likes her drink, doesn't she?" he asked Eilidh, a few minutes into their drive.

"Yes, she does, but as far as I'm aware she doesn't seem to have a drinking problem, if that's what you're implying, Richard. She has a very active social life and drink's a part of that."

Richard nodded, unconvinced by the well-worn excuse for heavy drinking, but not willing to argue the point with Eilidh. Thankfully, it wasn't his problem to worry about.

An hour later, after encountering light traffic on the roads, they found themselves reversing into a space in an almost empty car park at Castle Penrhyn.

Richard opened the car door and got out, looking with great interest at the huge estate.

Despite not being a big fan of the countryside, he enjoyed breathing in the fresh oxygenated sea air and seeing before him the tranquility of the rolling, green landscape. Indeed, it would be hard to find anything more different to the City of Westminster's noisy, polluted congestion than the gentle hills and lush trees in front of him. Even though he was certain the novelty would wear off after a while, it was an attractive enough prospect for now.

He turned his eyes back to the car park.

Perhaps an overcast, autumnal weekday might explain why the imposing castle and its magnificent gardens had so few visitors but Richard was still taken aback to see the car park had only three cars in it. Maybe this was the norm for Penrhyn Castle but with such a meager number of visitors, how on earth did the

National Trust manage to stay on top of all the upkeep required for the place?

However, rather selfishly, he reckoned that if they were going to figure out what happened the night the Botticelli painting was stolen, it was better to have the area more or less to themselves.

They made their way along the road towards the grey walls of Penrhyn Castle and stopped to admire the view of the Welsh coastline, with the rough waters of the Menai Straits to the north.

When they turned to face south, they could see the dark peaks of the Snowdonia mountains, their undulating lines breaking up the horizon.

Large and forbidding, though, the grey castle dominated the surrounding landscape and its high stone walls loomed over them as they approached.

Despite its thick walls, fortress-like towers and narrow windows, Penrhyn Castle wasn't a proper castle by any stretch of the imagination. Having been completely rebuilt in the 19th century, Penrhyn Castle was a Victorian's fantasy version of a Norman castle and it wasn't constructed for defensive purposes, but for pleasure and comfort instead.

Richard and Eilidh made their way up to the front entrance, walking under the archway and then crossing the gravelly carriage forecourt.

They greeted the lady in uniform standing by the double doors. She seemed to have been primed about their visit because she called Peter Griffiths straightaway on her mobile and informed him the "police" were there.

Peter appeared less than five minutes later, which was a bonus for them as they were waiting outside, shivering slightly in the cool breeze. Like the typical Londoners that they both were, they had underdressed for the more northerly climate.

Richard had expected a longer wait for Peter to arrive given the size of Penrhyn Castle and reckoned that whatever office Peter used when he was on the premises must be close by, on the ground floor.

Peter Griffiths turned out to be a short, unprepossessing man, with round glasses and a balding head that had a few stray strands of russet hair artfully combed over.

After shaking hands with them both, Peter turned to lead the way into the castle.

"Is that the window the thief jumped out of?" asked Eilidh quickly, pointing across to one of the windows on the ground floor of the castle.

Peter stopped and looked at the window Eilidh was pointing at.

"No, I'm afraid it wasn't that one. It's the second window from the left. I can take you straightaway to where the thief escaped, if you feel you'd like to have a look around there and in the office, before reviewing some of the CCTV footage we have."

"Yes, that would be helpful," confirmed Richard, thinking to himself how ridiculous it was for Peter to consider they might not want to inspect the crime scene first of all. He could only hope the thief was as daft as Peter because it would make the robbery so much easier to solve.

As Richard walked into the castle, past the thick oak doors at the entrance and through a number of towering stone arches, he felt the hairs on his scalp stand on end.

Having been so dismissive of Natalia's stories of ghostly apparitions, he could now see and feel for himself the heavy, brooding atmosphere in the castle. He also understood, for the first time, how Gothic romanticism from the past could revisit a place like Penrhyn Castle and weave its spell amongst the people visiting there.

But even so, he absolutely refused to believe in ghosts...

3

Nkiruka

Nkiruka felt a small hand pat her cheek and groaned.

Keeping her eyes firmly shut, she turned over and tried to get back to sleep. Two minutes later, she sat bolt upright.

Staring across to the bedroom window, she saw the light creeping in through the edges of the blackout curtains.

She reached across her daughter, pulled the alarm clock towards her and saw it was 7.38.

"Oh, my Lord! Oh, my Lord!" she muttered to herself, as she swung her feet off the bed and onto the cold, wooden floor.

She stood up, leaving her five-year-old sleeping under the cocoon of the duvet, and shivered in the early-morning coolness.

Yawning, she stretched out her arms and legs, feeling and hearing her joints crack as they released their stiffness.

Then, with a sigh, she turned and bent over her sleeping daughter.

"Ada, wake up!" she said, shaking her gently.

No response.

"Ada, for heaven's sake, wake up!"

Ada opened her eyes and stared up at her mother with such a look of trust that Nkiruka felt her heart turn over. Her anger at having had her sleep broken for yet another night dissipated. But despite Ada's lovely hazel eyes gazing up at her like an endearing fawn's, Nkiruka's resolve remained unchanged. She was still going ahead with the plan to drop Ada off at her mum's house, that very morning, for a three-night stay.

Her mum would have happily babysat Ada at Nkiruka's house in Islington but Nkiruka knew that if she carried on this sleep deprived she would end up making some serious mistakes at work. Forgetting to switch her alarm clock on last night was the least of her blunders and she couldn't afford to start messing up at work, especially with Superintendent Lionel Grieves breathing down her neck.

She was already skating on thin ice after her most recent homicide case, where she had devoted a lot of time and resources to proving the killing was related to a notorious south-side gang. Something that hadn't impressed Lionel one little bit, given they hadn't found out who the actual murderer was. Lionel was first and foremost a results man and anything that didn't clock up positive statistics for the police force was a complete waste of time as far as he was concerned.

Nkiruka picked up her daughter and gave her a hug.

"Come on, darling. Let's get you dressed and take you to *Papa* and *Nne nne*'s house. I've laid out your Scooby-Doo jumper and trousers for you to wear."

She put Ada down and watched as Ada raced off to her bedroom, her braids swinging from side to side.

Ada didn't need much incentive to get dressed and go to her grandparents' house. There she had different toys to play with and her grandparents' undivided attention, whereas at home Ada had two frazzled parents who, often as not, found themselves falling asleep in front of the TV in the evenings.

Nkiruka grabbed some clean clothes from her cupboard and disappeared into the en suite bathroom to get ready for the day.

She was going to be late for work again but so far Lionel hadn't noticed her tardiness, which was a relief. Trying to explain to a sixty-year-old confirmed bachelor like Lionel that she was late as a consequence of having an insomniac child was always going to be mission impossible.

Still, Lionel owed her a few favors these days given that she'd been working plenty of overtime during the last month. A colleague had been off sick for the better part of six weeks and it had been mayhem in their department. Nkiruka had stepped up to the plate and done more than her fair share of work, never once pointing out to the others that she had a five-year-old daughter waiting for her at home.

Putting on her tights, Nkiruka reminisced about her pre-coronavirus mornings, when she had actually felt alive and fit. Ada hadn't always been this bad, she thought to herself. It was the first Covid lockdown that had destroyed their slumber, for Ada had been sent away to stay with Nkiruka's sister for thirteen weeks and during that time she had only seen her parents through a glass window.

Frustratingly, when Ada came back home again, she began the soul-destroying habit of checking on her mum and dad during the night. Things were marginally better now, in that there were some nights when Ada slept through until morning, but those nights were few and far between.

Tom, Nkiruka's husband, had early on decided to leave them to it and went to sleep in Ada's bed as soon as Ada appeared at their bedside.

Nkiruka would not have put up with this craven behavior for one minute had it not been for Tom's job as a nurse. Knowing that the consequences of screwing up a patient's care in hospital was always going to be more serious than making mistakes in a homicide case, Nkiruka turned a blind eye to his nighttime disappearing act. At least on the days when Tom was off work, Nkiruka was the one who got to escape to the spare bed.

Brushing her teeth vigorously, she stared at the dark shadows under her eyes. She looked exhausted and already she was dreading a day at her desk, micromanaging her team and the cases they had been allocated.

She shook her head at herself in the mirror and then, without further ado, put on the rest of her clothes, washed her face, and carefully applied her make-up. She dabbed foundation over the dark hollows of her eyes, hoping to look less haggard, by which time Ada had turned up in the doorway wearing her favorite pink and red stripy tights and a bright orange tutu.

Nkiruka glanced out of the bathroom window at the overcast October skyline and then looked back at

Ada who was watching her with a stubborn tilt to her chin.

Nkiruka sighed.

She wasn't prepared to have a battle of wills over her daughter's tutu, which she knew Ada would win hands down that morning. A thick anorak and Ada would be ready for the outdoors. Besides, Ada had plenty of clothes at her grandparents' house and Nkiruka's mother was more than a match for Ada's iron will.

Without saying a word, Ada reached out, took Nkiruka's hand, and walked her downstairs, the thick layers of her orange tutu brushing up against the wall and making a swishing noise as she moved.

Once they reached the bottom of the stairs, she led her mother to the kitchen with a look of suppressed excitement in her eyes.

Ada has been down to the kitchen already, thought Nkiruka suspiciously. What was the little mischief-maker up to now?

As Ada waited beside her, she peered in through the kitchen doorway and then smiled with pleasure.

The table had been laid out for the pair of them, with a large vase of pink and white roses at its center, a bright-pink bow tied round its middle. The sweet, heavy scent from the roses filled the room. It was patently obvious the beautiful roses weren't a cheap supermarket offering but from an expensive, upmarket florist.

Bless him, thought Nkiruka.

Tom was leaving the house at five in the morning for his shifts that week and this somehow made his thoughtful gesture all the more special. He must have hidden the flowers from her yesterday evening...

"Isn't that sweet of Dad, Ada? You know, you have the best daddy in the whole world. Come on, let's eat up quickly and get going."

Ada obediently climbed onto her chair. With two hands, she grabbed the cereal box and shook some Cheerios into her bowl. Nkiruka watched her daughter as she carefully poured the milk over her cereal and tucked in.

Ada was a perfectionist at heart and if any of her Cheerios ended up scattered around the table, or the milk splashed out of her cereal bowl, then all hell broke loose. Perfectionism was a pain in the neck to live with and Nkiruka could already see many troublesome years ahead of her, but as far as Ada's breakfast went that morning it was a real blessing. Ada would leave no mess behind for her to clear up, and exhausted as she was Nkiruka was thankful for small mercies.

Nkiruka went over to the kettle and switched it on.

Tom had already placed her favorite mug next to the kettle, with the coffee granules in it and a teaspoon.

That man is going to get lucky tonight, she thought to herself, as she waited for the kettle to boil. Always assuming she didn't pass out with tiredness first, of course.

By the time Ada had finished her cereal and orange juice, Nkiruka had downed her mug of coffee, eaten two pieces of marmalade and toast, and packed her hefty work bag.

Nkiruka cleared up the kitchen and then turned to look at Ada, who was busy putting on her Start-Rite shoes.

She reached down and fixed up Ada's braids.

"Ada, go fetch Roo!" she said, remembering Ada's favorite soft toy.

Roo, a teddy from Australia Zoo, had been given to Ada by her adored Uncle Chibuzo, who combined a job in environmental science with wanderlust. He popped in and out of their lives whenever he stopped by London and had stolen her daughter's affections with the quirky gifts he brought her from around the world.

At the moment, Chibuzo was working in an American research station in Greenland and, from time to time, sending them random photos of caribou, musk oxen, and lemmings. No doubt his next present would be suitably ethnic, like a Nordic sculpture or a sleigh and husky dog toy.

If they had left Roo behind, Nkiruka would have had Ada on the phone in tears at some point during the day, begging for her cuddly toy.

Nkiruka's mother would never hesitate to call her at work either.

Neither of her parents seemed to appreciate the importance of her job and had called her so often during working hours that Nkiruka had resorted to owning two mobiles: one for work and one for home business.

Nkiruka's mother had been a successful architect and her father was still working as a well-known sculptor, but both her parents seemed to be under the impression that Nkiruka spent a lot of her time at New Scotland Yard either standing or sitting around, as she waited for evidence and facts to emerge relating to her homicide cases.

Actually, in some instances, it wouldn't be far from the truth but Nkiruka knew that the huge pressure to complete cases, as well as the horrors of her job, were an alien concept to the pair of them. Which was no bad thing, really, and despite her parents" lack of understanding, Nkiruka was happy to keep them blissfully ignorant.

Ada was already making her way up the stairs to fetch Roo, with her small legs rocking her from side to side.

Having pre-packed Ada's overnight bag so it would be ready for the following morning, Nkiruka checked her briefcase one more time to see if she had everything and then ran upstairs to fetch her AirPods from her dresser.

When she came out of her room she bumped into Ada, clutching her kangaroo.

"Well done, darling. Right, we had better hurry or mum is going to be in big trouble."

"Your boss is going to get you into trouble?"

"Maybe. But don't you worry, honey, I can handle the boss. Remember, your mum has superpowers when she's at work."

Ada nodded solemnly.

Nkiruka laughed and gave her a quick kiss.

Once they were downstairs she put Ada's warm navy anorak on top of her tutu.

The anorak was flattening down the tutu's stiff layers and Nkiruka hoped Ada wouldn't start to protest about this, but Ada had already lost interest in what she was wearing and was eager to get going.

As they left the doorstep, Nkiruka could see the bustle of the outdoor market had started up at Chapel Market, further confirming her lateness that morning.

The familiar market smell of over-ripe fruit and

street rubbish assailed Nkiruka's nostrils and she thought longingly of the sweet aroma from the roses sitting in her kitchen.

Holding on to Ada's hand, she walked impatiently past the few stragglers who seemed to be in no rush to get to work that morning, and turned the corner.

When they reached her green Hyundai, Nkiruka dumped their bags in the boot and then helped Ada climb up onto her car booster seat.

She drove the car through busy traffic to her parents' house in Camden and, after resisting her mother's eager attempts to get her to stay for coffee, she kissed Ada goodbye.

Leaving her car at her parents' house, she walked to Camden Town Tube Station and took the Northern Line to Embankment. From Embankment it was usually only a seven-minute walk to New Scotland Yard but because it was 9.20, Nkiruka ended up darting in and out of the stream of pedestrians as she raced to the office, arriving at the security barriers out of breath and sweaty.

As she crossed the security barrier, she made a vow to improve her fitness levels in the New Year.

She took the lift up to the sixth floor, and as soon as she entered the open-plan office she sensed a different atmosphere to the normal early-morning buzz she was used to.

She stood by the double doors and looked around, confused by the silence.

It was as quiet as her local public library. Nobody was chatting or standing about in huddled groups; instead all the staff who were in that morning were seated at their desks, with their heads bent to their work.

Looking at the solemn faces in front of her, Nkiruka tried to figure out what she might have missed. Racking her brain, she tried to remember if she had read anything relevant while sitting on the underground train to work that morning. She could think of nothing in her work emails, or even on the online news, that could shed a light on the eerie quiet on her floor, but no doubt she would find out soon enough.

Fixing a smile to her face, she started to walk across to her desk at the far corner of the room.

She didn't get very far because DI Stephen Ainsworth came across to her and blocked her way.

"Ma'am, DI Webster has been trying to get in touch with you. He asked if you could call him urgently."

And with those few words Nkiruka knew the rest of the day was going to be a challenge for her tired mind.

"Of course, I'll call him as soon as I've dumped my stuff at my desk," she answered, trying to sound bright and breezy.

"Great, thank you, ma'am."

Nkiruka watched as Stephen Ainsworth scurried off, his awkward, lanky gait and prominent eyes reminding her of a hare. Taking note of Stephen's bulging eyes, she asked herself if he might have a thyroid problem.

As she continued to walk to her desk, she shook her head in disgust at the erratic way her brain was working that morning. It wasn't like her to be jumping to daft conclusions about a colleague's state of health. She really felt like giving her head a good slap to wake it up.

Her tiredness notwithstanding, it was not a good start to her working day.

She hurried past several colleagues, deliberately avoiding any eye contact with them, and reached her corner of the room with a sigh of relief.

Sitting down heavily at her desk, she dumped her bags by her chair and let her legs stretch out in front of her. After staring blankly at her computer screen for a moment, she reached down and dug into her bag's side pocket for her mobile. Looking down at her phone, she saw there were no missed calls or even a voicemail from Johnny.

It seemed as though Johnny might have tried to reach her on her desk phone, which could possibly mean that whatever situation he was dealing with wasn't too serious. She was going to keep her fingers crossed.

Leaning back on her chair, she called DI Jonathan Webster's number. "Hi Johnny. Everything alright?" she asked.

There was a dry laugh at the other end.

"No, I'm afraid not. We need you to come out to Hampstead Heath, as soon as possible. It's Hampstead No 1 Pond. We're parked by Hampstead Heath Tube Station on South Hill Park. There's been three murders committed in the park last night, by the same perpetrators we think, and it looks as though one of the bodies has been severely tortured. I've never seen anything like it in my life before, Nkiruka... I mean, seriously, I puked up when I saw the state of him. The press will have a field day when they find out about it. Forensics are on the scene now."

"Who found the bodies?"

"An old geezer who was out walking his incontinent dog at the crack of dawn this morning. Proper shook up he was, poor sod. No way was he involved. A puff of air would have knocked him over. In fact, I'm surprised he didn't have a heart attack when he came across the bodies."

"OK, Johnny. I'll be there as soon as I can," said Nkiruka, thinking that if a seasoned police veteran like Jonathan Webster had thrown up, it had to be bad.

She wondered briefly if anyone from West Hampstead Police Station was involved and present at the scene. It didn't matter. Either way, Johnny would be keeping an eye on things and would stay at the scene, or near the scene, until everything had been dealt with.

She put her phone back in her bag and looked around.

Katie Hill, a sergeant, was seated at her desk diagonally across from her, her head bent as she read through a file.

"Katie, fancy driving me to Hampstead Heath and taking a look? Johnny's called me out there."

Katie's friendly face looked up and nodded back at her.

"Yeah, we've heard about that one. Johnny and Steve rang up an hour ago trying to find you."

Nkiruka ignored the pointed reference to her lateness and continued to listen to what Katie had to say.

"Apparently, an old man was tortured to death. His gut was cut right open and everything was spilling out, they said. Sliced to bits with something sharp by the looks of it."

"Unusual."

"I'd say that's an understatement," said Katie,

primly. "It's pretty horrific. Johnny said they think the three men were killed by the same people. Different methods, though. Steve told me he hasn't seen a case like it in the last ten years."

Nkiruka thought about this for a moment.

"Is that why everyone's so damn quiet this morning?" asked Nkiruka, lowering her voice.

Katie giggled.

"No, don't be daft. Lionel came in here searching for you..." Katie looked at her watch, "twenty-five minutes ago, and blew his top when he saw what he called "lack of hard graft" going on. Threatened to cancel overtime for the entire month if people didn't get back to their desks right away."

Nkiruka made a face.

"Great. I look forward to speaking to him later."

Katie smiled sympathetically back at her but was too wise to commit herself to saying anything to Lionel's discredit. She knew which side her bread was buttered on.

"Well, come on then, let's get going," said Nkiruka, picking up her briefcase again. Katie glanced down at the work on her desk, a worried frown on her face.

"I've still to fill in the paperwork for that incident in Finsbury Park, Nkiruka, and Lionel wants me to collate some reports for him this afternoon."

"Oh, forget the bloody paperwork, Katie. That can wait. If Lionel has a problem with that, tell him to speak to me."

Katie nodded, resigned to obeying her instructions, but if Nkiruka read her correctly, also happy to be given a chance to get involved in a murder that was a cut above the norm for their department.

Katie generally didn't offer herself up to doing any offsite work, preferring instead to be a pen pusher within the department. The rare times when she would volunteer to go out on a job tended to happen if, and when, her interest was awakened with a case.

Most of the other sergeants at New Scotland Yard had the opposite problem to Katie. They were eager to prove themselves and desperate to get some time away from their desks, often moaning between themselves about the bureaucracy and paperwork. Therefore, it never ruffled any feathers when Katie ended up staying behind at the office, working on the administrative side of things.

Katie locked her computer and stood up.

Picking up her small handbag, she scanned her desk anxiously one last time to see if she had missed anything, and then smiled at Nkiruka, indicating she was ready to go.

Both of them began to walk towards the lift in companionable silence.

Nkiruka was pleased to have Katie with her. She was good company, unfailingly cheerful, and raised the morale in the office when she was there, not least because she was "hot as fried plantain," as Nkiruka's mother would have said. She was in her early thirties and petite, with long auburn hair and green eyes. Pretty enough to induce some serious crushes in the men who worked with her.

Nkiruka, who was very tall, often felt like she was the Leaning Tower of Pisa when standing next to her, but despite this minor inconvenience she appreciated Katie's down-to-earth manner and her willingness to muck in when needed.

As Katie drove them towards Hampstead Heath, Nkiruka reflected on the fact that one way or another she wasn't going to be able to escape North London that day.

Even though she had both parents living in North London, she didn't spend any of her leisure time in Hampstead Heath. She preferred the quieter, lesser-known parks at the weekend, like Antrim Gardens, Primrose Gardens, or Montpelier Gardens.

Large, wild, and ungoverned spaces like Hampstead Heath didn't appeal to her because they were precisely the kind of locations where crime tended to flourish and that only made her feel edgy when she walked about in them.

4

Nkiruka

It took them three quarters of an hour to reach their destination, with Katie weaving her way along the city's back streets with the expertise of a taxi driver.

Once the car was parked, they crossed the road and started walking across the Heath towards Hampstead No 1 Pond.

In amongst the autumnal woodland colors, there were strands of bright-yellow crime scene tape visible from quite a distance.

It didn't take them long to spot Johnny. Just outside of the barrier was the stocky outline of a broad-shouldered man, standing with his legs far apart and his arms crossed as he spoke with the uniformed policeman next to him.

A typical Johnny pose, thought Nkiruka in amusement, and a stance that was probably developed to perfection during his youthful stints as a nightclub bouncer.

Feeling re-energized by the fresh air, Nkiruka

picked up pace and called out to Johnny, leaving Katie to follow behind her.

"Hi Nkiruka! How are you doing?" asked Johnny, with his usual breezy bonhomie when she reached his side.

For some reason, his cheeriness grated on Nkiruka that morning. She questioned if what she felt was envy and decided it was quite possible. Johnny was looking hale and hearty, when she felt like an old sock that had done several rounds in the washing machine.

Seeing the frown on Nkiruka's face, the sergeant Johnny had been speaking to excused himself and quickly walked away.

"So, anything else you want to tell me?" asked Nkiruka, not wanting to waste time beating about the bush.

She listened to Johnny relaying as much information as he could about the three murders and watched the forensics team, in their white suits, working over the crime scene.

It didn't take her long to realize that Johnny had nothing much to add, so it was going to be a waiting game until forensics finished their preliminary work.

They had erected a white tent over the bodies and were weaving their way in and out of it as they methodically worked through their procedures. Depending on who was in charge of the forensics team, Nkiruka could either be given a detailed, onsite report or else be blocked from receiving any information until the official pathology report came out.

Whoever was in charge would also decide whether she'd be allowed to inspect the bodies at the crime scene, but given her high ranking and in an exceptional homicide case like this one she would expect to be called into the tent at some point.

If she wasn't invited into the tent, she would kick up a fuss.

She was in the mood for confrontation that morning and wouldn't shy away from asserting herself, if need be. From here on in, the murders were going to rest heavily on her shoulders, and she felt she had every right to get involved at each stage of the process.

It was a chilly day and she was glad to have on her coat and scarf. The wind was tugging on her scarf, teasing it back over her shoulders, and she could feel the drafts penetrating through the thick outer layer of her duffle coat.

Across the pond, gusts of wind were causing ripples to spread across its mirror- like surface, and under their force the thinner branches on the trees were waving back and forth.

Nkiruka noticed Katie was seated a short distance away on a low-lying tree branch, looking demure as ever and without a hair out of place, busy texting on her mobile.

She turned and scanned the surrounding landscape.

On the other side of Hampstead No 1 Pond there were a number of buildings, their windows gazing out over the water like cavernous eye sockets. Some of the windows were lit up with an orange glow.

They were going to have to make enquiries at those waterfront apartments and find out if anyone had seen anything last night, thought Nkiruka. Most of the windows had a clear view across the water.

Nkiruka couldn't figure out why the bodies hadn't

been deposited under the water with something heavy, like a rock, tied to their legs. After all, Hampstead No 1 Pond was large and deep enough to qualify as a reservoir. It was almost as though somebody wanted the bodies to be found.

But why?

She frowned again.

She was jumping to conclusions which was a dangerous thing to do with a complex crime. What the hell was wrong with her this morning?

She sighed, bent her head downwards so her scarf covered her nose and mouth, and tuned back into what Johnny was telling her.

"...so, the two other bodies are of two men. A young man, who at a guess looks to be in his twenties, and a middle-aged man," continued Johnny. "Shot at point blank range in the back of a head. It must have been a gun with a silencer because everyone knows Hampstead Heath is a haunt for gay sex at night. Not the ideal setting for a murder, I wouldn't have thought. We should let out an appeal for witnesses because this close to the road there were bound to be people hanging around."

Nkiruka nodded in agreement.

"It's what they did to the old man that is the real shocker. He has cuts over every bit of his skin, some deeper than others. It would have taken some time, and I can't figure out how they did any of this when he was still alive. They gouged out both his eyes, and his lips and nose are a bloody mess. They also cut open his stomach and pulled out his intestines. You can tell he suffered by the angle of his body. His head was arched right back with the mouth stretched wide open."

"Was there anything in the mouth? A gag or something?" asked Nkiruka.

"No."

"How much blood was there around the bodies?"

Johnny looked sideways at her.

"Some, I think. I'm afraid I didn't examine the ground too closely at the time. I was taken aback by the state of the old man. I could ask Steve, the sergeant from West Hampstead Police Station."

"No, it's OK. Forensics will pick up on it."

They stood watching in silence for a few moments as the white-suited forensics team moved in and out of the tent. The forensics teams reflected such a sense of purpose in their work that it often seemed to Nkiruka as though they were following through the steps of an elaborate ballet, a sensitive and complicated performance whose moves were only ever understood by those of their profession.

"Not today, I'm afraid," boomed a cheery voice from behind them.

They turned and saw that two female swimmers, clad in their wetsuits, were getting turned away by a policeman further down the path.

Nkiruka wrinkled her nose in disgust.

Swimming in cold water, with the amount of bird shit and God knew what else in the pond, did not appeal to her.

She could see from where she was standing several swans on the water and a big cluster of Canadian geese at the edge of the pond. Those birds like to poop, she thought, as she remembered what she had seen on the lakeside at Kew Gardens.

"When is the Underwater Search Unit going to get

here?" she asked Johnny, wondering if they would find anything else in the sludge-brown water.

"They said they'll be here by lunchtime."

Nkiruka nodded.

"Chief Inspector Ezemonye?"

Nkiruka turned and saw a slight man with a balding head and a white goatee coming towards her. His white plastic hood and mask were pulled down.

"Yes?"

"I'm Dr. Philip Berger, the forensic pathologist on this case. I wonder if you could come with me?"

"Certainly," said Nkiruka, without hesitation.

She walked up to the sealed area and put on the white plastic overall handed to her, as well as the paper shoes, plastic gloves, and face mask. Thankfully, her overall was on the large side so her long legs fitted into it without any problem. Her short skirt, though, was scrunched up around her hips.

She followed Dr. Berger as he walked into the tent and went up to the bodies. Nkiruka sniffed as she entered the tent.

Even with her tight mask on, Nkiruka could pick up the stench of blood and the metallic, sickly-sweet odor that death brought to the human body. Since she had been promoted to Chief Inspector she wasn't out at homicide locations as much as before but even as a DI she had never grown accustomed to the smells that permeated around dead bodies.

Dr. Berger pointed to two clothed bodies, lying side by side.

"These two were dumped here together. Both were killed with a single bullet to the back of the head, through the occipital bone and at very close range. Both were left fully clothed. I can't, on initial inspection, see that there's any damage or injury to their bodies but I will look at that more closely in the lab. The old man, as you can see, is slightly further away and completely naked."

Nkiruka gazed down at the two clothed men and felt a twinge of sadness when she saw how young one of them looked.

She turned slowly and walked with measured steps towards the bloody and naked mess that was all that was left of the old man.

She noticed that unlike the other two, who had darker skin, the old man had pasty white skin on the body parts that weren't covered in cuts or blood. His abdomen was split open like an over-ripe tomato and the colon was hanging down the left-hand side of his body in a contorted loop.

She looked enquiringly at the pathologist.

"This man has been tortured. At a guess, it looks to me as though he had a heart attack at some point in the process. Some of the cuts, here and here, for instance," said Dr. Berger, pointing to the legs and chest, "look as though they were done after he died. There's little evidence of blood flow around those cuts, unlike some of the other ones. But again, I won't be able to confirm that until I'm in the lab. What might interest you is that the dead bodies have all been transported here by car and dumped. The guys have picked up on car tracks to and from the road right up to this point."

"I guessed as much. There's a lot goes on in the Heath at night and no way would they have been able to torture the old man and not be seen or noticed by someone. What I still don't understand, Dr. Berger, is why the bodies were dumped here, so close to the water. It's as if someone wanted them to be found. After all, they could have put weights on them and dropped them deep into the water."

Dr. Berger shrugged.

"That's your remit, Chief Inspector, not mine. What I can tell you is that whoever did this didn't do it alone. There's no sign he was tied up. Two of them at least must have held down the old man while he was getting cut. The lines are straight and neat, almost obsessively so. I haven't seen anything like this before. It's almost like something you'd expect to happen in the Middle Ages when they used to hang, draw, and quarter people."

"They must have been wrapped up in something," said Nkiruka, looking around. "There doesn't seem to be much blood spilled."

"We've picked up a few black plastic fragments. Looks to me as though they were wrapped up in bin liners before they got here, which were then removed."

"Which would have taken up more of their time and put them at a greater risk of being seen or caught," added Nkiruka.

"Possibly. You'll have to appeal for witnesses of course. I don't expect you'll ever find the car or van. If they have any sense at all, they'll have got rid of it by now."

"Any documents or ID on the bodies, at all?"

"Nothing at all. Not one single item revealing their identity. The labels on their clothes," he indicated the two clothed men, "suggest that they were from abroad. They're not recognizable clothing brands. Might be worth looking into."

"Hmm. What's your guess about the time of death?"

Dr. Berger scratched through the white plastic at his chin.

"At a guess, I would say yesterday morning for all three. But again, I would prefer to give a more scientific time once I've had a good look at them in the lab."

"OK. Thanks. I hope you don't mind me asking but when will you have the pathology report ready? I think my boss will want me to move fairly quickly on this one."

Dr. Berger gave Nkiruka an understanding look.

"I'll treat this case as a priority, so at a guess it'll be done by the end of next week. I imagine it's going to create quite a stir in your department."

"Yes, it will. This is the first time I've seen something like this in the time I've been working in Homicide."

She was going to have to get a criminal psychologist to try and write a profile on the murderers and she had no doubt their report was going to make interesting reading. She struggled to see how anyone could make sense of what had been done to the three men but it was worth a try.

Dr. Berger was looking distracted, his thoughts clearly returning to the dead men. He nodded in dismissal to Nkiruka and turned back to the bodies again.

Nkiruka walked out of the tent and stripped off her outer layers, depositing them in the bag left open by forensics. Sometimes forensics liked to double-check the protective kit for any evidence that might have attached itself, unintentionally, onsite.

Nkiruka was hoping forensics would follow through on their meticulous work and check their used kit that day because she knew the kind of pressure she was going to be under to get the case resolved. Her team were going to need every tiny little scrap of evidence they could get their hands on and she didn't want anything to be missed.

She walked across to where Katie and Johnny were standing, chatting amicably to each other.

"Right, you two, fancy getting a coffee before we head back?"

Johnny grinned.

"There's a nice café on Fleet Road."

"There is, is there?" said Nkiruka, raising an eyebrow to him. Johnny blushed.

"It took them a while to set up so I went and grabbed myself a takeaway coffee. Glad I didn't eat anything though," he added, looking ill as he remembered what he had seen in the tent.

"I'm only pulling your leg, Johnny," said Nkiruka, amused by his explanation. "As you know, I'm hardly in a position to judge. Timekeeping's never been my forte and I'm sure there's plenty of room for improvement for us both. Right, lead the way, I need some caffeine. My mind really isn't working right this morning and I need it to kick into gear."

They walked away from the pond, enjoying the sun that had broken free of the clouds and was transforming the landscape around them into a halcyon scene. Mounds of red, yellow, and orange leaves were sitting loosely on the muddy ground, with uneven patches of green grass poking through and fighting for their place amongst them.

Feeling her spirits lifting, Nkiruka marveled at the change in the atmosphere, reflecting to herself that the weather had a lot to do with one's mood.

Johnny's café turned out to be a large two-story eatery called The Heath Mix and it was busy inside, which suggested it was a good place to stop for a morning coffee.

They found a recently vacated table by the window and sat down, relieved to be away from the cool air outside.

Nkiruka shook off her coat and laid her thick scarf across the back of her chair. Katie, meanwhile, reached across and grabbed a menu from an adjoining table.

Nkiruka stifled a pang of jealousy as she watched Katie studying the menu. Six years on, she had still not lost the baby weight and with the stress of her job she doubted she ever would. Katie, meanwhile, looked as though she was a walking advert for Weight Watchers and David Lloyd gyms combined. Healthy living oozed out of her.

"Right, what's it to be? My shout today," said Nkiruka.

"I'm going to have some chocolate fudge cake and a cappuccino. I didn't have breakfast this morning," stated Katie, shooting down Nkiruka's preconceived ideas about her health.

"A tea for me please, Nkiruka," said Johnny, eyeing up the menu with trepidation. "And seeing as you're paying today, a bacon roll, too."

"No problem," said Nkiruka.

She waited until the waitress reached them and added a scone, "with loads of jam, please," and an Americano to the list.

"We've got quite a problem on our hands, haven't we?" remarked Johnny, as they watched people walking up and down the pavement outside.

Nkiruka glanced around at the tables near them. Although people were pretending not to look, she could tell their neighbors were interested in a sergeant in police uniform turning up at a café with a tall black woman in tow.

"Yes, we do, Johnny. But we'd best discuss it in the car or back at the office," Nkiruka remonstrated.

Johnny looked around and nodded his agreement.

"Yes, we don't want to end up with a crowd of rubberneckers messing up the crime scene over at Kenwood House," said Katie, in a loud voice and glaring across the room at a woman who was staring openly at them. It was doubtful, though, that any of the customers would head over to Kenwood House on the off-chance there was something to see.

Nkiruka chuckled but felt too weary to say anything else until she had drunk half her coffee and felt the caffeine begin to work its magic on her fuzzy brain.

"Ah, that's hit the spot," she said, putting her coffee mug down.

She lifted her knife and smeared a thick layer of butter and jam onto her scone.

As she took a huge bite out of her scone, Nkiruka caught Katie watching her with a fascinated eye.

She wiped away the crumbs from her mouth with a paper napkin and then looked across at Katie, who was daintily eating her cake with a fork.

"Sorry. I've learnt to eat quickly because of Ada, my daughter. There's never any leisure time to enjoy sitting and eating. I'm going to have to re-educate myself when life gets a little easier," she said apologetically.

Johnny grinned.

"Don't bother me, ma'am. The men in blue eat like that every day at the canteen."

"I know," agreed Katie, to their surprise. "The only other people I've ever seen eating like you guys at the canteen are public schoolboys, who have been educated at boarding school and have learned to shovel in as much food as they can in the quickest possible time."

Johnny shrugged dismissively as he drank some tea.

"Don't know anything about boarding school, I'm afraid. Out of my league."

"Did you go to boarding school, Katie?" asked Nkiruka, interested.

"No, but my ex-boyfriend went to Eton."

"Impressive," said Johnny, holding his bacon roll in both hands with his elbows resting on the table. "Shame it didn't last. You could've been onto a good one there."

Nkiruka and Katie stared at him.

"You know Eton, man. Half of them end up being prime ministers and CEOs, don't they?"

He looked across at their puzzled faces.

"So?" prompted Katie.

Johnny put his roll down and rubbed his fingers together.

"So those boys have plenty of dosh."

Nkiruka rolled her eyes as she polished off the remains of her scone.

"If I was after 'dosh'," remarked Katie. "I wouldn't be working for the Metropolitan Police, would I?"

"Yeah, right. You don't convince me, Katie.

Everyone could do with a little more of the ready," contradicted Johnny.

Privately, Nkiruka thought that with her good looks and intelligence Katie could do a lot better than the Met but who knew what factors had influenced Katie's decision to join the police force? In any case, Katie was already a firm favorite of Lionel's and it was obvious that before long she would be destined for better things at Scotland Yard.

"Are you OK, Johnny?" asked Nkiruka, beginning to feel worried about his financial state.

"Yes, of course I am. Just saying, all of us could do with a little extra, couldn't we?"

Johnny took another bite out of his roll and chewed it.

"Glad I didn't put any tomato ketchup on it today," he said cheerfully, through a mouthful of food. "Don't want to be reminded of this morning."

Nkiruka looked down at the strawberry jam left on her plate and felt a little sick. She got up, put her coat and scarf on, and went to the counter to pay the bill.

By the time she came back, both Katie and Johnny had finished and were waiting for her at the door.

"I'm just going to go to the toilet. I'll meet you at the car," said Nkiruka, conscious that her pelvic floor muscles had not recovered since Ada either.

The other two nodded and made their way outside.

Nkiruka checked her phone as she stepped down-stairs to the toilets. Miraculously, there were no messages from her parents.

She tucked the phone away in her bag and felt a huge sense of relief. Ada was obviously having a great time and had forgotten all about her.

5

Richard

"OK. Here we are," announced Peter, as they stood beside an inconspicuous white door.

Richard sniffed.

The potent fumes of freshly applied gloss paint lingered in the air.

Having walked through the castle's Entrance Gallery into the Grand Hall and then through a narrow corridor on the other side, they were now outside the room the Botticelli painting had been stolen from.

Like a tour guide, Peter gestured to the door in front of them.

"This is the office and the room the thief broke into to steal the Botticelli. In the olden days it used to be used as the Steward's Office but these days it serves as the castle office. It's always left locked at night. The thief broke the mortice locks on this door by force, all three of them. Whoever did it had substantial strength because the locks were found scattered right across the office floor."

"A little clumsy, isn't it?" asked Eilidh. "Noisy and

time consuming, I'd have thought. Most professional criminals use lock-snapping as a technique to break in, which is much faster."

Peter shrugged.

"I wouldn't know, I'm afraid. That's the way they broke in here."

Richard and Eilidh turned to look at the newly painted, repaired door and noticed a keypad beside it.

"The insurance claim for the stolen painting has been submitted, along with all the police evidence for the break-in, so we've updated the security to the office now," explained Peter. "We're using a permission-based, cloud-hosted system, which means we can know who has used which key, where, and when. We'll soon be expanding it to other areas of the castle, too."

Right after the horse has bolted, thought Richard. It smacked very much of complacency, which in his experience wasn't unusual for a historical building out in the sticks.

"Am I right in saying that you don't normally keep works of art in the office?" asked Richard.

Peter flushed.

"That's correct, yes. It was unprecedented to have the Botticelli here in the office but we had to get some of the paintings in the Breakfast Room moved to a different place before we could hang the Botticelli up."

Bent over, Eilidh was busy scrutinizing the door to the office.

"The security on this door's good," she said, sounding satisfied. "I can't see anyone being able to force open a door with this system on it. It would alert someone right away, if they did."

"Yes, that's true. Inside you can see where the

alarm sensors are on the door. Hopefully that's enough of a deterrent in future. In fact, we're going to be doing this on all the rooms that aren't open to the public. A bit late, I know," said Peter, shamefaced. "The robbery has been a wake-up call for us and we are trying very hard to improve the security in the castle. Although, who knows if the family will want to continue keeping their paintings here after what's happened?"

No one bothered to answer Peter's question. Any platitudes coming from them weren't going to make him feel any better.

"The public rooms are secure. Very secure. They have laser scanners on the wall spaces where the paintings hang," added Peter, as though trying to prove the security at the castle hadn't been totally incompetent.

"Who knew that the Botticelli painting was in the office?" asked Richard.

"The curator for Penrhyn, Stephanie Meadows, and the administrator, Sandra Holt. Baqir Malouf and Dylan Evans, the security guards on duty at the time. As I've told you already, the security guards knew there was a valuable item in the office. In any case, it only took them two minutes to reach this passageway after the alarm went off from the window in the Housekeeper's Room. They were both patrolling in the near vicinity at the time the alarm sounded."

Peter looked thoughtful for a moment.

"They're all long-term, trustworthy staff, including the other two security guards, Damon Usher and Neil Fernsby. They're dedicated to the castle. I'd say the same about all the staff and volunteers here."

Peter began to pace restlessly up and down the

corridor, the heels of his feet rising upwards as he did so.

"Stephanie Meadows has worked for us for nearly 18 years. Sandra Holt for 7 years. Dylan has been with us for about 10 years and, if I remember rightly, Baqir for 8."

Peter rubbed his forehead. "They have work experience in their respective fields and excellent recommendations. There isn't a huge amount of job availability in this part of Wales so people tend to stay put in their roles and appreciate their jobs. No one else knew anything about the Botticelli in the office, and it's general policy, as you'll know, not to talk about security matters with anyone. But I guess you can't always stop people talking, can you?"

"No, especially over a beer or two, I imagine. Who else uses the office during the day?" asked Eilidh.

"I don't know who exactly used the office that day but the painting was in its crate, so it wouldn't be visible to anyone dropping in."

"It still might be helpful for us to know who was in the office that day," Richard affirmed in a quiet voice, wondering for a moment if Peter was being deliberately obstructive.

But Peter nodded, accepting Richard's point.

"I'm sure Sandra Holt will be able to tell you who was in here. She's very efficient."

Covering the keypad with his hand, he imputed the code numbers and then with his key card opened the door to the office.

They walked into a room that had two desks in it and a number of metallic chairs, randomly arranged in the middle. All the furniture seemed very functional compared to the grandeur of the pieces seen in the rest of the castle, and the carpet had faded in places from a rich burgundy to a pale rose-pink.

"There's two other entrances to this room?" asked Eilidh in disbelief, seeing the two other doors in the room.

"Yes, regrettably, but they're now all secured, too. The door the thief broke in through is the one I showed you."

Peter crossed his arms, looking for a moment like a ruffled vicar, his black shirt and trousers adding to the overall effect.

A sheep rather than a wolf, thought Richard. Quiet, gentle, and helpless. He might know a lot about curating paintings but competence wasn't exactly shining out of him. Not a man to have on your side in a crisis, he concluded.

"Can you show us where the painting was sitting before it got taken?" asked Eilidh.

"The painting was placed here, next to Sandra's desk," said Peter, walking across to the far side of the room. "Between the wall and the desk."

He pointed to a large plywood crate that was leaning against the wall.

"That's the crate the painting was in."

Richard and Eilidh followed him over.

"Well, she certainly has a very tidy desk," remarked Eilidh, glancing down at the large oak desk. "Either that or she doesn't have much to do."

"Oh, believe me, Sandra has plenty to do," said Peter curtly, looking over the top of his glasses at them. "She always clears away her desk top. She's very good at her job."

"I'm sure she is," agreed Richard, trying to appease him.

Given Peter's over-the-top defensiveness, it seemed to Richard the man had to be half in love with Sandra Holt. There was, after all, nothing like an office environment for romance to blossom and grow.

Eilidh, meanwhile, was examining the area under the desk and along the wall.

"Forensics have already had a good look around there," commented Peter as he watched her.

Eilidh looked up at him and smiled sweetly. "I know but it's interesting, nevertheless." She stood up and dusted down her trousers.

Eilidh then went over to the wall and studied the open one-sided crate that was tilted against it, her slender fingers prodding and feeling the uneven edges of the wood panels. Next to the crate was a rectangular, badly chipped piece of wood that had clearly been pried off during the robbery.

"It would have taken some time to get the painting out of its container," Eilidh concluded, as she looked at the screws that kept the other sides of the crate together. "It looks as though the thief levered open the crate on one side and then I presume there was packaging cushioning the painting too. You said it took just two minutes for the security guards to come along to this corridor. There's no way the burglar could've opened the housekeeper's window, broken open this door, cracked the lid off the crate, removed all the packaging, and sliced the canvas out of its frame, within those two minutes. It's impossible."

"Yes, I agree. For whatever reason, the window was unlocked and opened from the inside, not the outside.

There's no damage at all to the window. The CCTV footage shows the thief outside, running away with the canvas, but there's nothing showing him entering the building," explained Peter.

"So of course he was already inside the castle when it was locked up for the night," stated Richard.

"I have to admit, it certainly looks that way." Peter turned to face them, seeming distressed. "I just don't see how it could've happened. The staff and volunteers check the castle from top to bottom before leaving. You can imagine what would happen if they inadvertently locked a member of the public in the castle after hours, especially with the ghost sightings in the place. We'd get sued and goodness knows what else. The National Trust as a whole is extremely careful about these things."

"It has been known to happen," said Richard, scratching at his fast-growing three o'clock shadow. "In 1961 a man once got himself locked into the National Gallery overnight. The builders were doing maintenance work to the Gallery and had left a toilet window open, so he managed to escape with Goya's *Portrait of the Duke of Wellington*. He actually threw the frame into the Thames. The painting went missing for a long time and then was eventually found, following a tip-off, in a left-luggage locker at Birmingham's New Street railway station."

Eilidh had stopped inspecting the room and was leaning against the desk, looking at Richard with interest. This was a new story to her, too.

"The thief came forward to confess in July 1965, a whole two months after Goya's painting was recovered. He made the mistake of confiding in a third party about the robbery and he was worried they might contact the police. He apparently decided to preempt them." Richard pushed his fringe out of his eyes and gave Peter a resigned look. "I'm afraid there's no common pattern of behavior in art theft. Each and every burglary of valuable art or artifacts is unique. Which, of course, makes it all the harder to solve them."

"But this situation is very different to the one you're describing, if you don't mind my saying so," insisted Peter, folding his arms. "I'm loath to contradict you, Richard, but I can tell you Penrhyn's always well-staffed and they do keep a close eye on everyone who comes in as a visitor. You can see for yourself we aren't snowed under with visitors. There's no building or maintenance work being done at the moment. I simply cannot believe that a visitor was left in the castle after it was shut to the public. It doesn't make sense to me."

"Yet there seems to be a significant section of the castle closed to the general public," argued Eilidh. "I mean, this place is massive. If they did manage to wander off, it would be quite easy to hide out of sight. Especially if they already knew the castle well."

Peter shrugged and said nothing, defeated for the moment by her reasoning.

"Do you only have CCTV externally?" asked Eilidh.

"Yes. During the day there's volunteers and staff in all the public rooms."

Richard shook his head disapprovingly.

"Not enough, I'm afraid. Professional art thieves are often very intelligent. They would find it easy to suss out the weak spots in the castle and work out how to get around the staff members."

"If the National Trust has the money, I'd advise putting 24-hour CCTV inside the castle, too," added Eilidh.

Peter smiled at her, with a certain amount of pity in his small grey eyes.

"Money? It's the lack of it that's always an issue. The National Trust as an institution is always short of cash," announced Peter, his hands on his hips.

He moved over to a chair and sat down.

"Please don't quote me on this, but time and time again the organization will come up with ambitious projects that drain an incredible amount of their resources. Some useful, others not so much. It's a big lumbering giant that is always trying to reinvent itself in the modern world."

Peter sighed wearily.

"Now, with a Botticelli masterpiece stolen, I hope they'll be prepared to financially support a more comprehensive CCTV system throughout the castle because, I agree with you, it's needed," he said, nodding his head. "I presume national museums in general have the same issue?"

Peter turned to look at Richard.

"Yes, I'm afraid so," agreed Richard, feeling depressed all of a sudden. "Sadly. Poor security, insufficient or poor-quality staffing, lack of training, and inefficient administration. They're all symptomatic of money shortages and, of course, these failures also pose security risks."

Richard sat down on the edge of Sandra's immaculate desk and leaned back.

"Government support has dropped for many of the smaller museums, as well as the larger," he continued.

"Unfortunately, it's all tied into efforts to reduce the national debt. In some ways, I understand it. If you have to choose between funding for a hospital or funding for a museum, you're always going to support health first. Art's a measure of our civilization and history, but no one can argue it's an essential service."

By the time Richard finished talking, Eilidh was smiling to herself.

Richard knew why she was smiling and blushed. He was back up on his favorite hobby horse again and she had heard it so many times before.

"Right," he said, standing up. "Sorry for going on. As you can see, Eilidh has often heard me ranting about this problem but it's not one that's going to change any time soon. Could we maybe go and have a look at the window the thief used to escape out of the castle, please?"

Peter nodded and stood up.

"Of course, follow me. It's just a short distance from the office, in the Housekeeper's Room."

He held the door open for Richard and Eilidh, closing it firmly behind them once they were outside the office.

"Do you spend much time here yourself, Peter?" asked Richard curiously, as they walked back along the corridor.

"Stephanie Meadows and I have many meetings here at the castle to discuss the management of the art collection. That'll be the case even more now that we're starting to update all the security. We've quarterly meetings with the Penrhyn Family Trust here, too."

They turned left and found that opposite the

entrance to the Grand Hall was another closed white door.

Peter used a standard key this time to enter the room.

"This used to be the Butler's Pantry. Back in the day, the butler would see to the cleaning and storage of the family's silver and assemble the wines." He pointed at the windows at the far end of the room. "This room overlooks the entrance forecourt so the butler would always have advance warning of any carriages arriving. These days, though, we call it the Housekeeper's Room, not the Butler's Pantry."

Peter walked over to another doorway, which was right next to the entrance they had come through, and peered upwards into the space above it.

"In bygone days this spiral staircase was used to access the butler's bedroom. There's a locked door at the top of the stairs."

"And how do you open that door?" asked Eilidh, leaning backwards and having a look herself.

"Only the security guards have a key to the door at the top of the spiral staircase, and Sandra Holt has one other copy in her desk. The guards keep the key in a locked cupboard at their base, which is where we'll go to study the CCTV footage of the thief. The spiral staircase is never used. There's no need for any of us to have access to the first floor via those stairs."

The Housekeeper's Room had two built-in dark wood cupboards on either side, each stretching across the full length of the wall and with every single door appearing to be locked. There were four large wooden tables placed in the center of the room, each one of them covered with pieces of blue and white porcelain, laid out in neat lines.

Whoever was in charge of the room seemed to have a tendency towards OCD, thought Richard, looking at its meticulous tidiness. They would have a severe shock if they got a chance to see some of the desks back at Scotland Yard.

As Peter passed by one of the tables, he picked up one of the porcelain pieces and showed it to Richard and Eilidh.

"Look at this beauty. This is an 18th-century Delft Tulipiere Vase. A five-finger vase made by De Metalen Pot. It looks beautiful with tulips in it. Stunning piece..."

He put it down carefully and surveyed the room.

"These are out for dusting," he explained. "They're very fragile and easily broken, so it's necessary to have a specialist to work on them."

When he saw Eilidh looking at him in disbelief, he smiled.

"I promise you it does. Many of the items in this castle are very valuable, it isn't just the paintings."

Richard, who usually liked to examine antiques of any color and type, had ignored the porcelain treasures on view and gone over to the window to check the locks.

"This seems a very easy window to open. There's no key lock on it," he said.

"Yes, it's easy to open from the inside," admitted Peter. "This room's out of bounds for the public and at least the window is alarmed."

"Too bad the office and the door to this room weren't alarmed. That might have saved the painting."

"Yes, well, as I've said many times before we are reviewing all of our security in light of the robbery."

"What I don't understand is why the burglar opened the window from the inside, and then came back out into the corridor with the painting," remarked Eilidh. "That's where the guards saw him, isn't it?"

"Yes, they did. We're assuming he's a male. His face was covered in a balaclava."

"Mmm. I suspect we'll never find out why he ventured out into the corridor," said Richard. "It's obvious he was somewhere in the castle beforehand and broke into the office a good bit before the alarm went off. When had the security guards last checked on the office?"

"They checked the office at around two in the morning, as their last stop on the ground floor, before heading up to the public rooms on the first floor and then the second floor. Nothing was out of place at that point. As I said, at the time the exterior alarm went off in the Housekeeper's Room, they were already nearby."

"OK. Let's have a look at the CCTV footage." Richard sighed. "I think that's all we can do at this stage. Was the door broken into this room, too?"

"No."

"*No?*"

"No," repeated Peter. "The door to this room was open and it wasn't broken into."

"So, the thief had a key to this room and not the office."

"Yes, it certainly looks that way. A key to the Housekeeper's Room would be relatively easy to get hold of. Lots of people access this room at different points in the day. The cleaners, for example, as well as the staff that oversee the tea room and public toilets. Staff members responsible for cleaning, repairing, and restoring the artifacts also spend time in this room."

"So how many keys are there?"

"There are seven keys in circulation. The keys have to be signed out if they are given to any other staff members or visitors. I know, it's not an ideal system. It's based on trust."

"Is it easy to get a copy of the key?" asked Eilidh.

"No key's impossible to copy but it wouldn't be easy because it's a patented key," explained Peter.

"Small consolation," remarked Richard.

"Yes," said Peter, shortly.

Richard and Eilidh looked at each other, thinking the same thing. The castle was a rabbit warren of a place with easy access to a myriad of rooms. It had been only a question of time before something like the Botticelli theft happened.

Peter made his way to the door.

"If you come with me, I'll take you to what used to be the Housemaid's Tower. It's used now by the guards and holds all the CCTV footage."

They walked back past the office, along the corridor and then came to a stop two doors down, in front of a thick wooden door that had *"Private—Staff Only"* on it.

Peter opened it, without any hesitation, and led them through a small hallway to another door at the far end.

"In the past, this used to be the place where the junior female members of staff used to sleep. They were strictly segregated, of course, from the male servants. The men slept over at the Footmen's Tower, at the corner of the stable block. We use one of the rooms in this section as the base for the security guards."

Peter knocked loudly on a door, before opening it cautiously.

"OK if we come in?" he asked, peering around the door.

Richard didn't hear the answer but Peter then replied, "Good. Thank you."

Peter pulled the door wide open and ushered Richard and Eilidh into a small room where a young man was drinking from a mug.

He had a thick mop of brown hair and was dressed casually in a pair of combat trousers and a khaki T-shirt. His thick boots had left a small trail of cut grass across the dark wood floor so Richard surmised he must have entered the castle through another nearby door as the front entrance was some distance away.

"This is Rhys Hopkins, who's the lodge keeper at the entrance of the estate," said Peter. "Rhys, this is Eilidh and Richard from the Art Crime Unit."

Rhys stood up shyly and shook hands with the new visitors.

He had the fresh-faced look of someone who spent a lot of time outdoors, with a network of red veins on his cheeks and a fan of wrinkles at the corner of each eye, as though he spent a lot of his time screwing his eyes up to the sun's glare.

His eyes were bright blue in color and Richard thought their expression was open and guileless.

Rhys's smile, by contrast, was somewhat reserved but such reticence seemed to be a natural part of him. His manner was that of a man who was an extreme introvert.

"Right, well, as I said before this room is used by the night-time security guards. Rhys has access to it during the day as well. This is the incident book," Peter said as he picked up a large red notebook from a table by the window. "And should Rhys be fed back anything of importance by the other staff members, he writes it in here. Likewise, the guards write in it if anything's amiss or there's something of note during their watch, so Rhys can take action the next day, if need be."

He turned to Richard and Eilidh.

"By the way, in case you're wondering, the Bangor police have already checked the incident book to see if anything untoward happened prior to the robbery. Nothing occurred that merited them having a look into it, at least as far as they were concerned."

Putting the incident book back down, Peter looked over to where Rhys was sitting on the edge of the table, cradling his mug in his hands, and smiled at him.

"Rhys is our technical whizz kid. Our resident geek, if you like. He's in charge of maintaining and managing the CCTV equipment and will help us go over the footage of the thief."

Peter pulled up three chairs to a large screen at the far end of the room.

The whole room was piled high with equipment, and everywhere they looked cables were hanging down or trailing along the floor. Whizz kid or not, Rhys didn't seem to be particularly organized.

Richard noted there were four screens actively monitoring the perimeter of the castle.

"Rhys has put together all the CCTV footage we have of the thief. It's not much, I'm afraid, but you might find it useful. Take a seat," urged Peter, signaling the chairs.

Walking across the room, Richard and Eilidh sat down on the chairs Peter had laid out for them and waited for the CCTV footage to appear on the screen.

Sitting on the uncomfortable chair, with his arms and legs crossed, Richard smiled to himself. He was sure the pair of them were looking like two school kids waiting for morning assembly to begin.

There was something of the school teacher, too, in the way in which Peter Griffiths was orchestrating their visit. Maybe his behavior stemmed from the custodial responsibility he felt towards Penrhyn Castle and its art collection. If so, Richard didn't blame him for this, because he felt just as possessive about his Unit back in London.

Rhys put down his mug, came across to where they were sitting and switched on the monitor.

He then moved to the computer next to it, and using the mouse found the relevant file and double-clicked on it.

For a few seconds Richard and Eilidh sat very still, staring intently at the black- and-white scene in front of them.

Then they suddenly saw the thief let himself out of the window in the Housekeeper's Room, feet first.

Richard winced as he saw the thief frenziedly tugging the rolled-up canvas through the window opening.

What a way to treat a five-hundred-year-old master-piece, he thought. It really beggared belief. The robbery was obviously not a professional heist but, even so, no one with the slightest appreciation of art could have treated the old painting in the way the Penrhyn thief had. What's more, should the painting ever be found, restoration work would no doubt have to be done to it in order to repair the damage caused by such carelessness.

Within a few seconds, the thief had the canvas secured and then he set off, running across the forecourt at speed.

He was clutching the canvas in one hand, noted Richard, with a small part of it hanging loose.

Despite the small screen, Richard was inclined to agree with the guards' earlier description of the thief. He did indeed look athletic and muscular in build.

A minute later, the bulky figure of the security guard struggled through the window, landed heavily on the ground and bolted after the thief.

The thief turned back when he heard the noise on the gravel behind him and then he seemed to increase his pace. Both figures were soon out of the CCTV range, even with Rhys slowing down the footage.

Richard realized he had been holding his breath and tried to relax.

Soon, the second security guard appeared out of the front entrance and ran across the forecourt, but by then both the other men had gone through the archway and into the grounds some time ago.

Rhys moved forwards to the mouse again.

"And here's a short footage of the thief outside the carriage forecourt," said Rhys, sounding more confident now. He seemed to enjoy the technological aspects of his job and appeared more at home in front of the computer than chatting to the visitors.

Still gazing at the screen, Richard and Eilidh watched as the thief shot out of the archway and turned left. Shortly afterwards the security guard appeared and turned left, too, but it was evident from the footage that the guard was running out of steam and had slowed down considerably. The angle of the second camera wasn't as comprehensive as the first one and it wasn't long before the thief and the security guard were both out of sight.

The second security guard appeared after a moment, looking right and left, before turning at what seemed to be the other guard calling out to him and then he, too, disappeared off the left-hand side of the screen.

"The security guard thinks the thief was heading towards the walled garden," said Peter. "Unfortunately, from there you can make your way down to the lower level and after that..."

He shrugged.

"But no car that they could see, is that right?" checked Richard.

Peter nodded.

"Yes, if you know where to stand, you can have a good view from the castle of all the surrounding roads."

Richard and Eilidh looked at each other.

"Well, I think, if you don't mind, we'll now take a look around the grounds," said Richard, voicing what they were both thinking. "That's the last piece of the puzzle. I'll register the painting on the Art Loss Register, as well as Interpol's Stolen Works of Art database, and I'll use all my contacts to keep an eye out for anyone trying to sell the painting on the black market. It's all we can do at present, I'm afraid."

"I appreciate that," said Peter, with a glum expression on his face. "I take it you have little hope of retrieving it in the near future."

"With art theft, anything is possible, Peter, but my advice to you would be don't get your hopes up. These things can take a long time to resolve, if at all."

Peter nodded.

"Yes, I understand, but I have to believe that it'll come back to Penrhyn one day. The alternative is too tragic."

Richard smiled at Peter in commiseration. He knew and understood only too well how he felt.

"The motive for the theft is a tough call," Richard said, trying to give Peter some morsels to keep him going. Richard had already reached some conclusions about the case, not that Peter was going to like them. "Sometimes the return of a top-tier painting is used as a bargaining chip to reduce the prison sentences of senior criminals or gang leaders, but I doubt that's the situation here. The theft isn't professional enough, I'm afraid, for that to be the case. Top-tier paintings are also sometimes used as collateral amongst criminals, but again this doesn't seem likely in this instance."

"The thief could have wanted to keep the cash for himself," suggested Peter.

"If so, that just proves my point, Peter. No matter what way you look at it, your thief must be a novice at this. Selling a Botticelli painting on the sly will be an extremely difficult thing to do. It could even end up being dangerous for him, depending on what kind of an art dealer he decides to do his business with."

Richard took off his glasses and rubbed his eyes.

"There's another scenario too, of course. Some unscrupulous, wealthy person could have sent someone in to steal the Botticelli, so they could keep it in their possession, hidden from the world. But that doesn't wash either, I'm afraid. The robbery doesn't seem well planned, and if the Botticelli had been stolen to order the guards wouldn't have seen the thief. The fact they did is too clumsy for a true professional."

Pausing for a second, Richard ran his fingers through his hair. He was badly needing a haircut. *Another job for the weekend*, he thought.

"The painting isn't widely recognised or well-known yet, so that does narrow down the field a bit," he added.

He looked up at Peter, uncertain how he would take his next deduction on the robbery.

"So, you think it's an inside job, after all?" asked Peter, speaking for him.

Both Peter and Rhys were now watching Richard with apprehension in their eyes.

"I can't tell you for sure, obviously, but if I was a betting man I'd say yes. It seems to have all the hallmarks of it, to be honest. It seems more of an opportunistic crime than a meticulously organized robbery."

Rhys and Peter nodded, assimilating this. Neither of them looked particularly enthralled by the idea of working alongside an untrustworthy member of staff.

"I hope we find out who it is, if that's the case," said Peter quietly. "It's a huge risk having a member of staff around who could do such a thing."

"That's where your security measures need to be watertight," remarked Eilidh. "If the security's tight enough there's not much harm any staff member can do to the paintings."

By now, Peter was looking as though he was

carrying the weight of the world on his shoulders. It was time to give the poor man a break.

Richard stood up and stretched.

"You've been very helpful today, Peter, thanks."

He glanced out of the window. The dark grey clouds suggested there might be rain at some point.

"Eilidh and I will have a good look around outside now, if you've no objections."

"Of course not. I've a meeting with someone at four o'clock in any case." Richard began to button up his jacket.

"We'll return to the castle to speak to the security guards this evening. We're staying in Bangor for the night and then we'll pop back in the morning, as arranged, to speak to Stephanie Meadows and Sandra Holt. Martin Thompson, the DI at Bangor, has agreed to follow up with the other interviews. He'll be in contact with me about the case but do feel free to get in touch if anything else comes up."

"Good," said Peter, shaking hands with Eilidh and Richard. "I'll leave you both to it. I'll be here tomorrow morning, too. You can pick up a map of the gardens at the entrance of the castle. I'm afraid I've got to dash now. There's a conservator-restorer waiting for me in the Grand Hall."

Peter walked over to the door and opened it.

"By the way, Peter, just out of interest, why did it take you so long to bring us in?" asked Richard, keen to get an answer to a question that had been bothering him ever since he left London.

Peter turned around slowly and looked Richard straight in the eye.

"Truthfully? Because we wanted to delay, or rather

avoid, having to make this theft public, of course." Peter sighed and placed his hands on his hips, rocking backwards and forwards nervously on his toes. "Now they know about the robbery, the Penrhyn Family Trust will have serious misgivings about keeping their paintings here at Penrhyn, under the stewardship of the National Trust. Quite aside from the fact that claiming back the insurance for the painting is going to be a titanic battle."

He shrugged, lifting the palms of his hands up in surrender.

"All the prospects were so awful for us that we wanted to be certain the painting was irrecoverable before we opened Pandora's box and announced the Botticelli had been stolen."

6

Richard

Richard was feeling tired the next day and was not in the best of moods.

They had checked into The Penrhyn Inn, Bangor, the night before but, unluckily, so had a large and rowdy group of young men on a stag night. The high-light of the party seemed to be the groom and his best man running up and down the street outside, stark naked, to the cheering and catcalls of their chums.

From the start of the festivities Richard was sorely tempted to pull rank on them because he wanted to get some sleep. He was sure that even earplugs, had he bought any, would not insulate him from the noise they were making outside. Whoever was in charge at the inn was either turning a deaf ear to the commotion or was in a padded room on the other side of the building.

By the time it was one o'clock in the morning and the members of the stag party had tied the naked groom to a lamppost at the front of the inn, Richard had decided enough was enough.

He got dressed and, with his police ID in his hand,

was about to make his way downstairs to confront the drunken idiots, when Eilidh, who also happened to be outside her room, grabbed hold of his arm and stopped him.

Eilidh had been quite right, of course. The last thing the men needed to know was that there was an off-duty policeman staying at the inn, too. In their drunken state, God knew what mad antics they could potentially come up with, and the fall out of that didn't bear thinking about.

To complicate matters further for Richard, Eilidh had been standing on the landing in a T-shirt and a diminutive pair of pajama shorts that exposed her long, slim legs and this hadn't helped his sleep later on either.

Even after the inn had quietened down, he couldn't shift Eilidh's image from his mind for the few remaining hours of the night. Hacked off, he lay sleepless on his bed, wondering if Eilidh, like him, was lying awake and gazing out of the window at the night sky.

Proving she was made of stronger stuff than him, Eilidh was in good shape at the breakfast table the next day. She looked fresh as a daisy and as though she had slept the full nine hours, which of course she couldn't have done.

How Eilidh had managed to find the time and energy to be so groomed was also a matter beyond his comprehension. Eilidh's trousers and jacket were looking spotless and ironed that morning, and her short blonde hair was styled and she had a full face of make-up. In addition to this, her wide, chocolate-brown eyes were sparkling with good health and her smile was jovial.

Hideously jovial, in his opinion.

When he had first walked into the breakfast room, he had spotted Eilidh sitting at one of the tables, reading the newspaper while she ate her fried bread.

Tempted to disappear upstairs again until he felt in a better mood, he had retreated back to the stairs but Eilidh, having caught sight of him, called him over before he had a chance to escape.

Noting his exhaustion with a cheeky laugh, Eilidh poured him a cup of coffee and pushed it across the table without saying a word.

He drank it gratefully, trying at the same time to smooth down the tufts of hair sticking up on the back of his head. He hadn't bothered to shave either but was resigned to the fact that he was going to look for the rest of the day as though he'd been dragged through a hedge backwards.

Once he felt a bit more human, he placed his breakfast order and then looked around the dining room.

The dining room was completely empty, even though every table had been laid for breakfast. Richard was sure most of the other guests were recovering from their antics of the night before.

He sighed. The lucky sods didn't have to get up to work.

His own bedroom in London was up on the top floor of the building and far, far away from any noisy bachelor parties. Not something he'd ever appreciated before but he was going to from now on.

He picked up his newspaper and had a look at the headlines. Realizing that he wasn't the only one having a bad day, he started reading while he ate his breakfast and felt himself relax as he lost himself in some world-encompassing problems that made his own appear trivial by comparison.

For several minutes, peace reigned at the breakfast table.

"So today it's Stephanie and Sandra and then back to London we go," said Eilidh in a sing-song voice, breaking the silence in the dining room.

Richard looked over the top of his newspaper at Eilidh.

"Yes, but after our interesting chat with the security guards yesterday evening, I'd like to do a thorough search of the gardens at Penrhyn Castle this morning, before we leave for London," said Richard, overriding his exhaustion and trying to summon up some energy for the day. "I'm prepared to gamble on the fact that eight out of ten thieves, if they're getting chased, dump the stolen goods as soon as possible in case they get caught. The thief was seen walking in the castle grounds that night by another staff member, according to what the security guards said."

Richard folded his newspaper and put it down on the table.

"If I were the thief, scurrying around on the night of the burglary, I'd have quickly hidden the painting somewhere, with the intention of returning for it when it felt sufficiently safe to do so," he continued. "And should the thief be an insider, familiar with Penrhyn Castle and its grounds, I'd expect the odds of this happening to increase."

Eilidh's big eyes widened.

"So, you think the painting's lying about somewhere on the castle grounds?"

Richard rubbed his forehead, feeling weary.

"I've no idea, frankly, but I can't come up with anything else at present. If the painting did make it out of the castle grounds on the day of the theft, it's either hidden in someone's house or it's making its way abroad through the usual black-market channels. In that case, the essential thing would be to find out who was the inside contact for the theft."

"That'll take some time, though," cautioned Eilidh.

"Yes, and it's not going to be an easy task, what with Peter Griffiths having already given the staff a good telling off for putting out unfounded accusations amongst themselves. I can see him turning his protective wrath onto us if we come across as too heavy-handed. I really hope the Bangor police manage to do the interviews without any interference from Peter. Might be wishful thinking, though."

Richard started buttering another slice of toast.

"We should definitely do a search of the grounds. At least the parts where the thief was seen," he said, firmly. "Anything and everything's possible with art crime."

Reaching across the table, Eilidh poured the remains of the coffee into his cup, before catching the waiter's eye and asking him for a refill.

Richard studied the waiter when he came over to pick up the coffee pot.

With bloodshot eyes and cracked, dry lips, he didn't look much better than Richard that morning. He must have had a rough night of it, too. Given it was Thursday and not the weekend, the city of Bangor was turning out to be party central.

Richard had some fellow feeling for the lad. There was no expression whatsoever on the waiter's face, just a blank gaze, and he was struggling with the basic task of serving them their breakfast. Earlier on, instead of the cooked breakfast Richard had ordered, he'd brought Richard a toast rack with four pieces of overdone toast in it, some butter, and a choice of jam and marmalade. Feeling too tired to protest, Richard had meekly accepted the burnt offering for his breakfast.

Finishing his piece of toast and marmalade, Richard turned his attention back to what Eilidh was saying to him.

"Bangor police are getting statements from everyone at Penrhyn Castle who knew that the Botticelli painting was in the office and they'll be sifting through alibis. The report should be on our desks by the end of next week. We'll see if anything comes out of that," said Eilidh, hopefully.

Richard grunted. Things were never that easy, in his view.

He reached out for his third piece of toast, spread a layer of butter on it, and then slathered it in marmalade.

Looking down at the glutinous coating on his toast, he thought it was interesting that the Brits had brought marmalade, fried eggs, fried bacon, fried toast, and black pudding to the breakfast table. Whereas the Continentals instead consumed pastries, croissants, cooked meats, cheeses, or simply artisan bread for their morning meal. There was no doubting who had the better palette.

Richard didn't think the guests at the inn would care about gourmet food. If the Penrhyn Inn guests had a tendency to be hung over in the mornings, then a cooked English breakfast, packed full of fat, was going to be perfect for soaking up any excess alcohol.

Eilidh, meanwhile, had finished her cooked breakfast and was now working her way through some toast
and jam. As she was of slim build, the amount of food
Eilidh managed to get through always took Richard by
surprise. She had to possess a fast metabolism because
there was no other explanation for a level of food
consumption that would have satisfied Obelix. He also
knew Eilidh well enough to know that she wasn't a
fitness fanatic either, so he had no idea where she
managed to put it all.

Swallowing some more coffee, Richard felt his
morale and mood begin to improve.

He pushed his plate away and thought back to their
evening interview with the two security guards at
Penrhyn Castle, Baqir and Dylan.

Both the guards had been more than happy to talk
about the burglary. Which wasn't surprising, really,
thought Richard, because in all likelihood the Botticelli
robbery had been the highlight of an uneventful and
boring job working as a night-time security guard.

Richard was already impressed with their honesty.
With no CCTV inside the castle, the security guards
could have done whatever they wanted to at night. The
fact the pair of them hadn't been discovered fast asleep
on one of the beds during the robbery or, indeed, getting
drunk in the kitchen quarters had to be a point in their
favor.

During the interview, the two guards had given
them no further clues or insight into who the thief was
or what his motive might be.

However, Baqir had given them one interesting
snippet of information. He told them that Alfie, the
head gardener at Penrhyn Castle, had seen the thief

walking in the castle grounds during their search in the early hours of the morning.

Alfie was one of the three staff members summoned from Llandygai on the night of the Botticelli burglary and, according to Baqir, Alfie was convinced he'd seen the thief in the light of his torch, walking quickly through the Rhododendron Walk and in the direction of the Ruined Chapel. However, when all the staff went to have a look around the chapel, they saw nothing to indicate the thief was there.

"Then again, lots of the staff say they see things at Penrhyn Castle," Baqir Malouf had said dismissively. "It could just as easily have been a fox moving about in the undergrowth and that would be enough for them to say it was a ghost or, if not, the thief. Why not? The more the merrier. They seem to buy into the spooky stories surrounding this place. Total nutters, they are."

Dylan Evans remained silent, with his eyes averted. Seemingly, he didn't agree with this.

"Really?" Eilidh had asked, interested. 'do they often see the ghosts that are meant to haunt this place?"

"Yes, all the time," said Baqir, rolling his eyes. "Once a place gets a reputation, everyone wants to join in the fun."

Baqir, who was a laidback character, was sitting comfortably on the sofa in the guards' base, legs wide and with his swollen stomach protruding over the top of his trouser belt. If Richard hadn't seen for himself the CCTV footage of Baqir jumping out of the window and running after the thief, he wouldn't have believed it had happened.

"So, you guys haven't ever seen anything out of the

ordinary here? I mean, anything superstitious?" asked
Richard, distracted by this new topic of conversation.

"I have," said Dylan, looking sheepish.

Baqir grinned and winked at Richard and Eilidh.

"I really have," insisted Dylan, glancing across at his
colleague. "I often see a woman in the Lower India
Room. She's dressed in old-fashioned clothing. Big skirt
and all that. Used to give me a fright, so it did, but I'm
used to her now. He doesn't see her."

Dylan nodded his head towards Baqir.

Baqir shrugged, turning the palms of his hands
upwards.

"I'm sorry but I don't buy into this ghost crap," said
Baqir. "Wouldn't be working here if I did."

"That's true enough," agreed Dylan, a soft-spoken,
elderly man with a gentle manner. "There's a few staff
that have left Penrhyn over the years because they get
scared. Mostly staff that work in the castle shop. The
shop used to be the castle kitchen in the olden days and
the staff say they can hear voices in there, when the
shop has no one in it. They also claim that some of the
stock gets moved around and messed up after the shop
has been closed."

During their drive from Chester, Richard had read
about some of ghost sightings at Penrhyn Castle on his
mobile phone. If just half the ghost stories were real,
Richard wasn't sure how anyone continued to work at
the castle. Most people wouldn't be as gutsy as Dylan,
thought Richard. *"I'm used to her now"* had to be a
novel way of dealing with a ghost. Most people would
have screamed and run away, himself included.

Ghost sightings aside, he was intrigued by what the
security guards had said about Alfie, the head gardener.

Alfie was convinced he had seen the thief later on that night and this was well worth investigating because, if accurate, it meant the thief had been in the castle grounds for far longer than they had assumed. Had the thief ended up hiding outdoors until the coast was clear?

Richard's plan was to get up to the castle early and have a look along the Rhododendron Walk and around the Ruined Chapel before leaving for London again. Maybe Alfie's sighting would run true. Every good detective had to follow up on the thinnest of leads at the end of the day.

It didn't take Richard and Eilidh long to finish their breakfast and check out of The Penrhyn Inn.

As he walked to the car with his carryall, Richard felt as though he was shaking the dust from his feet and devotedly hoped he wouldn't have to return to The Penrhyn Inn in the near future. In fact, he'd be willing to pay good money to avoid spending another night there.

They made it up to the castle by 8.30, Rhys waving them in at the entrance when they sounded their horn.

After parking the car, they started to make their way towards the Ruined Chapel, walking next to each other in companionable silence and admiring the views.

With it being so early, little birds were out in force everywhere, hopping between hedges and trees, their songs ringing out vibrant and strong amongst the dense vegetation.

Richard had once read in a newspaper that birds had evolved louder songs in cities to compete with noise pollution. He could believe this, for although his flat was up on the top floor of his building and had double glazing, he was used to falling asleep to the background rumble of traffic when he went to bed. A city like London never slept.

He did sometimes ask himself if the cultural shift to electric vehicles would make London a quieter place to live in but he knew he would be a good bit older before that change fully bedded in.

As they drew nearer to the Rhododendron Walk they passed several mature oak trees that were in the process of shedding their autumnal leaves and, not long afterwards, found themselves bypassing a little wood-land copse which had several chestnut and lime trees in it, with thick swathes of fern filling the empty spaces beneath the trees.

A robin suddenly appeared on a holly bush in front of them and seemed so eager to follow them along the pathway that Richard wondered if the gardeners, or maybe even the visitors, were in the habit of feeding it.

They soon reached the Heather Slope, the cold, bitter wind making Richard wish he had brought his winter coat with him. The wind was causing his eyes to stream with tears but he noticed that all it did for Eilidh was to bring an attractive pink flush onto her pale cheeks. She was sturdier than she looked and didn't even have to lean forwards to counteract the strong gusts.

The south-west side of the estate was exposed to the full brunt of the elements and two trees were upended there, plucked out of the ground by the wind and with their squiggly, matted roots exposed.

Lichen had made its home on the fallen tree trunks, the grey fronds dribbling across the bark, but the moss was even more vigorous than the lichen, and large sections of the felled trees were already smothered with its thick, green padding.

Richard could tell it wouldn't be long before the dead trees would change color from grey-brown to a luminous lime, sinking into humiliating obscurity in what was an already very green landscape.

The damp, exposed conditions obviously favored the moss, helping it to thrive in that part of the estate. It could be seen everywhere, tinting the surroundings bright green and creating a mysterious, other-worldly atmosphere for anyone who happened to be passing by.

Further along the walk, Eilidh and Richard made a point of avoiding the Walled Garden, as well as the Bog Garden below it, and instead traced a path adjacent to an old yew hedge.

Richard felt that given the constraints of time, they should focus solely on the area around the Rhododendron Walk and the Ruined Chapel, which was where Alfie claimed to have caught a glimpse of the burglar.

It didn't take them long to reach the Rhododendron Walk, and once there they spent a substantial amount of time exploring the area.

They foraged along the arched walkway and around it, watching for any signs of trampled undergrowth and trying to spot likely hiding places. They peered under every single one of the rhododendron and azalea plants, in case it had occurred to the thief to hide the canvas beneath them.

Crazier things had been done with art theft, thought Richard, three quarters of an hour later, when he ruefully inspected his scratched, dirty hands and damp knees. The walk, up to that point, had been lovely but it was looking increasingly likely it was going to end in frustration and disappointment.

Once they had conducted a thorough search on the ground covering the Rhododendron Walk, they went up to the medieval-style chapel and started to investigate it, too.

There was little left of the old chapel. No roof remained, one wall was completely missing and the two facing walls were crumbling to bits. Only one stone wall was relatively intact and it had a beautiful arched window positioned at its center. Richard supposed that the window, at some point, must have had stained glass panes in it but those were long gone.

Slowly and carefully, Richard and Eilidh hunted around the chapel, trying to find subtle signs indicating the undergrowth had been disturbed or perhaps even damaged, something that they were sure would have happened had the thief been moving about the place in the pitch-dark or even hiding there.

They found plenty of proof that people had been trampling around the chapel's exterior. The night of the burglary had been a wet one and the staff who had gone to look for the thief had left muddy tracks with their boots around the perimeter of the chapel. Yet Richard and Eilidh established pretty quickly that there was nothing indicating to them that someone had been sheltering or hiding inside the chapel recently.

They were no experts at this kind of thing, though. Forensics, for example, would have noticed the tiniest disturbance in the undergrowth and more importantly, like African bush trackers, they would have been able to read what it meant, too. There was no chance, sadly, of getting forensics back out to Penrhyn Castle on the basis of slim and disputed evidence from the castle's head gardener.

Richard stood back from the chapel and tried to think where he would seek to hide if there were several staff members searching for him with torches during the night.

The chapel didn't offer much protection, that was for sure.

There was a certain sadness in seeing what was once an attractive building disintegrating with the passage of time. Richard, who loved anything with a romantic, melancholic atmosphere to it, had a soft spot for ruins. He liked their historical associations and was convinced that every ruin had an interesting story to tell.

Maybe one day he would try and find out what had happened to the Ruined Chapel at Penrhyn Castle but given that Penrhyn Castle itself was a Norman imitation, he wouldn't put it past the former owners to have created a ruin to add some antiquity to the scene. He could see them creating a fantasy world of their own making, so to speak, in the mold of Michael Jackson's Neverland.

The two standing walls of the chapel were barely there and didn't look particularly stable or solid. In fact, it seemed as though some of the climbing ivy and undergrowth was helping to prop the old edifice up.

The odd brick had loosened, and then fallen, from the crumbling walls and this had left a random pattern of empty holes in the brickwork.

In this part of the estate, nature had the upper hand over the manmade construction, demonstrating its power as it did with so many other abandoned buildings across the globe, given half the chance.

The vegetation was surviving the weather far better than the old chapel and was flourishing within the building, as well as outside of it.

Inside the chapel, ivy cascaded down the walls, with its thick fronds reaching all the way down to the ground. Emerald-green grass provided a soft floor to cushion their steps. In Richard's eyes, the chapel was slowly transforming from a stone place of worship to a green palace.

It looked as though some effort had been made to thin the trees surrounding the chapel, but even so there was a fully grown cedar tree nearby, reaching out and touching the wall with its majestic branches.

A bushy eucryphia tree was shielding the chapel's other flank.

To the north of the chapel, in the far distance, Richard spotted the distinctive red bark of a few straw-berry trees dotted amongst Douglas firs and the less flamboyant birch trees.

After half an hour of surveying the ground with no result, Richard let out an exasperated shout.

When Eilidh poked her head above a low-lying tree branch and looked at him, her hair ruffled and her cheeks flushed with bending down so close to the ground, he chuckled. To her credit, Eilidh really got stuck in when she was working on a case.

"It's not going to happen for us today, Eilidh. I feel it in my bones."

"Well, now that we're here, I'm happy to keep going," said Eilidh calmly, as she bent to look at the grass once more.

Admiring her tenacity but deciding he'd had enough for the time being, Richard walked over to a sheltered spot inside the chapel, where there was a pile of fallen brickwork buried under a thicket of honeysuckle.

Drained, he sat down on top of the bricks and enjoyed feeling the sun warming him up with the little heat left in its rays at that time of year.

He watched as a magpie, which had been observing them with interest from a distance, flew across to a nearby tree and started cackling manically, lifting and dropping its black tail as it did so.

It was time to call it a day, thought Richard, as the magpie took off again and disappeared into the woodland.

A rustling of leaves distracted him and when he turned he saw a grey squirrel appear from under the ivy cover, then move across the wall in the erratic, disjointed manner so common to rodents.

Richard tilted his head to one side as he watched the squirrel disappear under the ivy again.

He got up and went over to inspect the thick blanket of ivy coating the wall.

Reaching up and tentatively feeling around the edges of the ivy curtain, he found that he was able to lift up a large section with ease and look underneath it.

Straightaway, he could see that someone had deliberately ripped the ivy from its tenacious grip on the wall. The trailing, curled fingers of the ivy strands were broken off and hanging loose right across the uneven brickwork of the chapel.

"Eilidh, could you come and hold up this ivy for

me, please?" called Richard, feeling the ivy envelop him in its smothering clutch.

Eilidh promptly appeared from the other side of the chapel and pulled the heavy ivy away from the wall, walking back with it as far as she could.

Richard bent down and went under the ivy cover again.

In the dim light, he could now see that midway up the wall there was a ledge where another arched window, now long bricked up, used to be.

Richard reached up on his tiptoes and started to feel with the tips of his fingers along the uneven stone window ledge.

It wasn't long before he felt the soft folds of some kind of cloth.

His heart beating quickly, he pulled the crumpled material down and held it gingerly in his hands.

Bending low again under the ivy canopy, he shuffled out into the bright glare of the sunlight and turned to look at Eilidh.

"It feels like canvas," he said, with barely suppressed excitement.

Eilidh said nothing but came forward and held on to the top of the cloth as Richard began to ease out the creases with great care.

Sure enough, soon they were looking down on two angel heads, both executed in the unmistakable style of Sandro Botticelli and smiling right back at them.

7

Richard

They stood still for a few minutes, their heads bent low and their arms wide open as they held on to opposite ends of the canvas, almost as though paying homage to the artwork painted 500 years ago.

"I can't believe we found it. Talk about a needle in a haystack," said Eilidh in a stunned voice.

"It was definitely an inside job," muttered Richard to himself. "Somebody knew that ledge was there and was planning to come back for the painting later on."

He took in every detail of the painting; from the delicate way the garlands were portrayed to the linear perfection of the angels' contours. He loved the contrast between the aqua-grey coloring of the River Arno and the terracotta and orange hues of the buildings in the distance.

It was hard to believe, on that sunny, autumnal day, that something so beautiful had been bought with the profits from slave labor.

"Well, it looks most likely to be someone who works in the gardens, don't you think?" asked Eilidh, trying to figure things out. "I can't imagine any of the staff working inside Penrhyn Castle spend much of their time exploring the gardens."

"I think the field of candidates is narrowing. Firstly, it had to be one of the few who knew the painting was in the office that night. Secondly, as you say, it had to be someone familiar with the gardens. Some of the staff here are such long-timers, though, that it could easily be any one of them... But I guess right now I don't really care who the thief could be, because the most important thing is that we've found the painting. Nothing else matters. I suggest we put this treasure into the boot of our car and go up to the castle for our chat with Sandra and Stephanie. We don't want to tell them we've recovered the painting because their answers to our questions could then be very different."

Eilidh stared at him.

"You're not going to tell them you found it?"

"Not yet. Let's get the interviews done and then we can bring it in. Peter said he would be here later this morning, too."

"Fine. But don't blame me if something happens to it in the meantime," said Eilidh, looking horrified at the idea of leaving the valuable painting in the car boot, even for a short time. "You do realize that even if we do figure out who is the most likely candidate for the burglary, we still have no proof? I guess we'll just have to live with that."

"Yes, that's true but a word of warning into Peter's ear about a staff member won't go amiss. I mean, it's not good to have untrustworthy members of staff hanging around the place. I'm sure he'll find a way to juggle things so there's no future opportunity for anyone suspicious to have easy access to the paintings, although the risk factor will always be there."

"I suppose so. Somehow, I don't think it's the end of art theft at Penrhyn."

"Oh, I'm hopeful it will be," said Richard, firmly. "The castle has a stunning collection. Absolutely beautiful. It would be tragic if anything happened to it. The security's getting enhanced, by the looks of it on a daily basis, and if whoever took this painting tries to do so again, he might find it impossible to get away with it. He'd be a fool to try again. These paintings aren't easy to sell on either. They're so distinctive, even to the amateur eye, and trying to fence an Old Master is always going to be extremely risky. Easy to get betrayed by someone along the way, especially if there's a reward offered for its recovery."

Richard carefully rolled up the canvas, tucking it under his long rain jacket for the walk back.

He looked at his watch.

It was nearly half past eleven, the time of their meeting with Sandra Holt and Stephanie Meadows. He hoped they would still be available for a chat by the time they got to the castle.

"We'd better hurry up, Richard," remarked Eilidh, voicing his thoughts.

They made their way back at a faster pace than before, and once they reached the car park they found to their surprise quite a number of cars were parked in it.

In the distance there was a group of joggers making their way across the Elysian Fields, with several sheep dotted amongst them, looking like bits of cotton fluff against the mountain and sea view.

Richard opened the car boot and gently placed the rolled-up canvas in it, covering it with a thick tartan car blanket.

There was other paraphernalia tucked to one side of the boot; torches, food, water bottles, a first aid kit, and a high visibility jacket. Out of habit, Eilidh always packed emergency gear for long car drives, even at the height of summer. She was, after all, someone who liked to be in control of every situation, but Richard found her precautions hilarious. It wasn't as though they were travelling by night through the Yorkshire moors or Scottish Highlands.

He slammed the boot shut.

Eilidh stood to the side, shaking her head.

"It would serve you right if that was gone when you came back for it."

"It won't go missing," said Richard, confidently.

He could see Eilidh was finding his assurance irritating. He was sure that, given half a chance, she would have hidden the picture somewhere else in order to shake him out of his complacency. She would have relished, too, seeing the look on his face when he found the painting had somehow vanished from the boot when they came back for it. If that were to happen, Eilidh would be his first and only suspect.

More and more cars were slowly winding their way up the road to the car park, so Richard and Eilidh walked at full speed to the castle entrance, hoping to beat the incoming crowd and therefore avoid having to wait in line behind them. They were late enough as it was.

Richard wasn't surprised to see so many visitors converging at the castle that morning. It was turning out to be a sunny and crisp autumnal day, perfect for capturing the last remnants of warm weather before the winter made its presence felt.

Jane, the same lady who had let them in the previous day, was at her standpoint at the entrance to the castle.

"We've a meeting with Stephanie and Sandra," said Eilidh, a little out of breath. "But we're running a bit late I'm afraid."

"Not to worry, I'm sure they'll be available," said Jane, with a motherly air. "I'll give Sandra a call."

The average age of the staff at the castle seemed to be fifty plus. Looking at Jane, Richard wondered for a moment whether she was a volunteer or a paid-up staff member. He wasn't sure what motivated people to volunteer at the National Trust but he honored them for it. He could imagine an added bonus for any volunteers would be that when they were in the twilight years of their life the job would help to keep their mental faculties sharp and bring them a sense of purpose they might not otherwise have had at that age.

As a group of visitors began to make their way across the forecourt outside, a large, tweed-suited lady, with her red hair tied up in a severe bun, walked up to Richard and Eilidh from the Entrance Gallery.

"Hello. I'm Sandra. I'm glad you could make it. Please come with me to the office," she said, smiling at them both.

They followed Sandra to the now-familiar office, Sandra marching in front of them with secretarial efficiency.

As Sandra seated herself behind her desk, they sat down on the two chairs placed in front of it.

Eilidh took a small notebook and pen out of her bag.

While she looked in her notebook for an empty page to write on, Richard peered over her shoulder and was surprised to see she had written a large number of notes in it, most of which seemed to be about the Penrhyn robbery. She was certainly putting him to shame with her zealousness.

He turned to look at Sandra and waited for Eilidh to begin the interview.

"Thank you for making the time to see us today, Sandra," said Eilidh. "We're wondering if you could tell us exactly who knew the painting was in this office. On the day before the burglary happened, of course. There seem to be an awful lot of staff running Penrhyn Castle."

"Yes, with the volunteers, there are rather a lot of us working here. Peter told me you wanted an exact list of those who knew about the Botticelli painting and I can tell you that very few did know about it," said Sandra, her freckled, plump face looking serious. "We're very close-lipped about security in the castle and the staff members and volunteers are regularly trained on maintaining security routines and roles. Only two security guards, who were on nightshift duty during that week, were told about there being a valuable item in the office. Baqir and Dylan. The other two weren't told anything. We were hoping to have the painting out of the office the next day, when Stephanie was in, and have it hanging up in the Breakfast Room."

"So, it was only yourself, Stephanie, Baqir and Dylan who were in the know?" pressed Eilidh.

"And Rhys, of course. He runs the CCTV system

in this place and is responsible for any incidents that happen during the day."

There was a tentative knock on the door behind them.

Before they had a chance to respond, the door opened and a lady walked in.

"Ah, this is Stephanie Meadows, the curator for Penrhyn," said Sandra, looking relieved to see her.

Stephanie was exactly how Richard thought an art curator should look. Ethereal, with long black hair, she was a slight figure, graceful in her movements and relaxed in her manner.

She was wearing a black T-shirt with a white skull and cross bones on it, black jeans, and a pair of bright-red DMs. An original and trendy choice of clothing for someone who seemed to be well past middle age, Richard thought, but what did he know? Eilidh would be a better judge of that kind of thing.

"Hello. I'm so glad you managed to make it here. I've been very keen to meet you both," Stephanie gushed, as she shook hands with them. "What an absolutely fascinating job you have."

Eilidh nodded at this and Richard smiled to see her do it. So, the shine hadn't worn off during her stint at the Art and Antiquities Unit. A little surprising, in his view, but good news.

"Yes, it's very fascinating," agreed Eilidh.

"Frustrating, too, at times," she added, looking pointedly at Richard. Richard looked back at her with his best poker face.

Giving up on riling him, Eilidh turned and faced Stephanie again.

"Anyway, Stephanie, we were in the process of

trying to establish who knew the Botticelli was in the office the night of the robbery. It seems to be a very limited list."

Stephanie perched herself on a nearby desk.

"Of course. It was only Sandra and myself that knew the Botticelli was here. Rhys, Baqir, and Dylan were aware we had a valuable item in our custody. That's it, I'm afraid."

She rubbed her forehead for a moment.

"Peter Griffiths knew Professor Balboa was returning the Botticelli to the castle but I don't know if he knew it was being kept in the office for the night or not. Actually, I don't think he knew the painting was here in the office... I'm afraid to say, it was my decision and my mistake to put the painting in here. The Botticelli painting deserved to have a special place in the Breakfast Room but we needed to shift some of the other paintings around first."

"He did know it was in the office," chipped in Sandra, succinctly. "I informed him as soon as the painting arrived. He had asked me to keep him informed."

"Oh, well. There you go then," said Stephanie, shrugging and smiling at Richard and Eilidh. "That makes six of us. Not many to choose from, wouldn't you say?"

"No, there aren't," agreed Richard. "I don't suppose there's any chance somebody could have overheard you talking about it, at all? It's easily enough done."

"No. I'm very conscious of the importance of our artworks and I wouldn't be gossiping about them to anyone," said Sandra, looking upset at the aspersion.

Richard looked at Stephanie and saw her smile sadly. She shook her head at him.

"Wasn't me. I spend most of my time here on my own, I'm afraid. I'm usually working on presentations for the artifacts in the castle, checking the inventories are in order, making sure the cleaning is up to date. I also make sure the security systems are functioning well, in addition to keeping a close eye on the conditions the paintings are kept in. It isn't easy to get the temperature and humidity consistent and correct in an old stone building like this one, I can tell you. It's a real challenge."

"The guards were only informed when they came on nightshift," added Sandra, as an afterthought.

"That wouldn't give them much time to plan a burglary then, would it?" said Stephanie, jokingly.

Richard was taken aback by Stephanie's devil-may-care attitude but maybe she was simply deflecting her genuine sense of guilt and distress about the loss of a unique masterpiece. He would always view the loss of a Botticelli artwork as a tragedy. Every single Botticelli painting added to the understanding and appreciation of the renowned artist and, as far as he could recall, there were only twelve of Sandro Botticelli's paintings in the UK, most of them in the National Gallery, London. No matter which way he looked at it, losing a Botticelli painting wasn't something he felt able to joke about.

"It's possible we'll never find out who the thief was but it's important, as far as the castle's collection goes, that the security system here is as good as it can be," said Richard, trying to get across to Stephanie the seriousness of the robbery.

"I agree with you, Richard. World-class paintings deserve world-class security," Stephanie replied, crossing her arms. "We've learnt from this, thankfully. The National Trust is supporting the additional measures we're bringing in. We aren't swamped with visitors here at Penrhyn Castle, so managing the security of the paintings shouldn't be beyond us. It really shouldn't."

Richard was satisfied with her response, thinking that it was as good an answer as he could hope to get.

Before he could say anything else, there was a sharp knock at the door and Peter Griffiths popped his head in.

"Great! I'm glad I've caught the pair of you before you left us. I just wanted to let you know that we're very appreciative of everything you're doing to help us find the painting."

Peter walked into the room and slowly closed the door behind him.

The others stared at Peter in shock because he was behaving like a man who'd received a blow to the solar plexus. He was bent over, with his arms crossed over his stomach, and he was looking thoroughly distressed.

Peter sat himself down on a chair next to Eilidh and Richard and, after a slight pause, he leant forward with his elbows on his legs and sunk his head into his hands.

The others watched him in bemusement.

"I've just had a painful meeting with the trustees of the Penrhyn Family Trust. They're not best pleased as you can imagine," said Peter at last.

He groaned.

"There was talk of suing the National Trust for negligence. I'm not sure where we stand on that one."

"It's not negligence to have a painting in a locked office, inside an alarmed castle with two security guards on duty," said Stephanie hotly.

Peter looked at her in despair.

"We've no choice but to wait and see what they decide," he said. "Maybe we should be taking some legal advice. I did go over the new enhanced security we're putting in place here with them. That seemed to mollify them a little."

"No museum or gallery can claim to be a hundred-percent secure," added Sandra.

"Yes, but the Rembrandt painting's now in the Cardiff Museum," said Peter. "Will they turn their eyes to there?"

"I don't think it'll be as simple as moving the paintings from one place to another, Peter," said Richard, thoughtfully. "There's the legal aspect of the family trust to consider, too. I'm prepared to bet it'll probably be quite specific in terms of where the paintings can be kept. The *Catrina Hooghsaet* painting was sold by the family trust through Christie's and then the anonymous owner, after an export license was refused, loaned it to the Cardiff Museum. Very different."

"Yes, we'll have to look into that I guess, if it comes to it," agreed Peter, halfheartedly. "I'm really worried that this won't be the last painting to be stolen if we don't beef up the security very soon. I mean—"

"I think we can help you resolve one of your problems, Peter," interrupted Richard, deciding it was time to let Peter know about the Botticelli and give him some good news for a change. "If you can come with us, we'll show you what we found this morning in the castle grounds."

Looking confused, Peter followed them out of the castle and walked with them to the car park.

He watched with interest as Richard opened their car boot and pulled out the coiled canvas.

Eilidh held on to the other end of the canvas as Richard unraveled it. Ten seconds later, Peter burst into tears.

"Definitely not the thief," muttered Eilidh, humorously, as she watched Peter wiping away his tears with a handkerchief.

Richard was inclined to agree with her.

As far as he could tell, Peter's tears were spontaneous and natural. No thief could fake that well.

8

Nkiruka

Nkiruka was absorbed in a crime report, written by a new DI at Scotland Yard, when she heard a phlegmy cough resonate above her head.

Looking up, she stared directly into the small, sharp eyes of Superintendent Lionel Grieves.

He didn't say anything, instead tossing onto her desk a tabloid newspaper with the bold, black headline:

Serial killer on Hampstead Heath.

"Shit," said Nkiruka.

"Yes, my thoughts exactly," said Lionel.

Nkiruka pulled the newspaper towards her and started reading the article.

"It makes good reading, I give them that," remarked Lionel. "They got their ugly little hands on a five-star storyteller."

"But who?" Nkiruka asked herself.

"There's no point trying to find that out, Niki. Complete waste of time. Everyone's been gossiping about the murders in here, as far as I can tell, and you don't need to tell me that the idiots at West Hampstead Police Station haven't been spilling the beans left, right, and center, because I wouldn't believe you."

Nkiruka didn't reply, her heart sinking as she read lines like *"evil killer tortures old man," "his eyes were gouged out," "stomach was cut open and then his entrails pulled out,"* and lastly: *"What are the police going to do about this? Our experts agree that it is only a matter of time before he strikes again."*

Nkiruka snorted.

As though every serial killer had to be a man. Usually the case, but not always.

"Oh, for goodness sake!" exclaimed Nkiruka as she gazed down at a disturbing photo of the old man's face. "That photo wasn't taken by our people, was it?"

"Probably. It would only take a second with a mobile phone. It's grainy and taken at a bad angle, but it does the job. Could have been any police officer hanging about the crime scene that day."

Nkiruka shrugged and nodded, her lips pursed disapprovingly.

"Dare I ask where you're at with this one?" asked Lionel, crossing his arms and tapping his foot impatiently against her desk leg.

This was an ominous sign with Lionel.

Nkiruka knew him well enough by now to recognize when his body language was signaling his displeasure. Lionel reminded Nkiruka of Mount Fuji, the unstable volcano in Japan she had studied as part of Ada's school project. It really didn't take much these days for him to explode and scald everyone in sight with his anger.

"Well, we're still waiting for more detail from the pathology report," said Nkiruka, stalling for time. "And DI Webster is keeping me informed. Not much else has come in yet."

"Not good enough, Niki. Next thing is we're going to get those hounds camping out here, at New Scotland Yard, and I'm going to need regular bait balls to feed them. So how about this case becomes top priority with you and you help an old, decrepit man out for a change?"

Nkiruka gave him a grim smile.

"I'm not going to flatter you, Lionel. There's no glossing over your age or your looks, I'm afraid."

A flash of admiration entered Lionel's gimlet eyes and seeing it she relaxed a little. Lionel always had time for the people who stood up to him.

"We're focused on this case, Lionel," she added, hoping to placate him. "I've full confidence in Johnny Webster's abilities, and we'll certainly do our best to try and dig something up soon, so you can pass it on to the press."

"See that you do," muttered Lionel gruffly, as he nodded at her and walked off. Nkiruka sighed.

She pulled the paper towards her and started rereading the article, feeling herself getting angrier and angrier as she did so.

She felt incandescent with rage by the time she finished it. Some stupid blabbermouth in the Met had stirred up the hornet's nest of the British press and as a result was going to make her working life a living hell. She really could have done with a little more time before the story came out. If she ever got her hands on the idiot in the police force responsible for the newspaper article, she wouldn't be answerable for her actions.

To add insult to injury, the paper had incorrectly reported several important details about the case.

For a start, there wasn't one serial killer on the loose, the murder and torture of the old man had been the work of more than one person.

Which, actually, in many respects was even more worrying and confusing, so it was probably a good thing the paper had got the number of perpetrators wrong. As it was, there would be enough hysteria over just the one killer.

The paper also stated that the murdered men had in all likelihood been looking for a sexual encounter on Hampstead Heath and implied that the murderer had some sort of a vendetta against gay men.

Again, Nkiruka disagreed with this conclusion.

The two younger men were found wearing foreign clothing. The youngest of the two men was wearing items of clothing with Ellus and Osklen fashion labels, which Nkiruka had since discovered were luxury Brazilian designer brands. Rich and from Brazil, would Hampstead Heath really be a location on their radar? Nkiruka somehow doubted it. Quite aside from the fact that the pathologist had confirmed over the phone that there was no evidence of any recent sexual activity on the bodies.

The gist of the story in the newspaper was that the murderer might strike again.

To add fuel to the fire, they had quoted a few experts on serial killers. Great titillation for the readers, but in Nkiruka's view the three dead men were linked to each other and all the signs were pointing to the fact that their killing was very much a targeted and specific event.

The criminal psychologist she had consulted had agreed with her and said that in his opinion the level of ferocity used in the murder of the old man indicated a revenge killing of some sort.

He suggested they look into the old man's past to find clues for the motive behind the murder, which, of course, wasn't going to be easy if the man came from Brazil.

Brazil did not have the same established rapport and cooperation on intelligence matters with the UK as Europe did, even after Brexit. And Brazil wasn't part of the Five Eyes alliance, of course. Digging up information on the old man was going to be tricky, and the Brazilian connection was likely to present a number of logistical problems for them.

They hadn't as yet communicated with the Brazilian embassy. So far, no one had reported the men as missing or raised the alarm, which was strange given how easy it was to get in touch with a mobile phone these days. The old man was unlikely to have owned a mobile phone but the other two would certainly have used one. If the men were from Brazil, as they were assuming, it seemed nobody over there had clocked their disappearance yet.

Nkiruka was a hundred-percent sure that the motive was going to be the key to finding the murderers but it was obvious, even at this early stage, that the investigation was going to be complex and difficult to resolve. No matter which way she looked at it, it was going to take time to produce results and this was not going to suit Lionel's hasty agenda in the slightest.

She sighed again and pushed the newspaper to one side.

She had to figure out a way forward soon but she was going to wait for the pathologist's full report first. His report would at least present her with some concrete facts, which would be very welcome given that everything else she had on the case right now was pure conjecture.

However, before the pathology report landed on her desk, things began to move at a fast pace.

Mindful of Lionel's instructions, Nkiruka had requested the homicide team in charge of the Hampstead Heath case to treat it as top priority and to keep her in the loop every step of the way.

Two days later, DI Johnny Webster came to her desk, full of suppressed excitement.

"Nkiruka, Claridge's called the West End Central Police Station yesterday morning because three of their hotel guests seem to have disappeared. They haven't turned up at the hotel for the last four nights. They were supposed to have checked out of the hotel yesterday but their luggage was left untouched in their rooms and they didn't make an appearance to pay their bill. They've not responded to the calls, texts, or emails Claridge's have sent them either."

"Please don't tell me Claridge's moved the luggage left in their rooms," said Nkiruka, with a sense of foreboding.

"Yes, I'm afraid they did. The hotel's full and they needed both rooms. They've kept their bags in storage, though, and at our request forensics went through the luggage this morning. The hotel has also retrieved three passports and the men's plane tickets from the safe in one of the rooms."

"Excellent," said Nkiruka, rubbing her hands together in glee. "We'll finally get their identities. A huge step forward."

She looked down at her watch.

"Phone Claridge's and tell them we're coming out to them this afternoon. I've got a number of things to get done this morning but I'll meet you downstairs at three, Johnny, if that suits you?"

Johnny nodded.

"OK. I'll drop Lionel a quick email to let him know about this latest development."

It had only been a question of time, at the end of the day, and at least now they had a chance to chart a way forward in their investigation, rather than treading blindly into the unknown. Similar to the unwinding of a spool of thread, more and more information was bound to come to light as a result of finding out the men's identities.

The offending newspaper was relegated to a drawer in her desk and she spent the next few hours concentrating on her other homicides.

Thanks to Johnny's foresight, when they left New Scotland Yard to go to Claridge's that afternoon they took a marked car, always useful in case they were forced to park on any double yellow lines in the city center. It saved any hassle with over- zealous parking attendants.

"Posh gits, aren't they?" commented Johnny, as he worked his way through busy traffic.

"Yeah, they certainly seem to be wealthy. If they're the Hampstead men, that is.

I'm sure they will be. Trouble is, if the murdered men turn out to be *"posh gits,"* it's only going to make this case even more high profile, and with the press harassing us for information on a daily basis, it's not as though we needed to be under any more pressure. I've a hunch this whole thing is going to turn out to be a bloody nightmare."

Johnny grunted his agreement.

Looking down at her fingernails, Nkiruka noticed they were looking unkempt and scraggy. A sign of the sleep-deprived times she was living in.

She began to scratch off the loose bits of nail polish and decided she would get her nails painted at the weekend. In truth, she had no excuse for letting herself go as far as her nails were concerned because painting her nails was not a chore for her. In fact, it was one of her favorite rituals and she always worked on them while sitting in front of the television, basking in the warmth of her living room fire with her legs stretched out on the sofa.

"We'd better contact the Brazilian embassy as soon as we get their names," she said after a minute, wiping the tiny shreds of nail polish off her skirt and onto the floor.

"Yep."

"And we're going to get forensics back into the hotel to see if they can find anything of interest in the men's hotel rooms."

"In their rooms?" asked Johnny, glancing across at Nkiruka.

"Yes, of course. I don't give a damn what the hotel or their guests think about it. We need to get our hands on any little thing that might be significant."

"There's not likely to be much there for forensics to find if Claridge's employs decent cleaners, which given their prices I imagine they might."

"I don't care. We're sending them in anyway."

Johnny grinned, finding Nkiruka's assertiveness on the matter entertaining.

Nkiruka suspected Johnny was somewhat awestruck by the Mayfair hotel and if he were on his own would be inclined to suck up to the staff working there and would prefer to avoid causing them any inconvenience. In many ways she could understand his point of view because their department, on the whole, tended to deal with members of the public from murkier and far less privileged backgrounds than the Brazilian men appeared to come from.

But with Lionel waiting impatiently for some progress on the Hampstead Heath murders, Nkiruka couldn't afford the luxury of being a people-pleaser. She had to make sure procedures were followed through correctly and to the highest possible standard, regardless of how Claridge's might feel about her bothersome requests.

They parked near to the entrance to Claridge's and exited the car.

Nkiruka looked up at the elegant red building and wondered what it must be like to be a guest at the hotel.

Even at the mature age of thirty-nine and after working in the Met for eighteen long years, she still found it intimidating to enter a place like Claridge's. This wasn't anything to do with the hotel's opulence or the extortionate prices it charged for its rooms but instead due to the building's historical associations. She felt little better than an imposter entering a location that had in the past belonged to a less diverse society and it was a feeling she found hard to shake off.

With her rational mind, she knew it was ridiculous to think in this way in the 21st century, but it was hard to deprogram oneself after a childhood in which she had been called names at school because of the color of her skin. There were idiots at every school but the ones at South Hampstead High School, like homing pigeons, zoned in on difference and, as a private, fee-paying school, the number of black students was very small. She knew that, for them it hadn't just been about skin color, it was about anything that stood out. A vulnerable, autistic boy in her year had been picked on more than her but that hadn't made the name-calling any easier to live with.

She bit her lower lip at the painful childhood memories.

Then seeing that Johnny was ready, she nodded at the doorman and walked in through the double doors.

She made her way to the front desk and presented her ID to the glamorous receptionist behind it.

"Hello, I'm Chief Inspector Ezemonye and this—" she turned to indicate Johnny "—is Detective Inspector Webster. We're here about your missing guests." The receptionist's eyes widened as she looked down at Nkiruka's ID.

She had on the thickest pair of false eyelashes Nkiruka had ever seen and her eyes reminded her of Bambi's.

She turned to look at Johnny and caught him gazing at the attractive receptionist with open admiration.

Cross at his unprofessional behavior, Nkiruka

kicked him on the shin to get his attention and then gave him a cold stare.

Unabashed, Johnny shrugged his shoulders and turned around to study the foyer instead.

"If you can wait here for a minute, please, I'll call the manager straightaway for you," said the receptionist in a soft voice.

Nkiruka nodded and moved to one side, leaning on the desk with her elbow.

Johnny, meanwhile, was enjoying himself. Scanning the foyer with a big smile on his face, he was behaving like a child who had just arrived at Disneyland for the first time.

Nkiruka decided to ignore him.

To occupy the time, she picked up one of the leaflets lying on the desk and proceeded to read about the tourist attractions on offer in London.

The caliber of the hotel guests that stayed at Claridge's was evident, for the leaflet recommended the London Eye Private Champagne Tasting Capsule, Truffle rolling classes with master chocolatier Paul A. Young, afternoon tea at The Goring, a £20,000 haircut with Stuart Philip (official hair stylist of the BAFTA awards), and a visit to Mr. Salvatore Calabrese's bar at the Playboy Club, where you could spend £5,500 for a cocktail.

Eyebrows raised, Nkiruka read on.

For those guests who wanted to be more adventurous the leaflet suggested a London-in-the-sky experience, where some of the top London chefs would bring their expertise to a table 25 meters in the air, a private helicopter tour with The London Helicopter company, or a day trip on the Belmond British Pullman train.

As she was unlikely to ever try any of the delights on offer, Nkiruka returned the leaflet back to the desk pile.

It was quiet that afternoon and there was no one sitting on the chairs laid out in the foyer's distinctive white white-and-black tiled floor. Two men and a lady were milling around separately near the entrance, waiting to be joined by their friends or family, before heading outside.

"Chief Inspector Ezemonye!" called out a deep voice with a discernible French accent.

Nkiruka turned and saw a tall and powerfully built man in a grey suit approaching them from the other side of the room, smiling broadly from ear to ear.

For one, totally insane, moment, Nkiruka thought she'd been whisked away to the 1st century BC and was watching a gladiator loping across the arena towards her. Broad and muscular, the hotel manager was a Russell Crowe look-alike and he seemed like a fish out of water in the dainty, plush foyer. A heavyweight boxing ring or a cinematic battle scene would have been a more appropriate location for him, thought Nkiruka.

With a chiseled face, wavy hair and warm, brown eyes, he had quite a presence and, in spite of herself, Nkiruka felt her pulse beat a little faster. Having admonished Johnny for his response to the pretty recep-tionist, she was also feeling something of a hypocrite.

"Hello. I'm delighted to meet you. I'm Henry Bisset, the duty manager," said the gladiator, when he reached the front desk.

He held out his hand.

Taken aback by his effusive welcome, Nkiruka shook it without saying a word.

It was rare for Nkiruka to meet a man who could silence her. Very rare. She was sure that Tom, who often tired of her chatter at home, would have loved to have asked Henry for some helpful tips.

Henry turned to Johnny with a smile and shook his hand, too, asking for his name.

Nkiruka liked that Henry hadn't ignored Johnny or treated him as someone less important than herself. For some reason, she'd expected the staff working at Claridge's to be five-star snobs and she realized that some of her prejudices would change as a result of her visit, which was a positive thing. Everyone needed their narrow perspectives tweaked and changed occasionally. It was healthy.

"If you'll come with me, I'll take you to the room where all their things are being kept at present," said Henry, pleasantly.

"Eh, what about the passports and tickets?" asked Johnny, anxious to get a hold of them before they left the front desk.

"Ah, yes! But of course. Mariana, can you get the envelope out of the safe with the passports and tickets belonging to our missing guests?"

Mariana nodded and disappeared to the back office.

"Mr. Bisset, we would like forensics to do a sweep of the bedrooms the men stayed in, if you don't mind," said Nkiruka, gathering her scattered wits together. "We know the West End Central Police Station have already had forensics checking out the luggage the men left behind but there's a slim chance there might also be something important left in the rooms they stayed in. Would you be able to arrange a convenient time with the current guests in those rooms? It would be very helpful."

Henry nodded his agreement straightaway, which surprised her. Nkiruka felt herself warming up to him even more.

She opened her handbag and pulled out a small card.

"That's the number of the Borough Forensic Manager, Dr. Alessandra Cappelli. I've spoken to her already and she'll be expecting your call. If you just explain you're calling from Claridge's, she'll be able to get things organized."

"Perfect. Very good," said Henry, giving the card a cursory glance and then tucking it into his jacket pocket.

Mariana came back with an A5 envelope and handed it over to Nkiruka. Nkiruka opened it up carefully and pulled out the passports.

Johnny, unable to stop himself, was peering over her shoulder, riven with curiosity.

"Mmm. As we thought, Brazilian nationals," muttered Nkiruka. "*Paolo Oscar Axel Fernandes. Luca Alvaro Barboza. Alonso Raymundo Fernandes.* So, two of them are related. Johnny, you must get in touch with the Brazilian embassy ASAP. Try and keep them onside, I want to know as much as I can about these three men. I imagine anything important in their background history is going to be based over in Brazil. Speaking to family members would be very, very helpful. We'll just have to hope they'll consent to cooperate with the investigation."

Nkiruka passed the envelope and passports over to Johnny and then she cast an eye over the plane tickets.

"Interesting... Alonso was due to fly back to Brazil but the other two were heading to Switzerland. Only one had a return flight from Switzerland. Luca Barboza. Strange. It would be worth looking into their travel plans in more detail."

She handed the tickets to Johnny and turned to Henry, who had been waiting patiently while they perused the contents of the envelope.

"What taxi service do you use for your guests?" Nkiruka asked Henry.

"We normally use Waterloo Cars if one of our guests wants us to order a taxi."

"It would be helpful for us to find out if the on-duty receptionist on the day the men went missing called up a cab for them. I imagine reception might well have done so given the old man was elderly and frail. Unless they were picked up by someone else, of course, but given the chain of events I think that's going to be unlikely."

"Of course. I'll look into it."

"Thank you very much, Henry. Right, if you could kindly take us to their luggage now, please, and we'll endeavor to be as quick as possible."

Henry nodded and led the way across the foyer and through a staff entrance at the far end.

They entered into another world where gorgeous finishes were no longer required and the utilitarian side of hotel life could be seen all around them. A series of offices were lined up along the corridor and, at the far end, they could hear the noise typical of a busy kitchen preparing for the evening's menu.

Henry stopped before a locked door and, using his

key card, opened it up and switched the fluorescent light on.

They walked into a large room that contained shelves and shelves of random articles, from men's and ladies' shoes to books, from electronic items to clothing and toiletries.

"This is the lost property office," explained Henry. "It's a shame because many people tend to leave their things behind when they check out of the hotel. I'm sure at times they leave them deliberately. The clientele in this hotel don't value their possessions in the same way as us lesser mortals do. You'll find all sorts here, from Chanel jackets to Jimmy Choo shoes, and, of course, we can't take any chances. We keep everything, listed by name, as well as room number, for a whole year before we dispose of them. It's part of the excellent customer service we like to provide to our hotel guests. We'll get the stuff posted, too, if they tell us they want their items back."

He walked to a table at the back where three large suitcases were reposing. A smaller suitcase was on the floor, next to a black cello case.

"Flip me, they didn't bring that thing with them, did they?" asked Johnny, pointing to the cello.

Henry smiled.

"Yes, I'm afraid so. One of them was a musician."

Nkiruka went over and unzipped one of the bags on the table. The lock on it had already been broken open by the forensics team.

She started lifting the items out of the bag, passing them over to Johnny who piled them up neatly on a shelf.

Inside the bag there were a number of items of

clothing, jumbled together untidily in a big bundle and, judging by the fashionable holes in the jeans and trendy logos on the T-shirts, Nkiruka guessed this was the younger man's suitcase.

She lifted out a washbag, a Kindle, a laptop, and a thick ring binder, which had what appeared to be chemistry notes in it.

She felt a twinge of sadness invade her professional detachment. The young man had had his future taken away from him, and all the time, effort, and money that had been invested into getting him to this point had been in vain.

One by one, they went through the suitcases, removing items to inspect them carefully before replacing them again. There was no need for them to write a list of the contents, as forensics had already informed Johnny that a complete list of the Brazilians' possessions would be with them in the next day or two.

The only item of real interest to emerge from their search was a sheaf of medical forms filled in for Dignitas in Switzerland on behalf of Paolo Fernandes.

Henry had sat himself down on a chair and was busy frowning at his phone, no doubt working his way through emails and messages. He was leaning forward as he worked, his muscular shoulders hulking over and filling the space around him, much like a prize boxer seated at the corner of a boxing ring.

After half an hour of sifting through the luggage, Nkiruka turned her attention to the cello.

Unclipping the locks, she opened the worn leather case and lifted it out.

It looked like a pretty ancient instrument to her.

There were multiple scratches crisscrossing the wood surface and the varnish had worn away in places.

She plucked a few of the strings and then put it back in the case. She looked up at Johnny from her position on the floor, puzzled. "I don't suppose you know anything about cellos do you, Johnny?" As she expected, Johnny shook his head.

"I think we ought to take this with us. It looks old and it might actually be very valuable. After all, they weren't short of a bob or two, were they? Some rare, old musical instruments are worth an absolute fortune."

"That's true," agreed Johnny. "But you're going to have to find a good expert in antique string instruments to get a proper valuation done."

"Yes. We can easily do that. In central London, there'll always be someone in the know. Henry, is it OK if we take this cello with us? We'll sign for it, of course."

"Absolutely. No problem."

Henry stood up and fetched a large binder from a desk at the side of the room.

"Here we go," he said, flicking through the pages and stopping at one whose table of items was half filled in. "If you can just put in your details and "*Paolo Fernandes cello*" on this line."

Nkiruka filled in her contact details and then thought about something.

"This cello was the old man's?"

Henry nodded.

"Yes, according to his grandson, he used to be an accomplished musician when younger. Mostly he played the Double Bass but this cello had sentimental value for him, having been gifted to him in his early twenties, and he didn't want to leave it behind in Brazil apparently."

He shrugged.

"Most of our guests have their little eccentricities. Their wealth has given them that entitlement. We've become very good at accommodating their individual wishes within the hotel. We have an on-call courier whose sole purpose is to fulfil any requests from our hotel guests, however unusual or complicated they may be."

Henry grinned.

"At a cost to them, of course."

Nkiruka glanced across to Johnny, who was looking enthralled at this insight into the world of the rich and powerful.

Before Johnny could ask Henry what outlandish requests the hotel had attended to on behalf of their guests, a question that she could see was on the tip of his tongue, she pointed to the cello.

"Johnny, could you carry the cello to the car for me, please?" Nkiruka's quiet voice was like a bucket of ice-cold water.

"Sure, ma'am," replied Johnny, reverting to his obsequious self.

A state of mind which Nkiruka knew would, at most, last a few minutes.

They walked back to the foyer, carrying the cello, and Nkiruka thanked Henry profusely for his cooperation.

Johnny left his card so Henry could call him once he'd ascertained as much information as he could about the day the three men were last seen at the hotel. They also agreed with Henry that Johnny would arrange to return to Claridge's, to speak with the staff members who had been on duty the day the Brazilian men disappeared.

As she left Claridge's, Nkiruka wished other places would be as open to the presence and interference of the police. Henry had been a proper, old-fashioned gentleman in her view.

Her parents would have approved of Henry's traditional courtesy, for they were convinced that the younger generation's morals and manners were in sharp decline. Nkiruka tended to agree with them, but then again she did come across a lot of damaged teenagers in her line of work and she often had to ask herself, who was at fault? The parent or the child? Some would argue the older generation had got it completely wrong and as a result everyone was now paying the price.

Johnny, realizing that he might be carrying a cello worth a ton of money, took his time making adequate space for it in the car, securing it with a box of radio equipment and his hold-all, so the cello wouldn't rock from side to side when he drove off.

Meanwhile, Nkiruka began to do a search on her phone for a dealer in antique cellos. She found a shop called *Delbanco and Amati*, near Covent Garden, that claimed to be dealers, experts, and restorers of rare, antique and modern violins, violas, cellos, and their bows.

Sounded good to her.

"Hey, Johnny, how do you fancy a trip to Covent Garden?"

Johnny groaned.

"Really? At this time of the day? We'll hit the rush hour."

"Come on, it won't be that bad. Let's strike while the iron's hot."

"Oh, alright. We can stop at Punch and Judy for some food. Good pub grub."

"You've got to be kidding, right?" asked Nkiruka, staring at him in disbelief. "We're not leaving the cello in the car."

"Nkiruka, we're in a police car," said Johnny in a sarcastic voice, reverting once more to his irreverent, cheeky self.

"I don't care. Nowadays, people have no boundaries whatsoever. A police car wouldn't stop someone breaking in."

"We could take the cello into the pub with us."

Nkiruka looked at him.

"We're not getting food until we're back at the office, got that? Try explaining to the Fernandes family why their granddaddy's precious cello was damaged or stolen, on top of everything else. Lionel would love that one."

Johnny sighed.

"Fine. Real killjoy, you are."

"Yeah, well, I won't say what you are."

"I can take it," said Johnny with a grin, as he indicated and moved into the flow of
traffic.

He gave Nkiruka a sidelong glance.

"Any ideas about the case after this afternoon?"

Nkiruka watched as raindrops began to fall and slide down the windscreen and prayed the rain would stop by the time they made it to Covent Garden.

"No, Johnny. No new ideas. More facts and evidence, that's all we have, but it'll come to fruition.

I'm sure of it. What we need at the moment is a motive, not a suspect."

In the end it took them near enough three quarters of an hour to reach Covent Garden, when at the right time of day and minus the road works, should have taken them only fifteen minutes.

They parked and made their way past a crowd watching a man on stilts outside Covent Garden Market, and then winced as they listened to the shrill notes of an electric violin being played by a busker.

The busker glared at them, no doubt thinking they were going to join him on the cello. Given the busker's lack of talent, Nkiruka reckoned that they stood a good chance of providing some stiff competition if they decided to set up next to him.

Eventually, after walking up Neal Street and turning left at Short Gardens, they entered Neal's Yard, a small alley hidden away from the outer crust of city life.

Nkiruka decided that *Delbanco and Amati* had to be a specialist shop with an established reputation and, as such, wasn't needing to be seen on a main thorough-fare because Neal's Yard was a little-known, hidden enclave in the city of London.

Tucked away in a quiet courtyard amongst brightly colored facades, cafés, and gift and health-food shops vied for custom.

Nkiruka walked in front of Johnny, shielding the cello case by sandwiching it between them as they made their way through the pedestrians.

"Ah, there it is," said Nkiruka, stopping and pointing to *Delbanco and Amati*.

It was a large shop taking up three separate windows on the corner of the courtyard.

The windows had metalwork shielding the glass, in the shape of long, extending musical notes. The woodwork surrounding the windows was painted bright green, contrasting nicely with the black paint on the metalwork. The high wall of the building was covered in bold blocks of color: orange, pale-pink, wine, purple, china-blue. And the name *Delbanco and Amati* was neatly scrolled across the shop front in dark blue lettering.

"Well, I never," remarked Johnny, looking at the colorful shop in surprise.

"That's London for you," said Nkiruka, feeling a sense of pride in her eclectic city.

She took a few steps forward and pushed on the shop door, before realizing it was shut.

Looking down, she saw a doorbell and rang it. Immediately, the door buzzed open.

Nkiruka and Johnny walked into a room that looked more like a warehouse than a shop. It extended down the full length of the building and every wall was covered with stringed instruments.

A young lady with long blonde hair came up to them.

"Hello. How may I help you?"

Nkiruka displayed her police badge.

"We're looking to see if one of your experts can tell us if this cello is valuable or not. It's important for us to find out as it's linked to a homicide case."

The lady nodded.

"I'm sure Stefan will be able to help you. He's

downstairs in the workshop. I'll take you there right now."

Nkiruka and Johnny followed her as she led them down some creaky wooden steps into the basement.

The workshop had a potent, earthy smell; a heady mix of fresh wood shavings, pine resin, polish, and linseed oil. The smell matched the scenery, for everything down there was made of wood, from the floor to the worktable and shelves. The walls were also lined with wood paneling, and if it hadn't been for the strip lighting the enclosed room would have been extremely dark.

Nkiruka gazed at her surroundings, relishing the smell of freshly cut wood which was reminding her of a childhood holiday spent near Aviemore, in a primitive log cabin situated on the edge of the Cairngorms National Park, Scotland.

At the workshop table sat a middle-aged man, with a mane of blond hair and a pair of half-moon glasses perched on his bulbous nose.

Next to him, a large table lamp was angled over a violin, and there was a miscellaneous collection of little tins and bottles scattered about the work surface.

A box of horsehair was open, with half its contents emptied onto the table.

The man looked up with some reluctance when the two visitors approached him.

"Stefan, these are members of the police force and they're looking for some help in identifying their cello."

Stefan stood up and came across to meet them, looking down at the cello case with interest.

"So where is the cello from?" he asked, placing a hand on the black leather case.

"A wealthy man from Brazil brought it to London with him," explained Nkiruka. "We're investigating his murder and wondering if this cello could be relevant in any way. If it's very valuable there might be a few people out there wanting to get their hands on it."

"Let's have a look. It's always possible, of course. A cello can be worth millions if it was made by someone like Antonio Stradivari. As you probably know, he was a famous Italian luthier, one of the most celebrated in the world... Only recently, in fact, a violin made by him sold for 9 million pounds at a Christie's auction," Stefan informed them, as he unclipped the cello case and opened it.

Stefan took out the cello and examined it with a great deal of curiosity.

He looked at the wood on the front of it, letting his long fingers run over the surface as though checking for miniature cracks.

For the next two minutes he checked the bridge, the finger board, the string placement, and then fiddled with the pegs.

"Well, this is a first," he said at last, a puzzled expression on his face.

"Is it an antique?" asked Johnny, impatiently.

"No. No, I'm afraid it isn't," said Stefan, looking across at them. "No luthier past or present ever made this cello. It's actually not functional as an instrument. The pegs are wrongly placed for a start. The finger board is far too long and the bridge isn't high enough."

Stefan rubbed his chin for a moment, perplexed.

Then he reached over and removed the bow from the case.

Holding the cello upright, he sat himself down, ran the bow across the strings, and started playing it.

The blood-curdling noise that emanated from the cello made them all cringe.

Stefan had made his point. The instrument was a dud and not a viable cello. It was, in effect, a badly conceived copy of the real thing.

Nkiruka and Johnny looked at each other, wondering what to do with this new turn of events. Why would the old man be carting around a cello that didn't work?

"This is also very heavy for a cello," remarked Stefan, lifting it up and feeling the weight of it in his strong hands.

He started tapping the wood at the front and back of it.

"There's more bulk around the back. Whoever made it must have put at least one other layer of wood into the cello. Strange..."

"But why would someone go to the trouble of making an imitation cello? And why would its owner treasure the cello enough to bring it with him from Brazil?" asked Nkiruka, feeling like a large sinkhole was opening up under her.

Nobody answered her heartfelt plea.

Just at the point when she thought the case couldn't get more complicated, it now had.

Stefan put the cello and bow back in the case and then shut it.

"If you ever find out what the story behind it is, please let me know. It's certainly very intriguing. I can honestly say I've never seen a cello like this before or even heard of anything similar to it," Stefan said, getting up and walking over to his former place at the worktable.

He sat down and began to inspect the violin in front of him, his mind switching back onto his workload once more.

Stefan picked up what looked like a bottle of glue and began squeezing minute dabs onto the violin's surface, carefully wiping away any excess with a cotton bud.

He seemed to be utterly enthralled with the instruments he worked on. Nkiruka, meantime, was still staring down at the cello.

She pulled herself together.

She passed the cello over to Johnny and, after thanking Stefan for his input, they went upstairs and left the shop.

Nkiruka and Johnny didn't speak again until they were seated in the car with the cello secured behind them.

"Now what?" asked Johnny, reasonably enough. "Do we return this to Claridge's?"

"No," said Nkiruka, firmly. "I'm not done with it yet. Who gets a fake cello made and then insists on travelling across the Atlantic Ocean with it?"

Johnny tapped his forehead.

"Someone who's not in their right mind, that's who. The old man was elderly. If he was going gaga there's any number of crazy things he'd be capable of."

"Sorry, Johnny, but that doesn't wash with me. The wood on that cello's old and worn. The case is tatty. This isn't something new, done on the spur of the moment. That cello has been around for some time."

They both sat in silence for a moment, watching the

pedestrians stream up and down the pavement next to them.

"I suggest we go back to Scotland Yard and I'll see if I can get the cello through one of our X-ray machines. That might be able to tell us something else," said Nkiruka at last.

Johnny sighed.

"OK, boss. But if you don't mind I'm going to go for some food when we get back to the office."

Nkiruka opened up her handbag and, after searching around for a bit, took out a Cadbury's Dairy Milk bar.

"Here, this'll keep you going. Only don't tell my daughter because it comes from her supply."

"Lucky girl," commented Johnny, accepting the chocolate bar gratefully.

He sat munching it while Nkiruka went through her phone messages, and five minutes later they were making their way over to Scotland Yard with the fake cello in tow.

9

Richard

Richard heard the knock on the door of his basement office and went to open it. DI Webster had phoned him the day before, requesting a meeting with them. Intrigued, Richard had agreed to it on the spot even though he had a backlog of art theft cases to get through on his desk.

The last time he'd worked with members of the Homicide and Serious Crime Command was on the robbery of El Greco's masterpiece *The Spanish Princess*, and he was interested to see what Homicide wanted from him this time.

"Hello," he said amicably as he saw the two on the other side of the door. "Come in and make yourselves comfortable."

A tall, elegant lady standing next to DI Webster smiled at him and strolled into the room, seating herself on a nearby chair.

She was confident and assertive in her manner so Richard could only assume she was senior in rank.

Which meant in turn that whatever case they were going to discuss was fairly high profile.

So far so good, in his view.

Johnny Webster followed her in, carrying in his arms a thick cardboard folder and a black cello case.

Richard knew a little about Johnny Webster, but only as a result of Eilidh's recent transition to the department. Since her move to the Art and Antiquities Unit, Eilidh had kept in touch with her old colleagues from Homicide and she frequently filled Richard in on the gossip humming around the upper floors of New Scotland Yard.

Usually completely in the dark with what was happening in other departments, Richard was fast discovering that Eilidh was both a valuable informant and a talented officer in his little section. It went without saying that Eilidh was always the one who stepped up to manage any of the Scotland Yard politics affecting them, because when problems arose she always knew who to contact.

Richard went over to his desk and sat down.

"Hi, I'm Chief Inspector Nkiruka Ezemonye," announced the regal-looking lady, tucking her long legs under the chair and crossing her ankles. "We're needing a helping hand with one of our homicide cases, Richard, and I've been told you're the one to talk to about our latest find. I'm hoping you'll be able to help us out with it."

"I must confess I'm very curious," admitted Richard. "It's been a while since I've had anything to do with the Homicide and Serious Crime Unit."

Nkiruka smiled and nodded, as though it made

perfect sense to her that Richard would be keen to get involved with one of her homicide cases.

Richard wasn't offended by her assumption. Many of his other colleagues behaved the same way.

Sadly, they assumed that working with old artifacts and paintings was dull work for a police officer. Art theft was seen as the least exciting or interesting crime field within the Met, and the Art and Antiquities Unit occupied the bottom rung in the eyes of those working there. This superiority complex didn't bother Richard as long as no one interfered with his line of work. "Each to their own" probably summed up best how he felt about it.

What Eilidh thought about the negative light in which their department was viewed, he didn't know.

For now, she'd given up any pretense of doing some work and had swiveled her office chair around so she could get a better view of their visitors.

She was also looking with interest at Johnny's cello case.

"It's not about the triple murder and the old man's cello, is it?" she asked, irrepressibly, from her side of the room.

Nkiruka turned her head and frowned at Eilidh.

"I'm surprised you guys know about the cello," complained Nkiruka, seeming cross that the news about her case was evidently spreading like wildfire around Scotland Yard.

Maybe she was also annoyed because if they already knew the facts pertaining to the Hampstead Heath case, her presence at their meeting was far less necessary than she had anticipated and a waste of her time. Having not met Nkiruka before, Richard couldn't hazard a guess on that one.

Behind Nkiruka, Johnny was looking up at the opposite wall, his face rigid and immobile. He was standing just like The Queen's Guard at Buckingham Palace, who somehow manage to stare fixedly into the distance while the tourists take photos and gaze admiringly at their bearskin hats.

If Richard didn't know better, he'd have assumed Johnny to be a complete imbecile. He restrained the urge to laugh.

In all fairness, he thought, were Johnny's face to be described as a work of art right then, it would be named *A Study in Blank*. For reasons best known to himself, Johnny was enacting the pose of a complete blockhead.

Richard saw Eilidh glance apprehensively at Johnny and then look away again.

The penny dropped in Richard's mind. It was obvious to him now that Johnny had been the one to inform Eilidh about the murders, as well as the cello. And it also seemed as though Johnny didn't want Nkiruka to find out that he'd been passing on updates about their homicide case to Eilidh.

Curiouser and curiouser, as Alice in Wonderland had once said.

"A lot of people know about the Hampstead Heath case. Hard not to, when it's been in all the papers," said Eilidh, trying to shield Johnny.

Nkiruka appeared to accept this as her face relaxed a little.

"I know, there's been a lot of publicity surrounding it," she agreed. "But it's hampering the investigation rather than advancing it."

There was a depressed silence in the room. Having made her displeasure about the media attention known, Nkiruka seemed to be in no hurry to explain the reason for their presence at the Art and Antiquities Unit and Johnny clearly wasn't in the mood to step in and do so on her behalf.

"OK," said Richard at last, wanting to move onto the subject at hand. "So how can we help you, Nikirusa?"

Instead of correcting his mispronunciation of her name, Nkiruka turned around slowly until she was facing Richard and scrutinized him with the intentness of a lioness about to pounce on her prey.

Beginning to feel amused by her behavior, Richard bit back a smile, schooling his face to look serious as the last thing he wanted to do was offend her.

Then he caught sight of a slight crinkling at the edges of Nkiruka's shining, dark eyes. There was a hint of humor reflected in their depths, too.

Relieved, Richard allowed himself to smile at her. Assured of her friendliness, any residual tension in him just melted away.

He was fast learning two things about her; she did things at her own measured pace and she also had an ingrained sense of fun, which was as rare as gold dust amongst the Chief Inspectors in the Met. Struck by this affinity, he began to wonder if she was going to turn out to be a kindred spirit. It had to be said, he didn't meet kindred spirits very often at Scotland Yard.

"You can call me Niki, if you like," Nkiruka informed him graciously, accepting his difficulty in pronouncing her name.

She grinned at him from her chair, transforming

chameleon-like from a regal princess to a cheeky schoolgirl.

"Thank you," he said, smiling back at her.

Strangely, Richard felt as though he had somehow passed Nkiruka's likeability test and had been rewarded with her nickname as a result. His gut instinct told him that if Nkiruka had taken a dislike to him, she would have made him squirm for a good deal longer. For sure, nobody would want to get on the wrong side of her.

Richard watched as Nkiruka slipped back into her adult, professional persona, folding her arms and leaning back on her chair.

She was wearing a short-skirted, royal-blue suit with a white shirt that day, her long legs tapering down to a pair of flat-soled, black shoes. She looked both smart and efficient.

"We're needing some help with something we found inside the cello," confessed Nkiruka, finally getting to the point of her visit. "We ran the cello through the X-ray machine upstairs and the security staff said it looked to them as though there was some sort of a wooden tube inside the cello." She sniffed. "As you already seem to know, the cello belongs to one of the murdered men on Hampstead Heath. Given we are trying to dig up some information, as soon as possible, on the murders, and that the cello itself isn't valuable—in fact, we've been told it's unusable—we felt within our rights to look inside it."

"Well, I'm afraid I know next to nothing about musical instruments, although I imagine they'd fall under my jurisdiction if they were valuable," warned Richard, worried that she was going to ask for his opinion on the cello.

"Not to worry, Richard. The cello itself is sort of irrelevant. I mean, we still have to ask why the owner was hiding things in a fake cello, but that's not really why we're here. We suspect what we found inside of it could be significant. Johnny, can you show them?"

Johnny put his cardboard folder on the floor and opened up the cello case.

When he lifted out the cello, Richard felt his jaw drop.

The cello was dented and splintered in several places, exposing the white wood under the varnish. The entire front of the cello was hanging loose and was only held in place by the strings.

"Man, who did that?" asked Eilidh, peering down at the mangled cello.

"I'm afraid I did," admitted Johnny. "The wood's frailer than it looks. Fell to bits as soon as I put a chisel to it."

He pulled up the front half of the cello, so they could take a look inside it.

Nestled tightly within the main body of the cello was what seemed to be a square tube, made of four strips of wood tightly glued to each other. Two latches were attached to the tube, securely clipping it into place on the top and bottom of the cello's cavity.

Johnny unclipped the wooden tube from the cello and held it between his knees to demonstrate how it worked.

Taking off the lid at one end, he lifted the tube up until it was horizontal, showing them that it was completely hollow inside.

"The tube was holding the paintings inside of the

cello," explained Johnny, putting the tube down and turning to the cardboard folder.

He stood up, opened the folder and carefully placed two small, canvas oil paintings onto Richard's desk.

Richard immediately opened his desk drawer, took out his white gloves and put them on.

Picking up his magnifying glass, he then bent his head close to the table's surface as he examined the pictures.

There was total silence in the room while everyone else watched Richard studying the cello's hidden artwork.

Both the oil paintings were glowing with bright, garish colors and the draftsmanship was very naïve in style.

One painting had a couple in it, the lady dressed in white and the man in black, both sitting on a bench. A brown animal, which looked like it was meant to be a horse, was looking down on them and between them a bright yellow and red sun was shining.

The other painting was colored entirely in shades of purple apart from the white figure of Christ, his arms stretched out in a crucifixion pose and with a yellow halo hanging over his head. Two purple angels were kneeling on either side of Christ, playing their violins.

After a few minutes, Richard straightened up.

He let out a sigh of disbelief, feeling his heart begin to beat with excitement as he looked down at the paintings.

There was no doubt in his mind that the paintings resembled the distinctive work of the Russian-French artist, Marc Chagall.

"They look a bit childlike to me," said Johnny, with a smirk. "A kid could've painted them."

Richard smiled.

"I can see why you'd think that but these two pictures look to me identical to the work of a world-renowned artist called Marc Chagall. He was a Russian-French artist of Belarusian Jewish origin. He was part of the modernist movement and used cubism and expressionism in his work."

"Surely, if he was Jewish he wouldn't be depicting a crucifixion," objected Eilidh, pointing at the purple painting.

Richard glanced across at it.

"He wasn't a practicing Jew but he had a strong Jewish identity. Chagall depicted the crucifixion in many of his paintings but as part of a universal message, rather than a religious one. It's important to remember that as a Jew he lived through two World Wars. He had to leave France because of the Nazi persecution of Jews so he was never, ever, going to forget his roots. He always identified as Jewish."

He moved the two paintings towards the desk light and bent down to have another look at them.

"These could be fake copies but I've a feeling they could be the real deal... They are very similar to much of his other work. Chagall had a unique and distinctive style."

Turning to his computer, Richard did a quick search on Marc Chagall and his screen soon filled up with many images of his paintings.

"Marc Chagall grew up in Belarus, which was part of Russia back then. Later he lived and worked in France, but as I said he had to escape France during the

Nazi occupation," said Richard, scrolling through the Chagall paintings on the computer screen. "He ended up in New York for a time, again spending lots of time in the areas where there was a Jewish community, but France was where he returned to in the end. His paintings have general appeal but even so, it would be ridiculous to say his artwork wasn't Jewish. His art was full of links to his Jewish identity and folkloric past."

"What do we do now?" asked Johnny, keen to move past the academia of the matter and onto the practicalities.

Richard leaned back on his chair.

"You can leave these paintings with us, for a start. This room's probably the most secure room in this building. It looks like I'll have to do some research and reach out to a few Chagall specialists to see if there is a record of these paintings anywhere. And we'll have to get someone to take a look and see if they can authenticate them. As for why they were in a cello, I have absolutely no idea."

"If these paintings are by Chagall, they'll be worth a fortune, won't they?" asked Nkiruka.

"Several million pounds, for sure," affirmed Richard.

He saw Johnny swallow in shock.

"You're saying those paintings are worth several million?" asked Johnny, as though he couldn't quite believe it.

"Yes. Each."

Johnny was silent. Small beads of sweat were accumulating on his forehead and he was looking worryingly pale.

"Johnny has been in touch with the Brazilian

embassy," said Nkiruka, who, unlike her colleague, was unfazed. "We hope to get a call back from them today. We'll have to inform the relatives about these paintings. Logically, they'll belong to them now."

"Hold your horses with that one, Niki," interjected Richard, alarmed by this. "Please don't tell the family about the paintings until I've done a little more research on them. I mean, the paintings were hidden inside a cello and they've technically been smuggled into the country. I think we need to establish ownership first."

"I don't get you," demanded Nkiruka. "Are you suggesting the paintings are stolen property?"

"Look, I don't really know anything at the moment but you have to remember Chagall was an artist who worked through two World Wars and during that period many valuable artworks changed hands illegally. By the time it was the Second World War, Chagall was already well-known and renowned, although he was disparaged by the Nazis for being a Jew. I think we should establish the paintings' provenance before we let the family know that their father, or grandfather, was travelling to Europe with two Chagall paintings hidden in a cello."

Nkiruka nodded at this.

"OK. We'll hand these over to your care, Richard. Several million pounds worth of artwork is enough of a motive to kill someone for, wouldn't you say?"

"I wish it was the motive for the murders, Nkiruka, but in my experience nothing's that simple. If someone wanted the paintings, they wouldn't kill the owners until they'd managed to get their hands on them, would they?" asked Richard.

"Yes, but they tortured the old man, didn't they?" argued Johnny, disagreeing.

"Maybe he told them about the paintings."

Nkiruka shook her head. "No, Richard's right. It doesn't make sense. No one's been asking for the cello. His family let him travel on a plane with it, so they clearly didn't know anything about the paintings. I think you're doing the right thing, Richard. Let's not tell the family about the paintings until we find out a little more about where they came from. If you could keep me informed, as much as you can, I'd appreciate it."

"Of course. I'll do my best. I understand it's like balancing on a tightrope," commented Richard, sympathetic to Nkiruka's situation. "If you don't tell the family now about the paintings, you'll inevitably have to explain to them later on why it took you so long to inform them. I'll try and get some results as fast as I can so we don't end up getting into trouble with the family members, but as you say it doesn't seem like they knew anything about the paintings. I think we should focus on the old man and his past life. We need to dig up all we can on him to try to understand how he was in possession of two Chagall paintings and, more importantly, where he procured them."

Nkiruka nodded and stood up.

She took a business card out of her pocket and laid it on Richard's desk.

"That's my number and email. Call me any time you want. I've got Lionel pleading with me for information on a daily basis because we've got the press whipped up in a frenzy and baying for details on this case. He wants them off his back. The drama of these murders, of course, is doing wonders for newspaper sales, so I don't think they're going to let up any time soon."

"The press will move on to other things before long," announced Eilidh, with authority. "They always do. The murders will soon be yesterday's news. You just have to hang in there."

Nkiruka looked amused as she listened to Eilidh's sage advice. Other DCIs might have taken offence at being preached to by a younger subordinate but Nkiruka was not one of them.

Noting her response to Eilidh, Richard knew he was going to enjoy working with Nkiruka on the case.

"You used to work in Homicide, didn't you?" asked Nkiruka, smiling at Eilidh. Eilidh nodded.

"Well, that should be useful, I suppose," remarked Nkiruka. "It's good to have someone who's a link between the two departments. I imagine the units work very differently to each other."

"That's true, for sure. Procedures are somewhat laxer in this unit." Eilidh grinned at Richard's exaggerated look of outrage.

"What made you join the police, Niki?" asked Eilidh, interested.

"My name."

Nkiruka burst out laughing when she saw the confusion on Eilidh's face.

Mystified himself, Richard was fast coming to the conclusion that Nkiruka was a compulsive tease. There was definitely a playful, naughty side to her character. He wondered for a moment if it had ever got her into trouble with her superiors.

"My name in Igbo means 'the future is greater,'" explained Nkiruka patiently. "I figured that if I was

going to make a difference in the world and
contribute to the greater future, what better place to
start than as a black woman joining the Met as an
officer?"

Eilidh nodded her approval of this. Nkiruka tapped
Johnny on the shoulder.

"Come on, Johnny. Let's go and get some proper
work done."

Johnny clipped the wooden tube back into the
bashed-up cello and settled the instrument into its case.

He hoisted the cello case up as though he was
getting thoroughly fed up of lugging it around. Johnny
would no doubt be dumping the cello in the evidence
room at the earliest possible opportunity.

"Right, folks. Good to see you. Keep an eye on those
two paintings," instructed Johnny, with a cheerful nod
at Eilidh and Richard. "And make sure you don't spill
the coffee on them!"

Richard went across the room to hold open the
heavy security door for Nkiruka and Johnny, and once
he'd seen them off the premises walked back to his desk
lost in thought.

He stood in front of his desk for a while, looking
down at the Chagall paintings with Eilidh by his side.

"Who knows what suffering these paintings have
witnessed?" he mused to himself. "The secretive
manner in which they were transported does make me
wonder if they've a horrible, dark story to tell us. We
shall find out soon enough."

"You're very melancholy today, Richard," remarked
Eilidh, patting Richard bracingly on the shoulder.

Richard turned and smiled at her, appreciating the
gesture.

Their eyes met briefly and then Eilidh looked away, uncomfortable. Richard heaved a quiet sigh.

Their relationship had always been professional and amicable, with neither of them wanting to dive down into the more complicated, tempestuous waters of a closer liaison. Uncertainty was abhorrent to both of them, but in recent days Richard had begun to wonder if it was worth challenging the self-imposed boundaries they had set up between each other. After all, life was short and no one knew that better than the people working in their building.

Taking their relationship to the next level was always going to be risky, though.

Most of the week, they worked together as an efficient, productive team on art theft, and any awkwardness could easily jeopardize that, ending up, in the worst-case scenario, with one of them moving on to another department.

Eilidh's right, he thought to himself. He was becoming morose. It was time to get busy again.

Dragging his chair back up to the desk, he sat down and looked at his computer screen.

"Right, I'm going to have a look at the Art Loss Register and see if there are any Chagalls reported missing," he stated.

He sat for a few minutes doing some research on his computer while Eilidh went back to her caseload, lugging the files across her desk and piling them up neatly on her right-hand side once she had finished with them.

"Mmm. This is interesting," muttered Richard, suddenly. "These two might fit the bill. *"Purple Crucifixion"* and *"Lovers on the Bench."* No one could accuse

Chagall of being over-imaginative with the titles of his paintings, which in our case is very helpful. There's no image of the paintings, though. They were reported stolen by Esther Sariya Dorin, formerly of Domhof, Aachen, Germany. She notified authorities in 1952 that both Chagall paintings were stolen during the Night of Broken Glass, 1938. She died May 1993, in Brooklyn, New York."

Richard leaned back on his chair and rubbed his chin.

"It doesn't say whether Esther Dorin has any living relatives."

"What the hell were the paintings doing in Brazil, if they were stolen in Germany?" asked Eilidh, perplexed.

Richard crossed his arms.

"Mmm. That's a very good question. It's difficult to say, really, isn't it? What I do know is that several Nazis managed to escape Germany after World War Two and hid in South America. They're still searching and finding them to this day."

"Who's finding them?" demanded Eilidh, unbelieving.

"Nazi hunters, mostly. Prosecutors in Germany. Of course, most of the Nazis are dead now but there's a few out there, nevertheless, who are unaccounted for."

"So, the murdered man could be an ex-Nazi?" asked Eilidh, sounding excited.

"Don't get carried away, Eilidh. We need to do two things before we can jump to that conclusion. Firstly, we need to track down a living relative of Esther Dorin and find out what her story was. The quickest way to get that sort of information would be to get in touch with the FBI, given she died in New York. Secondly,

Nkiruka needs to find out a lot more about the three murdered men. If the old man turns out to be an ex-Nazi, then it could also give a tenuous motive to his murder. Someone might have wanted revenge for the past. The murder itself was highly unusual and distinctive. Extreme torture in a homicide isn't usually seen in this country."

"OK. So, assuming the old man was an ex-Nazi who stole the paintings on the Night of Broken Glass, does that mean these paintings belong to the heirs of Esther Dorin?"

Richard nodded.

"Yes, I would say so. If we can prove that the old man was an ex-Nazi, I've no doubt these two paintings would be seen as the property of Esther Dorin's living heir. Nazi treasures are getting recovered and returned to their rightful owners all the time. Legally, though, it could be tricky. There's a long way to go before we can start that kind of a proceeding. We need to get these two paintings authenticated as soon as possible. I wonder who'd be best placed to help us authenticate them..."

He picked up his mobile and began to scroll through his professional contacts.

Eilidh, by now used to Richard's frequent moments of abstraction, turned back to her computer.

"The foremost specialist in Chagall paintings, here in London, is Dr. Gabriel Autry from Goldsmiths College," reported Richard after a while, sounding satisfied. He put his mobile down on his desk. "I hope if I speak to him, he might be able dig around and find me an image or photo of the stolen paintings, so we can confirm they are the same as these two. Chagall's works were usually well documented because he was a successful artist during his lifetime, unlike many in his line of work."

Richard leaned forward to look at the two Chagall paintings again. He was struggling to keep his eyes off them.

"We'll also request the SCC Laboratory to verify the paintings. I know they've examined a few other Chagall paintings in their lab and I think they would be best placed to certify that the age and technical elements in these two paintings correspond with Chagall's work. I'm pretty sure that for the sake of rectifying a potential war crime, they'd be willing to do that for us for free."

"When are you going to tell Niki and Johnny what you've discovered?" asked Eilidh, her head tilted to one side.

Richard could tell she was mindful that Nkiruka and Johnny were under Lionel's thumb with the Hampstead Heath murders. Not the kind of situation Eilidh would ever envy anyone being in.

She knew, too, of course, that informing the pair of them that the two paintings might have been stolen by an ex-Nazi would put a completely different complexion on their homicide case.

"No time like the present," replied Richard, picking up the phone and with his other hand pulling Nkiruka's card towards him. He dialed the number on the card and waited.

"Hello?" asked an impatient voice on the other end.

"Niki?" asked Richard, not recognizing the voice on the other end of the phone.

"Yes, Richard, it's me. Will it take long? I'm afraid I'm about to head into a meeting."

His cut-glass accent, unlike Nkiruka's, was very easy to identify.

"It's about the two Chagall paintings. We've still to do some more research on them but it looks as though the Chagall paintings were possibly stolen by a Nazi before the Second World War kicked off. I believe they're the two Chagall paintings listed on the Art Loss Registry as having been taken during the Night of Broken Glass."

"Lord have mercy! You think the old man was a Nazi?"

"As I said, we have to do more research on this, Niki. Quite a bit more research, actually. But I thought you should know, as no doubt you'll be seeing the family members soon."

"Yes, we've a Portuguese Family Liaison Officer lined up to meet with them." "Well, make sure they're good at their job. We need to dig up as much informa-tion as we can about the old man and his past life."

"Yes. I think we've reached the stage where I might get directly involved with the family, too. There's a number of questions I'd like them to answer. Hmm... I always thought the key to solving this case was going to be the motive. We're getting there, slowly but surely. Thanks for the tip-off. I'm going to have go now, Richard, sorry."

"No worries. I hope to be able to give you more info on the paintings soon." Richard hung up.

"Right, Dr. Gabriel Autry's going to be my first port of call. Eilidh, could you get in touch with Dan Wain-wright from the FBI in New York and ask him to kindly find out if there were any descendants of Esther Sariya Dorin, formerly of Brooklyn, New York? Remember, she died in May 1993. I'll text you his number. He's based at the White- Collar Crime division of the FBI. We've worked together a couple of times before."

"Sure," said Eilidh, looking pleased to be actively involved in the Chagall case.

Richard could see she was hooked. Right then, she had the same hungry look in her eyes he'd seen countless times before. Her face was taut with the hunter's instinct that always came to the surface when she was pursuing a lead on a case that interested her. This suited Richard just fine. Basically, chasing down precious works of art and artifacts that had been stolen and restoring them to their rightful owners was what their unit was all about.

Eilidh had behaved the same way when they were searching for El Greco's portrait, The Spanish Princess. Richard was just thankful that this time Mike Telford, the unconventional private investigator who worked with Eilidh to track down The Spanish Princess, was uninvolved because the two of them together were quite happy to cross red lines for the sake of retrieving stolen artwork.

To be fair to Eilidh, though, her law-breaking actions when searching for The Spanish Princess were mostly done on her ex-boyfriend Igor's behalf. Mike, meanwhile, never had qualms about breaking the law. He worked and lived by the mantra that the ends justified the means, and at least in this criminal investigation Richard was spared the headache of dealing with Mike's potential misdemeanors. For which he was devoutly thankful. However, there remained a lot for

Richard and Eilidh to do to bring the case to any sort of completion and to see justice served as well.

Picking up the phone, Richard called Goldsmiths and asked to speak to Dr. Gabriel Autry. Dr. Autry was able to see Richard the following morning, which only confirmed Richard's view that academics in the arts had a ridiculously light timetable compared to their colleagues in the sciences.

He arrived at Goldsmiths art department, the red-brick building on the south side of the River Thames, at ten o'clock the next day.

Their meeting didn't last long.

Once he understood what Richard was searching for, Gabriel looked up a database put together by Fabien Moreau, an academic based in Paris, who had dedicated his life's work to researching Chagall.

There were only two black-and-white images of *Purple Crucifixion* and *Lovers on the Bench* on Fabien's database, but it was enough to confirm they both matched the paintings residing in Richard's basement office at New Scotland Yard.

10

Nkiruka

Nkiruka knocked tentatively on Lionel Grieves' office door.

"Come in!" his voice bellowed from the other side.

Holding onto her case file, Nkiruka walked in, and when she saw Lionel was on the phone she sat herself down in front of his desk.

While Lionel grunted to whoever was on the other side of the phone, Nkiruka looked around the office, taking note of the fancy leather desk set, the Romanesque sculpture sitting on the filing cabinet and what looked to be an original oil painting of several race horses on the wall.

Nkiruka wouldn't put it past Lionel to actually own a horse but she thought the race course painting probably harked back to the days when he might have frequented betting shops. Lionel was too refined in his tastes to do that now.

Five minutes later, Nkiruka was starting to feel impatient as Lionel continued to talk on the phone, giving instructions to the hapless individual on the other end.

She took her mobile out of her jacket pocket and started looking through the emails that were flooding into her inbox.

The detective inspectors working for Nkiruka dealt with most homicide investigations themselves, sending her the completed homicide reports once their cases were closed. But they also knew when to bring to her attention a sensitive or problematic murder enquiry and request her support.

One hapless individual, Lucy Moore, who'd been promoted recently to Detective Inspector, was struggling to find her feet. She was sending Nkiruka endless enquiries about her homicide cases, which she should have been more than capable of solving herself.

Just as Nkiruka was going to tackle another annoying email from Lucy, Lionel slammed down his phone.

"Niki, sorry about that. Independent Police Complaints Commission. Wankers, the lot of them, but got to handle them with kid gloves these days."

Nkiruka burst out laughing. More at the thought of Lionel trying to handle anyone "with kid gloves" than anything else.

Lionel grinned at her, but a moment later he looked serious again.

"It's no laughing matter, Niki. You'll find that out when it's your turn to be in my shoes."

Nkiruka didn't acknowledge the implied compliment. She'd rather resign than take on Lionel's job and she suspected he knew that, too.

Lionel fidgeted with a glass paperweight on his

desk, at one point lifting it up and down in his hand as though assessing its weight.

"OK. So, Niki, I've asked you here because we've got a potential problem looming with that torture case of yours. As if it wasn't enough of a headache already. I don't suppose you've ever heard of an actress called Juliana Margarida Fernandes?"

"No. Why? Should I know her?"

Lionel sighed.

"No. Not really. Can't say I ever heard of her myself before. I've been informed she's one of the most famous soap stars on Brazilian TV, if not the most famous. Which is a massive achievement, apparently. I mean, we're not talking Coronation Street or East-Enders, here. Soap opera viewing figures over there blow us out of the water."

Lionel leaned back on his chair and then picked up a half-finished Rubik's cube from his desk.

Watching him, Nkiruka couldn't help smiling because it was so typical of Lionel to reach for the gadgets during a meeting in his office. She'd often wondered if Lionel had been diagnosed as having ADHD as an adult. He found it hard to sit still and focus on one thing for any length of time, yet on the other hand his endless font of energy was a real plus for the people working for him.

Lionel looked at his Rubik's cube, slowly turning it in his hands as he tried to figure out the quickest way to complete it.

"She acts in a soap opera called *A Riqueza do Amor*. In English that translates as *The Wealth of Love*," said Lionel, as he started clicking away at his Rubik's cube. "Sickly stuff by all accounts. I've got it on good authority that the program's full of mush but that's beside the point. Soap operas are a big deal in Latin America and have a huge following. This woman has friends in high places in Brazil and—this is where it matters to us—she also happens to be the daughter of Paolo Fernandes, the old man who was left tortured and murdered on Hampstead Heath."

"Ah."

"Yes, exactly. The publicity on this case is going to be enormous over there, too, now. Nothing like a famous and beautiful Brazilian woman to add to all the drama we've got going on here in Scotland Yard. And she's not our only problem because she wasn't Paolo's only child. He had four children and the four of them, of course, are on their way to London as we speak."

Lionel pulled on his ear, always a sign of his inner agitation.

"We're setting up a press conference with them, at their request, for four days' time," he continued. "They want to appeal to anyone who might have any information on the murders. Which is fair enough, in my view. The young murder victim, Alonso, was the son of Paolo's only son, Oscar. This info, by the way, comes courtesy of our resident Portuguese translator, Sergeant Benison Farrell."

He tugged his ear again, then reached for a packet of nicotine gum lying on the desk and popped a white piece into his mouth. As far as Nkiruka was aware, Lionel had not managed to kick his habit but chewing the gum seemed to give him a boost when he needed it.

"I suggest you hook up with Benison Farrell because I'm expecting you to meet with the family and figure out what the hell those three men were doing when they came over to London. Benison told me some tosh about Paolo making his way to Switzerland for some private medical treatment, accompanied by his carer Luca, but I'm afraid I don't buy it. I mean, the States is far closer. Why travel all the way to Europe? And why stop in London, if that's the case?"

"I was planning to meet with them anyway," Nkiruka assured him. "We've on stand-by a Portuguese Family Liaison Officer. I want to be as involved as possible with the family because, as you know, we're struggling to find a motive for the murders. I believe the answers are to be found in the old man's past life and Richard Langley agrees with me on this. He thinks Paolo Fernandes might have a secret identity."

Lionel stared at Nkiruka.

"Cut to the chase, Niki," he growled. "What the hell's Richard Langley doing in this investigation?"

"It's not always easy to 'cut to the chase', Lionel," said Nkiruka, dryly.

He was beginning to irk her. She hated to be rushed but Lionel, unfortunately, had the attention span of a small gnat.

She sighed.

"OK, Lionel, as you wish. To sum up, the murdered men brought a cello to London. Paolo's cello, in fact. We discovered the cello couldn't function as an instrument, so we decided to run it through the X-ray scanner here and inside the cello we found a hidden compartment, containing two paintings..." She ran a hand over her buzz cut. "Richard Langley thinks they're the two Chagall paintings listed on the Art Loss Register as having been stolen by a Nazi before the Second World

War got started. In 1938, on what's called the Night of Broken Glass."

Lionel had stopped chewing his gum.

"Are you telling me the old man was a Nazi?"

"We're going to need the cooperation of his family to ascertain that. If they don't want to help us, then we can, as a last resort, contact the police in Rio de Janeiro for their help. The name on the old man's passport was *Paolo Oscar Axel Fernandes*. Axel is a German name. Just saying."

Lionel chewed his gum for a bit, his thoughts somewhere else.

"What's Richard doing about this situation?"

"He's going to get the paintings verified and he's working to find out what their background story is. He doesn't want us to mention the paintings to Paolo's family until we know for sure if they were stolen or not. Should he discover that the two Chagall artworks were stolen by a Nazi around the time of the Second World War, then their rightful ownership would have to be legally established."

Nkiruka looked down at her open file.

"That could well be a long and difficult process, according to Richard. Especially if the present-day heirs don't have strong evidence proving their family bought and owned the paintings in the first place."

Lionel looked at her.

"How much would those paintings be worth?"

"Millions according to Richard."

"Damn it! Those paintings are going to complicate matters. Even more than they are already," concluded Lionel, sounding depressed. "If the family ever find out we've withheld multi-million-pound paintings from them, all hell will break loose. The three of you have got to keep your mouths shut about this. I'll get in touch with Richard and ask him to keep me informed and up to date with his progress on the paintings. Bloody hell. What a mess."

He tugged at his ear while his thick jowl continued to masticate the nicotine gum.

Observing him dispassionately, Nkiruka thought Lionel was looking like a bald cow chewing some cud. Not a pretty picture, by any stretch of the imagination.

She bent down and put her case file into her briefcase.

Determined not to become consoler-in-chief to Lionel's current woes, Nkiruka decided it was time to wind things up and get back to the other pressing matters on her desk.

"I'll let you know of any new developments on the case, Lionel. DI Webster's going to be coordinating the meeting with Paolo's relatives."

Nkiruka looked pleadingly across the table at Lionel.

Nice and civilized as Lionel's office space was, she had a lot of work to get through and she didn't want to be putting in any overtime that evening. Ada and Tom, as ever, would be waiting for her when she got back home and she had worked late the day before.

"Is there anything else you wanted to discuss with me, sir?" she asked, itching to get away.

Lionel looked amused.

"Got to get back to the desk, have you? I've never heard you be so polite to me before."

"First time for everything," said Nkiruka, as she

stood up. "The day I call you Superintendent Grieves you'll know I'm in deep shit."

She heard Lionel chuckle behind her as she exited his office and closed the door.

Once she was back at her desk, she quickly logged onto her computer and googled Juliana Margarida Fernandes.

The actress had a Wikipedia page dedicated to her but then so did many not very well-known people.

Clicking on Images, Nkiruka's screen flooded with professional photos of a tanned, blonde-haired woman, posing in a variety of glamorous outfits at red carpet events. In some of the snapshots, Juliana was receiving awards in front of a massive audience.

Lionel wasn't exaggerating. The woman was bloody famous.

Nkiruka shrugged.

Juliana's dad wasn't going to get any special treatment as a result of his daughter's fame and, as far as Nkiruka was concerned, that was all that mattered. They would continue to work towards seeing justice done for the three murdered men and they would treat the case with the same care and attention they did every other problematic homicide. No more or less.

She pulled a can of Diet Coke out of her desk drawer and popped it open, kicking off her shoes at the same time.

Starting to work through her emails, she reached for the Coke can and drank it slowly, finding comfort in the drink's familiar, sickly-sweet flavor. It was tastier by far than the watered-down coffee from the drinks machine on their floor.

She had spent just over an hour responding to the messages in her inbox when her desk phone rang.

She picked it up, still half-absorbed in the email in front of her and, balancing the phone on her right shoulder, she waited for whoever it was to speak.

"DI Webster?" asked a female voice.

"He's tied up just now," said Nkiruka, realizing that Johnny must have forwarded his calls to her phone while he was out of the office.

It was a bad habit of his and she'd told him off for it several times before. She didn't have time to answer calls for her detective inspectors, but any scolding from her was like water off a duck's back as far as Johnny was concerned. He only paid heed to her when it suited him to do so.

"Could you tell me when he'll be back? He's not picking up his mobile and it's important."

"No, I'm sorry. Is it anything I can help you with?" asked Nkiruka, intrigued in spite of herself.

"I highly doubt it," said the voice humorously, sounding as though the idea of Nkiruka helping her was very entertaining for some reason. "If you could just tell him Bella Matthews called, please."

"Will do," said Nkiruka, pleasantly.

"Thank you, I appreciate that very much."

The phone clicked as the caller hung up.

Nkiruka put the phone down and continued to read through her email.

Bella Matthews.

For some reason, Nkiruka couldn't get the name out of her head. It certainly rang a bell...

Frowning, she stared at her computer screen but all

she could see in front of her eyes was the name Bella Matthews.

Bella Matthews.

"No, please, no!" she muttered to herself, as she suddenly remembered where she'd last seen it.

She opened her bottom desk drawer and starting hunting around in it.

At last, locating what she wanted, she pulled out a folded copy of a tabloid newspaper.

With her hands shaking, she opened up the newspaper's front page and found the article she was looking for.

Serial killer on Hampstead Heath.

Directly underneath the headline was the name "Bella Matthews."

She was a journalist for the paper and it appeared she was in contact with Johnny.

Nkiruka felt her blood boil as the repercussions of his betrayal hit her.

She wondered how much money Johnny had received for the story. It was front-page news. What was that worth?

She was going to wipe the floor with him.

In fact, given the extent of his misconduct he'd be deemed suitable for immediate dismissal.

Chewing her bottom lip, Nkiruka considered her obligation to inform Lionel of her discovery. Lionel, for one, wouldn't mess about and he'd have Johnny out on his ear, no questions asked.

Quite right, too.

However, there was a hitch in this plan because,

despite her burning rage, Nkiruka was fond of Johnny and had a soft spot for him.

She wasn't sure she could put a finger on why, though.

Possibly it was something to do with Johnny's tough upbringing. At the end of the day, Johnny had been moved from one foster family to another, like an unwanted parcel in a "pass the parcel" game, from the time he was born. The odds had been stacked against him and yet he had somehow managed to overcome his difficult childhood to emerge into adulthood as the ultimate survivor.

Nkiruka would be the first to admit his attitude stank at times, but in spite of this glaring defect, he'd earned her respect because of everything he'd achieved despite life cutting him little slack.

While putting himself through a part-time course at college, to make up for the qualifications he had missed out on during his turbulent school years, Johnny had worked as a laborer on a building site. He had then attained a BSc degree in Civil Engineering from Southampton University, during which time he spent three years sleeping in a bedsit and working weekends as a waiter at a Pizza Express restaurant. During his last year at university, he did a stint as a bouncer in a local nightclub.

Interestingly, his references had been unanimous in declaring him to be dependable and hardworking. God only knew how or why he had ended up at Scotland Yard but he'd done well for himself until now. A little more respect from Johnny would have been welcome but Nkiruka was someone who liked straight-talking and Johnny had that in abundance.

Up until this point, he'd been a stalwart of hers, proving his loyalty to her time and time again. What's more, Johnny knew how to behave professionally when it counted, which made her wonder what had induced him to give in to temptation and cross a red line on this occasion.

It was most unlike him.

She was convinced he had to be in financial difficulty to have felt the need to approach the "journos" he hated with a vengeance.

She looked at her watch.

It was half five. If she was going to get home for 7:30, she needed to get a move on and sift through the rest of her emails.

She liked to take her time with big decisions and act with a cool head. Many years ago, an Australian boyfriend in the force, exasperated by the time it took her to make up her mind, had given her the Aussie nickname "*Slowey.*" Needless to say, their relationship didn't last long.

In her cautious and considered way, her preference was always to sleep on things before taking drastic action and she was sure that by the following morning she would know for certain what to do about Johnny's misbehavior.

Dismissing him from her mind, she put the newspaper back into her desk drawer and plowed on through her emails.

By half past six Nkiruka was seated on the underground train as it shuddered, shook, and thrust its way through a long black tunnel, moving gradually closer to Islington. The train was a noisy, voracious monster, carrying in its belly the hapless souls who had boarded it along the way.

For once, Nkiruka had found a vacant seat to sit down on and in the heat of the train she could feel herself beginning to nod off. She was sure the day would come when she would wake up at the end of the Northern Line without her briefcase or her handbag.

Trying to stay awake, she adjusted her mobile phone to Radio 5 Live so she could listen to the news through her AirPods. The news had a habit of upsetting her and she was unlikely to fall asleep listening to it.

She wasn't a political animal but she had recently begun to dislike the bias shown by different broadcasters in their reporting. She could understand why these days so many conspiracy theories were flying around and filling up the internet. Most people had cottoned on to the fact that despite living in a democracy, there were limits to a journalist's impartiality and truth-telling. The truth was always filtered through the lens of those reporting and editing the news and the obvious bias annoyed her, just as much as it did everybody else.

She nudged her briefcase, which was on the floor between her legs, and then moved her ankles closer together to keep a better hold on it.

The best part of her day was coming up soon.

There was something special about opening her bright-yellow front door and feeling the sense of calm that came from leaving the frenzied world outside and coming home.

Her home was a time capsule for her, a precious slice of life that she carried within her every single day and a place where her mental sanity was strengthened.

No matter how many horrific things she saw in her line of work, going home erased every single one of them from her mind. Her small double upper with Tom and Ada was where she belonged and where her future would always lie. She didn't need anything else.

Dedicated to her job, she was nevertheless someone who worked to live and didn't live to work. She never considered herself irreplaceable at the Met and, unlike a few of her colleagues, she didn't have an inflated ego.

She also gave credit where credit was due because thanks to the wonderful upbringing her parents had given her, her self-esteem was sound and she never felt the need to prove she was an invaluable asset to New Scotland Yard, or the world at large.

Her tube stop arrived before long and the station loudspeaker blared out "Angel" and "Mind the gap" in a deep-throated voice as she walked off the train.

She exited Angel Underground station, made her way to Upper Street and then cut across to Chapel Market.

The curbside vendors were long gone but the mess they left behind lingered on. Pieces of trodden fruit lay scattered along the street and two stripy plastic bags were drifting further and further away down the road, pushed onwards by the breeze.

A small sock, starkly white against the tarmac, was lying right next to the pavement.

Nkiruka smiled when she saw it.

She had no idea why so many toddlers, when strapped into their pushchairs, relished pulling off their socks and chucking them away. Maybe they enjoyed watching their parents having to run back to fetch them, like a dog would.

Nkiruka had long since come to the conclusion that some children were in charge of their parents, rather than the other way round. She was also convinced many children were far cleverer than their parents gave them credit for and she had often spotted a look of malicious satisfaction in a child's eyes as they watched their mother or father running around in circles after them, like headless, helpless chickens.

Ada was a classic example in this respect, thought Nkiruka, with grim insight into her own life.

If she had to sum up her experience of motherhood, she would say it was about knowing which battles to pick in order to survive mentally intact at the end of the day. In her opinion, nobody could teach a mother this useful skill before a child was born because every child came into the world with their own very special character. Every single child responded differently to their parents' authority. How on earth could you prepare for the unique mix of DNA that was going to arrive in your home? It was impossible.

Dropping her briefcase, she stopped at her yellow front door and rummaged in her handbag for her key.

Attached to the keyring was a heart of colorful Hama beads, made by Ada one Sunday morning when she was bored and the rain had kept them indoors.

Nkiruka opened the front door and walked up the stairs to their double upper.

Like a castle with a postern, Nkiruka's house had a robust dual entry system. She appreciated this, familiar as she was with the ingenious methods determined criminals used to break into people's homes.

She opened the multipoint lock at the top of the

stairs, standing on a mat that said: *"don't knock unless I married you, birthed you or ordered food from you."*

The smell of Jamaican curry assailed her nostrils as soon as she walked into her home. Tom found cooking therapeutic and relaxing, something she was forever grateful for as her cookery skills were practically non-existent.

It wasn't through lack of trying. Her mother had slogged away with her in the kitchen, trying to ingrain in her an understanding and appreciation of food, but none of it had worked. Nkiruka somehow managed to burn the simplest of recipes, although she had got to grips with the basics such as cheese on toast, a boiled egg or pasta.

When Tom wasn't around she stuck to salads, but Ada was beginning to get fed up with her limited repertoire in that area too.

Nkiruka dumped her bags on the floor and braced herself as Ada ran out of the kitchen and rugby tackled her legs.

Hugging Ada to her, she looked up and saw Tom poking his head out of the kitchen.

"Hello, love. Nice to see you home on time," he said cheerfully.

Turning a deaf ear to what she felt was implied criticism, Nkiruka smiled back at him. She had indeed been late a lot recently.

Tom had a thick head of strawberry blond hair and a pair of piercing, bright-blue eyes that had riveted Nkiruka's heart from the first time she looked into them. To this day she couldn't help getting lost in their icy beauty.

Nkiruka and Tom had met at St Thomas's A&E,

when he happened to be the nurse on duty and had to stitch up a deep wound on her head caused by an angry suspect.

The suspect, during an interview, had unexpectedly pulled out a knuckle duster from his back trouser pocket and her reflexes hadn't been quick enough to avoid the blow. This was a rare oversight from Nkiruka because, despite being measured and careful in her thought processes, she was usually very quick with her physical responses. Even more so after years of putting her long legs to good use in kickboxing classes.

Not that she regretted the incident or the permanent scar on her head, because it had brought Tom and her together. Their subsequent romance was the old cliché in reverse, ending up with the nurse proposing to his patient, many months later, over a bottle of champagne in Enish (Nkiruka's favorite Nigerian restaurant in Lewisham).

All of which felt like a lifetime ago, she thought, feeling the nostalgia from the past begin to overwhelm her.

She walked into the kitchen and poured herself a glass of rosé wine from the open bottle on the table.

Sitting herself down, she turned and looked at her daughter who, puppy-like, had sat down next to her.

"So, Ada, how was your day today?"

"I've got a new teacher called Adeline."

"Oh, yes? What happened to your last teacher? What was she called again?"

"Mum! I can't believe you can't remember her! Miss Hipsley, of course."

"That's right. I remember now. Miss Hippo."

Ada giggled.

Tom, who had a quirky sense of humor, loved to make up ridiculous nicknames for Ada's teachers. Nkiruka was sure that Ada was going let the nicknames slip one day and they were going to end up blacklisted by her school.

Times had changed, though. Nicknames were now common as muck but no doubt the older generation still thought this was disrespectful behavior, especially at school. Nkiruka could only remember one teacher at her school who had a nickname, a dragon of a woman named "Spitfire" for good reason.

"What happened to Miss Hippo?"

"I don't know. They said she had to take some time off to go be with her mother. Her mother's not well."

"Oh, that's a shame... Is Adeline nice?"

"Yes. She lets us call her Adeline and not Mrs. Charpentier. She also says she has a tortoise at home and she's going to bring it in next week so we can have a look at it. She's fun."

"Sounds like it."

Nkiruka wondered what name Tom would conjure up for Mrs. Charpentier.

Tom drained the jasmine rice over the sink and then he started to serve up soft mounds of it onto the three plates laid out in front of him.

"How was your day, Tom?"

"Not too bad. Two cardiac arrests. One case of suspected meningitis. Another biker with a fractured collarbone and a broken ankle."

Nkiruka tutted.

"The authorities have to do something for the bikers. There's too many accidents."

"Yes, I agree. We've a long way to go before we

catch up with the Dutch, that's for sure. Traffic in London's crazy. The big lorries can't see the cyclists half the time. It's really about time the government got cycle paths extended throughout the city and made them safe."

He took the saucepan off the cooker and began to spoon the curry out, heaping up layers of chicken, carrot, and white potato on top of the rice.

Once everyone had their plates, he sat down, smiling with genuine pleasure at Nkiruka and Ada, seated on either side of him.

Outside they could hear the voices of the night-time folk as they walked past, probably on their way to enjoy a few drinks at The Joker, a pub on Penton Street. Or maybe even The Three Johns, a bar around the corner, on White Lion Street.

"I've got some good news today," announced Tom, after swallowing a spoonful of curry to make sure it tasted good. "I've been made matron at long last. Starting in three weeks' time."

"That's wonderful, Tom!" exclaimed Nkiruka, delighted for him.

She leaned over and planted a kiss on his lips, breathing in the citrusy smell of his grapefruit shower gel. Tom liked to wash away the antiseptic smell of hospital when he got home and she didn't blame him, especially when he had to deal with so many other unpleasant smells in his line of work, too.

"What's matron?" asked Ada, puzzled and wondering what all the fuss was about.

"It means a very important nurse, Ada," said Tom, widening his eyes for special effect.

"Oh. I see," said Ada, sagely nodding her head as if

she was twice her age and understood fully the implications of a nursing promotion.

Nkiruka and Tom began to laugh as they ate their stew.

This is what Nkiruka loved best about her home life. The laughter. No one could deny that young children laughed so much more than adults. What change happened in between? Life, undoubtedly.

Nkiruka lifted her glass and chinked it against Tom's.

"Here's to a glittering career as matron."

"Here's to you catching the Hampstead Heath baddies," said Tom, conscious Ada was listening to his every word.

Ada took over the conversation after that, chattering away like an excited parrot about her friends at school until it was her bedtime.

Later on, after tucking Ada up in bed, Tom came downstairs and sat down on the sofa next to Nkiruka.

She was curled up in the right-hand corner of the sofa, gazing into the far distance, with a glass of wine in her hand.

As soon as he sat down, she lifted her feet onto his lap. Another habit of hers.

She had cleared up the kitchen earlier, as she always did after a family meal, so the evening was theirs to enjoy.

In front of them, a small fire was burning away at the two logs in the grate, chasing away the chill of the evening as their antiquated heating system made the radiators in the room clink and clank in an effort to pump hot water round them.

Hanging on the walls of their lounge was Tom's

precious collection of Keith Haring's Pop Art prints.
Nkiruka wasn't sure what Richard Langley would make
of Tom's motley art collection but Ada certainly
approved of their cartoonish quality and bright primary
colors. Nkiruka liked them, too, and thought the prints
stood out nicely against the lemon-yellow paint on the
walls, making the room feel cheerful and cozy, even on
a grey day.

"Out with it then," said Tom with calm authority
after a few minutes of companionable silence.

Nkiruka, who had been gazing into the fire with a
frown on her forehead, put down her wine glass and
sighed.

"It's Johnny. A journalist called Johnny's phone
today. I'm pretty sure he's been leaking information to
the press about the Hampstead Heath case."

"Stupid bastard."

"Yep. And I'm not sure what to do about it."

"You have to fire him now, Nkiruka. It's called dere-
liction of duty. This is serious shit he's done this time."

Nkiruka looked at him. Tom stared back at her.

He knew the expression on her face too well and
she could tell he was reading her mind already.

"You're not considering letting him off, Nkiruka?
Please don't tell me you're weakening on this," begged
Tom. "If Lionel were ever to find out, you'd both be
fired on the spot."

"I think everyone deserves a second chance," said
Nkiruka, conscious she was tilting her chin in just the
same way as her stubborn daughter.

"Second chances? Blimey! By the sounds of it,
Johnny has had more than his fair share of chances,

Nkiruka. From what you've told me, he's like Scotland Yard's version of the cat with nine lives."

Nkiruka smiled.

"He sails close to the wind sometimes but his heart's in the right place. He hates the press with a vengeance so he must have been felt desperate to sell them a story."

"So what? Nkiruka, most of us mortal beings are in desperate situations at some point. We don't all go running to the press to sell them some juicy piece of gossip, especially when it's against all the basic principles of our profession. Bloody hell, Nkiruka, you're far too tolerant. He's been riding roughshod over you for years."

He was sounding angrier and angrier.

"Only because I let him. He toes the line when I need him to."

"I would hope so," growled Tom, crossing his arms.

By now he was so furious he couldn't even bear to look at Nkiruka.

She decided she needed some new tactics to restore some badly needed peace to the evening.

Putting her feet down, she reached across and started to massage his shoulders, which were hunched up with tension.

"Oh no, you don't," he said crossly, pulling down her hands. "You don't get to turn me up sweet."

As he held onto her hands, Nkiruka leaned in and started kissing him playfully on the neck.

"Nkiruka! What the hell do you think you're doing?" admonished Tom, in quite another voice.

She kissed his lips, feeling the tightness in them

gradually yield and their familiar soft plumpness return under her persistence.

As Tom started to respond to her kisses with more and more urgency, she completely forgot about her workday troubles and felt herself begin to exist in the moment, the here and now, which unfailingly brought her tranquility.

For her, this was what home was all about.

With their discussion stopped, there was now no more tension between them.

The only noise in the room was the crackle of logs burning in the fireplace and the contented murmurs coming from their kissing on the sofa.

"You're incorrigible," concluded Tom, as they came up for air.

"I know, honey. But that's why you love me."

11

Richard

"Here we are," said Eilidh, driving the car into Wentworth Road.

The road was typical of a London suburb. Rows of neat semi-detached houses stretching all the way up the road with a few trees breaking up the monotony of the landscape. Most houses had a driveway in front of them, again not an unusual feature in an over-populated and congested city, where space of any kind was at a premium.

Eilidh parked the car next to two tennis courts and reached across to the cup holder to pull out her cappuccino, bought on the way at the Starbucks on Finchley Road.

While she drank her coffee, Richard, who had finished his coffee some time ago, looked out at the quiet, peaceful street.

Golders Green was a relatively unknown part of London for Richard but Eilidh's aunt had lived nearby in Templewood Avenue, right up until she died of pneumonia two years ago, so Eilidh had a fair grasp of their location which was handy for them both.

Richard deeply mistrusted satnavs and was convinced they never picked up the quickest route. Given that he seldom ventured out to North London, had he insisted on driving to Golders Green the journey could have taken them far longer.

Each London district was a unique cultural microcosm and, just like Chinatown or Brixton, had its own identity. In a city the size of London, people tended to stick to their local communities. About 20,000 Koreans lived in or around the suburb of New Malden, for example, making it the biggest Korean community in Europe. A large Serbian community was based in Notting Hill and Shepherd's Bush. Richard had, in fact, attended the wedding of a Serbian school friend that Easter, at the Serbian Orthodox Church in Notting Hill.

Even though he wasn't familiar with the geography of Golders Green, Richard was well aware that the area was known for its Jewish population and for having the largest Jewish kosher hub in the UK.

"Right, let's go," said Eilidh, smacking her lips contentedly as she put her empty cup down.

Richard smiled to himself. Eilidh would have been shocked had she known how many times he had been tempted to kiss those self-same lips.

He opened his car door and let himself out, waiting for Eilidh to gather up her things, before the pair of them then crossed the road in tandem.

They walked up to number 35 which was where Rachel Lea Dorin, Esther Sariya Dorin's daughter, lived.

It was amazing how much you could discern about a person from their front garden, thought Richard, looking at number 35's.

The garden had seen better days, that was for sure.

The landscaping of it held promise. There were pretty rose bushes arranged around the edges of the two grass patches on either side of the pathway. On the right-hand side, which was a larger expanse of grass, there was a healthy-looking cherry tree with a few autumnal leaves holding on for dear life to its branches.

But what should have been a very attractive front garden was marred by the sheer quantity of weeds over-running the grass, flowerbeds and even the path. The grass hadn't been cut in a very long time and the flower-pots by the front door had withered plants in them.

At one time the garden had been well looked after but clearly no more, which suggested the inhabitants now found themselves in difficult circumstances and taking care of the garden was beyond them.

If the front garden was showing signs of neglect, Richard wondered what the back garden, out of public view, was looking like.

Eilidh rang the doorbell and they waited.

The door, with the dark blue paint peeling off it, opened and a young girl smiled at them from behind a grimy doormat.

Signs of neglect were everywhere, thought Richard, looking at the messy hallway behind her.

"Hi, there!" said Eilidh. "Natalie Abergel?"

"Yes, that's me. Please come in. My mum's in the kitchen at the back of the house," said Natalie, a dark-haired girl with a pretty, pale face.

"Thank you very much," said Richard, letting Eilidh precede him into the house.

There was a hockey bag lying in the hallway alongside a large shoe rack. Richard guessed it belonged to Natalie for she looked about the right age to be playing hockey at school. A girl who was maybe 15 to 16 years old was his educated guess.

Unless, of course, he was completely mistaken and she was playing hockey at club level.

They walked through to an open-plan kitchen with a large L-shaped sitting area at the far end.

Lying on the sofa, facing the television, was a woman with two blankets wrapped around her and propped up by sofa cushions.

When she heard them stepping into the kitchen, the woman turned to look at them and revealed a pale face that was gaunt and ravaged, with a network of lines sketching deep grooves along her forehead and on either side of her nose.

It didn't take any intuitive skills to inform Richard and Eilidh that she was a seriously ill woman.

"Forgive me if I don't get up but I'm afraid my multiple sclerosis is playing up again. It's been particularly bad this month, which was a bit of a downer after I'd been in remission for the better part of eight months," explained the recumbent lady, with a very slight hint of an American twang in her voice.

If she was American, she had lived in Britain long enough to tone down the American nuances in her speech.

"Hello Rachel. I'm Eilidh Simmons and this is Richard Langley. We're from the Art and Antiquities Unit at Scotland Yard, as I think we explained to you over the phone," said Eilidh, seating herself next to the reclining woman.

"Yes, that's right," said Rachel, nodding gently as she reached up with the TV control and switched the television off.

Richard sat down on a sofa chair, feeling himself sinking slowly into the comfortable padding.

Were the sofas extra-padded for the sake of Rachel's illness? He felt his ever-ready compassion stirring and hoped, for Rachel's sake, their visit would be a success.

"Would you like a drink?" asked Natalie, politely.

"No, thank you," said Eilidh, smiling up at her. "We've just had a coffee in the car. Rachel, thank you for agreeing to speak with us, especially when you're feeling so unwell."

"It's OK," said Rachel, a smile glimmering on her lips. "Having the police in the house makes for a little variety in an otherwise very dull day." She looked up at her daughter and gestured to the sofa. "Sit down, honey. Come and join us."

"It's OK, mum. I'll just sit here."

Natalie dragged a kitchen stool from the breakfast bar and perched herself up on it, a little distant from everyone else, as though not wanting to intrude in what didn't concern her.

Instinctively liking the self-effacing girl, Richard thought about the hidden burden Natalie had to be carrying inside of her due to her mother's illness. It couldn't be easy for a girl of her age to see her mother in the grip of a degenerative disease.

"So, Rachel, am I right in understanding that your mother was Esther Sariya Dorin? Formerly of Brook-

lyn, New York?" asked Eilidh, leaning towards
Rachel.

"Yes, indeed she was. I was brought up in New
York but came to England after my marriage with my
husband. He was a senior accountant with KPMG in
London and I requested a transfer to the office of
Hogan Lovells in Holborn, which is where I worked as
a lawyer for 30 years. At least, I did when I was in
remission. I've taken retirement now," she said, a sad
smile on her lips.

Eilidh nodded.

"I'm afraid my husband's not in the picture any
more, if you wanted to talk to him," Rachel continued,
candidly, as she rearranged the blankets around her.
"He found his secretary was sexier than I am and more
willing to accommodate his hugely inflated, middle-
aged ego."

Taken aback by her cutting words, Richard recognised that inside the frail body lying on the sofa in front
of him was a formidable lawyer with a razor-sharp
mind. They would have to be careful not to underesti-
mate her during their interview. Rachel was nobody's
fool.

"Well, we've come to chat to you about your
mother, Rachel. We're wondering if Esther told you
anything about her life in Germany, specifically the
Night of Broken Glass? You see, we're hoping there
might be something from your grandmother's past that
could help us with one of our homicide cases."

Rachel was silent for a moment.

A melancholic expression came into her face and
lingered, as though in her mind she had travelled back
in time to her mother's side.

"She did indeed talk to me about that night. The Night of Broken Glass... She was only a young fourteen-year-old girl, working in her father's watch shop, back then. The watch shop was a very profitable business until the Nazis came and took my grandfather away. My family couldn't maintain the business after that happened because my grandfather was the watch specialist and he hadn't trained any of the women in his craft." Rachel's smile was a little skewed. "He was an old-fashioned, chauvinistic man. The women had to be working at home or helping out in the business but with no responsibilities. He'd be horrified if he saw me at my work today."

"So, there was no one to take over the business after he was gone?" prompted Eilidh, after Rachel appeared to have sunk into quiet abstraction again.

Lifting her head up to look at Eilidh, Rachel grimaced.

"No. There were two nephews doing an apprenticeship in the business but, don't you see, they took them, too. They rounded up the men. Most were taken away. That's what happened because of The Night of Broken Glass."

Richard wished that Eilidh had done some background reading on the Night of Broken Glass. She was an excellent interviewer, with the ability to build up rapport with just about anyone, but she hadn't fully absorbed the repercussions of that period of history, and as a result she was looking a little shamefaced at her lack of knowledge.

Eilidh reached across and squeezed Rachel's hand sympathetically.

"I'm so sorry to hear that, Rachel. It's utterly tragic.

It's hard for us, who don't have that history, to comprehend how that must have felt for your family. I know it's very painful for you to relive it but it's important we try to find out as much as we can about what happened to your family during the Night of Broken Glass. Did Esther ever give you any specific details?"

Rachel looked perplexed, as though confused by her question.

"Did they break into your mother's home, for example?" added Eilidh, deciding to cut to the chase.

"They did indeed break into their flat. It was an event my mother was never going to forget because it was the last time she saw her father. I remember her saying that theirs had been a happy and close community in Domhof until the Kristallnacht. They helped one another." Rachel chuckled. "Just as they've done with us, here in Golders Green. The Golders Green Synagogue has been fantastic, really helping us out when I've been ill, haven't they, Natalie?" Natalie nodded from her stool. "They do a meal rota for us every week, which is so kind of them, and help me get to my hospital appointments."

Rachel turned to face Eilidh again.

"Anyway, sorry, I'm digressing. My mother remembered how lovely it was to have close family members nearby in Domhof because she missed that a lot in New York. When they went to America they left many of their extended family members behind in Germany. Not everyone wanted to leave behind businesses they had worked for all their lives. Many stayed put in Germany after the Kristallnacht. I never heard what happened to the other family members during the war. She never spoke about that."

She sighed.

"My grandfather had wanted a boy, of course, to carry on the family business but he loved his nephews. He knew them from a young age and was proud of them. The Nazis took the boys away, too, but I know they would have helped my grandmother out with the business, had they been spared. I'm sure of it."

Aware that Rachel would probably soon tire, Richard decided to intervene before the family reminiscences became too random.

"It would be really helpful, Rachel, if you could give us a very precise description of what happened the night the Nazis took away your grandfather. As best you can, of course. It might help us get a little closer to solving a case we're trying figure out at the moment."

Rachel turned to him in surprise.

"You're working on an active case to do with my parents? From Kristallnacht?" she asked, watching Richard intently.

For the first time that afternoon, she seemed to grasp how crucial her mother's memories were to them.

"Yes, we are actually," said Richard, deciding honesty was probably the best policy in this conversation.

"Why?" demanded Rachel, looking confused.

"Well, it's a little complicated. I promise you as soon as we have proof confirming what we suspect, we'll inform you. But at the moment, I'm afraid, it's just conjecture. That's why your mother's memories are so important."

He could tell the cogs in Rachel's mind were whirring at breakneck speed as she tried to figure out a present-day connection with her parents.

Her eyes were focused and alert as she stared at them.

"I wonder... Tell me, has it got anything to do with the two missing Chagalls?"

Bull's eye.

Richard smiled at her.

"There are two Chagall paintings involved, that's true."

Rachel sat up abruptly and tossed away her blankets as she swung her feet down.

"You've found them?" she asked, leaning forward excitedly.

Richard lifted up his hands. "Whoa, hold on, please, Rachel. What we need right now is to have a better understanding of what happened to your mother and her family that night. This isn't only about the paintings, Rachel. There's been a murder, too."

"Ah, OK," she said, subdued.

It was clear she didn't understand why a murder would be mixed up with the Chagall paintings, which was fair enough, but it seemed she was also too polite and respectful to inquire about it. Richard couldn't help but feel relieved. Explaining how Paolo came into the current scenario would be time consuming and, at this stage in the investigation, unprofessional, too.

Despite her knowing there was a death somehow linked to the paintings, he could sense Rachel's elation and he didn't blame her for it. She wasn't stupid. Marc Chagall was a world-renowned artist. The implications of what he had told her had the potential to change her and Natalie's life for the better. Not only for the better, actually, but to the point where both their futures would be unrecognizable.

"What is it you want to know?" she asked Richard eagerly.

"Can you tell us, in as much detail as you can, what happened when the Nazis came to your mother's home?" repeated Richard, hoping that this time around they would get some solid answers to their query.

Rachel looked thoughtful.

"I can try but, to be honest, I think what might be of more benefit to you will be my mother's diaries from that time. We had them translated when we came to London. My poor mother gave them to me before I left New York for London. I think she felt it was her legacy, really. I can pull out the diary that covers the Kristallnacht and get the translation for you, if that's of any use?"

Richard was so surprised to find out that there was written evidence from Rachel's mother that he was speechless.

"That would be wonderful," affirmed Eilidh, seeing that Richard had been stunned into silence.

Rachel looked across at her daughter, perched up on her stool.

"Natalie, my love, could you bring down the cardboard box from the office?"

"Sure, mum," said Natalie, standing up and walking to the door.

"Do you need any help with it, Natalie?" asked Richard, worried that the box of diaries might be heavy.

"No, thanks anyway. There's not much in it," Natalie called back from the hallway.

It was refreshing, reflected Richard, to imagine what it was like to have everything that one held most dear fit into a small, lightweight container.

A woman's legacy left in a cardboard box.

While they waited for Natalie to return, Richard thought about the possessions he had carted around during his short life, which included his precious collection of Art Nouveau ceramics and a room overflowing with books, most of them heavy tomes filled with artwork.

One small box of possessions really put things in perspective, he thought.

He remembered it had taken his parents the better part of six months to clear out his grandmother's house in Wimbledon after she died. What would he be leaving behind when his time came?

He also thought about Chagall and how he had escaped to New York during the Second World War. He wondered how many possessions Marc Chagall had brought with him when he arrived in the USA. So many immigrants fleeing war or poverty arrived with nothing at all.

12

Richard

Meanwhile, Rachel had lain down on the sofa again. She was looking pale and tired, but peaceful, as she waited for her daughter to reappear.

Eilidh, tactfully, hadn't tried to engage her in conversation. She was sitting with her legs crossed, staring in a trance at a stoneware, Siamese cat splayed out on top of the coffee table.

It was a tasteful artifact, obviously handmade, with the cat's slender legs and face shaped with a great deal of skill. The mocha color on its tail, legs and ears blended in nicely with the dark wood of the coffee table.

Before long, Natalie came in carrying a white cardboard box and placed it carefully in front of her mother.

Rachel sat up, took the lid off it and started pulling out a variety of colored diaries, laying them to one side.

She then lifted a thick, red A4 book out of the bottom of the box and held it for a moment in her hands, stroking its hard leather binding.

"This is the complete translation of all the diaries in

the box. My ex-husband had it done for me one Christmas. The translator did a fantastic job and the diary entries in this book are clear and fluent. It's very moving to read, even in English."

"Would it be possible to have a quick look at the originals first, please, Rachel?" asked Richard, who liked to start from the beginning when he was looking into things.

"Yes, of course," she said, indicating the diaries on the table. "But they're all written in Hebrew. You won't understand them."

Richard picked up a diary and started looking through it carefully. The first page had the name Esther Sariya Dorin inscribed on it in English. As Rachel had pointed out, the rest of the book was scrawled in Hebrew and he couldn't make head or tail of the writing, apart from the dates of each day.

He had a cursory look at the other diaries but they were identical, with Esther's name written at the front of them in English and the rest written in Hebrew.

He put them down again, handling the books delicately, in much the same manner as Rachel had done. He wasn't underestimating their sentimental value to her for a minute.

"Could you read us the passage she wrote on the Night of Broken Glass?"

"Not from the Hebrew, I'm afraid. I never learnt to read it properly. Mum put extra sheets of paper for the Night of Broken Glass in her diary. Unsurprisingly, because it was a grim time for my family. What happened scarred mum for life."

She put down the A4 book she was holding in her hands and picked up a turquoise blue diary.

"This is the one," she ruminated, as she turned its pages. "See? Here it is."

She opened a page in the diary and showed them three folded sheets of discolored paper, filled with inked writing.

"This is what she wrote about the Night of Broken Glass."

She opened up the papers and laid them flat on the coffee table in front of Richard.

Richard leaned forward and stared down at them, wondering if it was possible to discern the state of Esther's mind from the style of writing or the condition of the paper. The ink wasn't blotched so she hadn't been crying when she wrote it. Did it differ from the writing in the rest of the diary? Was she scribbling with the agony of a broken heart? He couldn't honestly tell by the writing but he felt humbled at seeing a piece of living history.

He wondered if the translator would be willing to attest to what had been noted in the diaries, for that would also convince the sceptics, who might wonder if the diaries had been conveniently made up for the purpose of claiming ownership of the Chagall pictures.

If the diaries mentioned the two Chagall paintings, Richard felt sure there was sufficient evidence for Natalie and Rachel to lay a strong claim to them.

Would it be enough to settle the matter outright? He didn't know.

Claiming ownership of a stolen artwork these days could be a tortuous, time-consuming legal nightmare unless the proof was iron-clad and conclusive. Rachel didn't appear to have time on her side, so the more evidence there was to support her claim the better, because he wasn't convinced Paolo's relatives were going to hand over the artworks to Rachel and Natalie with their goodwill and blessing.

People were funny where large amounts of money were concerned. Once the Brazilian family found out about the two Chagall paintings and their rightful heirs, it was very possible that they would decide to fight tooth and nail for ownership and Rachel, able lawyer though she might be, did not seem to have the financial or mental resources to argue her case.

"This is very helpful," said Richard. "Could I have a look at the translation for that

night please, Rachel?"

"Sure", she said, picking up the leather bound A4 book and deftly turning the pages until she found the section in question.

She passed the open book over to Richard and he started to read it.

9/11/1938

We heard the thugs out in the streets of Domhof from about seven o'clock in the evening. It wasn't the first time there were fights after dark in our area. There were often street fights between the boys from the two local schools in our district but nothing like this. There seemed to be so many of these young men and they were only interested in destroying buildings, not in fighting each other. They were hitting windows along the street. Damaging cars. We saw many of them from our bedroom window, walking past our house, but after Mama caught us staring out of the window and told us off, we went to our bed. We could still hear the noise they made outside, which kept us up until the early hours of the morning.

The nights have always been scary for me. Mama keeps my bedroom door open so I can get some light from the hallway. I think the night brings out the worst in all of us and it's when our fears become more vivid and real, both in our imagination and dreams.

Last night felt different to normal though. Evil was in the air.

10/11/1938

This morning we went out with Papa to the watch shop.

The windows were smashed, most of the watches we had in it were taken. But to Papa this wasn't the worst news. The worst news for him was that the men had burnt down our synagogue last night. The synagogue represents who we are as a people, he said shaking his head. He had tears in his eyes and I have never seen him cry before. Not even when Bubbeh died. It made me feel afraid.

We swept up the broken glass lying on the shop floor and outside on the street and placed the boxes scattered about the shop onto the counters.

Then we went to help out the other shop owners on our street.

Alya Fischel's clothes shop next door had the glass broken on her shop front. Her stock had been tossed to the ground but it wasn't damaged. It was OK.

Elena Haber's kosher grocery shop was an awful mess, the fruit was mashed up and the wooden boxes containing them damaged and broken. Bottles of milk had been thrown across the shop and splattered onto the floor and were already starting to smell rancid. Red mince from the meat counter had been flung at the clean white walls and bits had remained stuck on, like blobs of paint. It really looked like the men had decided to have a food fight in her shop.

The delicatessen next to hers, belonging to Max Fischer, was untouched. Looking worried, he was helping Elena tidy up.

Mendel's bookshop, my favorite place to go at lunchtime, was trashed too. They had set it on fire and he said it was only the quick action of neighbors that stopped the fire from spreading after they left.

But common to all was the shattered glass. There was glass everywhere, crackling underfoot. On the road, the pavement, in the shops.

Papa began to phone around for glaziers to come and replace the glass on the shop front. He was finding it hard to get through to anyone. There were probably many in the same situation, calling desperately to restore some kind of normality to what had been brutalized.

He has always been so strong but today he seemed old and frail to me. As though he had aged many years. They left his watch tools behind which he was pleased about. He said with the tools he could rebuild the business and that we would get an insurance payout for the damage done to the shop. We would rebuild, he kept repeating.

At lunchtime he sent me and my sister home, saying there was nothing more to be done for now.

We found Mama shaking as she sorted out the laundry. She had been visiting neighbors affected by the crisis. Unlike Papa, Mama isn't a strong person. She suffers from anxiety and worries about us with great intensity. Something like this is not good for her mind.

We spent the afternoon helping her with household chores and preparing the food for dinner.

We didn't speak much. There wasn't much to be said.

Just when I thought the day couldn't get any worse, it did.

We are living a nightmare. Papa has gone. We cannot believe it. Mama hasn't stopped crying.

She just sits on the kitchen chair in her dressing gown, letting the tears slide down her face and the mucus from her nose drip down onto her lap. She doesn't care. She doesn't seem to even know we are here. We run and fetch her tissues, trying to console her with our hugs, yet our hearts are afraid and broken too.

They took Papa away with them and we fear the worst. We have heard of the internment camps. There are whispers that Jewish dissenters are sent there, anyone who falls foul of the authorities. We fear the worst.

Five of them came in when we opened our front door. They took our stuff. And they took him. No explanation, no accusation.

They grabbed him and left.

His last words to us as they frog marched him to the door were: "Take care of each other and remember I love you."

That was it.

He's gone.

They went through the flat and they took all the silverware from the dining room,

they took Mama's gold necklace off her and took her purse out of her handbag.

Wolves. They reminded me of wolves. Hungry, fierce, violent.

The strangest thing has just happened.

We heard banging at the front door again and ran to open it.

Mama didn't move. It was like she didn't care what happened to us or her any more. One of the young men who took Papa away came back.

He looked so young. Too young to be so brutal.

I remembered him. While the others grabbed what they could, stuffing the sacks they carried with them, he stood silently staring at the things in our flat. He spent a little time looking at the two paintings Papa had bought Mama for their 20th wedding anniversary.

This time when he came in, he marched straight past us, still carrying his revolver. He walked into our sitting room. We saw him reach up and take the two paintings off the sitting room wall.

With the meat knife from the kitchen he cut the pictures out of their frames and rolled them up.

Without saying a word, he walked out of our house with them both. I hope those paintings curse him forever more.

Mama didn't move from her chair in the kitchen. I don't think she even noticed

what happened.

Richard closed the book and put it down carefully on the coffee table.

"It's so sad to be reading this. Awful, in fact. I hope better things happened in the future for your mother?"

Rachel looked pensively at him.

"Yes and no. She was very young when she arrived in New York. She ended up working as a sales assistant in a jewelry shop for most of her life. It wasn't very well paid. My dad worked as a tailor. They did all right and it was enough. Enough to put me through school. I was a late and unexpected child for them. A blessing, my mother always said. They had a lot of community support in the end too, which was lovely."

"What about your grandmother?"

"She didn't fare so well. She died five years after they reached America, of a stroke. She was young for that to happen but then she always was a fragile creature and more so, probably, after they took grandad away."

"The diary also mentions a sister?"

"Yes, Aunt Talia. She died of breast cancer, poor soul. She was only sixty years old. She never married."

Richard nodded.

"I'm afraid I'm not sure how these diaries will play out as far as ownership goes. Unfortunately, what I read doesn't mention that two Marc Chagall paintings were taken from your parents' house. That's going to be the sticking point."

"Yes, that's true. You're right. I was thinking the same thing when you were reading the diary." She leaned back onto the sofa cushions. "We do have a receipt for the paintings, though. You know, Chagall was well-known by the time my father bought those paintings, so I'm sure the gallery he bought them from would have made a record of having sold them to him, too. If the gallery still exists, that is. It's always possible, isn't it? It was a gallery near the Champs Élysées in Paris called The Bluebird Gallery."

She sat up again and pulled the box to her.

"It was a really big deal when he bought those paintings for my mother. My mother said he must have used the better part of a year's profits to buy them. So extravagant. I've a receipt for them in here somewhere," she said, rummaging in the box again.

She lifted a sheaf of papers out of the box and ruffled through them.

Pulling out a dog-eared, yellowed piece of paper, she reached across and handed it over to Richard.

"My grandmother always kept that receipt with her because it was all she

had left of his present to her."

Richard looked at it.

It was a creased, handwritten receipt confirming that two paintings by Marc Chagall had been bought at La Galerie L'Oiseau Bleu, Paris:

05/07/1936
La Galerie L'Oiseau Bleu 3 Rue de Marignan Paris
75008

Crucifixion Violette—Marc Chagall—
10,000 franc payé Amoureux sur le Banc
Marc Chagall—10,000 franc payé

"This is as good as it gets," said Richard, pleased.

"With a little research we should be able to connect this gallery with the sale of the two paintings. Even if it has shut down now or changed hands, it must be possible to track down those connected to the previous owners. After all, Parisian art galleries have a strong tradition of record keeping and a sterling reputation in good practice, as you'd expect in the city of art. The better-known galleries in Paris, for example, kept meticulous records of the Impressionist works they sold, which has been invaluable to our present-day art historians."

Richard reached across and placed the receipt on top of the diaries.

"In the meantime, I suggest you keep these diaries and the receipt very safe. You'll need them."

Rachel frowned.

"Would you mind keeping them, Chief Inspector?" she asked, suddenly looking anxious. "Life's so uncertain right now and I'd never be able to live with myself if I misplaced or lost them. If you already have the paintings in your custody at the moment, you might as well have these, too."

"Yes, I understand, Rachel. It won't be a problem for our department, at least not in the short term. It makes sense for us to keep these diaries and the receipt with the two paintings while we try to establish ownership. It's useful evidence in this investigation, at the end of the day. All you have to do is sign them over to our custody and we'll take care of them for you. Hopefully, it won't be for too long. We'll keep everything safe until your ownership's fully settled with the paintings," he said, reassuringly.

Relief had eased the lines on Rachel's face and

Richard felt glad he was able to offer her a morsel of comfort when she was so ill.

"Should your ownership be validated beyond doubt, I would then suggest you arrange for one of the big auction houses to pick up the paintings directly from us," he advised. "Those artworks aren't the sort of things you'd want to have in your home unless you can afford around-the-clock security. But for now, we'll keep them secure."

"Thank you, Richard, that's a weight off my mind. Natalie, my love, can you fetch a plastic bag from the cupboard, please?"

Natalie stared at her, baffled by the request.

"It's so we can put the diaries in it," explained Rachel, smiling at her.

Obediently getting down from her stool, Natalie went off to fetch the plastic bag.

On a scrap piece of notepaper, Rachel signed over the diaries and the Chagall receipt to Scotland Yard.

She seemed to be weakening for she leaned back after this, with her eyes half-shut and a frown furrowed on her brow. Her energy levels had been ebbing and flowing at different points during their meeting but now it was clear it was time for them to go.

Watching as Natalie came back into the room with a large plastic John Lewis bag, Richard could read the boredom written all over her face.

Natalie had no idea what was at stake with the paintings and for the last half hour had looked as though she was itching to leave the room to do something more interesting.

Her mother, by contrast, knew very well what was

tied up in the two small paintings sitting in his office at Scotland Yard.

Eilidh, meanwhile, no doubt intrigued by all the history under discussion, was casually flipping through the pages of one of Esther's diaries. Not that she could understand any of the writing.

"Rachel, if you don't mind, I think we'll take everything in the original box, rather than putting it in a plastic bag. It's not raining outside and the box will be better than a plastic bag for protecting them from damage," suggested Richard.

Rachel shrugged.

"Sure, whatever you think is best."

Eilidh reached across and started putting the diaries and papers back into the white box.

As Richard stood up to go, Rachel turned her head towards him and smiled.

"You know what's so bizarre, Chief Inspector? The Nazi, or Nazi sympathizer, who took my grandparents' Chagall paintings. He must have known they were painted by Marc Chagall. Chagall's work is so distinctive. I've thought about this a lot. Why did he come back to my grandparents' house after the others had gone? I think it's because he couldn't afford to let the others see him take away paintings by a famous Jewish artist. A painter, moreover, who had been openly disparaged by the Nazis in Germany," she remarked, as she spread the blankets over her legs again. "But that young Nazi knew their worth, that's for sure."

On reflection, Richard had to agree with what she said. It made sense.

13

Nkiruka

"Johnny, take a seat," said Nkiruka, holding open the door to Room 319.

As Johnny walked past her into the room, he glanced around and noticed there was no one else attending their meeting.

He raised his eyebrows at her as he sat himself down, his legs stretched out in front of him.

"We really should stop meeting like this, Nkiruka," Johnny said in a sultry sotto voice.

He was a superb mimic.

Nkiruka could feel her lips twitching. Not today, she said to herself, trying to override her instinct to smile.

This was the crux of the problem she had with him. Johnny was able to make her smile or laugh and that mattered a lot in a job as grueling as theirs but, of course, it also meant he was her Achilles heel when she had to be firm with him.

She sat down and toyed with her pen as she summoned up the courage for what was coming next.

When she looked up she saw that Johnny was watching her curiously through narrowed eyes and with his head tilted on one side.

He wasn't daft and he could sense something was wrong.

It was also obvious he had no idea what was on her mind as he waited impatiently for her to speak, his foot tapping a restless beat on the floor.

Like a lamb to the slaughter, she thought.

"Johnny, I believe you know Bella Matthews?" she shot out, studying his response to her question.

Johnny jerked himself upwards on the chair as though she had given him an electric shock to the backside.

"Yes," he said, looking apprehensively at her.

"Who also happens to be a journalist." Johnny's face turned bright red.

She was relieved to see he wasn't doing a good job of disguising his feelings. Had he acted innocent in front of her, she would have known him to be past the point of redemption. A liar was not the kind of character trait she wanted in one of her team members and there was no doubt in her mind that she would have fired him on the spot had she heard his denial. She had enough evidence to do so. Bella's redirected call to her phone had been recorded, for a start.

"Why, Johnny? Why did you do it?" she asked, quietly.

Johnny continued to gawk at her like a rabbit transfixed by car headlights.

Nkiruka could see there was a battle going on in Johnny's mind. He wanted to trust her with the truth of the matter but wasn't sure he could.

"Well, I..."

"The truth, Johnny. I don't want any bullshit from you. I'm not in the mood."

Johnny sighed.

You're not going to believe me."

"Try me."

"My foster brother's getting married in Australia this year."

"Yes, I knew that."

"So, I didn't have the cash on me to go. My mortgage is massive."

"That's it?" said Nkiruka, staring at him in disbelief. "You ruined your reputation, put your job at risk and sold a story to a tabloid newspaper, so you could go to Australia?"

Johnny now had a stubborn expression on his face.

"For my brother's wedding. Yeah. He's stood by me from the time I joined his family. I was fifteen years old when I moved in with them and I owe him a lot because he's always believed in me. He's asked me to be his best man."

Nkiruka didn't trust herself to speak.

"You don't know what that means to someone who's never known who his real parents were. Bloody hell, Nkiruka, I was abandoned in a supermarket car park as a baby, did you know that? In a cardboard box. Dumped like a piece of trash by my mother. So yes, I'm afraid it meant a lot to me to go to Australia and be the best man at my foster brother's wedding. He's the only real family I've got."

Gripping her hands together tightly, Nkiruka stayed silent although she was very tempted to speak. Not to speak, actually, but to yell.

There was no remorse or contrition in Johnny. Talking as though life had dealt him a rough hand and he deserved to have something back, he seemed blithely unaware that any criminal residing in Her Majesty's Prison Service could make the same argument in justification of their crimes.

Johnny would have been shocked to know that right then her overriding desire was to scream at him at the top of her voice and to punch the dumbass look out of his face. She was actually sitting on her hands in a bid to control herself.

While she waited for the flames of her anger to die down a little, Johnny squirmed and fidgeted on his chair.

She could see from his face that he knew his answer had been a big disappointment to her but he was still struggling to understand why she couldn't see his point of view and, not for the first time, she wished his moral compass wasn't so out of kilter with hers.

Despite his moral blind spot, though, he knew her very well. Nkiruka was never, ever, short of words and she'd lost count of the times when Johnny had complained about her incessant talking during lunchtimes or official meetings. Her lengthy silence was freaking him out and she wasn't surprised. The truth of the matter was, both of them were seeing a new and unpalatable side to each other that morning.

Ignoring Johnny in a bid for self-preservation, Nkiruka said and did nothing to allay his discomfort. She sat motionless and silent in front of him, her eyes hooded as she fought to restrain her impulses.

Realizing her silence might not be ending any time soon and deciding it wasn't worth taking the risk of speaking to her again, Johnny leaned forward, put his elbows on his thighs, and stared miserably down at the floor.

After another minute, Nkiruka gave herself a mental shakedown. She had to pull herself together and sort this out. Time was a valuable commodity and she was wasting it.

Despite her anger, she'd already made up her mind regarding Johnny's unprofessional behavior.

Her decision came at a cost. She was about to cross a line in her work that would leave her with a permanently guilty conscience. And yet, she was going to have to learn to live with it, because at the end of the day she was certain her decision was the lesser of two evils.

She let out a long sigh, feeling the weight of Johnny's troubled livelihood on her shoulders.

Hearing her sigh, Johnny glanced across at her hopefully and sat up.

"You know, Nkiruka, I accept I wrongly gave in to temptation but the truth of the matter is Bella Matthews is always sniffing around The Red Lion, trying to get one of us to spill the beans after a pint or two," he argued, holding his hands together.

The West End had definitely missed out on Johnny's thespian talents, decided Nkiruka, as she watched Johnny transform himself into a penitent supplicant. She wondered how long his meek stance was going to last. Not long, she reckoned, because eating humble pie was not a familiar role for him to play.

Looking at Nkiruka's uncompromising face, Johnny swallowed and then loosened his tie.

"She gave me her card once," confessed Johnny, at last, as he looked her in the eye.

"Summer last year, I think it was. I tossed it onto my desk at home and didn't think any more of it. Then lately, when I knew I couldn't afford the flights to Australia, it seemed such an easy thing to do to give her a story. A bit of gossip for some cash. It hasn't been an easy thing to live with, though. She got her pound of flesh off me and now she won't stop hounding me. It's like those fraudster cold callers. Give them an inch and they don't give you a minute's peace."

"You expect me to feel sorry for you?"

"No," said Johnny, shaking his head. "No, I don't."

"How much did she give you?"

"Fifty grand."

"Wow. That's some wedding trip you've got lined up."

Johnny shrugged and said nothing.

He wasn't going to argue back. Again, very unlike him.

Nkiruka began to feel sick as the adrenaline ebbed out of her.

She knew The Red Lion at Parliament Square. Loads of officers ended up there at the end of a shift because, like everyone else, they needed somewhere to let their hair down. Especially so in a job as grim and challenging as theirs. The thought that Bella Matthews was hanging on to the place, like a leech, trying to get a story from her officers when they were off duty and relaxing, made her furious.

She wondered if anyone else had succumbed to temptation. She would probably never find out.

"I trusted you, Johnny."

"Yeah, I know. I'm sorry."

Nkiruka smiled sadly.

"To be honest, I don't know if I'll be able to rebuild my faith in you again. And on top of all this crap, I needed your help in finding the murderers o the Hampstead Heath men. You're the best DI in my team."

"What do you want me to say, Nkiruka? I know I messed up. Are you going to bloody cut to the chase and tell me if you're going to let me go? Or are you trying to torture me as well?" exploded Johnny, having reached breaking point.

Nkiruka gazed out of the window for a moment.

The sun was shining and she wished she could be out in it, rather than sitting in a stuffy meeting room with Johnny.

She turned on her chair to face Johnny once more.

"I didn't like the sound of her."

"What?" asked Johnny, totally confused.

"I didn't like the way she was on the phone. Bella Matthews sounded like an arrogant bitch, excuse my French. I'm not going to let her take away a good man from his job, but Johnny, if I ever catch you doing anything like this again, I'll sack you for misconduct. No redundancy package either. *Nada*, understand? Don't take my goodwill for granted. You know I've my limits."

Johnny leant back in relief and put his hands behind his head.

"Nkiruka, thank you so much. You won't regret it. I'll be on the straight and narrow from now on, I promise you. I know I screwed up big time and, in any case, I haven't had a good night's sleep since it happened."

"As for that piece of filth, I want my revenge on her," said Nkiruka, oblivious to Johnny's heartfelt regret.

"Sorry, what?"

"I want to take her down, Johnny. Bella Matthews," she explained, as though speaking to an obtuse child.

"You can't, Nkiruka."

"Oh, I think I can. Wait until I tell Lionel she's haunting The Red Lion in search of a good story from our officers."

Johnny was looking terrified.

"Oh, don't worry, Johnny, I won't say a word about what you've done but that doesn't mean I can't try and hamper her efforts. I think an official warning from Lionel should go to all the officers about her, accompanied by a photograph, of course. And while I leave Lionel to work on that, I'll get an undercover officer in our team to feed her some made-up crap in the meantime. We could put together a good crime story for her. She's going to look a complete fool when the Met strenuously denies the report. That should put her in her place."

"For goodness sake, Nkiruka. Is it really worth going to all this effort?"

"Oh, yes, Johnny, it really is. I want to nail the bitch and I'm going to enjoy getting my own back on her. Anyway, none of this is going to involve you, so let's move on to more important matters."

She bent down and picked up her briefcase, feeling

her shoulders loosen up as she returned to her familiar role once more.

Pulling out her laptop, she smiled reassuringly at Johnny, who seemed shell-shocked by her vengeful behavior and was sitting bolt upright, with his arms crossed.

Whether he was crossing his arms for comfort or in self-defense, she had no idea, but it was body language that signaled he was feeling far from at ease with her.

"We've a lot of additional information on the Hampstead Heath case at this point in time. Enough, at any rate, to see if we can chase up any leads," summed up Nkiruka, determined to get them back to business matters once more.

She glanced at her written notes.

"I've noted down a few points of interest. Nothing was found in Hampstead No 1 Pond. It begs the question, what did they do with the old man's wheelchair, their wallets and phones? A wheelchair wouldn't be an easy thing to conceal and, what's more, an old man in a wheelchair is going to be somewhat conspicuous. Somebody must have seen something."

Nkiruka fiddled with the gold chain around her neck and then clutched the gold and abalone palm tree pendant hanging on it.

It was a gift bought on a whim during her honeymoon and reminded her of a world that existed beyond the narrow confines of Scotland Yard. Holding onto the palm tree icon brought a sense of perspective to her working life when she needed it, which she had to admit was fairly often in recent days.

She looked down at her notes again.

"Reception at Claridge's Hotel confirmed they

called up a disabled cab for the three men on the day they went missing but we still haven't heard back from Waterloo Cars, have we? Could you chase them up for me? If you visited them in person it might speed things up. It's taken far too long for them to get back to us."

Johnny nodded his assent.

"The pathology report told us nothing new other than noting that pieces of broken glass were used to torture the old man, slicing cuts through his skin. I think this detail is hugely significant because it ties in with what Richard has told me. According to the Art Loss Register and Rachel Dorin, the two paintings in the cello were stolen by a Nazi after the Night of Broken Glass. It seems obvious to me that the two things must somehow be connected. The criminal psychologist also said Paolo's murder had the hallmarks of a revenge killing. I think we must assume we're looking for someone who wanted revenge against Paolo, specifically with a view to what happened on the Night of Broken Glass, don't you think?"

"Possibly, but we don't really know what he did, do we? Stealing valuable paintings might not be his only crime."

"Yes, that's true. The level of ferocity used in his murder suggests it wasn't just about a couple of stolen oil paintings. We can only assume there's a strong connection with Paolo's Nazi past. In which case, were the killers unofficial, vigilante Nazi hunters? Could there be a connection with Rachel Dorin we haven't explored yet? Or could it even be possible that the murderers were sponsored unofficially by the Israeli government? We've had trouble with their special agents in this country before."

Johnny shook his head.

"The Israelis? No, that's nuts, if you ask me," he said, dismissively. "They have bigger problems to worry their heads about and I really don't think he was important enough for the Israeli government. I mean if Paolo, or whatever his real name was, was some big-shot Nazi, somebody would surely have found him before now, don't you think?"

Nkiruka shrugged helplessly, raising the palms of her hands up in surrender. "I'm only throwing ideas out there. I'm as much in the dark as you are." Leaning forward, Johnny pulled his notes towards him and smiled.

"Well, you can at least bin the Israeli theory, Nkiruka. An Israeli agent would be a lot subtler in their methods and would want to avoid any unnecessary publicity. There's nothing clinical or cold-blooded about these murders. I know what you're thinking, but I'm telling you now, it'll be a complete waste of my time approaching MI6 to find out if there were any suspicious Israeli spies here at the time the murders happened. I'm afraid I don't think that theory holds any water. Sorry."

Rubbing his chin as he pondered the problem, Johnny looked at Nkiruka.

"Even if he *was* a low-profile German Nazi, though, we have to recognize that it's unlikely the Jewish people would forget even the smallest of crimes committed against them during the Second World War," he said. "The same goes for the Nazi hunters working on their behalf."

"Do we start from the premise that the killers could be Jewish?"

"Yes, I suppose they could be Jewish," said Johnny, shrugging his shoulders. "But I don't think we can assume that with any certainty. We've nothing on Paolo but the history behind those two stolen paintings and a German middle name. He could be a criminal middleman or maybe he bought the stolen paintings off someone who was a Nazi, without knowing anything about their origin..."

He shook his head.

"No, that doesn't seem likely, especially seeing as he kept both paintings well hidden inside that cello of his. We've no actual proof he was a Nazi, but there's a chance we might find out more about him from his family. His original name would be very helpful, for a start."

In spite of his recent fright, Johnny's eyes were now intent and narrowed with interest.

At least they were now in familiar territory, thought Nkiruka.

Working together on a tricky murder investigation and arguing out their theories was a normal process in their day-to-day meetings. For some reason, debates had become an integral part of their working partnership. In this respect, they were like an old married couple, reenergizing their relationship with a fight over who was going to make the tea.

"The murders happened here in London. That's got to be significant. If there was a Brazilian connection, why didn't they just murder Paolo over there?" asked Nkiruka. "The way in which they killed the three men suggests a level of hatred that must be linked to his Nazi past. I'm not convinced we're going to get anything useful from his Brazilian family, either, unless Paolo told them something about his past misdemeanors or his former life in Germany."

"The family might well know something more about him. We'll soon find out. I think you're jumping to too many conclusions, Nkiruka," said Johnny, bluntly. "We should keep an open mind. There's no evidence showing Paolo was associating with people here in London. Even the Dorin descendant hadn't heard of him when I asked her. I would hazard a guess that the murderers were more than likely to have been following him from Brazil. For a start, how on earth did the murderers know Paolo was travelling to London? It had to be someone over there... But we could go around in circles forever on these questions. No matter what way you look at it, we still need more information."

Nkiruka shook her head.

"Rachel Dorin lives in Golders Green and has done so for a long time," she said, looking at her notes. "After speaking with her, Richard has a tenuous idea that Paolo may have been stopping in London to return the paintings to her. After all, they were only staying in London for a week before heading on to Switzerland, presumably to check into Dignitas, judging by the paperwork we found in their suitcases. We should verify that with Dignitas, too, by the way."

Johnny nodded, which meant he would get this done.

"The three men brought the cello with them to London," continued Nkiruka. "Why did the others not object to bringing the cello with them on such a long journey and insist it stay in Brazil? Paolo was a weak, very old man, when all's said and done. I don't get why they brought the cello with them. It seems odd to me.

But as you've rightly pointed out, the most important thing is to figure out who could have known about Paolo's visit to this country. I'm wondering if there was any correspondence between him and the killers. A man of his age would be a letter writer."

"Going down that route is a bit of a nightmare, if you ask me," remarked Johnny. "We've got the relatives here in London now. They're not going to be in a position to check out any correspondence he might have back in Brazil."

"They'll have plenty of relatives back in Brazil, I'm sure, with access to his house. I do wonder how much they knew about their father's past. After all, how easy would it be to keep your German identity secret from your family? For most of your life? He must have at least told his wife something about his life in Germany. I know she died a while back but maybe she told another family member his secrets. Anyway, we can find out more when we meet with them later on this afternoon."

Nkiruka suddenly noticed the two plastic water cups she had laid out on the table prior to their meeting.

She picked hers up and drank it, grateful for some water now the most dreaded part of her working day was over.

"I think we should also be looking at a link between where the murdered bodies were found and the fact that this Dorin descendant lives just up the road in Golders Green," suggested Johnny, his mind continuing to focus on the Hampstead murders. "The locations must be, what, three miles apart?"

"True but nobody seems to have known about the paintings and the cello was left behind at Claridge's.

Rachel Dorin is an invalid with MS and has a teenage daughter living with her. They're hardly in a position to murder three men and drop them onto Hampstead Heath, are they?"

"No, of course not, but surely it's possible the killers could have exacted revenge on their behalf, whether the Dorin family were aware of it or not..."

Another possibility, thought Nkiruka, feeling disheartened.

"We need to find out where the murders actually happened. I presume not too far from where the bodies were dumped," said Nkiruka, following this line of thought. "Give Waterloo Cars a kick up the backside, will you? We really need to know where they dropped the three men off that day."

"Yes. I'll get it done."

Johnny leaned forward to check his case file.

"Let's just accept we can't make any early assumptions about the killers' profile. There are too many options," said Johnny, rubbing his forehead and looking tired after his earlier ordeal with Nkiruka. "The murderers could have come from Brazil, having tracked him down and bided their time. I mean Paolo could have fallen out in a big way with the people who helped him hide his true identity all these years. Maybe he betrayed someone in business over there or did someone a bad turn. After all, it does sound like he was a nasty piece of work."

Nkiruka chewed a fingernail as she pondered this.

"You see, there are so many alternatives," said Johnny, looking at her perplexed frown with morbid satisfaction. "Maybe the killers are emotionally involved and invested in the Dorin family? Possibly some other relatives of theirs in London? Or a local Jewish group, with strong views on justice, who knew about the Dorin story? There are extremists in all religions. Maybe we should be checking out the synagogues in the area and find out if Rachel Dorin and her daughter have attended any of them."

"Yes, that would be helpful," agreed Nkiruka. "Richard did mention that Rachel and her daughter are currently supported by their local synagogue. The rabbis will know their congregations and the local community. That would be a good place to start."

"Yes, I agree," assented Johnny.

"Tell you what, once you've heard back from Dignitas and looked into where the men were dropped off by the taxi, I want you to arrange for us to go together to Rachel Dorin's synagogue. The rabbi might be able to give us some new insight into the killers' thinking or tell us of anyone they know who's particularly interested in tracking down World War Two Nazis. He might even be able to pinpoint someone who's been behaving out of character," said Nkiruka, trying to be positive and upbeat.

In front of her, Johnny was looking unconvinced by her optimism but that was his habitual manner and she was used to it.

She didn't resent his downbeat attitude because he grounded her on the rare occasions when she allowed herself to get carried away. Sometimes she would endorse a highfalutin theory from another DI in the team and then, often as not, Johnny would shoot the theory down in flames, bluntly pointing out how their ideas did not correspond with the facts of the case.

It had to be said, his combative nature did not win

him a lot of friends at Scotland Yard but Nkiruka, for one, valued his plain-speaking.

Nkiruka checked through her notes to see if they had covered everything.

"I've spoken to the attaché at the Brazilian embassy and he's going to do what he can to uncover more information about Paolo Fernandes. Without involving his family, of course," she added. "I suspect, though, we might get some answers directly from his children this afternoon."

Especially, she thought to herself, if they are bereaved and emotionally vulnerable. But would they be grieving Paolo's death? The best indicator of what kind of a man he was during his life would be the reactions of those closest to him.

Nkiruka glanced at her laptop and felt her heart race when she saw the time.

She scrambled up from her chair and while her laptop shut itself down, she shoved the rest of her things into her briefcase: an assortment of dog-eared papers, her phone, and a couple of chewed-up biros.

Picking up her empty water cup, she tossed it into the wastepaper basket sitting in the corner of the room and felt absurdly pleased when it dropped in at the first try. She hadn't been a goal shooter in the netball team at school for nothing.

"I've got to get going, I'm afraid. I was supposed to be attending a conference call meeting five minutes ago," she explained, hastily dropping her laptop into her briefcase and closing the clasp. "OK, Johnny, I'll meet you in the foyer at 2.30 then. Please don't be late."

She picked up her briefcase and raced out of the door.

Behind her she heard Johnny shout out: "I'll be on time!"

He'd better be, she thought, as she ran down the corridor to the lift. Johnny owed her a huge amount of brownie points.

14

Richard

By the time Richard reached the penthouse suite of St James's Hotel in Mayfair, the others were already there.

DCI Ezemonye and DI Webster were seated next to one another on separate armchairs, two middle-aged women were seated on a grey sofa adjacent to them, holding on tightly to each other's hands, and pacing by the window was an agitated man wearing an open-necked shirt.

A dark-haired young lady in police uniform was standing unobtrusively behind Nkiruka, her hands clasped in front of her, and Richard assumed she must be Sofia, the Portuguese liaison officer.

At the far corner of the room, a little separate from everyone else, was a striking- looking lady seated on a pink velvet armchair.

She could have been, Richard guessed, anything from fifty to seventy years of age due to her obvious use of cosmetic enhancements. Tall and slim, she had platinum blonde hair, tanned or spray-tanned skin, and a pair of piercing green eyes that complemented her bright-pink, dermal-filled lips.

Unlike the others in the room who were all looking relatively casual, she was dressed in what seemed to him to be a designer mint-green dress, with slits down the arms, and matching stiletto shoes.

However, it was actually her magnetism, of which she seemed well aware, and a sharp, almost predatory, facial expression that drew Richard's eye to her more than anyone else in the room.

Privately, he thought she had the potential to be a rare handful for any police officer to engage with.

He'd come across a couple of women of her ilk before in his line of work. They had been proprietors of fabulously expensive stolen pieces of art and neither of them had made his job any the easier because of their incessant and unrealistic demands on his team's time and resources. Their behavior, he felt, stemmed from an ingrained sense of entitlement and from having been spoilt from a very young age.

As he turned around to speak to Nkiruka, he clumsily knocked into the desk behind him and righted himself before he fell over.

Space was a little too tight for comfort in the penthouse suite and he was beginning to wonder if he was destined to spend the meeting standing up like poor Sofia.

"Sorry I'm late, Niki. I was held up," he said, apologetically.

Nkiruka didn't acknowledge his apology by so much as a flicker of an eyelid.

"Everybody, this is Chief Inspector Richard

Langley of the Art and Antiquities Unit," she said, waving a careless hand in his direction.

She stood up and picked up her briefcase.

"Richard, you're just in time. We're heading to a conference room downstairs.

The hotel has been kind enough to put it at our disposal this afternoon because there's not enough room in here for all of us," explained Nkiruka, as she straightened her suit jacket.

"That does makes sense," agreed Richard, as the others began to gather up their things prior to leaving the room.

He stood politely to one side as, one by one, the others walked out of the penthouse to the lift outside.

"Tut, tut, tut," said Johnny, in a low voice, standing alongside Richard as they watched three of the Fernandes family members taking the lift to the ground floor with Sofia. "What happened to you, mate? Supposed to be here twenty minutes ago. The boss isn't happy about it, I can tell you."

Richard shrugged.

"I was tied up in a meeting at the Royal Academy. It ran on a bit, as these things tend to do."

A look of respect appeared in Johnny's eyes.

"Rather you than me, Richard. You'll be lucky if Nkiruka lets you get a word in edgeways. She isn't in a forgiving mood today."

Before Richard could ask him about this intriguing nugget of information, Johnny had walked off to join Nkiruka, who was busy listening to messages on her mobile while she waited for the lift to return.

"So, you're the art detective?" asked a soft, accented voice behind Richard.

"Yes, indeed," said Richard, turning around and shaking the delicate hand that was proffered him.

He found himself enveloped in a waft of rich perfume and looking into a pair of unblinking, pale-green eyes.

The lady on the pink chair had noticed him or, at the very least, his interest in her.

"I thought so," said the lady with satisfaction. "You have unusual mannerisms, if you don't mind me saying so, and you don't look like a policeman." She stared at him with her eyes half-shut and he could feel himself about to squirm under her scrutiny. "Yes, there's definitely something of the Bohemian about you... I'm Juliana Fernandes, by the way."

"Pleased to meet you, Juliana."

Juliana seemed a little taken aback by his lackluster response but she smiled graciously up at him anyway, displaying the full force of her charm.

Looking down at her pearl-white, even teeth and glittering, feline eyes, Richard sensed she was used to being treated as somebody special by the people around her.

For a few anxious seconds he searched his memory for a possible explanation before suddenly remembering Lionel mentioning her.

She's the soap star, he thought.

Although Lionel had informed him, a few days ago, that a famous Brazilian soap star was part of the Fernandes family group, it hadn't meant anything to him at the time because he'd never watched a soap opera in his life.

As far as he was concerned, life was too short to waste it watching make-believe human drama on television. As most police officers would testify, there was plenty of angst and emotion going on in people's everyday lives anyway. Too much of it, in Richard's opinion. That there happened to be a demand for yet more drama and tragedy on the TV screen completely baffled him.

In any case, he would never squander his time watching a substandard soap opera on television when he could escape to far more exciting and exotic worlds with his books.

He glanced at the elegant lady next to him.

He didn't know if the Brazilian police were in the habit of kowtowing whenever they came across Juliana Fernandes but he doubted Nkiruka would stoop to doing this and he certainly wasn't planning to, either.

He guessed, though, that Johnny might bend over backwards for Juliana. Johnny was the kind of man who would be impressed by star dust from any country or continent, no matter how insignificant.

Richard smiled back at Juliana, disguising his less-than-charitable thoughts about her.

"I'm sorry for your loss," he commiserated, thinking to himself that under her self-assurance there seemed to be no sign of any genuine grief.

A spasm of distress appeared briefly on Juliana's expressionless, botoxed face. "I'm sad, of course, to lose my father but he was already a very old man and he'd lived a full life, you know? But my nephew? His death has devastated the whole family. He was a very bright and talented young man. His death's a total tragedy."

"Yes, he was too young to die," agreed Richard, nodding his head. "I very much hope we'll be able to catch their killers but it's not a clear-cut case, unfortunately."

"We'll be very disappointed if Scotland Yard doesn't find the murderers, Chief Inspector. We're putting our faith and trust in the British police," Juliana said, almost sternly.

"Rest assured, we'll do everything we can."

He looked behind him.

"Shall we make our way downstairs, Juliana?" he suggested, stepping over the threshold and into the corridor.

Juliana nodded and followed him out, shutting the door firmly behind them.

"We're intrigued to hear what you have to say to us, Chief Inspector Langley," remarked Juliana, as they walked along the corridor to where Johnny and Nkiruka were waiting for the lift to arrive.

It had to be the first time anyone had ever said such a thing to him, thought Richard, his sense of humor getting the better of him. Most people tended to switch off when he was in full flow.

"I'm very flattered," he said, uncertain where she was heading with her fulsome compliment.

"Yes, you see, my poor father was very interested in art," explained Juliana. "He has some beautiful and rare pieces of art in Brazil. He owns a small sculpture by Rodin, among other things."

Richard glanced down at her to make sure she wasn't pulling his leg. A Rodin? It seemed incredible.

"Goodness! I hope you have it well protected," he said, trying to sound blasé when in truth he was utterly gobsmacked at the thought of a Rodin sculpture sitting out on display in Paolo's Brazilian home.

"Of course," said Juliana, with a hint of bitterness in her voice. "My father always had the best security at his home. He was extreme in his desire to protect his possessions and he cared about them more than he cared about his children or grandchildren. It was a lifetime's obsession for him."

"Well, he was wise to have good security if there's a Rodin in his home," commented Richard, trying to be diplomatic and steer the conversation away from sensitive subject matters.

He wasn't quite sure how to respond to Juliana's outspoken comments. Reserved himself, he speculated whether her directness was simply a result of their cultural differences. He was sure Brazilians were bound to be less inhibited and uptight than the British, and although Juliana's style of conversation was making him feel like he was being hit by a sledgehammer, he had to admit he did admire her blunt honesty.

The lift pinged as its doors opened.

The four of them walked into the lift, with Johnny and Richard letting the ladies go in first.

Johnny hit the ground floor button and then turned around to stare admiringly at Juliana, who was standing next to him and staring up at the ceiling as if she wished she was elsewhere.

Juliana's potent perfume filled the enclosed space, making Richard feel nauseous, but her scent didn't seem to be putting off Johnny.

On the contrary, chuffed to be in such close proximity to a famous actress, he had a broad smile on his face.

As they descended at what felt like a snail's pace to

the ground floor, Richard caught Johnny's eye and saw him wink surreptitiously at him.

He smiled and felt himself relaxing.

It looked as though Johnny was prepared to go along with the flow and enjoy himself. Thinking about it, Richard decided he should try to follow his example and do the same.

There were high stakes for them at the meeting, though, in terms of finding out what Paolo's true identity was and whether he'd been in contact with the murderers.

Feeling a sudden craving for caffeine, Richard hoped the hotel would be providing tea and coffee.

When they reached the conference room, Richard found the hotel had indeed exceeded his expectations because at the entrance there was a sideboard with thermos flasks labeled "*tea*" and "*coffee*," as well as a large platter filled with foil-wrapped chocolate biscuits and a tray of china cups and saucers.

Johnny immediately designated himself as server and proceeded to pour out drinks for everyone while Sofia, the liaison officer, introduced the other members of the Fernandes family to Richard.

It turned out Paolo's only son was called Oscar and he was an architect with a busy and thriving practice in San Paolo.

Remembering Paolo's passport photograph, Richard thought the son looked very different to his father, for he had dark brown eyes and hair, a rounder face and his mouth was fuller and larger than his father's.

Oscar seemed highly strung that afternoon, tapping his pen on the conference table and shifting in his seat as though he had itchy underwear on, leaving Richard guessing whether it was the stress of his father's demise or being away from his business so long that was causing his uneasiness.

Then he remembered Alonso, Oscar's son, who had been murdered alongside his grandfather, and felt ashamed of himself for losing his empathy and forgetting for a brief moment the horror the Fernandes family were facing with their trip to London.

Christina and Pepa were introduced to him next, Paolo's eldest and youngest daughters.

Christina, the eldest-born daughter, seemed emotionally frail, clutching Pepa's hand and finding it hard to look anyone in the eye. Sofia explained she worked as an administrator at the university in Rio de Janeiro.

She was a small woman, with crow's feet on the edges of her eyes and lines around her forehead and mouth, so she clearly hadn't accessed the cosmetic aids Juliana had used to great effect on her own flawless skin. Christina's dark hair was brightened in places by her incoming white hair, giving her complexion a more luminous and gentler appearance than her stylish sister and making her seem far more approachable.

Pepa, a primary school teacher, was the youngest daughter and it was obvious she had a special and close bond with Christina. Bolder than her nervous sister, she had a full face of make-up and her hair was tinted an unfortunate shade of red, the streaks in it making her look like she was carrying a tabby cat on her head.

Pepa and Christina had the light-blue eyes of their father and his pale skin type, as well as inheriting his straight nose and thin lips.

Both sisters also looked considerably older than

Juliana, who had now seated herself next to Oscar and was gazing placidly out of the window as she sipped her tea.

Richard was almost expecting her to lift her little finger as she drank it. Juliana turned and smiled as Nkiruka introduced her to the group.

"May I ask where Luca's relations are?" Nkiruka asked Oscar, who seemed to be the de facto head of the family and, along with Juliana, the most fluent in the English language too.

"Luca's relations live in the Rocinha favela in Rio," Oscar explained. "They're very poor and Luca's salary was supporting his siblings and his mother. We offered to pay for them to come here but they preferred to wait until his body's repatriated and then use the money for his funeral. We'll, of course, be giving them ongoing financial support for the foreseeable future. They are devastated by his death and they want to see the killers brought to justice."

"Of course," said Nkiruka, a slight tremor to her voice.

Looking across at Nkiruka, Richard thought he could detect the glimmer of unshed tears in her dark eyes but he might have been mistaken. He sensed Nkiruka wasn't quite the toughie Johnny was making her out to be.

Johnny, meantime, was nodding along at Oscar's explanation for the absence of Luca's family, appearing to understand their perspective all too well.

As he drank some more coffee, Richard thought about Luca's family and how horrendous it must be to lose a close relative in a far-flung country. He could empathize with their agony. There was no closure

without the body. Having to wait for the paperwork and
bureaucracy of repatriating the body to get done, while
their loved one was lying dead in an anonymous
morgue across the ocean, seemed too cruel.

"Right, thank you for meeting with us today," said
Nkiruka, slowly, so Sofia could keep up with any
necessary translating. "We're terribly sorry for your
loss."

Nkiruka waited for Sofia to translate, but despite
the language barrier Richard had noticed that every
member of the Fernandes family seemed to grasp the
English language to some extent. Hopefully, that would
make their meeting a little less arduous.

Nkiruka glanced across at Oscar's rigid face.

"And we can only imagine how awful this is for
you. We'd like to find the perpetrators, but in order to
do this we need to ask you for any information you can
give us on Paolo, Alonso and even Luca, actually, that
might have a bearing on the case. For example, were
you aware of anyone over here who knew that the three
of them were travelling to London?"

Nkiruka paused for a moment while Sofia translated this for the family. Richard watched the facial
expressions on the siblings" faces.

Christina seemed uncomfortable.

The rest only seemed to be confused by the
question.

After Sofia had finished, Juliana shrugged her
shoulders as though none of this had anything to do
with her.

"I've nothing to say," she said in her impeccable
English. "I've a very busy life back at home and I saw
very little of the old man."

She looked at her family for a moment and then turned to face Nkiruka.

"We saw as little as possible of him. Paolo was not a kind or forgiving father and we have all been in some form of therapy during our adult years because of him," she added. "I hope you weren't expecting us to be the equivalent of *The Brady Bunch* because nothing could be further from the truth."

Her siblings seemed shocked by her candidness and they stared at her in a communal silent rebuke.

"*Quê?*" Juliana said angrily, glaring at them. "They're the police and we want to find out who did this. We're not going to get very far if we don't tell them how things were."

After a brief and awkward silence, Oscar sighed.

"Yes, what Juliana says is correct. We didn't see much of my father but we made sure he had everything he needed and was well cared for. Christina checked on him the most," he said, turning to his sister with a fond smile.

Sofia translated this and Christina smiled sweetly back at her brother.

"*Eu sabia que poderia te pegar se precisasse de você.*"

"I knew I could catch you if I needed you," said Sofia.

"*Claro, Christina,*" said Oscar. "*Mas você fez mais.*"

"Of course, Christina. But you did more," translated Sofia.

Oscar looked at Nkiruka.

"I knew a little about my father's past and it's one of the reasons I moved to San Paolo and away from Rio. I wanted some distance between us after what he told me. I warned my son not to go with him on this trip but he refused to listen to me. He loved his grandfather and couldn't understand my reluctance to go and see him. Paolo, of course, spoilt him rotten," said Oscar bitterly, his voice wavering and his eyes filling with tears. "*Idiota!* If only Alonso had listened to me he would still be alive and safe. Why my father decided to drag him over to London with him, I'll never know."

Oscar sobbed out loud and pulled a handkerchief from his breast pocket.

Tears began to stream down his face. As he wiped them away, Juliana, looking upset, put her arms around him and hugged him.

"Oscar, *acalme-se,*" said Pepa. "*Não foi sua culpa.*"

"Calm down. It wasn't your fault," repeated Sofia, looking embarrassed.

"*Você não vê, eu sabia o que ele era,*" said Oscar, in between gasps.

"Don't you see, I knew what he was," translated Sofia, softly, from across the table.

"Oscar, how much did you know about your father's younger years?" asked Richard, after a couple of minutes.

Again, he closely observed the family's expressions as Sofia translated for him.

He could see from the blank faces of the others that Oscar alone was the one who knew something about Paolo's former life in Germany.

Oscar, though, didn't answer Richard's question.

Bent over the table, he continued to sob and wipe away his tears while his siblings looked on, distressed and unhappy.

Christina was crying silently, too, now and Pepa

was casting resentful glances at Richard, Johnny and Nkiruka, looking understandably irate that their private grief was shared with the police in the room.

Once Oscar's tears had abated somewhat, Nkiruka, frustrated by their lack of progress, patiently repeated Richard's question to him.

"Oscar, what did you know about your father's past? I hope you understand we're trying to find the killers and bring them to justice," she said, her tone serene and reasoned.

As Sofia translated this, Oscar managed to pull himself together.

Gulping back his sobs and wiping his face a couple more times, he sat upright again.

He was in no hurry to speak, though. A few minutes passed, with everyone around the table waiting for him to talk.

Staring down at his hands, Oscar took in a few deep breaths to calm himself.

Thinking of the hefty workload on his desk back at Scotland Yard, Richard wondered if Oscar was ever going to tell them anything of value. It was quite possible their meeting would turn out to be a disappointment and a complete waste of time.

If so, he would prefer to get back to the office sooner rather than later.

"To be honest, I don't care about what happened to my father because he wasn't an innocent man. He had blood on his hands," Oscar said at last, pulling his shirt cuffs down as though finding some inner resolve in doing so. "But I want justice for my poor boy. He'd nothing to do with any of it and he never deserved to die."

There was quiet in the room as everyone waited to hear what else Oscar had to say but they waited in vain.

Instead of speaking, Oscar bent down and picked up his briefcase.

Opening the briefcase up, he pulled out a large, rectangular wooden box and placed it on the table. He handled the box as though it made him feel disgusted.

After dumping the briefcase back on the floor, he lifted up the lid of the box.

"Who tortures an old man like that?" asked Oscar, looking directly at Nkiruka as he held on tightly to the box lid. "Someone deranged, who's angry and wants revenge. That was my first thought when I heard what had happened in London. I immediately went to my father's house and searched through his desk, because he was an avid collector and I knew he wouldn't be able to resist keeping mementos from his past."

Pulling a medal and its ribbon out of the box, he laid it carefully on the table in front of him.

Everyone leaned forward to take a closer look.

Johnny, smitten with curiosity, was standing up and bending right over his half of the table to get a better view.

The ribbon was edged in black and white, with a thick red line in its center. The silver-colored medal was in the shape of a cross.

Richard recognised the shape of the cross straight-away. It was the type of cross used during the Middle Ages and was often associated with the crusading knights of the Teutonic Order.

In the center of the cross there was the relief of a Nazi swastika.

15

Richard

"It's the Knight's Cross of the Iron Cross. Awarded to Nazis for bravery before the enemy or for excellence in commanding troops," Oscar clarified.

His siblings gasped.

"*Ele era um Nazista,*" he told them, almost defiantly, as they muttered between themselves.

"He was a Nazi," said Sofia.

"But why would he tell you this and not your sisters?" blurted out Johnny, confused.

Oscar leaned forward, elbows on the table and his fingers interlaced, and looked him in the eye.

"I don't know. Maybe because I was his only son. Maybe because he was drunk. Maybe because after losing his wife, he felt his own mortality closing in. What do I know? He told me one night, only a few days after my mother had been buried. He was drunk, too, of course, or else I don't think he would've said anything about it. He was too careful for that."

"Do you know what his real name was?" asked

Nkiruka, quietly. Reaching into the box again, Oscar withdrew a tattered piece of paper.

"Yes, his German name according to the papers I found in his desk was...Wolfgang Max Axel Bormann and he became a Colonel in the 1st SS Panzer Division Leibstandarte SS Adolf Hitler," Oscar said, reading from the piece of paper he had pulled out of the box. He looked across at them. "My father told me that he served in both Poland and Italy during the Second World War. He also admitted he was involved in what's called the Lake Maggiore Massacres and the killing of the Jewish banker Ettore Ovazza in North Italy..."

Pepa interrupted and asked Oscar to translate for them.

While Oscar explained what he had just said in Portuguese to his sisters, the others sat in resigned silence waiting for his siblings to catch up.

Pepa, Christina and Juliana appeared stunned as they listened to what Oscar had to say.

Noticing the look of disbelief and denial on their faces, Oscar pulled out a pile of black-and-white photos from the box on his lap and put them onto the table.

"Some people have porn hidden in their rooms for their arousal, my father kept these instead," said Oscar, his voice harsh with suppressed emotion.

He turned a few of the photos around and pushed them across the table towards Nkiruka, Johnny, and Richard and then passed the rest to his sisters.

Richard picked one up from the pile and looked at it.

In the photo was a pile of naked, scrawny bodies, lying in a dirty, dug-out ditch.

The bodies looked as though they had been tossed in.

Picking up and studying another photo, he saw two Nazi soldiers posing and smiling as they carried a sack, obviously containing a body, towards a boat.

Bit by bit, Richard inspected every photograph, ignoring the chatter from around the table.

Some photographs were of Nazi soldiers smiling in front of the camera and others were simply close-ups of dead people, with each of their faces showing a different expression. In the throes of death, some seemed to be at peace, others were frozen in their distress or agony.

Across the table, Christina and Pepa started to cry.

Juliana, meanwhile, was looking frightened, as though she could sense turbulent waters ahead.

Richard wondered if she was worried about the implications for her career and her fans' perception of her, should Paolo's past become public knowledge.

It was very hard to tell what exact emotions were swirling around in the different minds of the Fernandes family but what was paramount in everyone was the shock.

Putting the last few photos down, Richard rubbed at his chin.

"Did your father ever mention the Night of Broken Glass to you, Oscar?" he asked, hoping some more evidence might be forthcoming regarding the origin of the Chagall paintings.

Oscar sighed, clasping his hands again.

"Yes, he did. He told me the Kristallnacht was the first time he'd killed anyone and that it left a lasting impression on him. I sensed that he grew indifferent to the killing later on in the war but those two nights really shook him up. He was very young when it happened."

"Oscar, did you not think that your father should've faced justice for some of his war crimes? Like so many of the other Nazis did?" asked Nkiruka, sounding cross.

Averting his eyes, Oscar waited while Sofia translated for Pepa and Christina, who were finding it hard to follow the conversation.

When Sofia finished talking, he crossed his arms.

With thick stubble encircling his chin, bloodshot eyes and the two half-moon grey shadows beneath them, Oscar looked a wreck of a man.

"Well, he's faced a justice of sorts now, hasn't he? And so have I... No, I didn't tell my siblings or anyone about it, and as a result I have to live with the truth that if I'd made Paolo's past public knowledge, my son might be alive today. Alonso would have been disgusted by his grandfather's behavior. He would have distanced himself, I'm sure of it. He would not have gone to London with his grandfather and would instead be living his life in Brazil."

Oscar sighed heavily.

"Believe me, it'll torture me to the end of my days. It wasn't an easy decision for me to make. Looking back, my God, I wish I'd been strong enough to expose him but I was repulsed by him and afraid of him at the same time. It was too difficult for me to move past the father-son relationship we had."

Oscar buried his head in his hands.

"Juliana's already told you, we were in therapy because of him. He frightened us as children," he continued. "My overriding instinct was to stay away from him as much as possible and he knew why I felt like that. I think he took pleasure in deliberately cultivating a close relationship with Alonso, to punish me for my disloyalty or whatever he thought it was."

He sighed again and sat in silence while Sofia began to translate again.

"I was a coward," Oscar admitted, suddenly, interrupting Sofia in mid-flow. "But, even so, his sins were not mine."

Oscar's head of thick brown hair was tousled by now, and consumed by his grief and anguish he looked a madder version of the man who'd sat down at the start of the meeting.

Richard felt sorry for him.

Oscar had a receding hairline, but other than that he looked extraordinarily young for his age. It made him look naïve and vulnerable. A weak man, no doubt. His rounded features lent a softness to his persona, which only emphasized how he'd been unable to stand up to his tougher and wilier father.

"Christina, do you know of anyone who was in touch with your father from here? Maybe even corresponding with your father before he left Brazil?" asked Nkiruka, turning her attention to Paolo's eldest daughter.

Christina seemed surprised by Nkiruka's sudden change of tack but she listened carefully as Sofia translated.

Stretching out his legs and leaning back on his chair, Richard was pleased Nkiruka had asked the question.

It had been clear to him from the start of the meeting that Christina was uneasy and had something to share. As the family member who had visited Paolo the most, she was bound to know the people who had been involved with her father.

"*Meu pai estava falando no telephone com un homem chamado Paul Abbott,*" said Christina quietly. "*Um investigador particular de Sharpes. Quando ele nos contou que ele estava indo para Londres, ele disse que ia encontrar com parentes de Joel Yurkovich. Ele tinha início da demência. Eu nâo tinha idéia que ele ia fazer. Ele não estava em seu juízo perfeito.*"

"She says that her father was speaking to a man called Paul Abbott on the telephone, who was a private investigator from Sharpes," explained Sofia. "When Paolo left for London he told her he was going to be meeting with relatives of a man called Joel Yurkovich. She says that, in her view, Paolo had the beginnings of dementia and she really had no idea what he was planning to do with these people. He wasn't in his right mind."

"Didn't she try to stop him? Given his age and possible dementia?" asked Nkiruka.

Sofia translated for this for her. Christina laughed mirthlessly.

"*Não. Ninguém poderia dizer a ele o que fazer. Luca estava com ele.*"

Her face looking sad, Christina shrugged.

"No. Nobody could tell him what to do," Sofia repeated to Nkiruka. "Luca was with him."

The more Richard heard about Paolo, the more he disliked him. For an elderly man to be such a tyrant to his fully grown, adult children proved what an unpleasant man he must have been throughout his life. It was a pity he hadn't been murdered early on, thought Richard, because then the world might have been spared some of the atrocities he had carried out.

He was well aware this wasn't a view any policeman should be advocating for but, privately, he believed that there should be rare exceptions to the rule of law with some dangerous criminals. For obvious reasons, he didn't tend to broadcast this controversial opinion and the few people he did confide in were like-minded and tended to agree with this point of view.

He recognised the major flaws in his reasoning, though. Who was going to judge whether a murder for the greater good was justified or not? He often wondered if the bosses at MI6 ever had this quandary.

Shaking off his vengeful thoughts on justice, Richard tuned into the conversation at the table again.

"Do you know who Joel Yurkovich was?" Nkiruka asked Christina, understandably intrigued.

This time Sofia didn't have to translate.

Christina shook her head.

"*Não, eu não sabia quem ele era.*"

It was obvious Christina had no idea who he was.

Nothing ever came easy, thought Richard.

Nkiruka was going to have to chase up the private investigator, Paul Abbott, to find out who Joel Yurkovich was and establish what on earth his connection to Paolo was.

Digging deeper into the case only seemed to bring to the surface additional, convoluted information and secrets, always with Paolo at the center of them.

The man was certainly complex.

The room had gone very quiet after Christina's denial and Richard decided to take the opportunity to ask a few questions that were bugging him.

"I wanted to ask a few questions, if I may," said Richard, thinking back to the Chagall paintings.

The Fernandes family nodded but looked warily at him. So much disconcerting, painful information had already cropped up during their meeting and now, before they'd had a chance to lick their wounds, they were no doubt wondering what Richard was going to hit them with next.

"We're in possession of two paintings that Paolo brought with him to London and we have good reason to suppose they were stolen from a family around the Night of Broken Glass. Did he tell you about them?"

After Sofia had translated this, every single family member looked mystified. They shook their heads, their eyes glued on Richard.

"I see. Juliana has told me that Paolo has many works of art in his house. Do you know where he acquired them all?"

Again, the family as one shook their heads but Juliana was also beginning to look suspicious.

"Are you suggesting he was also a thief?" she asked outright, clasping her handbag tightly.

"The Chagall paintings we've in custody seem to have been stolen from a Jewish family during the Night of Broken Glass. There's ample evidence for this and we're working on finding more, in order to make this a legally clear-cut outcome for the Jewish family they should belong to. But it seems, from what you're saying, Paolo was quite an art collector, and I wonder what other treasures he brought with him to Brazil and whether they were legally acquired. Do you know if he had an inventory or kept any receipts?"

"He'll have an inventory in his house," said Oscar, with certainty. "He was very, very meticulous. He does have a nice collection of artworks, although not substantial. I don't know if they are particularly valuable."

"Some of his pieces are incredibly valuable," argued Juliana, looking angry and upset. "You've no idea what you're talking about, Oscar. When did you last spend time with Paolo? He talked me through his entire art collection on several occasions as I was the only one in the family who appreciated art and liked to paint and draw. He has in his house a small Rodin sculpture, three Goya pen and ink drawings, a sketch by Tintoretto, paintings by Kazimir Malevich, Piet Mondrian, Francis Bacon, and a very small Cézanne painting."

Oscar looked bewildered.

"If you are planning to take his art away, you'll find yourself with a fight on your hands," said Juliana fiercely, turning to face Richard. "You can't make assumptions like this, and as for the paintings you've in custody, I presume they're valuable?"

"Yes, they are as a matter of fact. They're two oil paintings by Chagall."

"Madre mia!" muttered Juliana, shocked.

"Juliana, I'm warning you, do not follow in Paolo's footsteps. This stops now," rebuked Oscar. "We'll look carefully into his collection and we'll make sure that none of it has been stolen. If some, or all of it, has been stolen, we have to return the items to the people they belonged to. We must break the cycle now, don't you see that?"

"I don't see that at all, unless there's legal proof or evidence," replied Juliana, her face flushed.

"You'll find it very hard to sell those pieces if Paolo has no proof of purchase or even provenance for them. Given what we now know about the Chagall paintings, some of his collection might be traceable to war crimes committed during the Second World War and could well be reported as missing or stolen," said Richard calmly.

"We might not want to sell them but instead keep them in the family," declared Juliana. "I'd be happy to have my father's artworks in my house and pass them on to my children when the time comes."

"Não seja ridículo, Juliana," scolded Oscar.

"Você é aquele que está louco," repudiated Juliana.

There was no need for Sofia to translate their conversation. The heated tone in which Oscar and Juliana were speaking to each other said it all.

Richard sighed.

Juliana's attitude wasn't unexpected. Whenever there was money or items of great value people had a habit of becoming fiercely possessive. He could see there was a gargantuan argument brewing between Juliana and Oscar over Paolo's art collection.

He wasn't giving up on securing Paolo's art collection. He would sort it out, with or without the cooperation of his family.

As soon as the meeting was over he was planning to contact (hopefully with Sofia's help) the Brazilian NCB, which was Interpol's Bureau in Brazil, and ask them to go to Paolo's house before anything disreputable happened to his precious artworks. With the evidence from the Dorin family, plus the additional information Oscar had brought to their meeting on his father, they were well within their rights to confiscate Paolo's artworks until their legitimacy and provenance were firmly established.

"Right, is there anything else that you feel would be helpful for us to know?" asked Nkiruka, already gathering up her papers and putting them away in her briefcase.

"We, of course, appreciate your openness and honesty with everything you've told us so far."

"No, there's nothing else. Except Paolo also kept some gold items in this box and I don't know if he took them off his victims or not," admitted Oscar, lifting a bag out of the box.

He emptied out a big, tangled clump of gold items onto the table. He slowly separated out the pieces of jewelry.

In total, there were twelve watch chains, five brooches with different stones in them and a medley of rings: thirteen signet rings and six dress rings with large stones in them.

Pepa, Christina, and Juliana looked on, horrified, as they watched their brother picking out the individual gold items.

Richard looked down at the pile on the table.

"I should imagine that unless the items are very distinctive, Oscar, it will be near impossible to trace where they came from," he said, picking up one of the signet rings and inspecting it. "I'd keep these with a clear conscience."

His face expressionless, Oscar nodded and proceeded to put the items back into the bag.

"How long are you staying in London?" asked Johnny, interested.

"We leave in four days" time," said Oscar, looking weary. "All of us have work to get back to in Brazil. It would be a real bonus for us if you manage to find the perpetrators before we go, obviously. We want closure on this and the sooner the better. My poor wife is at home with her sister, doping up on sleeping pills and spending her days crying in the bedroom."

"We'll do our best, Oscar," reassured Nkiruka, pushing her chair back and standing up. "We'll devote as many resources to this as we can. I'm optimistic, with the information we've gathered here today, that we'll make some headway soon."

Johnny stood up and handed his card to Oscar.

"Feel free to call me at any time, should you feel the need. If there are any new developments, I'll let you know."

Oscar nodded, taking his wallet out of his trouser pocket and carefully inserting Johnny's business card in it.

"I'm truly sorry about your loss," said Nkiruka, earnestly, leaning forward with her fingers on the table. "And we do really appreciate you talking to us today. I know it must have been very difficult for you. Sofia and I will be with you for the press conference you're holding here tomorrow. In the meantime, we'll do everything we can to get to the bottom of this terrible crime and give you some form of closure."

Sofia translated as the Fernandes siblings sat subdued and quiet on their side of the table.

They smiled weakly at Nkiruka.

"Thank you for your help," said Juliana shortly, speaking for them all.

With that Richard, Johnny and Nkiruka left the conference room, instinctively knowing the family needed more time to talk without them there.

As Richard left the room, he turned to look at the family one last time and saw them looking at each other, devastated. Even Juliana, with her mask-like features, was managing to radiate her unhappiness as she sat stock-still in her chair, her head bowed.

He hoped for their sakes they would be doing something nice later on with what was left of the afternoon.

In his case the time would be spent signing off eight art theft files where his team had concluded there was no possible means of tracking down the stolen property or the thieves. Depressing stuff.

Each of the eight items was one of a kind, irreplaceable. Treasures that were now hiding out of sight, having vanished into the hands of professional art thieves. The stolen artifacts included an ancient Chinese jade lion from the Zhou dynasty, stolen during the early hours of the morning from the Fitzwilliam Museum in Cambridge.

There was also Mary Queen of Scots" pocket watch, which was taken from Traquair, the ancient royal hunting lodge in Scotland, during a false fire alarm.

Richard was under no illusion. He could well be retired by the time any of these items resurfaced, if at all.

Despite the pessimistic forecast for his afternoon,

Eilidh had unexpectedly good news on his arrival at Scotland Yard.

He walked into their basement office carrying two takeaway coffees in a cardboard holder and a couple of slices of carrot cake, having picked them up at Treats Takeaway on his way from Westminster Tube Station.

He knew the rest of the team were out of the office that afternoon on different assignments and Eilidh had never yet turned down the offer of a free coffee.

"Richard, they've managed to catch the Botticelli thief at Penrhyn," said Eilidh, spinning around on her chair to face him as he walked into their office.

"Really? How on earth did they do that? Did the Bangor police track him down?" asked Richard, genuinely astonished.

As time had passed he hadn't really expected the Penrhyn thief to be caught. He had been satisfied to have at least returned the precious Botticelli painting back to the castle, which was far more important to him than apprehending the culprit.

He went over to his desk, pulled Eilidh's coffee free from the holder and handed it over to her.

Eilidh took the coffee gratefully, sipping it as Richard logged into his computer and sorted out his paperwork.

"So, go on! Tell me what happened," said Richard at last, looking across at her while he laid out the carrot cake on a paper plate.

Eilidh snorted and then burst out laughing, setting down her coffee in a hurry as her shoulders and arms began to shake.

Richard looked at her, bemused. He struggled to see what she found so funny about the arrest of an art thief who had the gall to steal a phenomenally expensive painting from under the noses of the staff at Penrhyn Castle.

Smiling politely at her laughter, he drank his coffee and nibbled at some carrot cake as he waited for her to speak, enjoying feeling the much-needed sugar boost from the thick layer of icing kick in.

After a minute, Eilidh recovered from her laughter.

She watched as Richard helped himself to some more carrot cake and got up to nab a left-over corner with her fingers.

"Mmm. Tasty!" she exclaimed, with her mouth full of cake. Munching on it, she sat back down on her chair.

"Yes, I know, but you were going to tell me about the Botticelli thief," said Richard, patiently.

"Oh, yes," remembered Eilidh, starting to giggle again. "I don't know if you remember Baqir, the security guard?" Richard nodded. "Well, Baqir Malouf has excelled himself. He should be given a job by Scotland Yard because he's damn persistent... He wasn't happy to be taken on a goose chase by the thief on the night of the robbery but he's damn well got his own back on him now."

"How?" asked Richard, absentmindedly looking at the Post-it notes on his desk while she spoke.

"Baqir set up a camera inside the Ruined Chapel, linking it to his mobile phone and a few other devices. Sure enough, he caught the thief returning to fetch the painting from under the ivy."

"Well, it seems Peter did tell the guards what had happened then."

"Yes, he only told the four security guards, though, so they could take this into account when patrolling the castle. The robbery was a major security flaw."

"Yes, true."

"Anyway, Baqir had some patience because it's no joke to be constantly watching what's happening on a camera screen. Peter Griffiths told me that Baqir got some of his family members roped in, with them using their own devices and keeping an eye on the camera. Including, believe it or not, his house-bound granny," said Eilidh, trying not to laugh again. "She watched the camera on her TV at home, apparently. I'm not sure about the legality of it but Peter's quite willing to turn a blind eye and accept Baqir's antics as authorized surveillance by the National Trust. To be honest, if we'd had the time we might have thought of doing it ourselves."

"But there's no proof he was the thief."

"He confessed to it, Richard. Cracked really easily from what Peter says. He wasn't a hardened criminal."

"So, who was it?"

"Rhys Hopkins. He admitted to the theft after the Bangor police were called in." "Really? Gosh, I didn't see that coming."

"Neither did I but in retrospect it makes sense because he was part of the security team at Penrhyn and one of the few who knew about the painting in the office."

Richard nodded wearily and reached for some more carrot cake.

"Richard, are you OK?" asked Eilidh, looking concerned and putting down her coffee.

Rubbing his face, Richard sighed.

"Yeah, I'm fine. It was just a bit of a heavy meeting

with the Fernandes family." 'did you get any more information about the Chagalls?"

"No, no other evidence on the Chagalls, but Paolo seems to have quite a treasure trove at his house in Brazil, some of which could have been stolen during the Second World War. I've arranged to meet with Sofia and call Interpol in Brazil about it later this afternoon. I called Oscar, Paolo's son, on the way here. He sent me the address and the number of the housekeeper and I'll pass on her details to Interpol. The housekeeper can let the police in."

Richard sighed and shrugged.

"Thankfully, Oscar's quite happy for us to look into Paolo's art collection. It's far better to get the family's cooperation on this. Juliana, his sister, is going to be a pain about it but she's overruled by her siblings on this one, or so Oscar says."

"Will the Dorins get the Chagall paintings, then?" asked Eilidh, curiously.

"I still have to find evidence that their receipt for the paintings is genuine before that can happen and also that the *L'Oiseau Bleu* existed. If I can get Lionel on side, it might warrant a trip to Paris to establish if there are any comparable records there, or even records of the Chagall purchase itself."

Richard drank some of his coffee.

"I've discovered the *L'Oiseau Bleu* gallery was taken over by another gallery called *La Maison d'Art*," he said, putting his cup down again. "Not very original, is it? Anyway, the gallery staff weren't keen to talk to me over the phone. I think if I go in person, I could tap my contacts in Paris and also see if *La Maison d'Art* will be more forthcoming in providing information on their predecessor, as well as pointing us in the direction of the all-important records we need to prove ownership. We can't sit on these multi-million-pound paintings forever. Sooner or later, we're going to have to return them to the Fernandes family or the Dorin family."

"A trip to Paris? I'll be surprised if you manage to wangle that one from Lionel but then again, you always were a jammy sod," said Eilidh, getting up and grabbing another sliver of carrot cake from the plate on Richard's desk.

Richard swallowed the remains of his coffee, watching her.

"Fancy coming with me?" he asked suddenly, feeling emboldened. "Nothing ventured with Lionel, nothing gained."

"Yeah, of course, I'm always game," said Eilidh, surprised by the invitation. Standing by his desk, she popped the piece of carrot cake into her mouth. Richard smiled.

"Two heads are always better than one," he said. "Though I don't suppose you know any French, do you?"

Eilidh shook her head.

"GCSE French," she said, mumbling as she chewed and then swallowed the cake. "Which in this country, of course, means nothing that'll be of any use in France. I know the verbs inside out but I can't speak a word of the lingo. *Rien, monsieur.*"

"It's not going to be luxury. It'll be Eurostar and the cheapest hotel possible."

"Richard, are you going all romantic on me?" asked Eilidh, looking at him with a mischievous smile on her face.

She laughed out loud when she saw him lost for words.

Reaching down, she cuffed him lightly on the shoulder.

"Come on, Richard, anything in Paris has got to be a step up from a dusty basement office at Scotland Yard or a stag night at The Penrhyn Inn."

16

Nkiruka

Nkiruka reached out and grabbed the half-eaten plowman's sandwich lying on the paper serviette in front of her.

Taking a large mouthful of bread, cheese, pickles and chutney, she started chewing while she stared at her computer screen.

She was reading through the concluding statement on the rape and murder of a woman who had been returning to her flat, late one evening, from Waterloo station.

The woman's familiar route home had been scoped by the killer and she was forcibly led into Bernie Spain Gardens by her abductor, who had been carrying a knife. He killed her shortly after raping her but her screams during the ordeal were heard by pedestrians near the park, who called out the police. Arriving too late to save the woman, they found the body after rummaging through the undergrowth and they then secured the area for forensics.

The CCTV footage hadn't been clear enough to

identify the suspect although
near Bernie Spain Gardens ᵛ
wearing a distinctive red coat

    In the end, the police ha(
given by a couple of eyewitnes:
report seeing a woman strugglir
of Duchy Street. Why no one
there appeared to be a woman in distress was a ...
point. Nowadays, few people cared to intervene in
crimes, understandably fearful of the repercussions.

    The police identified the suspect's DNA from
semen found in her body and from a couple of stray
hairs on her coat. They then proceeded to turn the
focus of their enquiries to a short-stay homeless hostel
which was located in the close vicinity of the suspect's
first CCTV image.

    Using the physical description of the attacker given
by the two eyewitnesses, they found a DNA match in a
Hungarian man staying at the homeless shelter and the
police found he had a criminal record in Budapest
which would have easily secured him a place in HMP
Belmarsh.

    Munching another piece of sandwich, Nkiruka
leaned back on her seat.

    She felt uncomfortable with the nature of this
particular case because it was an absolute cliché to
think that the worst criminals came from either the
immigrant community or from deprivation. Some of the
most notorious criminals in UK history had led very
middle-class lives and were British. Take Harold Ship-
man, for example, or Jimmy Savile.

    Still, Lionel would be pleased to see another
completed case added to his spreadsheets and, despite

⸝ the tragedy of every murder she dealt ⸜iruka found it very satisfying to sign off a ρ⸝eted homicide case. The parents of the twenty-⸝ne-year-old woman would be grieving for the rest of their lives for a daughter who'd never given them cause for worry and had been a high-flying business woman at the time of her death, but at least justice had been served.

A justice of sorts, Nkiruka backtracked, fully aware that in their anger and grief, the relatives of such victims would probably prefer to have the rapist castrated and for a life sentence to actually mean life.

And that thought brought her mind back to Paolo Fernandes. Was he tortured and killed for his Nazi misdeeds?

She finished her last piece of stodgy sandwich and washed it down with a swig from her bottle of mineral water.

Looking at the bottle's plastic exterior, she wished she could magic up something more potent. The press conference with the Fernandes family earlier on that morning had left her feeling frazzled and in need of a strong drink. Right then, she was craving a soothing glass of Sauvignon from the bottle in her fridge and was counting down the hours for her work to finish so she could get home and enjoy one.

The journalists had done their research, of course, and after the Fernandes family had made their appeal for witnesses, they began to throw out a number of questions which Nkiruka couldn't, or didn't want to, answer.

Did the police have a profile of the killer?

No comment.

Why had the three men left Brazil to come to London?

No comment.

The Fernandes siblings squirmed in their seats at this question because their inability to answer it gave the impression they were uncaring or estranged.

Why had Paolo Fernandes been singled out for torture?

No comment.

Nkiruka had silently cursed Johnny for this question because it was Bella Matthews's article that had brought the public's attention to the fact that Paolo had been treated differently to the other two victims.

How far along were they in discovering who the murderer was?

No comment.

All the facts of the case would be presented in due course, she had added, but right now they were in the middle of an investigation.

And on and on it went, with Nkiruka fielding and dodging questions like an incompetent novice on the cricket field.

Nkiruka knew she didn't shine in press conferences. She came across in them as belligerent and suspicious. Which wasn't far from the truth, right enough. If she had to discuss her issues with the press, where would she begin?

She disliked the way journalists seemed to thrive on digging up titillating morsels about people who worked and lived in the public eye.

There was an element of the wolf pack about the press corps, too, she felt.

She disliked the way individuals in the UK were

made to think they just had to grin and bear the vicious coverage because they lived in a country with a free and independent press. Most of the victims of negative press stories were obligated to suck it up and very few had the power to dispute or challenge the journalists responsible.

She also believed that press standards in the UK had sunk to an all-time low in their partisan and cynical reporting. This was now affecting police work too because the consequence of dysfunctional journalism was that many people seemed to take with a pinch of salt much of what was reported in the media, preferring instead to believe the most ludicrous online conspiracy theories.

As for the license given to social media...

Feeling herself getting het up, Nkiruka sat up straight and moved her head from side to side, hearing the bones in her neck clicking into place.

She really had to get back to her yoga classes, she thought, as she tried out a few more stretches to release the tension in her shoulders.

Looking up as she extended her arms outwards, she caught sight of Johnny walking through the double doors into the office.

Forgetting, as usual, to hold the doors open, Johnny let them swing back into the face of the sergeant behind him.

Nkiruka chuckled as the sergeant swore loudly and fluently at Johnny. Startled and confused by the sergeant's anger, Johnny stared at her in dismay, causing several of the police officers working in the near vicinity to bend their heads and grin in amusement.

Muttering profuse apologies as the sergeant

stormed off, Johnny turned and started to make his way across the office to Nkiruka.

The altercation at the office entrance hadn't dented Johnny's enthusiasm in the slightest. His style of walking, as he came over to her desk, could best be described as the upbeat swagger of a footballer who'd scored a winning goal in the last five minutes of a match. He therefore had good news to impart to Nkiruka.

"Nkiruka, can you spare a few minutes?" asked Johnny, when he reached her desk. She smiled at him.

"Of course. Take a seat."

"I thought we could grab a meeting room. Room 417 is free," suggested Johnny, in a gruff voice, as though he half-expected she would turn down his request.

He was avoiding eye contact with her and it was obvious he was still smarting from their last meeting.

He would get over it, thought Nkiruka. Johnny always bounced back.

"Sure, let's go," said Nkiruka amicably, pushing back her chair and putting her screen saver on.

She swept the three files on her desk into a drawer and locked it up, pocketing the key.

In his eagerness to get on with their meeting, Johnny hurried out of the open- plan office, his arms swinging and his back as straight as it would be on parade.

Impressed by his energy given her own jaded feelings that day, Nkiruka followed close behind him, her long legs keeping up with the pace of his strides.

They reached the entrance and mindful of his lesson from earlier on, Johnny held the door open for Nkiruka.

"Thank you, Johnny," she said, politely, as she walked through.

This was a courtesy she was convinced Johnny would forget to do in the near future. Having been left to fend for himself when younger, Johnny had an "everyone for himself or herself" attitude.

He hadn't been set a good example in manners when growing up either.

According to what he'd told her, one of his many foster parents had drunk soup directly from the bowl and enjoyed coughing up phlegm and spitting it onto a specific location on the kitchen floor. If a napkin appeared at the table his foster parent would use it to blow his nose, while farting and burping had been the standard accompaniments to every meal in the house.

In spite of an unorthodox upbringing, though, Nkiruka reckoned Johnny did all right. Thoughtful, polite manners might not have been ingrained in him but Nkiruka valued his matter-of-fact temperament. With Johnny, what you saw is what you got.

There was never any risk of a misunderstanding with him because he said what he had to say and the words "hint" or "imply" were not a part of his vocabulary. In other words, Johnny was as blunt as a lead pipe.

Johnny had a hard edge to him too, probably stemming from his difficult childhood, and in many ways this served him well in the police force. Nkiruka knew that when he applied himself to an investigation he could be ruthless, his single-minded focus on a homicide often achieving results which other, less driven, detectives failed to accomplish.

The only problem was he was hopelessly inconsistent and she couldn't rely on his grit on any given case.

She hadn't as yet discovered the carrot needed to incentivize Johnny to push himself and produce the best of his substantial talent on every homicide case she put on his desk. Most of the time, the level of his involvement seemed to depend on which murder cases caught his interest or caused him the most outrage.

She glanced sideways at him as they made their way to Room 417.

The fluorescent lights above them were bleaching Johnny's pale-skinned face to an unnatural degree, so it seemed to her for a moment as though she was walking next to a ghostly specter.

The overhead lights and the shiny plastic flooring on the sixth-floor corridors made New Scotland Yard resemble a hospital more than a police headquarters, thought Nkiruka. Except, instead of the aroma of chemical disinfectant, there was the fusty smell of unwashed bodies combined with a strong tang of aftershave and perfume.

Many hospitals these days had expensive works of art on display in their corridors, in a bid to improve quality and patient care. Supposedly, research by Professor Ulrich showed that fine art in a hospital provided a restorative and pleasant environment, reducing stress and improving clinical outcomes. Nkiruka couldn't see why the Met shouldn't do the same and had already tried to persuade Richard Langley to advocate for it. So far, she hadn't been successful. Just as she was in her relationship with Ada, Richard was wary of picking battles he couldn't win.

Nkiruka did approve of the brightly colored toilets at New Scotland Yard, however. Tiled in the blue and yellow chequerboard of standard police vehicles or the red, blue and orange stripes of the diplomatic protection vehicles, most of the tongue- in-cheek toilets were inspired by police car liveries. The idea being, according to the architects who designed the place, that police officers needed to have a sense of humor to do their job. They were quite right about that.

Realizing she was falling behind Johnny's fast pace, she hurried to keep up with him. Johnny was looking preoccupied and didn't seem to be aware of Nkiruka's presence. His thoughts were taking him some place elsewhere, which meant Johnny was in the zone, with his brain working at full throttle. Johnny always appeared distracted when he was motivated and engaged with a homicide case. It was a good sign.

Opening the door for her at Room 417, Johnny stood to one side, clutching to himself the worn leather folder he liked to bring along with him to team meetings.

Nkiruka sat at the table and pulled her notebook and pen out of her briefcase. Johnny joined her and opened up his folder, looking serious.

"OK, Johnny. Shoot."

Rifling through his notes, Johnny found the annotated sheet he was looking for and placed it in front of him.

"You'll be pleased to know, Nkiruka, that I've made some progress on the Hampstead Heath murders. I'm hopeful it'll bear fruit. The Waterloo Cars taxi dropped the three men off at The Gaming Palace, a video game shop on Golders Green Road. I spoke with the taxi driver who took them there. He doesn't remember them going into the shop and none of the sales staff working in the shop remembers them coming in. An elderly man in a wheelchair coming into a gaming shop would certainly be remembered, in my view."

Nkiruka nodded in agreement.

"So, I made enquiries at the shop units on either side of The Gaming Palace. One is a hairdresser called Bellissima and the other is a Starbucks coffee shop," continued Johnny. "I've questioned the staff that were in both units on the day in question and only one person remembers seeing them. One of the hairdressers, Jenny Tyler, at Bellissima, had a last-minute cancellation and was sitting at the reception desk, by the window of the shop. From what she says, the men waited on the pavement for a few minutes and then met up with two young men."

Nkiruka stared intently at Johnny.

"I couldn't get a concise description of the unknown young men, by the way," Johnny hastened to add, seeing her interest was piqued. "Jenny Tyler, well, she's a bit of a dopey mare, if you ask me. Says she was browsing on her phone at the time and only glanced at them. Anyway, she wasn't able to describe them in any meaningful way, other than telling me that both men were of a big build with coarse features. "*Heavy-set young men*" were her actual words. Jenny's getting on herself so I'm not sure what she meant by "*young men.*" Could mean anything from fifteen to forty years of age, if you ask me. She says both had short, dark hair, both were sporting long beards and wearing casual sportswear, nothing distinctive."

"That's a real shame," said Nkiruka, disappointed.

"I know, right? I bet you if they'd been two gorgeous-looking studs standing outside the shop, she'd have memorized every single detail of their appearance," commented Johnny, cynical as ever.

Nkiruka sighed.

"Is it worth getting a police artist to work with her?"

Johnny shook his head.

"Not at this stage, no. She kept changing her mind. She said to me she was sure the two men had long hair and then reversed that to short hair. Hopeless. Personally, I think she'd drive a police artist demented. I would wait until we've a couple of suspects and then we might see if she can identify them out of a few faces."

"So, where does that leave us now?" Nkiruka asked.

"Well, Jenny says she saw them crossing the road and heading down Armitage Road."

"CCTV?"

Johnny shook his head.

Nkiruka sighed again, feeling defeated.

"But I think it's significant it's not far from Golders Green Synagogue."

"Meaning?"

"Well, it all seems so connected doesn't it? The Dorins live in Golders Green, they're supported by the Golders Green Synagogue and the men get dropped off on Golders Green Road. It's too much of a coincidence."

"It certainly appears so," said Nkiruka cautiously. "We're going to see the synagogue's rabbi later this afternoon, so we can give the rabbi a grilling and see what comes out of that. The synagogue's long overdue a visit from us but even so, to be honest with you, Johnny, I'm not sure the rabbi will be able to help us out much. I doubt anyone who could torture Paolo Fernandes like that would attend a synagogue like the one at Golders

Green. Murder and torture are anathema to the majority of people of faith, no matter what religion they come from."

"Yes, but it's about the relationships within the community, isn't it? The location's intertwined with the murders. That's obvious."

"Possibly, yes. The case is also tied up with the past. I suspect history is a matter of great interest to people of the Jewish faith and the Dorins have a pretty interesting family background in that respect, don't they? By the way, have you spoken to that private investigator, Paul Abbott?"

"I have actually, but hold on. I've found out more," said Johnny, lowering his voice to add some theatre to the moment. "I found out that a young man called Isaac Andelman used to work at the gaming shop on Golders Green Road during the holidays. I asked the shop for the names of staff past and present, and trawled through the list.

Isaac Andelman worked there when he was home from Brunel University, where he was apparently studying game design. Anyway, he apparently stopped working at The Gaming Palace a couple of years ago when he started making some serious money."

"And?"

"Joel Yurkovich's daughter is called Leila Andelman. Isn't it a bit coincidental that he has the same surname as the daughter of Joel Yurkovich, the man Paolo wanted to see?"

"I suppose. Depends on how common the surname is, I guess," said Nkiruka, determined not to get carried away.

Johnny huffed impatiently.

"Fine, but just for the record, I disagree with you. Anyway, it doesn't matter for now. I did speak with Paul Abbott. He says Paolo called him eight years ago. He remembers him because he was so reluctant to explain himself. Normally, Paul's clients give him an open dossier to work on but Paolo was very reserved, even evasive. He wanted Paul to locate for him the man who was landlord to a building in Germany, back in 1938. The building was 16 Domhof, Aachen, Germany. Turns out that the landlord was a man called Joel Yurkovich. Left Germany for the UK at the start of the Second World War, as so many others did. Paul located his address in Hampstead and their home phone number. That was it. Paolo paid him and he heard nothing more from him."

"Did he give you the address?"

"Yes, he did. He located it in Paolo's file. It's 3 Nassington Road, Hampstead. The only problem being that Joel Yurkovich passed away five years ago. The house is now owned by his only daughter, Leila Andelman, and her husband, Michael Andelman. So, whoever Paolo was planning on meeting in London, it wasn't Joel Yurkovich."

"Are you saying someone was masquerading as Joel Yurkovich?"

Johnny shrugged.

"Who knows? Paolo's daughter, Christina, says he was going to meet Joel Yurkovich's relatives. Any calls or mail sent from Paolo, or on his behalf, must have been sent to that house. Do the family know Rachel Dorin or her daughter? I reckon they must be connected somehow. There are too many coincidences here."

"We should ask Rachel Dorin and her daughter if they knew Joel Yurkovich. Maybe this rabbi at Golders Green Synagogue will be able to tell us something about the man too? I mean, this whole bloody thing is giving me a headache," complained Nkiruka. "I can only hope and pray we get a little more clarity this afternoon."

"We can drop by Rachel and Natalie's house after we see Rabbi Stanton."

"Yes, good idea. See if you can arrange a chat with Leila Andelman too. Does she have any children?"

"I don't know. Not registered at that address but I should imagine any of Joel Yurkovich's grandchildren would be late teens or early twenties by now and might have left home," said Johnny, pensively. "I won't get in touch with Leila Andelman until we've had a background chat with Rabbi Michael Stanton. Then we can decide if we think we should pursue that angle. I think the rabbi will probably be able to help us untangle all of the loose threads in a close-knit Jewish community. We don't want any of the Yurkovich family members, if they're guilty, to get suspicious. And if they're innocent, we don't want to upset them unnecessarily. We really should try to figure out what connects the two families before we start interviewing them as well."

Nkiruka nodded.

"You're right. We want to tread carefully." She looked at Johnny. "It would have been so much simpler for us if Paolo could've been more open with everyone about the paintings or his reasons for coming to London, but I guess that wasn't his style. If we could find out who met him and why they did so, we'd crack this one."

She playfully spun her pen on the table.

"Actually, I'm inclined to agree with you, Johnny. I think whoever murdered them is connected to the Dorin family in some way," she added. "And I'm sure that at least one of the people Paolo met with has a criminal record too because they'd access to a gun and I'd be very surprised to find the murder weapon is legally owned and traceable. It's a crying shame we couldn't get hold of the bullets..."

Johnny got up and walked over to the window, rolling up the blind so he could see out.

"It's no use lamenting the fact that Paolo didn't give out more information to his family," he said impatiently, speaking from the window. "If Paolo was heading to an end- of-life clinic, he wouldn't want an investigation into potential war crimes to get in the way of that. His secretiveness has complicated matters for us but having led a double life for so long, I imagine it would have been almost impossible for him to break the habit."

He walked back to the table and sat down in his seat.

"I still think it's an odd coincidence that an Isaac Andelman worked at that gaming shop. Same surname as the daughter of the man Paolo wanted tracked down," he said, persistent. "I'm not giving up on that angle yet. I'm going to do a little more research on him."

Nkiruka shrugged, her large black eyes watching him.

"OK, but don't go off on your own and do something stupid, will you? Someone capable of torturing the old man to that extent might be willing to do something reckless when backed into a corner."

Johnny grinned at her, amused.

"Aww, Nkiruka. I never thought I'd see the day when you cared what happened to me."

"It's no joke, Johnny. I care very much about you," responded Nkiruka, emphatic and almost, but not quite, aggressive. His obtuseness was getting her annoyed.

Raising his hands, Johnny acknowledged her point.

"OK, I'll be careful," he said softly, his smile the most genuine she'd seen on him yet.

Something was thawing inside of Johnny, which was no bad thing. But she was surprised nonetheless by his sudden mellowing and at a loss to account for it.

She got up, picked up her folder and made to leave.

"I'll meet you at the entrance at 2.30. Are you happy driving?"

"No, I asked Katie Hill to take us. Thought she could check out the synagogue while we're speaking to Rabbi Stanton."

This came as another surprise to Nkiruka. Since when had they identified a need to "check out" Golders Green Synagogue?

Besides, Katie usually turned down any such last-minute driving requests with the valid excuse that Lionel had loaded her down with important work. This was usually enough to send every single detective scurrying away to find someone else. Lionel had taken a liking to Katie's bubbly temperament and the pair of them had quickly reached a stage where Katie was working for him as a semi-official PA.

Of course, those of a skeptical frame of mind were free to assume that by taking on the extra work, Katie was also expectantly eyeing up a promotion or job opportunity from Lionel in the near future. She was no fool, Katie.

Nkiruka bent her head to one side and studied Johnny, who began to look uncomfortable under her searching gaze.

Nkiruka grinned. "Like that, is it?"

Johnny looked at her.

"I've no idea what you mean."

"You damn well do know what I mean. All I'll say to you, sir, is that she has good taste."

Embarrassed, Johnny didn't reply.

Smiling to herself, Nkiruka decided not to tease him anymore. Johnny had been showing a more sensitive side of himself recently and she didn't want to push him too far or erode his goodwill.

She got up and went back to her busy desk, leaving Johnny behind in Room 417, sitting at the end of the table and frowning down at his notes.

Johnny, so far, had the remit to focus single-mindedly on the Hampstead Heath murders because the torture of the old man and killing of three foreigners on British soil had made the case a top priority. In the meantime, she also had ten other open-ended cases needing to be chased up and reassessed that week.

17

Nkiruka

By the time she was ready to meet Johnny and head to the Golders Green Synagogue, she was running late.

Her tardiness was becoming a bad habit, she thought to herself, and it was something she would have to address soon.

Seeing three missed calls on her phone from Johnny, she didn't bother wasting time calling him back. Instead, she took the lift down to the ground floor and ran out into the foyer, only to see Johnny and Katie seated side by side on a sofa, looking very cozy and with their heads together.

She walked up to them and coughed loudly. Both of them jumped out of their skins.

"Jeez, Nkiruka, you nearly gave me a heart attack," complained Johnny, placing a hand on his chest.

Nkiruka looked down at them.

"Sorry about that," said Nkiruka, not looking or sounding in the least bit penitent.

"Shall we get going? We're running late as it is."

"Of course, ma'am," said Katie, standing up straightaway and behaving as if it wasn't Nkiruka who'd caused the delay in the first place.

Johnny, not so diplomatic, made a face and rolled his eyes at Nkiruka in open disapproval at her hopeless timekeeping.

The girl had class, no doubt about it, thought Nkiruka as they made their way out of the building. What on earth was she doing with a rough-and-ready street cur like Johnny?

Feeling a bit guilty about her uncharitable thoughts, Nkiruka had to admit to herself that love could account for a whole load of surprising pairings and, indeed, many would wonder what she and Tom had in common, too. In the end, there was no accounting for the effects of pheromones and sexual chemistry.

Ignoring Johnny's protests for her to sit up front, Nkiruka sat herself in the back seat of the car and tried to get some of her overdue work done as Katie drove them towards Golders Green.

She'd been distracted that morning with another detective's pending homicide enquiry, to the neglect of her own caseload. One of her detectives was off work for a week with mental health issues and the rest of her team were struggling to process the extra workload, which inevitably meant she had to step in to help get things completed in time.

Lionel, oblivious as ever to her staffing issues, was sending her irate emails on a regular basis, complaining about her team's lengthy delay in getting homicide reports signed off. No doubt their backlog was having a knock-on effect on his spreadsheets but Nkiruka estimated they still had a couple of weeks in play before Lionel really blew his top.

They arrived at the Golders Green Synagogue on Dunstan Road and parked near the entrance.

Dunstan Road consisted mostly of standard white, two-floor, semi-detached homes, with trees and greenery planted at intervals along it.

Tranquil, middle class and very dull, was Nkiruka's verdict on the street.

The nearby trees were lifeless and the sky was grey, which did not make the synagogue look welcoming, despite its red-brick exterior.

With a sigh, Nkiruka shoved her paperwork back into her briefcase and got out.

The weather had worsened during their journey and a few ominous-looking black clouds were looming overhead. Fastening the buttons on her coat in the chill November air, Nkiruka followed Johnny and Katie as they made their way to the entrance.

She was reconciled to the fact that Katie would be with them in the meeting, not having been credulous enough to buy into Johnny's assertion that Katie could "check out" the synagogue while they spoke with Rabbi Michael Stanton. She thought it highly unlikely any rabbi would be happy with a police officer wandering off and inspecting the synagogue as though it were a crime scene. Johnny's excuse for Katie's presence was a feeble one, at best, but you had to give the man credit for inventiveness.

Three police officers sitting in what was meant to be an informal interview was total overkill, but Nkiruka liked and respected Katie and wasn't going to object to having her there. It was always possible her feedback might be helpful, too.

They rang the bell and a young man, wearing a kippah, opened the door.

"Come in, come in," he said with a smile. "Welcome to Golders Green Synagogue."

"Thank you," said Nkiruka, stepping over the threshold.

"I'm David Sutro. Rabbi Stanton's expecting you."

Nkiruka followed the young man as he turned left and led them to an office at the far end of a long corridor.

He knocked on the thick wooden door.

"Come in," said a deep voice.

David opened the door and stood to one side.

"Enter, please," urged David, with a smile.

Once the others had walked in, he closed the door behind them.

"Hello! Welcome to Golders Green Synagogue," said Rabbi Stanton, getting up from his desk and coming over to greet his visitors.

Nkiruka was surprised to see he was wearing a pair of jeans and a grey hoodie top, with only the kippah on his head reflecting his position. He had a neat beard, kind brown eyes behind gold-framed glasses and a nice smile, which made Nkiruka think he would cooperate with them as much as he could. Goodwill seemed to radiate out of the man.

Rabbi Stanton shook hands with them while Nkiruka introduced everyone, and then went to sit down on the other side of his desk.

"Please take a seat," he said, gesturing towards the chairs in front of the desk. "I was eager to meet with you. I'm curious to find out what you need to know and how best I may help you."

There was a large window behind him looking out onto a picturesque, enclosed garden, with an autumnal cherry tree brightening up the horizon with its fragile, pink flowers.

Glancing at the garden, Nkiruka wondered how Rabbi Stanton managed to get any work done with such a restful view so close to hand. There was nowhere to hide where she worked. The whole point of an open-plan office was to encourage workers to apply themselves, driven by the sight of others beavering away on the same floor. With a view like the one Rabbi Stanton had in his office, she was sure she would end up daydreaming every single workday away, but then maybe, if you were a rabbi, a little meditation now and again didn't go amiss.

"Thank you for agreeing to meet with us, Rabbi Stanton," began Nkiruka.

"Please, do call me Michael. Most of my congregation do," interrupted Rabbi Stanton, with a smile.

Nkiruka smiled and nodded.

"We're hoping you could tell us a little about a couple of Jewish families living in this area, one of whom is very involved in your community," said Nkiruka. "Our detectives have already met with Rachel Dorin and her daughter, Natalie Abergel. We're keen to find out if there's anything you can tell us about their connection with another family, Joel Yurkovich and his daughter, Leila Andelman."

"Joel Yurkovich?" asked Rabbi Stanton, frowning to himself. "Yes, I knew a little of him, but didn't he pass away some years back?"

"He did indeed, sir," confirmed Johnny.

"Well, Joel Yurkovich used to attend Hampstead

Synagogue on 1 Dennington Park Road. We do have joint services very occasionally. And yes, he was friendly with Rachel Dorin. He knew her mother very well back in Germany and when he heard her daughter was local, he linked up with her," explained Rabbi Stanton. "It's quite an extraordinary story. He was the landlord of Rachel Dorin's grandparents' flat in Germany. Amazing how they both came to be living in London after leaving Germany."

Rabbi Stanton looked pensive.

"I'm not sure I should be telling you this..." He looked doubtful for a moment. "But he's dead so there can't be any harm in it... When Joel found out about Rachel Dorin's illness, he helped her out quite a bit financially. That much I do know. He was a very kind and generous man."

There was a pause while Nkiruka and Johnny thought about this.

"What about Joel's daughter, Leila Andelman?" asked Nkiruka.

"I don't know her as well as I knew her father. I was invited along to celebrate her son's bar mitzvah some time ago, along with a few other members of our synagogue. Goodness, her son was quite old by then. He was fifteen, if I remember rightly. It was a lavish affair, held in the Marriott Hotel Maida Vale. Yes, they're a very wealthy family."

"What's her son called?" asked Johnny, leaning forward in his eagerness to hear the answer.

"She has two sons, Isaac and... Ben, if I remember rightly. And a girl, but I can't for the life of me remember her name. She was the youngest of the three."

"This is all very helpful," said Nkiruka. "Thank you."

Rabbi Stanton smiled.

"Do you know if any of the Yurkovich family members continue to keep in touch with Rachel or Natalie?" asked Johnny.

Shaking his head, Rabbi Stanton looked confused.

"I'm sorry, I really don't know. You're better to ask the families directly. I've very limited information about the relationships between them, I'm afraid. We've a big congregation here at Golders Green."

"Do you happen to know if Isaac Andelman lives in Golders Green?" asked Johnny.

"I believe so. I do bump into him now and again. I've seen him at our local Sainsbury's and at The Book Warehouse. He doesn't attend our synagogue, though, but I wouldn't be surprised to find out he lives in Golders Green." Rabbi Stanton paused and looked thoughtfully at them. "Years ago, he used to work at the gaming shop on Golders Green Road. He was heavily into his gaming and I remember his mother complaining to me about it during his bar mitzvah. It used to drive her to despair but I think he does quite well for himself in game design now, at least that's what she told me the last time I saw her. He's apparently designed a series of successful Jewish video games that seem to have taken off, especially in Israel and the USA, I believe."

Nkiruka watched as outside the office a robin dropped down onto a large flowerpot.

The earth in the flowerpot interior was topped with a deep layer of water and within seconds the robin had jumped into the puddle of cold water and had begun to wash itself, spinning little droplets as it shook out its feathers.

Nkiruka loved robins. She remembered watching them splashing in the bird bath in her garden while she was growing up. In the days when she had plenty of leisure time and little stress in her life. Rarely was there more than one robin to be seen in her parents' garden because they were plucky little birds and defended their territory with stoical aggression.

She had always cherished the valor displayed by such a tiny, delicate bird.

Bravery was a quality she admired in people too. She held her husband in high regard because he dealt with life and death emergencies on a daily basis at the hospital, as well as the whole gamut of human emotions.

Her job was relatively tame in comparison. She mostly dealt with dead bodies and, in successful cases, their murderers. Bereaved relatives she often didn't see in person, unless the case was a high-profile one. Homicide investigations to her were often like a game of chess, a thinking man's or woman's game, with no, or little, risk to herself.

She turned her gaze back to the office and saw the others were watching her with some confusion on their faces.

Embarrassed, she realized she must have been daydreaming for far too long. She smiled apologetically.

"Forgive me," she said to Rabbi Stanton. "Your garden's very beautiful and it distracted me."

"Quite understandable," laughed Rabbi Stanton, with his easy manner. "I spend hours gazing at it myself. I'm very lucky to have such a nice view from my desk. I take it you aren't similarly fortunate?"

"No, we work in a concrete block," remarked Johnny, cheerfully. "There's a few trees outside, mind you, but not many of us get to see them from our desks."

"Thank you for your time, Rabbi Stanton," said Nkiruka, hurriedly, before Johnny started to embellish on his horrible working conditions. "You've been very helpful and I really appreciate that. More than you could possibly realize."

Rabbi Stanton inclined his head and stood up.

"Delighted to be of help. Any time, any time," he repeated as he shook hands with them.

He accompanied them out of the building and as they walked back to their car,

Nkiruka twisted round to speak to Johnny, who was walking behind her with Katie.

"Johnny, can you call Rachel and check if she's still OK for us to pop by her house?"

"Sure," said Johnny, moving to one side and taking his mobile phone out of his suit jacket.

Nkiruka left him to make the call and got into the back of the car again.

She looked at Katie for a moment, who was now sitting in the driver's seat and staring out of the front window of the car.

"I'm glad you've come with us, Katie. If we do get to drop by Rachel's house, I'd like you to come in with me, if that's OK? If we're going to find out more about Isaac Andelman and his connection with the Dorin family, it's probably going to take some delicate questioning to get the most out of Rachel and Natalie. Not Johnny's forte, I'm afraid."

"I understand," said Katie, turning her head to watch Johnny talking on his mobile through the side window.

"He's a gem, though," added Nkiruka, mischievously.

Katie smiled but said nothing.

A few minutes later Johnny opened the car door and flung himself into the front seat.

"Right, let's go to 35 Wentworth Road," said Johnny, putting his phone away. "I've spoken to Rachel and she's happy to see us. No problems there." Katie indicated right and pulled away from the curb.

"I've asked Katie to come in with me on this one, Johnny. Hope that's OK," said Nkiruka.

Johnny turned to look at her and raised an inquiring eyebrow.

"Too many cooks spoil the broth?" asked Johnny.

"Yes, something like that. I think they'll respond better to two females asking the questions."

"Sure thing. I can catch up on the footie news while you're both in there."

"Thanks Johnny. You're a star."

"I know you think I'm fantastic, Nkiruka," answered Johnny, with a tinge of humour in his voice. "You don't need to spell it out."

Nkiruka and Katie caught each other's eyes in the rear-view mirror. Nkiruka smiled as Katie giggled.

Johnny was a class act, she thought to herself a few minutes later, as she walked up the pathway to number 35. One in a million, for sure.

Having not met Rachel or Natalie before, Nkiruka was pleasantly surprised by the two of them. Both turned out to be engaging and open, and it was obvious to the meanest intelligence that a close bond existed between mother and daughter.

Natalie greeted them at the front door and once they were in the sitting room began to make tea and coffee.

Thinking of poor Johnny, sitting outside in the cold car, Nkiruka accepted a mug of instant coffee and a biscuit.

"Rachel, thank you so much for having us round at such short notice," said Nkiruka, turning to look at Rachel, who was lying on the sofa with her feet next to Nkiruka's hip.

"It's no problem. We're very grateful for all the help the police have given us so far. Chief Inspector Langley was so kind when he was here," replied Rachel, arranging the blanket on her legs so she could balance her mug of tea on her thighs. "It's a relief to know that he'll be taking care of authenticating the two Chagall paintings and establishing my grandparents' ownership of them."

Nkiruka nodded, thinking she must pass on Rachel's compliment to Richard. Police officers didn't get praise very often from the people they were trying to help. Each time they did was a moment to be savored to the full.

"We really wanted to ask you how well you knew Joel Yurkovich and his family. We think they might be involved in this case of yours, too," said Nkiruka, as she dunked her biscuit in her coffee.

"Really?" exclaimed Rachel, looking surprised. "I can't begin to imagine why. Joel was my guardian angel when I had to stop work. He knew my grand-parents and my mother back in Germany, you see. I think he felt awful after what happened to my family during the Kristallnacht and he always kept an eye on us. We were very sad when he passed away... Very sad."

"Yes, I believe he passed away some time ago, didn't he?"

"Five years ago," said Rachel, forlornly. "It still feels like yesterday. He left Natalie a small legacy, as well. Enough for her to get started on a flat of her own or to pay for her university studies."

They looked at Natalie, who in turn smiled from her armchair.

"I'm not leaving mum. I'll be going to university here, if that's what I decide to do," she said with great determination.

Katie nodded.

"I understand how you feel. I felt the same when my mother was frail."

"Oh, did she have MS, as well?" asked Natalie, interested.

"Nope, she had cancer. Ovarian cancer. In the end, she didn't last too long but I wouldn't have wanted to be anywhere but close by while she had to deal with it."

"Don't get me wrong, I understand Natalie's point of view, but no mother likes to be a bind, either. Children should always be free to fly the nest," said Rachel, looking upset. "Still, selfishly, I can't deny I'm happy for Natalie to stay here with me."

There was a silent but not uncomfortable pause, during which the four of them drank their beverages and thought about the far-reaching and personal implications of ill health.

"I presume the rest of Joel's family keep in touch

with you, given how close Joel was to you?" asked Nkiruka eventually.

"Actually, we don't keep in touch," said Rachel, a little defensively.

"I'm surprised to hear that given your past history together," commented Katie.

"Were the family estranged from Joel?"

"No, not at all," said Rachel. "They're an incredibly tight-knit group. A typical Jewish family unit."

"Oh, right," said Nkiruka, looking confused. Rachel looked pleadingly across at her daughter.

Natalie shrugged her shoulders in a fatalistic manner.

"The problem is me, I'm afraid," she confessed. "I'm dating her son, Isaac, and she's not happy about it. Leila Andelman, that is."

Rachel sniffed.

"Doesn't seem to think Natalie is good enough for her precious son, when in fact Natalie's an angel."

"Mum!" chastised Natalie, looking embarrassed.

"Well, it's true, Natalie. Leila's a stuck-up cow. There, I've said it now. Wasn't happy her father left Natalie a small legacy, even though they're now multi-millionaires because of what Joel left them. She's only interested in one thing," said Rachel, rubbing her thumb and forefinger together.

"We have Isaac around here all the time, or Natalie goes up to his when she can, because Leila won't let Natalie come over to hers," she added, bitterly.

Nkiruka looked across at Natalie, her half-eaten biscuit forgotten on her lap.

"It's true. It's a real pain," admitted Natalie. "She's always putting pressure on him to break up with me."

"And Isaac has his own place nearby, does he?"

"Yeah, he has his own detached house in Basing Hill," said Natalie, proudly. "He's made loads of money designing video games."

"What's his address?" asked Katie. "It might be helpful for us to be able to tie up loose ends with the Yurkovich family."

"34 Basing Hill."

"Thank you. Do you happen to know if Joel told Isaac anything about your family background, Rachel? With a view to the Kristallnacht?" asked Nkiruka. She put down her empty mug on the coffee table and then ate the remains of her biscuit.

"Did he, Natalie? I'm not sure but I think Joel would have told them about our story. It affected him as well, you see... Yes, I'm sure their family know about our past history," said Rachel, insistent. "Our connection to Joel was because of our shared past. Joel was forever inviting us to meals with them and trying to include us in any significant family events. He wanted them to accept us. It's sad Leila isn't honoring his wishes."

"Isaac told me that he knew a little bit about our background but I've filled him in too, of course. He said he found out more recently because his mum received a weird letter from abroad asking for information about us," said Natalie. She smiled as the others stared at her in surprise. "He said his mum told him the letter was from a madman and had something to do with what happened to our family during Kristallnacht. She threw it in the trash but he retrieved it and read it for himself."

Uncomfortable under their searching gaze, Natalie began to comb through her thick black hair with her fingers. She twisted her fingers around individual strands of hair, then tugged them loose, over and over again.

Watching as she fiddled with her hair, Nkiruka thought her repetitive movements were nothing more than a nervous mannerism or tic, not the actions of someone with a guilty conscience. Indeed, Natalie appeared to be entirely oblivious to the momentous implications of the mysterious letter.

"Isaac said the letter seemed to be from some crackpot, who was wanting to meet with mum and make some reparation for the past," Natalie continued. "But before he could do anything with it, his psycho mum caught him with the letter and screamed her head off at him. In order to avoid a fight, he told me he handed it back to her."

Bending her head, Natalie began to plait her hair.

"I think that was the end of it," said Natalie, looking up and realizing the others were waiting for her to say more. "I didn't demand that he get the letter back from his mum or anything like that. I don't want to ask him about it either because things aren't great with his mum and he's finding it hard. I don't think it was an important letter. I mean, if the man had been close to us, or if he really cared to find us, he would have known we live here in Wentworth Road. All he had to do was to ask around this area. Loads of people know us locally."

Nkiruka pursed her lips while she thought about this. She noticed Rachel was looking at her oddly.

"Do you know what that letter was about?" she asked Nkiruka.

"I've an idea, yes," admitted Nkiruka. "But I'm

afraid you're going to have to wait a little longer before
we can tell you the whole story."

Before she got asked any more questions by Rachel
and her daughter, Nkiruka stood and picked up her
briefcase.

"If at all possible, we'd appreciate it if you don't tell
anyone about our visit today," she said, knowing that
this instruction was unlikely to be adhered to. Still, one
never knew, once in a blue moon people did follow
police requests. "We'll explain everything in due
course, but at the moment we're at a very sensitive stage
in our investigation."

"Yes, of course," said Rachel, with a tight smile.
Natalie got up to accompany them to the door.

"Are you sure you wouldn't like me to ask Isaac
about the letter?" she offered. "Maybe his mother still
has it."

"That won't be necessary but we'll let you know if it
is," confirmed Nkiruka. "Thank you, anyway. It's best,
actually, if you don't mention the letter at all to Isaac or
his mother."

Looking relieved, Natalie nodded, her curtain of
loose, black hair swaying backwards and forwards as she
did so.

She opened the front door and waved them
goodbye from the doorstep.

Nkiruka and Katie walked to the car, which unsurprisingly had the engine running.

"Well?" asked Johnny, impatiently, as they got in.

"There was a letter sent to Leila Andelman's
house from someone who wanted to find Rachel and
Natalie, to make reparation for the past," Katie
informed him.

"Bloody hell! The old sod did try and get in contact with them after all."

"Yes, and apparently her son, Isaac, read the letter, too," said Nkiruka. "Isaac is dating Natalie, but his mum disapproves of him doing so. The fact that Isaac continues to date Natalie, in the face of his mother's anger, is significant. It suggests the young man is head over heels in love with her. I think, as soon as possible Johnny, you should arrange for some discreet enquiries to be done with the neighbors by Isaac's house to see if anyone saw the three men from Brazil there. His address is near here. 34 Basing Hill, Natalie said."

"Will do," said Johnny, with alacrity. "I'll also check out Leila's neighbors, too. You never know, Paolo might have ended up there."

"I would start with Isaac and steer clear of Leila, for now," suggested Nkiruka, as Katie indicated right and turned the car to drive them back to the office. "My gut's telling me that Isaac's the one we have to keep an eye on. Leila seems to want nothing to do with Rachel and Natalie and I wouldn't want to get her upset. We've no solid evidence as yet, apart from what is hearsay, and we're powerless to do anything until we find something concrete tying the Andelmans to the crime."

"OK. Fair enough," said Johnny, leaning forward to switch the music on.

For the rest of the journey to Scotland Yard, Nkiruka lost herself in the morass of emails that had arrived in her inbox during the time they had drunk coffee at Wentworth Road.

She didn't expect to hear back from Johnny for at least another week but once he had a bee in his bonnet there was no stopping him. Two days later, on a

Thursday evening, she received a text from him asking her to meet him the next day, first thing, at Room 417.

Intrigued, she didn't even bother to stop by her desk to drop off her coat and hat when she came into the office in the morning but instead walked straight to the meeting room.

"Morning, Johnny," she said, as she walked in carrying a takeaway Pumpkin Spice latte.

"Morning, Niki," said Johnny, looking worried as studied his notes.

"What's up?"

"I've spent the last two days making enquiries at Nassington Road and Basing Hill with Katie."

"I thought I said to leave Leila alone, if possible."

"It wasn't possible, in my view, Niki. We drew a complete blank at 34 Basing Hill. No one had seen anything, and believe me there were plenty of curtain twitchers close to Isaac's house. They knew about him too. A very helpful, pleasant young man, is how they described him. Very friendly and caused no bother until a year ago or so."

"Oh? And what happened a year or so ago?"

"I was told that approximately a year ago, he started having a rough, sleazy crowd around to his house for parties. Upset a lot of the neighborhood at the time, with the noise and the ambience. You get the gist. Bit of a daft thing to do on a quiet suburban street. However, after several neighbors complained to him, he stopped having parties there. He's no problem now, apparently. Spends plenty of his time at home, occasionally he's away with business. We covered the whole street, working from opposite ends."

"OK..."

"We made sure we turned up early in the day so people would feel safe opening the doors to us."

"True, though doing door to door during the daytime is going to be more conspicuous. Especially on a street like that one. What did you tell the residents? Did you mention why you were there?"

Johnny started to look uncomfortable.

"To be honest with you, I borrowed some gear off someone I know. He works as a parking attendant. He was game for it. I didn't want anyone to turn up in police uniform, but someone official-looking always helps to make things easier when you're doing door to door," said Johnny.

He glanced sideways at Nkiruka.

"We told them we were looking into disability access for a resident who was looking to move into the street. We said we were from the council, canvassing to see if people on the street objected to having a few additional disabled parking bays put in. We then asked if any of them had noticed an old man in a wheelchair visiting the road, back in October with his carers, but nobody had seen anything."

Nkiruka put her head in her hands and groaned.

"Johnny, you're incorrigible. This could blow up in our faces. If they ever find out you were the police, we could be in for serious liability."

"Well, what did you want me to do? Explain that a person of interest to the police is living on their street? That would put the cat among the pigeons, wouldn't it? What we don't want is for our investigation to put the wind up Isaac."

"I'm better not knowing, Johnny, when you do these things. Please, just don't tell me."

"Fine. Whatever," said Johnny, dismissively. "At least this way we get results, Nkiruka. When we did the same traffic warden routine at Nassington Road, we got a good outcome. Huge houses on that street, by the way. Must be worth a good few million quid. The residents were friendly enough, though. Anyway, on the 15th of October, at around 11 o'clock in the morning, two residents saw an old, disabled man exiting a people carrier and entering Leila's house accompanied by four others, one of whom was Leila's son, Isaac."

Nkiruka stared at Johnny.

"Before you jump to conclusions, I should tell you that the neighbors said Leila and her husband were on holiday in Italy that week. Isaac was house sitting for them because they've a dog. I checked it out. Michael and Leila Andelman were both in Bologna for the two weeks. They were away from the 9th to the 23rd of October."

"OK. This sounds very positive."

Johnny grinned at her.

"The residents near Leila's house weren't happy with Isaac at all, by the way. They were fuming. I'm pretty sure Michael and Leila must have had quite a few complaints hurled at them when they came back from holiday. Apparently, there were a couple of parties held at their house while they were away, with a lot of young people "making a ruckus" according to one old biddy. Estimates from the neighbors vary from fifty to a hundred young people."

Johnny looked at his notes.

"I asked for police records for the two nights in question from West Hampstead Police Station. The two parties were held on the 13th and the 19th. There were only forty there the first night the police came out to the house, ten the second night. Sounds to me like the neighbors had completely lost it by the second night."

"Doesn't seem like a big deal to me. Happens all the time when parents are away."

"It was a little more than some youngsters having fun and getting rowdy, though. It wasn't just drink, either. Complaints were made about anti-social behavior, people drinking and smoking in the street, loud music. The usual stuff. Smell of joints, too, apparently. As I said before, several complaints were made to the local police station by the neighbors. The reports state that on the 13th, seven ASBOS were handed out and five people were charged with possession of Class A drugs, namely cocaine. One of the party goers was charged with common assault. He'd punched a neighbor when he came to the door to complain."

"Stupid of Isaac to attract so much attention if he was the one planning to do Paolo, Alonso, and Luca in."

"I've a feeling it got out of hand, Nkiruka. I really do. Even when they weren't having parties, the place was like Clapham Junction apparently. People going in and out of the house at different times of the day. Who knows what they were taking during that week? An excess of amphetamines or cocaine would do the job."

Nkiruka looked at him doubtfully.

"If they were under the influence at the time, they would have made more mistakes, left a trail, left a mess for goodness sake, and made it easy for us. Discreetness isn't something they seem capable of, given the upset they've caused in the neighborhood. If that lot were in any way responsible for the murders, it seems they've covered their tracks up very well. Surprisingly well."

"Yes, I agree, it all depends on how well they cleared up after themselves," agreed Johnny. "We've established, though, that the murders didn't happen on Hampstead Heath."

"I don't think there's enough for us to issue a search warrant yet."

"No, there isn't. For that we'd have to go back and do some facial recognition with the two residents who claimed to have seen an old man in a wheelchair entering the property that week."

"Which could then send the street, Leila and her husband into total panic. People aren't daft, they'll connect the dots to our murder investigation," said Nkiruka, thoughtfully.

"Yes, exactly. The publicity has been huge with this case," said Johnny, having the grace to look shamefaced about it. "My suggestion would be to go and speak to Leila informally. A courtesy visit. We'll say we are looking into the disturbances that happened on the street during their holiday. Ask if there was any damage to the house and try to get her onside. If she lets us have a look around, all the better. If nothing comes of it, we'll have to work with the neighbors."

Nkiruka nodded her head. "A fishing expedition."

"Yes."

"OK, I agree. That's where we should start but you know, Johnny, you can't torture someone and not have anyone hear it. Not on a suburban street."

"I agree. I can't figure it out. If they weren't going to murder them at Nassington Road, then why bother taking them there in the first place? It doesn't make sense. I think we need to approach Leila and see what she can tell us about the parties. A good look around would be helpful. You never know, there could be a cellar. It would be hard to hear anything from there."

Nkiruka sighed.

"Fine. Try and arrange a meeting with Leila Andelman."

Johnny nodded and got up, rolling up his notes and holding them in a tight fist. Nkiruka smiled up at him.

"Well done, Johnny. I feel we're getting close."

Johnny relaxed for a second and smiled back at her. "Yes, it certainly feels that way," he said.

Once he left the meeting room, Nkiruka lingered on for a few more minutes, relishing the peace and quiet.

Before she left to go back to her desk, she got up and walked over to the window.

Looking out on the River Thames, her head against the window pane, she thought about the bereaved families living under the humid, tropical sun of Brazil, waiting for justice.

She hoped they would get it.

18

Richard

"You OK?" asked Richard, watching Eilidh as she pulled her luggage up onto the pavement.

"Fine," replied Eilidh, curtly.

For reasons best known to herself, Eilidh had brought a huge suitcase with her to Paris.

As soon as Richard saw the size of it at St Pancras International, he made a decision to detour to their hotel in Paris and drop it off. Otherwise, they were going to end up walking around Paris with Eilidh wheeling a heavy suitcase behind her and looking as though she was going to stay there for a month, not a night.

He had also texted his friend, Jean Aubert, and asked him to meet them at the foyer of the Hôtel d'Argenson at eleven o'clock.

Jean was an art historian who worked for the Institut National d'Histoire de l'Art on 2 Rue Vivienne, and like many other people who worked in the specialized field of art history he was quite a character. Lively, intelligent and friendly, Jean had given

Richard invaluable help with several other art crime cases.

The French in general had a cultural passion for art that Richard wished could be replicated in the UK. He was filled with jealousy whenever he heard what the French operating budget was for their Central Office for the Fight against Trafficking of Cultural Property, in other words the OCBC. He was waiting for an opportune time to put those statistics on Lionel's desk.

Eilidh and Richard had taken a taxi from Gare du Nord to the Hôtel d' Argenson, a 2-star hotel that best suited the meagre expenses budget Richard had at his disposal for such trips. Having used the hotel several times before, Richard felt it punched above its weight in terms of comfort and location.

They left Eilidh's suitcase and Richard's hold-all at reception and waited for Jean to turn up.

They didn't have to wait long.

A large, bluff man with a crop of unruly brown hair came through the doors and beamed as he walked over to them.

"Welcome to Paris, my friend," he said, shaking Richard's hand vigorously.

"This is my colleague, Detective Inspector Eilidh Simmons," said Richard, introducing Eilidh.

"*Enchante*," said Jean, bowing slightly as he shook Eilidh's small hand.

Eilidh smiled with amusement. Jean turned to look at Richard.

"What can I help you with, Richard? I understand it's about two Chagall paintings?" Jean asked, his eyes wide open with interest.

"Yes. We're trying to find some records for a gallery

that used to be on Rue de Marignan. That's where the Chagall paintings were bought from and we have the receipt for them. But if we're to establish ownership of the paintings we need to be able to certify the receipt, which means we need to find the gallery's records and prove the paintings and the place existed. *La Galerie L'Oiseau Bleu* has been taken over by another art gallery. They weren't very helpful when I called them."

Jean grinned.

"Yes, well, you know the French don't like the English too much. I personally blame it on Henry VI. The English have tried to control us too many times. If it wasn't for Joan of Arc, my friend..."

Jean laughed as Richard gave him a soft punch to the arm. He made a face at Eilidh.

"You see, he's very violent. This is what we French have to put up with."

"OK, Jean, enough messing around," said Richard, with an exasperated smile.

Richard knew Jean was quite capable of carrying on in this vein for the rest of the day, and more so if he had an audience like Eilidh to encourage him.

He reached into his briefcase and took out the tatty receipt for *L'Oiseau Bleu* gallery.

He handed it over to Jean, who looked at it pensively, stroking his chin as he did so.

After a minute Jean shrugged his shoulders.

"Personally, I think the best thing would be to try the online catalogue at the reading rooms in the Archives Nationales, Pierrefitte-sur-Seine. At least at first. What do you think, Richard? The catalogue has private records of national interest, along with state documentation, and the gallery must have had tax records, for example. There'll be something in there for this gallery, I'm sure. That's where I would start. If you want to see the original documents afterwards, as you know, you'll have to put in a request directly to the Archives Nationales. It can take time but I can do that for you, if you require it."

He looked at Richard.

"Yes, sounds like a good idea to me," agreed Richard.

"The online catalogue will give us a good indication if there's anything official out there for this gallery. With two Chagall paintings, I think there will be, and the staff at the reading rooms are excellent at tracking down any records. They're very experienced and I know they'll be happy to help us with this problem. Then afterwards, I'll accompany you to this unfriendly gallery of yours, Richard, and we can see if they have any further information for you."

"Thanks, Jean."

"No problem, Richard. I'd do anything for the sake of a Marc Chagall painting, you know that. What a shame you couldn't bring them with you because I'd have loved to have seen the originals..."

Jean sighed dramatically.

"Never mind. Who knows? Maybe one day, *mon ami*. OK, we can take my car to Pierrefitte-sur-Seine. It's quite a long drive but we can go for some lunch nearby afterwards. I've a parking permit for the Archives Nationales because of my work, so it's very easy for me to find parking there."

With that they left the hotel and got into Jean's antique light-blue Citroën.

"I apologize for the car," Jean said, looking at Eilidh

in the back seat. "It's very old but I'm passionate about history and it would go against all my instincts to drive a modern car."

"I like it," said Eilidh, touched by his concern.

"A woman after my own heart," stated Jean with alacrity, starting up the car and driving into the traffic.

Knowing how temperamental the Parisian traffic was, Richard was very thankful that Jean was doing the driving to Pierrefitte-sur-Seine.

As he looked out of the car window, Richard wished for a moment that they were heading instead to the national archives at the Hôtel de Soubise. Hôtel de Soubise was a beautiful building, previously owned by various members of the French aristocracy and now housing all the state records and documents from before the French Revolution.

The modern building housing the national archives at Pierrefitte-sur-Seine was an aberration, in Richard's opinion. He'd only visited the place once before but once was enough. Unfortunately, though, the ugly building at Pierrefitte-sur-Seine was where records made after the French Revolution were kept and so was best suited to tracing any history for the two Chagall paintings.

He smiled to himself.

C'est la vie, as the French would say, or quite simply, as the English slang went, sod's law.

Eilidh looked rather shaken by the time they arrived at Pierrefitte-sur-Seine.

Jean had interrupted his gregarious chat with car toots, rude gestures and fluent curses as he drove them onwards to 59 Rue Guynemer. His driving style was a novelty to Eilidh and not a welcome one, as Richard could see.

Once they were out of the car, Richard gave Eilidh a quick hug as Jean headed to the entrance.

"You OK?" he asked, concerned.

Eilidh nodded. "Yes, fine thanks," she said, quietly. "Thank goodness Jean never thought of joining the police force. I can only imagine what it would be like sharing a patrol car with him."

She turned and stared in surprise at the building in front of them.

Richard didn't blame her as this was a part of Paris most tourists didn't get to see and with good reason.

Diamond shapes seemed to be the running theme for the Archives Nationales in Pierrefitte-sur-Seine. The lower level was fronted with plenty of glass contrasting with the white, diamond-shaped metalwork on the floor above. The enormous ugly grey rectangle of a building, situated just behind the main entrance, was also completely covered in a pattern of diamonds. It wouldn't have surprised Richard if the architect had conjured up the building after some heavy poker nights.

They hurried after Jean, who was talking animatedly to the receptionist at the front desk.

After gesturing for Eilidh and Richard to follow him, Jean made his way to the scanning machines at the back of the foyer.

"It's good you didn't bring any of your luggage with you," commented Jean, as they went through security. "Because of the terrorist attacks no one's allowed to bring in large bags."

They followed Jean as he took them to a spacious, airy and bright reading room, which had a honey-colored parquet floor and brown desks, neatly lined up in rows.

A few solitary figures were scattered about the room, seated at their desks and engrossed in their studies.

There was no sound other than the tapping of a keyboard.

Jean went to a table near the door and pulled over two more office chairs.

"Here we go," he said, cheerfully. "Reception said Sylvie will be joining us in a minute to help us out. She's a talented researcher. If she can't find something for this gallery, nobody will."

Jean looked around and shuddered in mock horror.

"This place is very badly designed," he said to them in a low whisper, as though imparting top-secret information.

It was possible he didn't want to be overheard criticizing the building but with Jean it was sometimes hard to know what was said for dramatic effect and what was genuine emotion.

Jean sniffed with disgust.

"There's no proper café or canteen in this building, would you believe? The architect forgot to put one in. They've introduced a coffee stand now, with sandwiches and drinks, but it's pathetic."

Jean frowned as he looked over his shoulder at the sea of desks behind them.

"Maybe, the *con* of an architect decided people won't be spending hours researching here and will go somewhere else for their information *and* their lunch," he added, sarcastically.

Remembering that the French placed a great deal of

importance on their food and drink, Richard was inclined to agree with Jean's passionate criticism of the building. Forgetting to put a proper cafeteria inside a research facility did seem to him to be a surprising omission and only confirmed his view that the architect must have designed the building after a heavy night of poker-playing.

"Ah, there she is!" said Jean, as an elegantly dressed, middle-aged lady with a stylish black bob walked towards them.

"*Bonjour,*" she said, smiling at them.

"*Bonjour, Sylvie,*" replied Jean, standing up and kissing her on both cheeks.

They babbled together in incomprehensible French while Richard and Eilidh sat with polite smiles on their faces, their posture typical of two Brits confronted with a foreign language.

"Richard, can you show Sylvie the receipt you have for the Chagalls?" asked Jean, suddenly looking across to him.

"Certainly," said Richard, retrieving the receipt from his briefcase and giving it to her.

"Sorry, do you mind?" asked Sylvie, signaling the computer screen on their desk. Richard and Eilidh hastily moved away and Jean gave Sylvie his seat to sit on.

Sylvie made herself comfortable and then studied the receipt Richard had given her.

"I think this will be very easy," she concluded, much to Richard's relief. "This receipt has plenty of information on it. The date, the address, and the paintings... It won't take me too long to find out if there's anything on record."

She began her search.

Eilidh pulled a bottle of water out of her handbag.

"Ah, no! Sorry. No drinks allowed in here. It's forbidden, I'm afraid," said Jean to Eilidh in an urgent voice. "There are valuable and important documents that get viewed in here, too, you see."

"Sorry," said Eilidh, contritely, putting the water back in her bag.

"Don't worry," Jean said to her, with a reassuring smile. "After we're finished here, I'm going to take you to a fabulous place for lunch. *C'est délicieux*. There'll be lots of drink and food for us."

Richard resisted the urge to laugh.

Eilidh was looking startled at the thought of consuming a huge banquet at lunchtime but that was Jean for you. He never did things by halves and, what's more, he was an irresistible force, carrying everything before him with aplomb.

"OK. Here we are," said Sylvie, sounding satisfied.

The others turned and stared at the screen in front of her.

"Here are the 1936 tax records listed for the *La Galerie L'Oiseau Bleu*. And if you look here," said Sylvie, pointing at the screen. "You can see specifically the two Chagalls that were sold in July. They correspond with the ones on this receipt."

"That's fantastic," said Richard, absolutely delighted.

Sylvie smiled with pleasure.

"If you like I can print this off for you."

"Yes, please do. I wonder if there can be found any documentation with the name 'Dorin' on it for those paintings or is that wishful thinking?"

Sylvie pursed her lips.

"It's doubtful," she said, looking thoughtful. "But maybe we can try with the gallery's insurers? I wonder whether the insurers for *L'Oiseau Bleu* were officially notified of the sale. That might be a possibility and if so, we could possibly find the purchaser's name listed. too, along with the paintings..."

She looked up at them.

"If you can give me a little more time, I can check and see if there were any insurance records for the Chagall paintings. Back then there were very few big insurers in Paris and one of the largest, AGF, was government-owned in those days, so we'll definitely have their records on file. If you have the time for me to do so, I should be able to locate them. If they exist, that is."

"Of course," said Jean, getting up. "I'll show Richard and Eilidh around the building. Shall we come back in twenty minutes' time?"

Sylvie nodded and waved them off, her gaze fixed to the computer screen.

As soon as they were out of the room, Eilidh took a long swig of her water bottle and then offered it to Richard.

He took the bottle gratefully. Travelling always made him thirsty, for some reason. He was also craving a strong coffee.

As though reading his thoughts, Jean said, "We can get a coffee from the coffee stand, if you like."

Both Eilidh and Richard nodded their approval at this.

In the end, after they had located the coffee stand,

Richard bought the three of them coffee and they wandered outside to enjoy their drinks.

The sun was shining and the moat surrounding the building was glistening and reflecting off the windows.

Next to where they were standing there were some curious, metallic shapes breaking up the rigid lines of the building behind them.

They studied the building as they drank their coffee.

"You know, if you arrive here early enough," said Jean at length, gesturing at the greenery, "you can see the cockerels that live on the grounds. They like to walk around in the mornings. It's quite a thing to see."

"That would be an amusing sight. However, this place is a real contrast to the Hôtel de Soubise, isn't it?" asked Richard, looking up at the diamond facade towering above them.

Jean scowled.

"Yes, it's shocking architecture. It doesn't blend in with anything," he complained. "Just like the Louvre Pyramid. It disturbs me, the lack of aesthetic appreciation for the old architecture in Paris. We must revere what came before, not make a mockery of it with ugly, glass structures. The planning department in this city has a lot to answer for."

They finished their coffee and made their way back to Sylvie, who was waiting for them with several sheets of paper beside her.

She stood up when she saw them.

"Here you go, Richard," she said, looking at the topmost paper. "The AGF insurance company received formal notification from *L'Oiseau Bleu* in 1936 that its two Chagall paintings had been sold to a man named Jacob Alexander Dorin."

She smiled at Richard, looking deservedly pleased with herself. Richard looked down at the papers.

"I can't thank you enough, Sylvie. This is wonderful news. I'm positive this will be enough evidence to allow us to pass on the two paintings to the rightful owner. Her grandfather was the one who originally purchased them. I didn't know his first name but the surname's absolutely correct. This is fantastic."

"My pleasure," said Sylvie. "Is there anything else you need?"

"No, you've done enough for us, thank you," said Richard, gratefully.

Sylvie had a spring in her step as she walked with them to the entrance and waved them off.

Richard hadn't bothered explaining to Sylvie the convoluted story behind the two stolen Chagall paintings. Had he begun to explain it all, they would have ended up staying there for a long time and he was sure Sylvie had better things to do with her day.

And, of course, Jean had lunch plans for them.

Jean took them to *L'Escargot*, a small restaurant on Rue Gabriel Péri, a fifteen- minute walk from the Archives Nationales at Pierrefitte-sur-Seine.

The unintended result of their gargantuan lunch was that by the time they'd finished their meal and were making their way to *La Maison d'Art*, Eilidh and Richard had drunk far too much wine and were feeling decidedly groggy.

Without quite knowing how it had happened, the trio had managed to down three bottles of delicious red wine from the Loire Valley.

Richard put the blame squarely on Jean for their light-headedness because Jean had brushed away their objections to drinking wine when they ordered a substantial meal at *L'Escargot*. With typical Gallic conviction, Jean had insisted that in France one must drink wine and eat good food. It was a sacrilege to French cuisine and culture not to do so, he had added, and, in any case, they had to celebrate the successful results from their search at the Archives Nationales.

Carried away by Jean's exuberance, Richard and Eilidh had taken him at his word, but when they walked out of the restaurant, Richard felt the fresh air hit him like a bucket of cold water and almost reeled in shock.

Their visit to *La Maison d'Art* wasn't as productive as their visit to Pierrefitte-sur- Seine but they still came away with some valuable evidence.

The current owners had gutted the old *L'Oiseau Bleu* gallery, turning it into a modern edifice that sold the work of up-and-coming students from art colleges such as the well-known École des Beaux-Arts. Many a savvy art collector had made a small fortune by investing in the work of promising young art students because these students often went on to make a name for themselves later on. On this premise, it appeared the gallery was thriving.

The gallery's owners were able to provide Richard with some of the photographs they had taken of *L'Oiseau Bleu* before it underwent its present-day transformation and Richard was very grateful for them. The detailed photos of *L'Oiseau Bleu*'s facade were helpful additional evidence in his quest to confirm the provenance for the two Chagall pictures.

The owners also informed Jean that the previous

owner, Anton Voland, was now an old man and was living out the rest of his days in a residential home on Rue Tronchet, near a large Catholic church called *L'église de la Madeleine*.

Richard decided they should go and visit Anton in the morning, before they caught the Eurostar back to London. Jean, who was becoming increasingly intrigued by the unravelling story of the two mysterious Chagall paintings, offered to accompany them there, too.

With typical generosity of heart, Jean designated himself tour guide for the rest of the afternoon and took them around the Rodin Museum, a place that had long been on Richard's to-do list.

By the time they left the Rodin Museum and said goodbye to Jean, it was early evening and they were ready for some more food.

Jean had recommended that they go to *Le Français Cuisiné*, a small restaurant that had an excellent reputation for affordable, good-quality food and which was located near their hotel, on Avenue Percier.

Taking Parisian chic literally, Eilidh turned up for this meal in a cream mini-dress with knee-high, brown suede boots. She looked so stunning that she took Richard's breath away and he could barely take his eyes off her. As a result, he was pretty much monosyllabic on their way to the restaurant.

However, this feeling didn't last very long. To Richard's surprise, Eilidh insisted on ordering yet more wine at *Le Français Cuisiné* and then, obviously hungry after a long day, she opted for the steak tartare.

"Eilidh, are you sure you want to order a steak

tartare?" asked Richard, dubiously. "You do know it's raw, don't you?"

"Oh, please, Richard," said Eilidh, impatiently. "Stop fussing. I always like my meat undercooked."

Richard looked at her.

He wasn't convinced Eilidh understood that her meat would turn out to be raw beef or horsemeat but he wasn't going to argue with her, a task he knew would be pointless. Besides, he was secretly looking forward to seeing the expression on her face when the dish was placed in front of her.

Not disappointing him, Eilidh's face was a picture when she saw the heap of red meat, with a raw egg yolk balanced on the top.

Looking revolted, she poked at the food gingerly with her fork. Richard burst out laughing.

"Ha-ha," she said sarcastically. "OK, Richard, you were right. I don't like my food this undercooked, thank you very much. I mean, is it even hygienic?"

"It will be," Richard assured her.

Making a face, Eilidh began to eat it gamely but in the end she only managed to work her way through a third of it.

They decided to order up another basket of bread and a duck pâté starter for her. Feeling a little sorry for Eilidh, Richard shared his Coq Au Vin dish with her, too, slicing small pieces of chicken and passing them to her on his fork.

They finished off their meal with a fig tart each, which they washed down with their remaining wine.

Replete with food, they then made their way back to their hotel, admiring the buildings around them and enjoying the nightlife.

By the time they reached the hotel foyer, Richard was already thinking ahead to their interview with Anton Voland the next day and the questions he would like to ask him, but as he made his way to the stairs, Eilidh tugged on his arm.

"The night's still young, Richard. Let's have a drink at the bar."

In the background, the melodious notes of a piano could be heard. Richard looked at her, worried.

He was tempted to stop at the bar but it wasn't like Eilidh to be so chilled out and he could tell she was more than a little tipsy. He didn't socialize with her enough to know if she routinely let her hair down when she was away from work but he did know that she was someone who liked to be in control.

He wondered what was causing her to relax in this way. Maybe, as he'd hoped, Paris was working its magic on her.

Having visited Paris several times already, Richard was convinced that the goddess Aphrodite had poured an amorous potion into the river Seine when the city was built. From literature to art and architecture, the city was infused with romantic ideals. And now even Eilidh, usually impervious to sentiment, was succumbing to its *joie de vivre* atmosphere.

"OK," he said, at last, with a smile. "I've had quite a lot of wine today, so I might just stick to a *digestif*. That's an after-dinner brandy."

"I'll have one of those, too," said Eilidh, walking to the bar.

"Really? You wouldn't prefer to have a limoncello?"

Eilidh sniffed.

"Nah. Too sickly-sweet for me."

In the end, Eilidh opted for a vermouth.

Eilidh looked at Richard thoughtfully as they sat on their cushioned seats at a corner of the hotel bar, with the piano playing quietly in the background. They'd been discussing the Rodin sculptures they'd seen earlier on but now something else was clearly occupying her mind.

"Richard, you're a sweet guy, how come you haven't been snapped up yet?" Richard smiled to himself.

"Well," he said, slowly. "I'm not sure there's a huge demand for men who are art historians. It's a real conversation-killer."

"Not necessarily. Jean seems to manage conversation just fine."

"Yes, but I think French men in general are very good at expressing themselves. Culturally, we're a little more repressed on the other side of the Channel."

"I can see that. A French accent helps too, of course. But even so, many men are fly-by-nights and you're very dependable."

"You're not selling me to myself," said Richard, wryly.

"Women like security in relationships," insisted Eilidh.

"And you think men don't?"

Eilidh wrinkled her nose as she thought about this.

"Some certainly don't, I'd say. I know it's wrong to generalize but my impression is that many men don't like to be tied down and I'd put you in that category sometimes, too. You seem to me to be a free spirit. For a start, you hate the bureaucracy, the rules and regulations we work with at the Met."

What Richard was hating was Eilidh trying to sum

him up. It was a real turn-off, in his view. But then again, maybe he was being rebellious, just as she'd implied.

"Eilidh, chaffing against restrictions at work is a very different thing to fighting against the ties you live with in a relationship," he objected. "You can't compare the two."

"Can't I?" asked Eilidh, with a provocative, lopsided grin. Richard rolled his eyes and finished his brandy.

They looked at each other, a strange kind of electricity sparking between them.

"Come on," Richard said at last, standing up.

He turned, took hold of Eilidh's hand and pulled her out of her seat.

He was keen to get Eilidh on her own before his nerves failed him and the suspense was killing him. It was now or never for voicing his feelings for her.

"Let's get upstairs and have another look at the documents Sylvie printed for us. I haven't had a chance to look at them properly."

Eilidh didn't demure and accompanied Richard up to his room, where they spread out the sheets of paper Sylvie had given him on the bed.

They were kneeling side by side at the foot of the bed, studying the printouts, when Richard, summoning up his courage, turned to Eilidh.

"Eilidh, can I kiss you?"

Undaunted, Eilidh stared back at him.

"Are you making a pass at me, Richard?" she asked, softly. Richard blushed.

"Yes, of course I am. Why wouldn't I? We're in

Paris and you know fine well I'm completely crazy about you."

"Actually, I didn't know, Richard. I did wonder sometimes, but you're so awkward it's almost impossible to second guess what you're thinking. You're cagey and sly, but I like your style..."

Richard lifted an enquiring eyebrow.

"Well?"

"Well, what?" asked Eilidh, determined not to give him an easy ride.

"Can I kiss you? I don't want to take advantage of you when you're totally tipsy, Eilidh."

"I'm tipsy but I'm not legless."

"Yes, but I'm not sure how you quantify that."

Eilidh grinned naughtily at him.

"I know what I'm doing, so don't you worry about me. And by the way, I could say exactly the same about you. There's plenty of Dutch courage in you tonight," she said, grabbing hold of his shirt and pulling his head down to hers. "Now shut up and kiss me."

Richard began to kiss her gently on the lips, tasting the vermouth she'd drunk earlier.

Wrapping her arms around his neck, Eilidh returned his kisses with increased fervor, teasing him with her tongue as she arched into him.

After a few minutes, she pulled back and looked up at him, her pupils dilated.

"Not bad at all. You're full of surprises, aren't you, Richard?" she murmured.

Richard didn't bother answering but feeling his knees getting sore on the hard floor, pulled her up and swept the papers off the bed.

For once, Eilidh didn't tell him off.

They collapsed onto the bed, tugging at each other's clothes, as they heard in the distance the piano in the bar playing Elgar's *Salut d'Amour*.

Richard remembered the piano the following day when they came down for breakfast and decided he would have to play Elgar's serenade at home, in memory of a night that had fulfilled his heartfelt wishes.

He wasn't sure how their relationship would pan out in future but right then, far away from Scotland Yard and in Paris, it felt idyllic. For now, he felt he couldn't care less about the road ahead.

At eleven they went to the foyer, where they had arranged to meet Jean before heading out to see Anton Voland.

Jean saw them holding hands and cocked an eyebrow.

"I see the city of love has lived up to its reputation," he remarked humorously.

Richard and Eilidh smiled at him and without the slightest trace of embarrassment walked out of the hotel into the Parisian sunshine.

Anton Voland turned out to be very pleased to see them and his mind was still sharp, much to Richard's relief. He was afraid that Anton might have ended up in a care home due to a reduction in his cognitive abilities.

He was a dapper man, dressed neatly in an open-necked shirt and jumper, with his grey hair combed back.

Anton remembered vividly the day Jacob Dorin walked into his father's gallery and bought the Chagall paintings. He was only a young boy, just starting his apprenticeship, at the time. The Chagall purchase had

stayed imprinted on his mind because his father had
discussed at length, with Jacob, what paintings would
be a suitable subject matter for a wedding anniversary
present and Anton had felt tremendously moved by
how much Jacob loved his wife.

Jacob Dorin told them that he had come to Paris to
pick up a couple of antique clocks from a customer. He
was making a name for himself in his field, he said, and
was beginning to make serious amounts of money.
Feeling flush, he ended up buying two of the most
expensive paintings in the gallery.

Anton was perfectly happy to testify to the
purchase, if needs be.

Aware that time was a luxury for a man who was
suffering from a weak heart, Jean offered to return to
the care home the following week to record on video
Anton's memories of the purchase.

Before they left, Anton smiled and spoke to Jean in
French.

"If you take anything away from this visit, please
remember to make use of the time left to you," Jean
translated for them. "I, too, was like the three of you and
now look at me. Time goes by so fast. Don't waste it."

"*Merci pour tout*," said Richard, genuinely touched
by his words.

As they walked out of the room, Anton lifted his
hand as though in a papal blessing.

But Richard already felt blessed.

After his night with Eilidh, a new horizon had
opened up for him and he was looking forward to
enjoying the time they had together.

Just as Anton had requested them to do.

19

Nkiruka

"Leila Andelman?" asked Johnny, as the bright-red door opened.

"Yes, indeed, come in," said Leila, a petite, dark-haired woman, casually dressed in jeans and a T-shirt.

On first impression, Nkiruka didn't think Leila matched the formidable image that had been conjured up in her mind after talking to Rachel and Natalie. Leila didn't remotely look like the battle-axe they had described.

Strange...

Leila took them through to the kitchen, which looked out on to an enormous garden, her black Labrador leading the way with his tail wagging.

After having walked past two Bentleys in the drive-way, it was abundantly clear to Nkiruka that the Andelmans were well off, but even if there was any doubt, once they walked into the house the ornaments and paintings on the walls would have made the matter plain to them. Every piece of furniture, every furnishing and decorative item, looked to be expensive and of good quality.

Nkiruka thought Richard would have relished having a good nosy around a house that had so many items on display.

"Would you like a drink?" asked Leila, politely, as they sat themselves down at the grey marble kitchen table.

"No, we're fine thank you," said Nkiruka. "We don't want to take up too much of your time today."

Leila's face clouded over.

"I'm sorry my son caused so much trouble on the street," she said, quietly. "I've no idea what got into him that week."

"Yes, there seems to have been quite a commotion on the street," agreed Nkiruka, in a mild tone.

Leila covered her face. "I'm so mortified. I mean, the ASBOs that were given out! And one of them punched Raymond, our neighbor, too. I couldn't believe it when I was told. And they were using drugs here, as well."

Looking despairingly at them, Leila clasped her hands together.

"What can I say? I can only apologize on my son's behalf for taking up police time that night and for his behavior and that of his friends."

"Isaac wasn't identified as being in possession of drugs," said Johnny, frowning.

Leila stared doggedly at him.

"Let's not kid ourselves, Detective Webster. Isaac didn't get caught with any drugs on him but that doesn't mean he's not a user. In fact, I know he is. But, you know, I thought he had that side of his life under control."

Nkiruka and Johnny nodded. Such situations were not uncommon.

"In many respects, I don't know who my son is any more," continued Leila. "It's hard to admit that as a mother, but it's true. You spend years of your life trying to provide them with the best of everything and then it's just thrown back in your face, time and time again. As a mother I'm a glutton for punishment. I keep trying to connect with him, bring him back to us, but, I don't know, it's as if a part of him has gone for good."

Johnny was looking surprised at Leila's frankness but Nkiruka, a mother herself, understood to a lesser degree the painful reality confronting Leila. Leila was now one of the many parents who were coming to terms with the fact that parenthood wasn't turning out to be the wished-for, lovey-dovey, fairy-tale experience they'd hoped it would be.

Nkiruka smiled at Leila with a great deal of compassion.

"It must be a great trial for you as his mother," she said.

Leila's bottom lip trembled and her eyes filled with tears as she nodded.

"Yes, it is. I'm sorry about the problems Isaac's behavior has caused with the police and the neighbors. I can promise you it won't happen again. We won't let anything like this happen again."

"We're not here to censure you, Leila," added Nkiruka, quick to reassure her.

"I know. I get that you need to investigate what

happened, given the disturbance, but I'm so ashamed. You've no idea how horrible some of the neighbors were to us when we got back from our holiday. What did they think we could do about it? We'd no idea what was going on while we were away. I got a snarky text from a neighbor informing me our son was a hell-born babe and that he was a danger to the neighborhood. That was it. She didn't even mention what had happened. Well now, of course, we've learned our lesson. We're not going to take any more risks. We'll be booking a house sitter next time we go abroad. Sad, isn't it, when you can't trust your own son?"

"Is this the first time you've had trouble with Isaac?" asked Johnny.

"No. No, of course not. He has his issues. Always has done, actually. But he's never caused trouble at our house while we were away before. Nothing like what he did recently. Other times he's made me cross with the thoughtless things he's done, but it was nothing really, in the whole scheme of things. Forgetting to lock up properly. Spilling wine on our carpets. Leaving dirty dishes in the sink or a forgotten pizza in the oven. You know, that kind of thing."

Leila gave a hollow laugh.

"He's never gone to the extent of having drug-fueled parties in our home. He's never done anything like that before. The drugs, drink and the ASBOs. I mean, good grief! He's house sat for us a few times but there's never been a problem like this. And certainly, no hassle with the neighbors."

She sighed.

"The mess they left outside was unbelievable. They completely trashed my garden. I sobbed my heart out for days. We didn't bring him up to be so inconsiderate, we really didn't. I think his mental health's deteriorating, actually. He finds it hard to be nice to us or to be grateful for anything we do for him and he treats us as though we're ruining his life. He's so aggressive, too."

She wiped away a tear.

"There wouldn't be a girlfriend involved, would there?" asked Johnny, sympathetically.

Nkiruka glared at Johnny, in the hope he'd pick up on her signal. She didn't think it was wise for them to push Leila too hard for information.

Brushing her hair away from her face, Leila looked out into the garden for a moment.

"He does have a girlfriend," Leila admitted. "We've fallen out over that, too. Natalie Abergel, she's called. The girl's still at school and has a very sick mother. There are too many issues in that family. My father knew them well and helped them out quite a bit. I felt strongly that Isaac could do with sorting himself out and I didn't see that happening with a girlfriend who was carrying a lot of emotional baggage herself."

She sighed.

"So there's been a lot of arguments over that, too, of course. Plus, I'm not convinced the girl doesn't see Isaac as her gravy train. He's a very wealthy young man and the girl's situation is precarious, to say the least. As his mother, it's natural for me to think like that. But he doesn't get it."

"Of course," agreed Nkiruka, hurriedly, as Leila looked at them for reassurance.

"One of the neighbors said your father used to be quite a character," commented Johnny.

Leila smiled.

"Yes, he was special, a real patriarch. Always

wanting to be involved in family affairs. He'd fond
memories of his life in Germany before the war
happened and he remembered Esther Dorin from those
days, too. That's Isaac's girlfriend's grandmother. It's
why he supported her daughter in every way he could
while he was alive, but the rest of us did worry he was
getting taken advantage of. Now the same thing is
happening with my son."

Nkiruka wondered how helping out a terminally ill
woman could be misconstrued as a malevolent ploy to
extract money. Unfortunately, some people were
willing to see the worst in others, not the best.

Looking at her watch, Nkiruka noted time was
ticking by.

"I'm sorry, Leila, to hear of your troubles with your
son," she said, softly. "I'm a mother myself so I can
understand how difficult the situation is. From a police
perspective, I presume, on the nights there were parties
held here, nothing was broken or stolen?"

Leila shook her head.

"Thankfully, my jewelry was left up in the safe. I
always put away the very valuable items in a locked
cupboard upstairs before we go away. They drank my
husband's best malt whisky, which was worth a fortune,
though. The paintings are worth a lot of money but
unless you're a connoisseur, you're never going to know.
At least Isaac had the sense to keep the others outside
for the most part. Isaac was aware it would cause an
irreparable rift in our relationship if our things were
stolen. I'm sure that's why he kept them outside, as
much as he could."

Leila turned and looked out to the garden with a
troubled face.

"They were outside for the majority of the time... Certainly, that's the impression I get from the neighbors," added Leila, bitterly. "They smashed a few glasses and raided our drinks cabinet in the sitting room, but they were in the garden most of the evening, with the barbecue and the heated chimneys. We have a wooden gazebo in the garden, too, and an informal den, right at the back."

Nkiruka and Johnny turned and looked at the pretty, pale-blue gazebo on one side of the garden.

"What a huge garden you have," remarked Nkiruka, with a smile. "I envy you. We don't have a garden and my little daughter ends up doing circuits of our sitting room when she's hyper."

Leila smiled.

"Yes, we're very lucky in that respect."

"What's that at the back of the garden?" asked Johnny, who was now standing in front of the glass doors leading out to the garden.

Nkiruka and Leila turned and saw he was pointing to a red-brick building partially hidden behind a privet hedge.

"Oh, that! That's actually a bomb shelter, would you believe? We always called it the Teen Den. My father had it built when he bought this house. The war was still on when he came here. I don't even know if he ever felt the need to use it. It was a great place for Isaac and Ben to hide out in as they grew up, as you can imagine. A playhouse hidden away from all the adults."

"Your father never thought to have it taken down after the war?" asked Nkiruka, curiously.

Leila shook her head.

"He never wanted it taken away. It's a bit of an

eyesore but we've grown some plants on the top of it and the hedge hides quite a lot of it from view." She turned to look at it.

"Ugly thing, isn't it? I'm not even sure it would save anyone from a bomb attack but it's solid enough. It has corrugated iron sheets lining the inside of it. My father told us we should never forget the atrocities caused by war and what people sacrificed for our freedom... He always said we had anaesthetized ourselves with material comfort and forgotten the past."

Leila smiled ruefully.

"The bomb shelter was his memorial after the war finished, if you like, and when we moved in with him, we respected that. Isaac and Ben loved hanging out in the shelter so we had it jazzed up a bit for them and their friends. Put in a Wi-Fi connection and a TV, that kind of thing. The bomb shelter's completely soundproof so it never caused us any bother. If I ever nagged Isaac too much about his gaming, he would disappear to the Teen Den for some peace."

"Where's Ben?" asked Nkiruka.

"Ben's training to be a doctor in the States," said Leila, mournfully. "We don't really see him these days other than on our weekly video calls. My daughter, Anna, is working in Bristol at the moment, as a teacher."

Nkiruka nodded as she turned to look at the garden again.

Interestingly, there was a ramp at the kitchen door, leading down to the terrace, and a paved path winding its way to the back of the garden.

"Would you mind if we took a look at the bomb shelter?" asked Johnny. "It's not often you get a chance to see a piece of living of history, is it?"

"Of course," said Leila, reaching forward and opening the door to the terrace. "You might want to see the damage they did to the garden, too."

As they walked outside she pointed to the paving stones next to the kitchen.

"All of this was covered with broken glass and stank of alcohol. Someone had been sick, too. Isaac had cleared up most of it by the time we got back but he still left plenty for me to do. I've had to bleach this whole area to get rid of the smell and I'm still finding tiny shards of glass on the ground. I used to be able to walk around here in my bare feet but not anymore."

She pointed to the grass.

"As for the lawn, you can see for yourselves what carnage they caused. We're in the process of getting quotes for returfing it."

The lawn looked as though a stampeding herd of buffalo had been kept there.

The ground near the house was a mud bowl, with the remaining turf torn and trampled. Several of the bushes on either side had broken branches as though someone or something had been hurled into them.

Leila led the way to the bomb shelter.

It was, as she had said, an ugly building but it hadn't been built for aesthetic consideration. The plain, red-brick building was rectangular in shape, with no windows and an ugly corrugated metal door at one end.

Nkiruka and Johnny looked at it pensively.

"Would we be able to take a peek inside, Leila?" asked Johnny, at last.

Leila looked surprised.

"Yes, of course," she said, bending down and removing a plant pot from against the wall.

"How strange!" she exclaimed. "The key's usually here, under this pot. I've no idea where it's got to."

She reached up and pulled at the door handle but the door remained firmly shut.

"Isaac must have taken the key with him," she said, looking cross. "I must remember to ask him to bring it back."

Johnny nodded.

He went and had a look at the side of the building, which was close to the back garden fence and covered with a thick expanse of climbing hydrangea.

"You'll be hoping they haven't left half-eaten food inside," joked Nkiruka.

"Yes, I hadn't thought of that possibility," said Leila, getting upset. "I'll have to get Isaac to come out this very evening and open it up for us."

"Oh! Are you growing vegetables?" asked Nkiruka, pointing at a small plot behind the bomb shelter.

Leila nodded and walked across to the small patch, which looked recently tilled.

"We used to have a proper glass greenhouse here but it was hard work and too hot for the plants we wanted to grow in it, so we had it removed. This is a mixed allotment," she explained, looking down at it. "We grow strawberries and rhubarb here, as well as carrots and sweet peas. It's a devil of a job, though, trying to keep the birds and rabbits away from it."

Leila reached up and tried to fix some of the netting that stretched across the patch of neatly furrowed earth.

"Nkiruka," said Johnny, in a strange, strangled voice. "Could you come and take a look at this, please?"

Leaving Leila to wrestle with the netting, Nkiruka quickly walked back to the side of the hut, wondering what had caught Johnny's eye.

Johnny pointed silently to a patch of overgrown grass, halfway down the hut's wall, where there seemed to be a number of square pieces of glass leaning against the brick wall.

Screwing up her eyes, Nkiruka turned sideways and slid into the gap by the fence. She moved towards the center of the bomb shelter and looked down. A pile of small panes of glass were leaning against the brick wall, some of them broken, some of them intact.

She wasn't in the most comfortable of positions, but she bent down as far as she could to take a closer look.

There was an unusual rust-like staining on several shards of glass.

She straightened up and, crab-like, walked sideways out of the tight space. She looked at Johnny.

They were both thinking the same thing.

"Leila, do you have any old bits of material we could use and a plastic bag, at all?" she asked.

Leila walked up to them, looking perplexed and worried.

"Yes, why?"

"We've found something by the shed that could be of interest. It might be nothing but it would be worth checking."

Leila didn't move, staring up at Nkiruka in confusion.

"Of interest, in what sense?"

"There's several panes of glass here and we'd like to have a closer look," explained Nkiruka.

"Oh, those," said Leila, dismissively. "Those were

from the old greenhouse. I doubt you'll find anything of interest in them."

"Well," said Nkiruka, gently. "If you don't mind, it would be good to inspect them. I'm not sure if it ties in with your son's stay at your house but several pieces look broken."

Leila shrugged.

"Those panes have been there for years so I'm not surprised if some of them are broken. OK. I'll be back in a minute but I think you're wasting your time, to be honest with you. You can do what you like with them. They're of no use to us."

While she went away to fetch the items, Johnny made a face.

"She's right, you know. It might come to nothing."

Nkiruka looked back at him, her face grim.

"I don't think so, Johnny. There's quite a bit of staining on them and I don't think that's anything but blood. Do you?"

Johnny shook his head.

When Leila came back, Johnny went and uplifted a few pieces of the glass with a cloth and then carefully placed them in the plastic bag.

They left shortly afterwards, assuring Leila that they would send a Community Support Officer along to try and soothe any ruffled feathers on the street.

Two days later, the DNA results came in for the blood on the glass panes. There was a positive DNA match for Paolo Fernandes.

Johnny went back to Leila's house with a search warrant, requesting access to the bomb shelter, and he brought a forensic team with him.

Leila and her husband were not best pleased to

have a fourth visit by the police to their property. They threatened to get their lawyers involved, but as soon as they realized it was connected to something their son had done they became very submissive. It seemed to everyone there that they were no longer surprised by anything Isaac might have been involved in.

The bomb shelter had been effectively cleared out by Isaac and his friends but in spite of this, forensics were still able to find strands of hair and more importantly, minute traces of blood for all three of the Brazilian men. They also found clear DNA in hair samples and fingerprints for three other people, two of whom had a police record for theft and dealing in Class A drugs.

Isaac Andelman was arrested at his home and taken in for questioning.

During his interview, under caution, he readily confessed to murdering the three men, on the very day they had picked them up from Golders Green Road, along with three of his friends, Mark Taylor, Jose Peres, and Peter Link. It turned out that both Jose and Peter owed Isaac a substantial amount of money and were willing recruits to the murders.

Nkiruka had always wanted to know what the motive was for the murders. As with many of her homicide cases, her hunger for an answer, sadly, was to go unsatisfied.

Isaac's lawyer blamed the murders on Isaac's unstable mental health and drug use and Isaac's psychiatrist also confirmed that Isaac was prone to drug-induced psychotic episodes.

The judge accepted their assessments as the explanation for the crimes committed, even though the police force had been shocked by the extent of the violence used and the criminal psychologist had profiled the crimes as instigated by revenge.

Nkiruka didn't buy into the judge's conclusions. The careful planning that had gone into arranging a meet-up with the Brazilian men suggested a level of clear thinking and premeditation that contradicted the notion that Isaac had lost control and was divorced from reality.

But at least Lionel was satisfied, as he now had four convictions and a completed homicide case.

Nkiruka was left to her own private reflections.

Had Isaac been influenced by his grandfather's experience of the Nazis during the war? Or had his love for Natalie Abergel pushed him over the edge once he found out more about her background story?

It was doubtful the answers would ever surface.

Whatever their motives, Isaac and his so-called friends hadn't given Paolo the chance to return the Chagall paintings to their rightful owners, nor had they given the world an opportunity to bring Paolo to the International Criminal Court in The Hague to face justice for his war crimes.

It seemed as though Isaac had decided that a painful death was the best form of justice that could be meted out to someone like Paolo, but as a wise man once said: *"An eye for an eye leaves the whole world blind."*

Epilogue

"Thirty million? Looking for bids for thirty million?"

Richard looked over the sea of waving mobile phones to the side of the room where there was a raised dais, filled with people.

A lady with a phone cradled to her cheek shouted something to the auctioneer.

"Yes! Excellent! Thirty million. Any bids for thirty-two million?" A hand went up and a man with a phone to his ear nodded.

"Very good, Dan. Raised to thirty-two million. Any bids for thirty-four million?"

Richard heard Jean swearing softly and fluently in French beside him. There was a tense pause in the room.

A woman standing next to the previous bidder, also with a phone in her hand, nodded.

"Ah, Clotilde, thirty-four million. Any further bids for thirty-six million?"

Another silence.

The bids were getting stretched at this point.

Records had already been broken and it was now down to who was the most determined to own the painting.

The auctioneer scanned the room.

"Thirty-six million?"

The auctioneer raised his hand with a gavel in it. On the dais, the bidder called Dan nodded again.

"OK, Dan! Excellent. Thirty-six million. Bids for thirty-eight million? Anyone ready to bid for thirty-eight million?"

This time the silence dragged on and there was a rustle of impatience in the room.

Richard looked at the wall behind the auctioneer, where Marc Chagall's *Lovers on the Bench* was hanging.

"Thirty-seven million then! Any bids for thirty-seven million?" At the front of the crowd, a seated man raised his brochure.

"Thirty-seven million! The gentleman bids for thirty-seven million. Bids for thirty-seven-point-five?"

The auctioneer looked around the room, craning his neck.

"Thirty-seven-point-five?"

The auctioneer's arm lifted again but Clotilde shouted out, just in time.

"Clotilde! Thirty-seven-point-five! Any further bids for thirty-eight million?"

Richard shuffled on his feet.

Next to him, Jean's eyes were shining with excitement. "Any bids for thirty-eight million?"

Another long pause in the room. Dan nodded and raised a hand.

There was a gasp amongst the crowd.

"Thirty-eight million, Dan. Thirty-eight million. Any bids for thirty-eight-point-five?

The silence stretched on and on this time.

It was obvious to everyone in the room that no matter what the cost, the anonymous bidder Dan was working for was set on owning the Chagall painting and had very deep pockets.

The auctioneer's gavel was raised again and then thudded onto the podium.

"Sold for thirty-eight million. Marc Chagall's *Lovers on the Bench* sold for thirty- eight million."

Like the popping of a champagne cork, the pent-up emotion in the crowd burst and the room was filled with a chorus of voices.

Jean turned to Richard and, no longer able to contain his feelings, gave Richard a big Gallic hug.

"Amazing, Richard. *Un miracle*. It's incredible, don't you think? A world record, I think, for a Chagall."

Richard grinned at him and nodded.

"Yes, I think so. The painting has had a real impact."

Shaking his head in disbelief, Jean turned to look at the painting at the front of the room.

"I cannot believe it. And to think it was hidden in a cello all these years!"

Richard's phone buzzed in his hand, and when he looked down he saw a text message.

"Well? How much dosh?"

Johnny Webster was taking a keen interest in the proceedings, too. Richard texted back: "38 *million*."

A few seconds later, the phone buzzed again. This time the text was unprintable.

Author's Note

If you enjoyed this book, please do post a review. It makes all the difference.

Acknowledgments

Thanks for this book go to my father, my husband and friends, who have collectively encouraged me to continue writing. Strangely, I would also like to thank two characters, Nkiruka and Johnny. They appeared in the book and suddenly took on a life of their own...

A Look At Book Three:
The Viking Hoard

An undeclared Viking hoard has been found on the remote Isle of Harris and Lewis, in the far north of Scotland.

When renowned Private Investigator Mike Telford discovers that items are being put up for sale—unbeknownst to the authorities—Detective Chief Inspector Richard Langley is alerted. Too bad an unexpected dent in the case evolves when the infamous treasure discoverer dies.

But not before he took three items to the police station for a corrupt officer to sell on the sly.

With the rest of the treasure hidden somewhere on the island, Richard and Mike find themselves in a race against time to find and protect the treasure from those who seek to use it for corrupt gain.

Will they find the remaining treasure before it's lost forever?

AVAILABLE NOVEMBER 2022

About the Author

Bea Green grew up as the daughter of a British diplomat and a Spanish mother. She spent every summer at her grandfather's olive tree farm in Andalusia. She graduated from the University of St Andrews in Scotland with an MA in English literature and currently lives in Edinburgh with her husband and two daughters.

Made in the USA
Coppell, TX
11 November 2023

24103220R00218